SPECIAL MESSAGE TO READERS

This book is published under the auspices of

THE ULVERSCROFT FOUNDATION

(registered charity No. 264873 UK)

Established in 1972 to provide funds for research, diagnosis and treatment of eye diseases. Examples of contributions made are: —

A new Children's Assessment Unit at Moorfield's Hospital, London.

•

Twin operating theatres at the Western Ophthalmic Hospital, London.

•

A Chair of Ophthalmology at the University of Leicester.

•

The establishment of a Royal Australian College of Ophthalmologists "Fellowship".

You can help further the work of the Foundation by making a donation or leaving a legacy. Every contribution, no matter how small, is received with gratitude. Please write for details to:

THE ULVERSCROFT FOUNDATION,
The Green, Bradgate Road, Anstey,
Leicester LE7 7FU, England.
Telephone: (0116) 236 4325

In Australia write to:
THE ULVERSCROFT FOUNDATION,
c/o The Royal Australian College of Ophthalmologists,
27, Commonwealth Street, Sydney,
N.S.W. 2010.

I've travelled the world twice over,
Met the famous: saints and sinners,
Poets and artists, kings and queens,
Old stars and hopeful beginners,
I've been where no-one's been before,
Learned secrets from writers and cooks
All with one library ticket
To the wonderful world of books.

LAWS BE THEIR ENEMY

When South African writer Howard Shaw is commissioned by a British newspaper to answer the thorny questions posed by the controversial laws of apartheid, his life is more than once in danger. But he has a constructive as well as an exciting role to play, since — through his newspaper articles — he makes suggestions on an alternative policy to apartheid. His compassionate quest, and his love for the beautiful Linda Mitchell, are played out against a background of conflict, violence, misunderstanding and terror.

Books by Frederick E. Smith
in the Ulverscroft Large Print Series:

LYDIA TRENDENNIS
THE DARK CLIFFS
OF MASKS AND MINDS
THE GROTTO OF TIBERIUS
A KILLING FOR THE HAWKS
THE WIDER SEA OF LOVE
THE STORM KNIGHT
THE OBSESSION
THE SIN AND THE SINNERS
WATERLOO
THE DEVIL BEHIND ME

633 SQUADRON:
OPERATION VALKYRIE
OPERATION CRUCIBLE
OPERATION COBRA

FREDERICK E. SMITH

LAWS BE THEIR ENEMY

Complete and Unabridged

ULVERSCROFT
Leicester

First published in Great Britain

First Large Print Edition
published 1996

British Library CIP Data

Smith, Frederick E., *1922–*
Laws be their enemy.—Large print ed.—
Ulverscroft large print series: adventure & suspense
1. English fiction—20th century
I. Title
823.9′14 [F]

ISBN 0–7089–3509–5

Published by
F. A. Thorpe (Publishing) Ltd.
Anstey, Leicestershire

Set by Words & Graphics Ltd.
Anstey, Leicestershire
Printed and bound in Great Britain by
T. J. Press (Padstow) Ltd., Padstow, Cornwall

This book is printed on acid-free paper

To

MY WIFE'S PARENTS

and other good friends

in South Africa

People crushed by law have no hopes but from power. If laws are their enemies, they will be enemies to laws; and those who have much to hope and nothing to lose will always be dangerous.

BURKE: Oct. 8th, 1777.

Glossary of South African Words

Apartheid: (pronounced Ap-ar-tate). Literally 'apartness', meaning separation of the races. A political catchword coined by the Nationalist Party before the 1948 general election.

Baaskap: Literally 'white boss-ship'. European supremacy.

Nationalist: A member of the South African Nationalist Party, the sponsors of *apartheid*.

Skolly: A street hooligan of a particularly vicious type.

Pondokkie: A makeshift hovel.

Coloured: Used as a noun, it denotes a member of a racially-mixed group descending from Europeans, Natives, and Asiatics (Indians and Malays). They number just under a million and live mainly in the Cape Province.

Dagga: Hemp or hashish.

Donga: A gully or ravine.

1

THE girl was clearly nervous as she came out of the squalid alley. She paused a moment, staring down the road. It was deserted, a long, untidy road flanked by dilapidated houses and an occasional factory. In the gathering dusk the flat-topped mountain that loomed over a small, wooden church opposite was slate-grey against the fading sky. The silence was intense and accentuated by the far-off mournful hoot of a train.

Sufficient light remained to show the girl to be in her early twenties, of slim build and average height. Her clothes showed good taste, and her dark head was uncovered. Her features were delicate, with slim, curved lips and large, melancholy eyes.

She began walking down the road. Her quick steps and the nervous play of her eyes suggested a highly strung nature, although the forbidding aspect of the district gave cause for her anxiety. A cat, crouched on a broken fence, eyed her balefully as she approached. Its lean body tensed as she passed by, its yellow eyes following her malevolently. Her footsteps came echoing back from the high factory wall opposite, making her turn her head to see if she were being followed.

She was within two hundred yards of the main arterial road that crossed the end of the long street when three men suddenly emerged from the shadows and spread across the pavement ahead of her. All were dark-skinned: two being Coloureds, the third a massive coal-black negro. The latter had a repulsive face with small eyes, a broad, flat nose, and blubbery lips, now agape with anticipation. One of the Coloureds was raggedly dressed, but the other wore a draped jacket of American style, wide trousers, and patent leather shoes. He had a thin, wolfish face, made more vicious by a long knife-scar that ran down one cheek. From his behaviour, it was clear he was the leader of the gang. He eyed the trembling girl a moment, then said something in Afrikaans.

The girl stepped back, her cheeks

deathlike. "*Nie*," she faltered. "*Nie*. Leave me alone."

The thug twisted on his heels, muttering from the side of his mouth to his followers. They let out a raucous laugh. The huge negro moved forward eagerly. The girl backed away in terror, one hand at her throat. She looked around frantically but there was no help in sight. A car stood on the opposite side of the road outside the factory, but it was empty. Her terrified eyes returned to the advancing negro.

None of them noticed a door open in the darkened factory opposite. A man, about to cross the pavement to reach his car, stopped dead at the scene across the road. He watched from the doorway with dismayed eyes, trying to find the courage to intervene.

The girl turned suddenly and tried to run, but the coloured gang leader was too quick. He leapt forward, catching her by one shoulder and pulling her round. She screamed and tried to pull herself away, but the hooligan pinioned her arms. He held her tightly a moment, then threw her towards the huge negro.

The negro caught her eagerly. His hands pawed her, then closed round her body. His face, lustful and hideous, bent over her. The gang leader stood alongside, mocking the frantic girl.

At that moment a car swung out from a side street and headed towards them. All three men looked round in sudden alarm. The negro's arms slackened and the girl seized her opportunity. Tearing herself away she ran onto the road, right in the path of the approaching car, and waved her arms frantically.

The car braked and a door was flung open. "Quickly!" a man's voice called out. "Jump in."

Sobbing with relief the girl scrambled into the car. The gang leader, seeing the car had only one occupant, snarled at his followers and leapt forward. He jumped into the car, clutching at the girl.

The driver cursed and drove his fist into the twisted, vicious face. The hooligan lost his balance and fell back on the road. Snarling like an animal, he was on his feet in a second, a long knife appearing in his hand. But before he or his slower followers could resume their attack, the car had gathered speed and was heading away. The watcher from the factory drew in a deep breath of relief, slammed the door on the darkened street, and ran inside to a telephone.

The girl sank back in the car-seat, her breath coming in dry sobs. The driver gave her time to recover before talking to her. Glancing over his shoulder, he saw the hooligans had vanished. He turned up the arterial road, then looked at the trembling girl.

"You're quite safe now. Would you like a cigarette?"

The girl tried to smile. "No, thank you."

He nodded, steadying the wheel with his elbows as he opened his case. Her unsteady voice came to him as he struck a match.

"I'm terribly grateful to you. I don't know what would have happened to me if you hadn't stopped."

"I don't know either," he said quietly, throwing the match out through his side window. "I know it's none of my business but I don't think a young girl like you should be wandering about alone in these parts, particularly at night."

Her voice was stronger now, more timid than frightened.

"It's never happened before — nothing like this."

He shrugged. "There's always a first time, you know." He threw her a quick, curious glance. "Do you come round here often, then?"

"Yes; quite often." She hesitated, then asked, "Where are you going now, Mr . . . "

"Shaw," he smiled. "Howard Shaw."

"Mine's Viljoen. Joan Viljoen."

"Well, Miss Viljoen; first we're going to the police and then I'm going to take you home — "

Her sudden protest took him by surprise. "Oh, no. Not the police. I don't want any fuss."

"The police won't make any fuss," he assured her. "And we can't let those hooligans get away scot-free, can we?"

She could not conceal her distress. "Please, if you don't mind, I'd rather not tell them . . . " She broke off unhappily, lowering her eyes.

He gave her time to explain, noting her

well-cut clothes. Her black hair, curled in page-boy style, made a soft frame round her sensitive features. He judged her above normal in intelligence.

The lights of Cape Town drew nearer, a great, gleaming kaleidoscope against the dark background of mountain. They entered the suburbs and the girl turned her eyes on the driver, examining him in turn. The passing street-lamps showed her a man in his middle thirties, with a high forehead, an aquiline nose, and a firm, well-formed mouth. Like herself, he was bare-headed. He had fair, curly hair, which receded slightly over his temples. Although his height was difficult to judge in the car, his hands on the wheel, long and sinewy, gave the clue to his build.

She had been too shy at first to confide in him. Now, to her surprise, she felt a sudden rush of confidence.

"I don't want to tell the police because the news might get my . . . a friend of mine . . . into trouble. You see, I do non-European social welfare work in my spare time, and my friend's father doesn't like it. If he heard about tonight, Brian would never hear the end of it."

He glanced at her curiously. “Why doesn’t his father like it? Or shouldn’t I ask?”

“He says it is bad for business for it to be known that a friend of his son’s does that sort of thing.”

He gave her a wry smile. “I know I shouldn’t ask, but what sort of business is affected by a little social welfare work? What does your friend’s father do?”

The girl gave an uncertain shake of her head. “He has so many interests I’m never quite sure. The newspapers call him a financier. He is very wealthy.”

There was no trace of conceit in her statement — rather the faintest undertone of disparagement.

“You may have heard of him,” she went on. “Trevor Mitchell is his name.”

Howard glanced at her with added interest. “Indeed I have. He’s a very important person out here.”

She nodded. “I suppose he is.”

“And what about his wife, and, most important of all, his son, your friend?” Howard asked. “How do they feel about your work?”

A shadow appeared between the girl’s

eyes. "Linda doesn't care one way or the other. She is his second wife — she's only two years older than Brian. But Brian — well, he works with his father, so I suppose he can't help being influenced a little. Not much," she went on loyally. "I think he is really afraid something might happen to me."

"Something nearly did happen to you," Howard reminded her. "You were attacked by non-Europeans, the people you go out to help."

She turned on him protestingly. "They can't help having hooligans among them any more than we can. Gangs like that prey on them much more than on us. They can't go out of doors at night for them. It isn't their fault."

"I'm not blaming anybody for anything," Howard said dryly. "But if you don't want me to report this to the police, you have to promise to be more careful in the future. Promise?"

She smiled at his wagging finger. "Thank you very much, Mr. Shaw."

They were in the centre of the city now. Howard pulled up for a moment and turned to her.

"Where do you want to be?" he asked.

She hesitated. "I was going out to see Brian tonight. He lives at Clifton with his father. But I can catch a bus here."

Howard shrugged. "If it's Clifton, you can stay where you are without a pang of conscience. I live out there myself — on Third Beach."

"Then you might have met Brian?"

Howard shook his head as he started up the engine. "No. I only got my rooms two days ago."

"It's beautiful out there, isn't it?"

"Quite beautiful," he agreed.

They threaded their way through the city, passed through the northern suburb of Sea Point and followed the winding coast road to Clifton. On the girl's instructions Howard drew up his car above Fourth Beach.

"You will come in for a little while and meet everyone, won't you?" she asked shyly.

Howard hesitated, then curiosity overcame him. "All right. Just for a little while."

"And you won't forget and mention anything of what happened, will you? I'll say you are a neighbour who gave me a lift home."

He crinkled his eyes in a smile. "I won't forget," he promised.

She led him down a flight of steps cut in a steep bank to a bungalow overlooking the sea below. She turned to him and smiled nervously. Then she pressed the door-bell . . .

* * *

The lounge was luxurious in brocade and satinwood. Two armchairs and a wide settee, their feet hidden in a deep pile carpet, were arranged round a nest of tables. A tall standard-lamp set them in a pool of light. In a corner opposite the door stood a cocktail-cabinet, in another a satinwood radiogram. The deep bay window overlooking the beach below was hidden by rich curtains that transmuted the light stolen from the lamp into the dull lustre of gold.

In one armchair Linda Mitchell was idly turning over the pages of a fashion magazine. She was a woman of rare colouring. Her hair, which she wore piled up on her head, was a fairer gold than the tan on her face and exposed arms, giving a vivid impression of health and vitality. In contrast, her eyes were an emerald green and ink-fringed with dark lashes. With a body matching the exciting qualities of her features, Linda Mitchell was an outstanding beauty.

In spite of this, a vague discontent showed behind her eyes and in the lines of her full red mouth as she stared down at the magazine. From one slim hand resting carelessly on the arm of her chair a cigarette was sending a thin corkscrew of smoke upwards. She put it to her lips and inhaled deeply, her eyes lifting and resting for a moment on her husband in the armchair opposite.

Trevor Mitchell was reading the financial page of the evening paper. He was fifty-six — twice the age of his wife — a man of medium height with a thick-set body now running to seed. He had a round, florid face with light, keen eyes and fair hair that had parted ways in the centre to expose a shiny expanse of scalp. At his elbow was a half-filled glass of whisky.

He looked up as a clock chimed,

meeting Linda's gaze. He frowned as he spoke.

"Brian must have stayed at the bus-stop. Damn silly business, waiting there. It won't bring her here any quicker."

She shrugged her slim shoulders. "He's in love with her. People don't reason things out when they're in love. At least, so I'm told." Her voice was deep-toned, a rich contralto.

Mitchell's face darkened. "The young fool had no business to get mixed up with her at all. It wouldn't have happened if I hadn't have been overseas at the time."

She met his resentful eyes coolly. "And what was I supposed to do? Chose his girl friends for him?"

"You could at least have let me know something about her and what she did."

"Why? Brian's twenty-five — old enough to pick his own girl friends. Why should I have bothered about it?"

"Your common sense should have told you I can't afford to get mixed up with people of her type."

Her green eyes narrowed. "My common sense? If your own son, who works with you, doesn't know or care whether his girl friends please you, where do I come in? Anyway, I like the kid. And what are you worrying about? She doesn't look as if she means things to go any further: she's refused often enough to get engaged. I'm beginning to wonder if she ever will agree."

Mitchell waved a fleshy hand in disgust. "That's probably an act to make him chase her all the harder. Unless she does it thinking it'll fool me. You know what I've got against her, well enough."

"What does Brian say about it? I suppose you've tackled him?"

"Oh, he's got it bad. He goes sullen and says he can't see what harm she does . . . "

She smiled cynically. "I may be dense myself, but what is the harm in social welfare work? Just how does it upset financiers?"

Mitchell's face set in grim lines. "I'll tell you how it upsets them. When you're dealing in credit it doesn't pay to become a suspect in any way. And you become one in this country today the moment you show non-European sympathies. Sure enough someone will brand you a Communist, a Socialist, or some such thing, and then the bottom drops out of your stock. In my game you make enough enemies without looking for more. To show too much non-European sympathy not only antagonizes business men, it gets the politicians' backs up as well. And they can do you some harm, believe me."

Linda's lips curled mockingly. "It's hard to believe your most implacable enemies could make a negrophile charge stick on you, darling."

He ignored her taunt. "You'd be surprised what is being said already. Brian's my son, and he's going round with a girl who spends most of her spare time doling out soup and clothes to unwashed Kaffirs and *skollies*. That's enough to involve me, and I don't like it."

She shrugged again. "Well; I don't see what you're going to do about it. He's pretty well gone on her or he wouldn't be worrying like this because she's an hour or two late. Where was she going tonight, anyway?"

"She 'phoned Brian at work and said she had to do some job or other in

Willisden," the financier grunted. "She said she would be round about seven." He paused, his eyebrows drawn together. "I wonder what the devil started her off on this nonsense in the first place?"

Linda tossed aside her magazine and rose. She was tall and lithe, with a superbly proportioned body. "They say some people are born that way," she yawned. "I'm going for a walk."

The telephone in the hall rang at that moment. Mitchell rose heavily, waving Linda back. "It'll be for me," he muttered. "I'm expecting a call from Hathaway."

He was out a couple of minutes. When he returned there was a curious, jubilant gleam in his eyes.

"That was Thompson, my works manager in the Willisden factory," he told Linda. "He was working late tonight, and as he was leaving he saw Joan attacked by three *skollies* on the opposite side of the road. Luckily for her someone in a car got her away. One of 'em had a knife."

Linda's eyes widened. "A knife! Was she hurt?"

Mitchell shook his head. "Thompson

thinks the car got her away in time. Good thing it did, because if I know Thompson he'd run straight back and lock himself in."

"Couldn't he have been mistaken?"

"No; he knows her. Brian took her round the factory two weeks ago. Besides, she was going out to Willisden tonight."

"Where will she be now?" Linda asked.

"Probably sitting in a corner somewhere reviewing her way of life," the financier grunted, moving towards the door. "I'm going up to the bus-stop to tell Brian. This might knock some sense into him, too. He has an excuse to stop her now, and I'm going to see he uses it."

He went out, to return a few minutes later with his son. Brian was a tall, broad-shouldered young man with a shock of dark hair and with pleasant, open features. Now, however, he was looking worried and was pale under his tan. His father was clearly making the most of the affair.

"You can give her an ultimatum, that's what you can do," he said as they entered the room. "Tell her it's you or the Kaffirs, and let her choose. Stop being so damned wishy-washy, man."

Brian shifted uneasily. "But why should I stop her? She likes the work."

"You know damn well why you should stop her," Mitchell growled. "I've told you often enough. Apart from that, she's going to get herself raped if this goes on."

Brian's face turned red. Avoiding Linda's amused eyes, he dropped disconsolately into a chair. At that moment the doorbell rang. The youth leapt to his feet and ran out. Mitchell met Linda's eyes. They waited curiously.

A few minutes later Joan Viljoen entered the room, followed by Brian and a tall stranger.

"Well; are you all right?" Mitchell asked the white-faced girl brusquely.

"Yes; thank you." Her timid reply was barely audible.

Brian introduced them to the stranger. "Dad; this is Mr. Howard Shaw who rescued Joan . . . "

Mitchell went forward with outstretched hand. "Good work, Shaw. God knows what would have happened to the girl if you hadn't turned up." He turned to Linda and drew her forward. "Meet Mr. Shaw, my dear. Mr. Shaw — my wife."

Linda moved forward with studied grace, holding out a slim hand.

"It seems we are in your debt, Mr. Shaw," she murmured.

Her voice was deep, throaty. She saw a look of sudden admiration cross Howard's face. Their eyes met and held as they shook hands.

Mitchell had turned again to Joan. "Take a lesson from this, girl, and stay among your own race in the future."

Reaction made Brian's voice fierce. "I'd like to go round the place with a tommy-gun. After all you've done for them, this is the gratitude they show . . . "

Mitchell eyed his son with satisfaction, then frowned at the girl's reply.

"They can't help having a few criminals among them," she protested. "It's not their fault this happened."

"Rubbish!" Mitchell scowled. "Don't be such a fool, girl. Learn your lesson before something serious happens to you."

Joan's eyes were enormous pools of

misery in which stirred a fine silt of resentment. For a moment it seemed she would answer the financier. Then she lowered her eyes and stood silent.

"Leave her alone, Trevor," Linda murmured. She slanted her green eyes enigmatically at Howard. "What about our guest? It isn't every day we have gallant knights to entertain."

Mitchell recovered his *bonhomie* quickly. He took Howard by the arm and led him to a chair. "What will you have, Shaw? Whisky? Brandy?"

"Whisky, thanks," Howard told him.

Chatting genially, Mitchell went over to his cocktail-cabinet. Brian took Joan over to the window bay, where they sat together. Linda sank gracefully into the armchair opposite Howard and appraised him under her dark lashes while he talked to her husband.

Broad-shouldered, easy-moving, an athletic build . . . An intelligent face . . . lean cheeks with high cheekbones . . . a strong jaw . . . brown eyes with crinkles of humour in their corners . . . Linda decided she liked what she saw. She put her mind to their conversation.

"You know, Shaw, the name's familiar," her husband was saying. "Wait a minute — you didn't write *The Green Sky*, did you?"

Howard nodded. Mitchell laughed triumphantly. "I never forget names. I remember now — I saw the reviews last year when I was in England." He approached with a tray of glasses. "Powerful stuff. I read it — thought it was a good job of its type."

"What was it about?" Linda asked with interest.

"Oh; about a poor devil from the Tyneside slums who was sent out to fight the Japs and then returned to his hovel. A grim yarn, but well done. Were you out there during the war, Shaw?"

Howard nodded again. Mitchell offered Joan Viljoen a glass of brandy. "Here; take this," he grunted. "It'll steady your nerves."

She shook her head timidly. "No, thank you."

"Don't argue, girl. Do as you're told for a change."

The girl sipped at the brandy, shuddering as the neat spirit bit her throat. Mitchell gave each of the others a glass, then seated himself, looking across at Howard.

"The reviewers said you were a South African living in England. How come you're back here?"

"I've taken on a job for *The World Observer*," Howard told him. "They're doing a series of articles on race relations. They want me to cover the *apartheid* laws over here — to find their effects on the non-Europeans."

Mitchell gave a grimace of disgust. "Has *The World Observer* started prying as well? I thought it was above such nonsense. We've had dozens of reporters here since '49, cocky little know-alls who have enjoyed a month of hospitality and cocktail parties, then gone back to damn everything we do."

Howard nodded. "There has been a good deal of criticism, I know."

"Downright, prejudiced slander, you mean," Mitchell grunted. "And written by people who weren't out here long enough to get their knees brown."

"Don't look so fierce, dear," Linda drawled. "Mr. Shaw has come to praise Caesar, not to bury him — if Shakespeare will forgive me. Didn't you say Mr. Shaw is a South African?"

Mitchell nodded. "True. You aren't likely to make the same mistakes. You'll know what these non-Europeans are like. Where are you staying?"

"I got a room two days ago on Third Beach — with a Mr. and Mrs. Dowson."

"On Third Beach!" Linda broke in. "Then we're neighbours! But I thought the Dowsons were away."

"They are," Howard told her. "I got the room through their agent. They are supposed to return the day after tomorrow." He laughed ruefully. "I hope they do. The bathroom is upstairs, locked up in their flat."

He had risen as he was speaking. "I'll have to be getting along now, I'm afraid," he told them.

Mitchell rose with him. "We're very grateful to you, Shaw. You must come round one evening."

"Thanks. I'd like to."

"You'd better come over for a bath, too," Linda murmured.

Howard answered her banter with a grin.

"We'll look forward to an evening, then, Shaw," Mitchell said. "Linda will arrange it, won't you, dear?"

"I shall be delighted," she murmured, her green eyes on Howard. "*Au revoir*, Mr. Shaw. Drop in any time you feel like a drink."

A faint, elusive perfume came from her. Her hand was cool and smooth. Howard met her eyes again, then turned hastily towards Joan and Brian, who were approaching. He smiled at the girl, trying to convey something of his sympathy in his voice.

"Good night, Miss Viljoen. I'm glad to have been of some use."

"Good night, Mr. Shaw," she said shyly. "I'm very grateful to you."

Brian and Mitchell saw Howard to his car. The financier grinned at Brian as they returned to the lounge.

"That's one reporter who should keep off this oppression nonsense. He'll know these non-Europeans for what they are — a rabble of crude, lazy devils whose only ambition is to get a bottle of wine into their bellies."

Brian cast an uneasy glance at Joan.

A flush of colour was mounting in her cheeks. Mitchell noted it with satisfaction. Linda turned towards him, holding out her glass.

"Give me a gin-and-lime, please. And can't we talk of something else but rabble and bellies?" she drawled.

Mitchell took her glass but ignored her plea. "Shaw won't be so keen on this equality rubbish — he'll know what living with 'em is like. And why should we give 'em it? Our ancestors had to fight and bleed for theirs — let these lazy brutes do the same. If they get it then, they deserve it. What's fairer than that?"

"Yet if they raise a fist against you, you call them criminals and have them arrested," Joan cried out.

Mitchell turned on her with a grin. "For a moment I thought you'd seen the error of your ways, m'dear."

"I'm not ashamed of my ways, Mr. Mitchell," she said quietly.

"Not even when they do harm to Brian's and my interests?" he asked ominously.

The girl made a helpless gesture. Linda

stood up. "Leave her alone, Trevor. She's had enough for one night."

Brian muttered his agreement. The financier ignored them both.

"I've no time for social reformers," he sneered. "They upset the normal progress of civilization by making people think they're better than they are. As a result there are strikes, riots, and God knows what else. And what are social reformers, anyway? Most of 'em are unbalanced, with a grudge against society. Nearly all of 'em have had something in their lives to turn 'em into cranks."

"Stop talking rubbish, for heaven's sake," Linda snapped.

Mitchell took no notice of her. His eyes had narrowed on Joan's face. She had turned deathly pale.

2

FROM the macadamized road that wound round the feet of the mountains, the four beaches of Clifton looked like curved scimitars. They were made of white sand that sank beneath the feet and were separated from one another by massive piles of granite rocks. From them the whole Table Mountain range could be seen — twelve great peaks over three thousand feet in height. They appeared to rise sheer from the sea itself, to form a panorama of rocky grandeur with the mimosa-covered slopes of Lion's Head almost overwhelmingly in the foreground.

Behind these beaches ran a grassy bank that was thick with trees and sweet-smelling bushes. It was dotted with gaily-painted bungalows of all shapes and sizes, some complete with small gardens, others with their front doors only a few feet from the sand.

One of these bungalows, perched above

the third beach, had its roof and windows painted a bright, pillar-box red. Like all the others, it was made entirely of wood, its walls stained black from many applications of creosote. It had originally been built as a single-storied building, but in recent years the space beneath it caused by the declivity of the bank had been boarded in to make two additional rooms — one of moderate size, the other tiny. In front of these rooms ran a narrow stoep that overlooked the beaches and the sea. Alongside the bungalow ran a flight of concrete steps that linked the beach with the road above.

A slim coloured maid stepped out from the upper flat of the bungalow and made her way down the steps to the stoep below. She walked carefully, balancing a tray containing a cup of tea. Reaching the first and larger of the two rooms, she tapped on the door.

It was opened a few seconds later by Howard Shaw in his dressing-gown and pyjamas.

"Hello. What can I do for you?"

"I've brought your tea, master," the girl said shyly.

Remembering under the terms of his tenancy he was entitled to morning tea, Howard took the cup from her.

"Thank you."

"What time does the master want me to clean out his room?" the girl asked.

"Any time after ten."

"Very well, master."

Howard watched her go with some curiosity. Unlike most of the servant girls in the neighbourhood, this girl was delicately built, shy and well spoken. She had a heart-shaped, elfin face — in fact, in spite of her brown skin and the tell-tale crinkles in her hair, she was attractive by European standards. He judged her on the twenty mark.

He took his tea out on the stoep. Fresh, salt-laden air greeted him and he took in deep breaths of it while gazing around. The early morning sun had not yet cleared Lion's Head, leaving the beaches below still in shadow. But a far-off fishing-boat was more fortunate and was picked out brightly against the blue-grey sea. A cormorant sped over the waves, its black head held low in search of fish. The tide was well out but the bottle-green fringes of seaweed on the white sand showed where its night excursion had ended.

As Howard sipped his tea, his mind was on his landlords, the Dowsons, who had arrived back the previous afternoon. He was beginning to think his decision to take the room without first seeing them had been somewhat premature, for they had proved a singularly unprepossessing couple. A series of heavy bumps on his low ceiling had heralded their arrival from holiday. He had waited until the more alarming of the noises had died away before going upstairs to introduce himself.

Mrs. Dowson, who clearly wore the trousers, if only figuratively, had proved to be a thin, narrow, acid-faced woman with a high-pitched complaining voice. Her figure was so unrelieved by contours that it was difficult to tell which was the back and which the front. Her curls were of the sparse and brittle variety, standing out stiffly from her head. They had vaguely reminded Howard of prim, virginal mouths uttering a series of maidenly oh-ohs at their harsh treatment with tongs the previous night. Her age was indefinable. Probably she was only in her late thirties, but whatever age it seemed impossible to believe she had reached it through the normal course of biological development. No imagination, however febrile, could conceive her as once a dewy-eyed, bright young thing.

Bert Dowson's development was, on the other hand, a much easier thing to conceive; if, indeed, such a development had ever taken place. The substitution of a pair of short trousers in place of his flannels would have put him back almost where he had been twenty-five years earlier — a corpulent, gluttonous schoolboy who stuffed his mouth with lollipops, dozed through lessons, and cribbed his way through examinations. Any augmentation to his natural gifts over the years would be entirely accidental — except perhaps one. Long association with his formidable partner had made sly cunning a prime necessity. He was round-faced, with close-set eyes and thick lips.

Their attitude to Howard had been ingratiating and yet had left him with no doubt of his fate if he transgressed any of their edicts. At the end of the introduction he had found himself hoping fervently their respective ways would cross as little as possible.

But there was no avoiding the daily meeting because of the bathroom, Howard reflected ruefully as he put down his cup and took up his shaving kit. It was one hell of a nuisance. Bracing himself he went upstairs and tapped on the bungalow door.

The vinegary face of Mrs. Dowson appeared. It slid into an unctuous smile as she recognized him.

"Oh, good morning, Mr. Shaw. You want to use the bathroom, I suppose."

"If it is convenient, yes."

She led him through her lounge where a child of eight, a smaller replica of her mother, was playing with a doll on the floor.

"Say good morning to Mr. Shaw, Audrey," Mrs. Dowson said as the child threw Howard a startled glance and grabbed up her doll defensively.

"Good morning," Howard said, looking towards the bathroom to make clear his intentions.

He followed Mrs. Dowson into it. A substantial pile of wet washing was heaped up in one corner. Mrs. Dowson caught his hastily-averted eyes and let out an exclamation.

"Lucy," she shouted. "Lucy; come here this minute. These maids," she offered Howard by way of explanation. "You can't leave them a minute."

"Don't bother about it. It won't be in my way," Howard said, having the uncomfortable feeling the maid was to receive the blame for an established practice. The girl's bewildered expression on receiving the upbraiding of her mistress confirmed his suspicions.

"Don't worry about it, please," Howard said again.

Mrs. Dowson waved her hand. "Let her move it. It's her own fault."

Howard stood in silence while the girl brought in a large pail into which she piled the washing. With averted eyes she carried it out.

There was a wail from the lounge at

that moment. "Mama, hurry up. I'm hungry . . . "

"Impatient brat," Mrs. Dowson grumbled, moving reluctantly towards the door. "Always wanting something. I hope she won't bother you when she has her tantrums. She has a bad habit of stamping her feet on the floor."

Howard's blood ran cold as he thought of his low ceiling. His smile was not a success.

"But children will be children," she pointed out. "They're all much the same, you know." She paused in the doorway, giving him a wintry smile. "I should lock the door or Audrey might come in."

"I will," promised Howard, with no other intention in mind.

* * *

Soon after eleven that same morning, Howard left his small saloon in a nearby car-park and made his way to an imposing building in Longmarket Street. He took the lift to the fifth floor, walked along a spotless corridor, and rang the bell of an oak-panelled door. A trim receptionist appeared.

"Good morning; my name is Shaw. I made an appointment with Dr. Morkel yesterday."

The receptionist gave him a bright smile. "Oh, yes; Mr. Shaw. Dr. Morkel is expecting you. Do sit down."

She went out. No more than thirty seconds had passed before there was the sound of hurrying footsteps in the corridor outside. The door burst open and there was a roar of welcome.

"Howard! *Ag*, man, Howard; it's good to see you again."

Everything about the man who advanced across the room looked square — his ruddy face, his stocky, powerful body, even his outstretched hand. His face was rugged: shrewd blue eyes were set under craggy eyebrows, curly brown hair cut short. In repose his features were pleasant: now they were split in a broad grin of welcome.

Howard jumped up and gripped the doctor's hand. "Hello, Jannie. How's the world treating you?"

Morkel chuckled, clapping him on the

back. "You look well, Howard. The climate over there must suit you."

Morkel's voice suited him, being deep and hearty. In spite of his excellent English, it had a faint, and pleasant, Afrikaans accent.

He turned to his smiling receptionist. "Fix us up with some coffee, will you, Miss Spillman? That's a good girl." He took Howard by the arm. "Come on, lad. We'll go into my office."

They entered a snug, well-furnished room. Morkel waved Howard into a comfortable chair, gave him a cigarette, then took his own chair behind a polished desk. He gave Howard a tremendous frown.

"You've been the devil of a long time looking me up, if you've been in the Cape nearly a week."

"I had to get a room first," Howard told him. "Hotel residents are allergic to tapping typewriters. Then I 'phoned over a dozen Dr. J. Morkels before getting you."

"If you'd answered my letters, you'd have had my new address."

"Which letter?" Howard grinned. "The

1947 one or the '51? If I hadn't had a month in Jo'burg and got all the news, I wouldn't have known you were down here. What made you come to the Cape, anyway?"

Morkel shrugged. "Opportunity. I was offered a cheap partnership in a good practice in '53, and I took it. I sold out last year, but it put me on my feet. Now I'm doing what I like — a bit of everything. I'm an assistant police surgeon; I'm in charge of a non-European clinic; and I have a small, but very lucrative private practice." He winked wickedly at Howard. "One day I'm lancing the carbuncles of some poor coloured devil with malnutrition, the next I'm consoling Lady so-and-so because her period is two days late this month and, oh dear, it is so worrying, isn't it doctor . . . ? You'll gather I can't afford to let my right hand know what my left is doing."

"I can follow that," Howard grinned.

"Now tell me about yourself. First your mother and sister — how are they?"

"Jane's very well — she is marrying a London boy next year. Mother was well when I left, but in her last letter

Jane told me she had had a nasty fall and hasn't recovered as quickly as was hoped. Of course, Father died two years ago . . . "

Morkel nodded, chin in hand. "Yes; I was sorry to hear that, Howard. So our little Jane's engaged . . . It seems only yesterday I was pulling her pigtails. Anyway; if her boyfriend is in England, that explains her staying there. But why hasn't your mother come back with you?"

"She didn't like leaving Jane. And she's dug in over there now. It has become her home."

Morkel nodded. "*Ja*; it's a long time since '39. All right. What about you? What has the Fatherland done to be honoured by the return of his prodigal son?"

Briefly Howard explained the purpose of his visit. Morkel listened with interest; his warm, shrewd eyes on Howard's face.

"I jumped at the chance," Howard finished. "Not that they're paying all my expenses — I didn't want to be too tied to them. I get a fixed sum for my articles which leaves me free to stay here as long as I like. This way I feel I can do a more thorough job than if bound by some time limit."

Morkel shook his head. "Surely *apartheid* has had enough publicity by this time! Good God; every newspaper in the U.K. has had a crack at us some time or other. What new angle are you trying to cover?"

"The non-European angle, Jannie. How the laws are affecting him. How he feels. Is he apathetic, or does he mean to kick back? If he does, how? That's what I'm after."

Morkel shook his head. "They won't kick back, Howard. If they had meant trouble, it would have happened before this."

"Some people think they will, Jannie. *The World Observer* makes the point that *apartheid* is a revolutionary step in the European's treatment of the coloured races he dominates. It's a full-blooded, positive policy that makes one point unmistakable — it means to keep the white man very much on top. Now the point is this — if the non-European here bows down to it, then *apartheid* from the European's point of view has been an unqualified success in solving the colour problem. And so Europeans in colonial territories elsewhere may become infected: if, indeed, they aren't infected already."

"As a Nationalist," Morkel scowled, although with twinkling eyes, "I resent your pathological imputation. The word is enlightened, my boy, not infected."

"Still a Nationalist, Jannie? You're in favour of these laws, then?"

Morkel's blue eyes were steady. "*Ja*; I am. And I'll stay in favour of them until something better comes along."

"Fair enough, Jannie. Fair enough."

Morkel took one of Howard's cigarettes. "So you think we're a test case, Howard? If *apartheid* works well here, it might spread throughout Africa and even further afield? But if our non-Europeans react unfavourably, then the disease remains in isolation — as no doubt you'd like to put it."

"Something like that," Howard grinned. "Obviously an adverse reaction here won't be a recommendation for its adoption elsewhere."

"There has been little trouble so far

and it has been in operation a good few years now," Morkel reminded him.

"True, but these things take time to get under way. In any case the laws aren't fully enforced yet. But resistance isn't the only thing I'm looking for. There is the humanitarian aspect. If *apartheid* is causing real and extensive suffering among the non-Europeans, then its publicity will strengthen the hands of all liberal-minded Europeans in other countries to resist *apartheid* there."

"So if you can't find mutiny, you hope to find misery," Morkel grunted.

Howard's face turned serious. "I don't know what I'll find, Jannie. I don't even know what I hope to find. Don't forget I'm a South African myself — I've known non-Europeans, particularly negroes, since childhood — and I know their strengths and weaknesses better than most people overseas. I've not come with any bias, Jannie. For all I know *apartheid* might be the best solution of a bad lot. I've come to find out."

A servant boy brought in coffee at that moment. Morkel pushed a cup over to Howard.

"All right, lad. So you're going to give us a square deal. How are you going to start the job? And why have you come to the Cape to do it? The Cape is still the most liberal part of the country, you know."

"That's one reason I came. Any bitterness here must be worse elsewhere. And there's a better cross-section of the coloured population here — Negroes, Asiatics, and Coloureds. I'm going to start by giving as accurate as possible a picture of the living conditions of both blacks and whites. Then I intend to get in among the non-Europeans to find out what is cooking."

"What about all the cross-currents?" Morkel asked. "The friction between the non-European races, the occasional Afrikaner-British friction? It all complicates the issue."

"It does here, but not overseas. Non-Europeans in other countries, unless they are particularly well-informed and liberal, don't forgive South Africa for its *apartheid* because half the white population oppose it. If they ponder the case at all, they argue that the laws were passed by a freely-elected government put in by the Europeans. So every white South African tends to get his dislike, whether a Nationalist or not."

"Which is damned hard luck on the Opposition," Morkel grinned.

"And the different non-European races don't really complicate things from *The World Observer*'s point of view," Howard went on, "because, after all, *apartheid* is directed against them all."

Morkel sat in silence for a moment, his craggy eyebrows drawn together in thought. He nodded slowly. "*Ja*; I see the general idea." He paused, then eyed Howard quizzically. "But, man, what a job you're going to have in getting the Kaffirs and Coons to talk in confidence with you. They're as tight as clams with Europeans these days. You're going to need some contacts."

"I know. How about you starting me off?"

"Me?"

"Just the man! You say you're in charge of a non-European clinic. Doesn't that mean you have a district where you go doctoring, vaccinating, and the rest of it?"

"Yes. Mine is Willisden."

"All right. Take me round some time. There must be plenty of non-Europeans there who look on you as the big white medicine man — I might get contacts from them. In any case I want medical facts and figures from you, as well as showing round the slum areas. Don't forget I don't know the Cape as you do."

"The bloody nerve," Morkel growled. "And me a Nationalist!"

Howard grinned. "That's another point. You're a study in yourself. A liberal European with an *apartheid* complex. It's as important to understand your type as to know about the rest. You can be useful to me, Jannie."

"Go to hell."

"I've made one contact already," Howard smiled, going on to tell about his encounter with Joan Viljoen and his subsequent introduction to the Mitchells. Morkel showed immediate interest.

"I know them all," he told Howard. "The girl is a typist at the Groote Schuur hospital and the Mitchells are a very important part of my fashionable practice. The old man pays me through his eyes and nose. He'd burst a blood vessel if he knew how many non-European patients he subsidizes. Hasn't he got a peach of a wife?"

"Yes," Howard said slowly. "He has."

"Man, she's really something — a biological masterpiece."

"How did he come to marry her?" Howard asked. "She can't be more than half his age."

"Money can get you damn nearly anything, Howard. I did hear she had been engaged to an engineer, but he was killed in an accident. After that Mitchell stepped in. I suppose she weighed it up in her sophisticated way and decided to become an old man's darling. She's deep, is that woman."

"What about the other girl, Joan Viljoen?"

"I know a little more about her — we often have a chat when I go to Groote Schuur. She's a nice kid. Now there's a European to quote in your articles to help offset the bad impression given by despots like me! A girl who genuinely believes an injustice has been done to the non-Europeans and in her gentle way does her best to right the wrong."

"Mitchell doesn't like her doing the work," Howard remarked. "I felt damn sorry for her last night."

"Of course he won't. He can't afford to give the impression he has any non-European sympathies. We've got fanatics these days who brand anyone a Red for giving a Kaffir sixpence. Things have hotted up since you were last over here. You'll have to watch your step, my boy, if you start saying nasty things about us."

Howard eased his lean frame from his chair. "Have more confidence in your laws. You might find me an *apartheid* apostle in two months' time. Now when are you taking me round Willisden?"

"Damn your nerve," Morkel grunted, hauling out his pocket-book. He fingered through it, then looked up.

"How will next Friday morning do?"

"Fine."

"Right. Then meet me here at nine-thirty." Morkel grinned wickedly. "And I'll taint and twist everything you see until you won't know your backside from your elbow."

Howard slapped his shoulder. "Thanks, Jannie. *Totsiens*. See you on Friday."

"*Totsiens*, Howard. Good luck, lad."

3

ALTHOUGH she was at least a hundred yards away, Howard recognized her the moment he swung round the bend. Her walk was distinctive: graceful with an indefinably seductive sway of slim hips. She was dressed casually in a sleeveless green sun-frock and sandals. Her head was bare, and the late afternoon sun turned her hair into a massed heap of pale gold.

Howard pulled up alongside her. "Can I give you a lift?" he called.

Linda turned without haste. "Mr. Shaw. How nice to see you again."

He jumped out, opening the door for her. "I take it you are going back to your bungalow."

"I am eventually," she murmured. "I was taking a walk. But I can never resist gallantry," she went on, sliding gracefully into the car.

Howard drove off. They rounded another bend in the winding coast road and a sudden panorama of the twelve mountain peaks came into view. Howard motioned to them.

"This is the finest stretch of coastal scenery I've ever seen. I needed only one look at it to make me snap up my room."

"Hadn't you seen it before?"

"No; I was born and bred in Jo'burg, and my family used to favour the South East coast for their holidays."

"Never mind," she murmured. "Now you can make up for lost time. How long do you intend staying?"

Howard laughed ruefully. "That all depends how long this job takes me. I shall have to watch myself. It won't be difficult to grow idle in a paradise like this."

Mocking lights glinted in her eyes. "From the speed we're travelling, it seems you have good reason for your fears."

Howard suddenly realized how slowly he had been driving since she entered the car. He laughed.

As he pulled up the car she turned lazily towards him.

"If you didn't sound so terribly industrious, I would offer to show you a little of our Cape scenery. I have an hour to while away. But, of course, I mustn't tempt you . . ."

"I'm easily tempted," he grinned.

Linda's green eyes appraised him. "I shouldn't have thought so, but I'll bear it in mind." She waved a slim hand at the mountains. "As we haven't long, I suggest we go up Kloof Nek. There is a good view of Clifton from there, and a charming café in the woods . . ."

"It's Kloof Nek," he said, letting out his clutch.

They drove another mile, then turned up a road that ran diagonally back to the ridge that linked Lion's Head with the Table Mountain range. Above them the ground rose steeply towards the buttressed peaks that towered against the sky, their rocks shaded a delicate rose-pink by the setting sun. Below, covered in flowering mimosa and aloes, the slopes ran down to the sea. At the top of the road, following Linda's instructions, Howard turned left and ran a short distance down a road lined with pines.

"Stop at this corner," she told him.

He pulled the car into the roadside. Through a wide gap in the trees the whole broad sweep of bay from Clifton to Llandudno could be seen. He nodded at her inquiring glance.

"Yes; it's superb."

They sat in silence for a few minutes, then she turned to him. "You'll be flattered to know that I've already read your novel, *The Green Sky*. And I liked it very much. It was very tough in parts, but very sensitive in others. Are you like that?"

"That's the hell of being a writer," Howard scowled. "Everyone psycho-analyses one through one's books as a matter of course. It's both embarrassing and damned unfair."

"I read somewhere that every writer must bleed a little on his pages. Isn't it true?"

"I'm not saying anything," he told her, suddenly aware of the faint, delicate perfume that seemed an integral part of her. He became acutely conscious of her nearness: conscious of her appeal. From a fleeting enigmatic smile that touched her lips, he felt she sensed his emotions. She turned to him, her voice innocent.

"Don't you think it might be a good idea to have tea now?"

"I think it would be," he said dryly.

They followed a path into the pine woods and after five minutes reached a stretch of lawn, on which stood a discreet café overlooking the bay. They had tea and cakes; the minutes slipping by unnoticed. Already impressed by Linda's elegance and poise, Howard now became conscious that there was an alert brain behind her sophisticated exterior. Her questions, however lazily put, were all shrewdly framed to further her knowledge of him. He decided Morkel had been very near the mark — Linda Mitchell was deep indeed.

The sun was a huge red ball low over the sea when she turned and reached for her handbag. The wealth of regret conveyed by the slight gesture was a revelation, although how much of it was genuine he could only guess.

He motioned to her bare arms as they entered the trees. "Aren't you feeling cold?"

"No. But I do wish you would take my arm. This path is very rough."

He obeyed in silence, her warm flesh burning his hand. The uneven path tantalized him, throwing her slim body sidewards to touch and touch him again. The smell of pines lay around them like incense; the trees were silhouetted black against the red horizon. From a deep kloof alongside the winding path came the busy murmur of a rivulet. Above, pink in the sunset, a mountain peak soared into the fading sky, its ravines and fissures delicately traced in pencil-thin shadows.

The path narrowed between a clump of bushes and Howard released Linda's arm, allowing her to precede him. She emerged from the shadowy tunnel, then gave a start and drew back. Seeing Howard was about to question her, she put a finger hastily on her lips.

"Look down there," she whispered. "Be careful they don't see you."

Howard moved curiously forward. Beyond the bushes, on the right of the path, the ground shelved into a shallow gully. A man and a girl were standing down there, engrossed in conversation.

The man, a non-European dressed in stained overalls, Howard did not recognize, but the girl was Joan Viljoen.

Howard drew back. Linda stared at him, a shocked frown on her face. "It is Joan, isn't it?"

Howard nodded. Without further hesitation, Linda stepped among the bushes, pulling aside the twigs until she had a clear view of the couple below. Howard watched her silently.

She turned and motioned to him. "Listen to him talking to her. Look at him!"

The man's voice was angry now, harsh and impassioned. In spite of himself, Howard followed her gaze. The light, although not good, was sufficient to show the man to be of medium height, well-knit, with features that in repose would have been almost handsome. Now they were drawn into a scowl that made his face a fierce mask. His fists were clenched and his whole body tensed with anger. He poured out a torrent of words on the distressed girl.

Even at that moment, Howard found himself impressed again by the girl's delicate appearance. There was a frail loveliness about her so often seen among consumptives or in delicate Dresden figurines, a frailness accentuated by the dark, incensed figure by her side. Her white face was anxious, full of solicitude. She put a hand pleadingly on the man's arm, only for him to shake it off impatiently. Her low voice rose, vibrant with concern. He listened a moment, then broke in harshly, drowning her entreaties.

Linda's voice was a mixture of anger and bewilderment. "Who is he and why is he shouting at her like that? Don't you think we should go down?"

"I don't feel she would like it," Howard said uncomfortably.

Linda turned back to watch. Howard, unable to understand Afrikaans, found himself listening to the tone of their voices. The girl's pleading, first low and anxious, then passionate with concern; the man's restless intolerance and fierce disagreement: both gave Howard the feeling that the man's anger, which the girl was struggling to quell, was directed more against a third party than against the girl herself.

The disagreement ended abruptly. After a last furious tirade, the man turned on his heels and walked swiftly back along the path towards the main road. Joan ran after him, but he ignored her. They both vanished among the trees at the farthermost end of the gully.

Linda's expression was incredulous as she drew back from the bushes. "What do you make of that?" She barely gave Howard time to shake his head before going on furiously: "She must be crazy. Walking out there with a Coloured, putting her hand on his arm, running after him . . . My God; I wouldn't have believed it. Who was the brute, I wonder?"

Howard remained silent. She looked at him sharply, transferring her anger to him.

"All right; I admit I was eavesdropping. But what else do you expect me to do when I see the girl Brian wants to marry fraternizing in the woods with a Coloured? Turn my back and say what a lovely sunset it is?"

Howard shrugged. "I suppose not."

"You suppose right," she snapped.

"Maybe it wasn't conventional, but I don't give a damn for conventions." She took cigarettes from her handbag, snapping the bag closed again. "Anyway; for all we knew he might have been going to assault her."

"I got the impression he was threatening someone else and she was trying to dissuade him," Howard commented.

She blew smoke into the motionless air. "So did I," she admitted. "But I'd like to have heard what they were saying. Don't you speak Afrikaans?"

Howard shook his head.

"Why the devil can't you?" she muttered. Then, seeing his wry smile: "All right; why can't I, either?"

She turned and walked moodily down the path. In a minute or two her anger seemed to evaporate. "I've never bothered about this work of hers," she muttered. "I've always felt that if she wants to go fooling about among non-Europeans, it's her own affair. Normally I mind my own business. But this is different. After all, Brian couldn't take her about more if they were engaged. That's what Trevor is worried about. Everyone is expecting their engagement at any time. This kind of thing could cause a hell of a scandal. Most people wouldn't worry about her belonging to a social welfare organization, but if it came out she had been wandering alone through the woods at night with a Coloured there'd be the devil to pay."

Howard made no reply. What she said was true.

She went on, voicing her thoughts aloud. "She had the sense to meet this fellow off the public road, but even then it was risky. We saw them: others might have done the same. Who was he, anyway?"

"Does Joan live around here?" Howard asked.

"Yes. She has two rooms in Kloof Nek."

"With her family?"

"No; I understand she is an orphan. But she's a quiet little thing; she never talks about herself. And I've never felt it my business to inquire, although" — and her red lips twisted — "I suppose as Brian's step-mother I should show more curiosity."

As they entered Howard's car, Linda gave a bitter laugh, "I wonder what Trevor would say if he heard of this."

"You won't tell him, will you?" Howard asked quickly.

Her green eyes flashed sparks at him. "I might have given you a lousy impression back there, but I'm not a sneak as well."

"Wait a minute," he protested. "I didn't mean it that way. But you were pretty down on her yourself a moment ago, you know."

"I'm not down on her at all. I blew up because that's my way, and because it's enough to make anyone furious to see a Coloured behaving like that before a European girl. But I know she was doing nothing morally wrong — I'd stake my life on that."

"So you really like her?"

"Of course I like her. God knows, I'm no Florence Nightingale myself, but I'm not such a cynic I can't appreciate the type when it comes along. That girl could be the best thing that has happened to our family for a long time. I wish she would agree to become engaged."

"Why won't she? She seems very fond of Brian."

"She is. That's the pity of it. Brian doesn't say anything but I think I know the reason. She knows Trevor doesn't like her and she's afraid he may turn on Brian if they make things definite. It's a shame, because although Brian is still a nice boy, he has been brought up among money and taught how to make more. That girl is the one person I know who might save him from it all."

"You talk as if money were a curse," Howard said, watching her face.

Her lips twisted. "Do I? Then I'm a damned hypocrite because I enjoy it well enough."

Howard turned the car from the grass verge and started downhill. The sunset had faded, leaving only a saffron pennant of cloud on the far horizon. The pale sky, robbed of its colour, was eagerly soaking up the gathering darkness.

Back on the lower coast road, Linda turned towards him mockingly. "You've had quite an exhausting time with me, haven't you? But I must say you've taken it very well."

Howard saw that the poised, sophisticated beauty he had met earlier had returned.

He smiled. "Not at all. It was stimulating, Mrs. Mitchell."

She slanted a glance at him through veiled eyes. "Would you care to be stimulated again next Wednesday evening?"

He pulled up the car on the road above her bungalow and turned to her. "What have you in mind?"

"A dance. Trevor and I were entertaining a journalist called Erasmus and his wife at the Berylsford, but this morning Trevor found out he has to go up to Jo'burg for the week. He hasn't postponed the date yet, so I'm wondering if you'd care to make up the four."

Seeing Howard's hesitation, she went on casually: "Don't worry. Trevor won't mind. We each have our own friends. In fact, he should be pleased — he is always telling me I don't bother enough about his social engagements." Hardness crept into her voice. "And as Erasmus is a very influential columnist in *Die Volksman*, the Afrikaans Nationalist paper, he should be doubly pleased. We must keep on the right side of the Press, mustn't we?"

"I'll be delighted to go, of course," Howard told her.

"Good. Then call round for me about eight-thirty. Don't bother to bring your car. We can all use mine."

She turned back before running down the steps. For a second Howard thought he saw devil lights dancing in her emerald eyes.

"Haven't you heard of Erasmus?"

Howard shook his head. "No. Should I have done?"

"I think you may find him a little unusual," she murmured.

"Good. It sounds as if we'll have an interesting evening."

"We'll do our best to make it one," she said. Their eyes met for a moment, then she was gone down the steps.

4

THE coloured man in stained overalls jumped off the bus at Upper Willisden and started down the long, dismal road opposite. He walked with hurried strides, oblivious of his surroundings. A dog snarled from the stoep of a ramshackle house as he passed by and threw itself savagely against a flimsy barrier of trellis-work, but the man gave no sign of hearing it. His footsteps reverberated from across the deserted road, harsh and impetuous.

He reached a solitary street-lamp that stood at the corner of an alley, and there, in the yellow island of light, he paused for a moment. For the first time he looked hesitant, not of his purpose but of his method of achieving it. His eyes, inflamed by bitterness and anger, stared across the road, first at a large factory that loomed darkly against the night sky, then at a small, wooden church, greatly dwarfed by comparison, that stood nearby. A second more, and he crossed the road.

He tapped on a side door at one end of the church. It was opened almost at once. In the yellow rectangle of light an old coloured priest peered out. He was clad in an old, black suit that showed the effect of much cleaning and pressing. His hair and beard were pure white, and the light at his back gave a silver halo to a face much wrinkled yet alive with a strange and impressive beauty. His deep and gentle voice was warm as he recognized his visitor.

"*Naand*, Michael. It is good to see you. Come inside, my son."

The man called Michael stepped into the small room. A naked bulb hanging from the ceiling showed it to be austere in the extreme. In one corner stood a gas-ring and a small wooden cabinet. A plain deal table and two hard-backed chairs completed the furniture. The floor was bare, except for a few square feet in front of a small paraffin stove, where lay a threadbare carpet. All was spotlessly clean.

The priest spoke in soft Afrikaans. "You are late home tonight, Michael."

Michael ignored the remark. He nodded towards the one small window. "Are they having a meeting tonight, *Eerwaarde*?"

The old man's face clouded. "So it is said, my son."

"Where, Father? In the location?"

The priest nodded slowly. He lifted up his wrinkled face. "Is that why you come to see me, Michael?"

Michael was already moving towards the door. He nodded, his eyes avoiding the slight figure who approached him anxiously.

"Go home, Michael, and let tomorrow bring you wisdom," the old man pleaded. "I saw your mother half an hour ago and she was very worried because you were late home. She was afraid you had done something foolish. Go home and show her you are safe."

Michael did not answer. The priest laid a gentle hand on his arm. "Violence does not kill violence, Michael. Hatred does not stop hate. Go home, my son, I beg you."

"Who mentioned violence?" Michael muttered. "I go to see Umzoni. I said I would go to another of his meetings."

The old man shook his head. "You may be going to see Umzoni, but only because you hope another will be there."

Michael's control broke. He spoke passionately, words pouring from his lips.

The priest sighed. "I know it was a wicked thing to do, my son. But he would not know what we know, and for the rest his mind is so blinded by evil that he cannot see the good others do. Feel sorry for him, my son, the way I do. If you will not go home yet, then sit and talk to me. I will make you some tea and find you something to eat . . . "

Michael's voice was a mixture of shame and sullen defiance. "*Nie*, *Eerwaarde*. I must go to the meeting."

The priest shook his head in distress. "I am afraid for you, Michael, and not only because of this thing. I have watched you since you were a child. Your passions are too easily aroused. Your pride is too strong."

Michael paused, his hand on the door. "You mean because of my dislike for the Europeans?"

"That is one thing I mean, my son. I

fear for what will become of you. Hate is a disease, Michael. It poisons and destroys both the mind and the body. Take care it does not destroy you."

Michael swung open the door. "This is a different thing — something I must do because I am a man. *Totsiens, Eerwaarde, en baie dankie.*" He turned away and vanished.

The darkness outside lay like a noxious mist around the church, a living thing seeking to douse the tiny oasis of light. The old man stared into it, then wearily closed the door. He walked over to a kettle on the gas-ring and made as if to fill it with water. Then, abandoning the task as if too severe, he sank into a chair and dropped his face in his hands.

* * *

The last of the houses had fallen away. In the distance the lights of the city were a nebula of stars under the shadow of the mountain. Ahead, camp-fires gleamed like watching eyes, and in the bushes and wattles a wind whispered of secrets hidden deep in the hearts of brooding men.

Michael turned off a sandy track and entered the location. At first the hovels were thinly scattered, but a few minutes later he plunged into a conglomeration of ramshackle buildings that were thrown together by the darkness into a dense, agglutinated mass.

He followed a narrow, twisted track that led him into the heart of the slum. Voices came out of the darkness, to be suddenly hushed at the sound of his footsteps; faint lights flickered and were gone. He walked on, his eyes watchful. A camp-fire stained the surrounding hovels crimson. He passed it and the darkness closed in again, more impenetrable than ever. Someone stirred beside him and muttered a command. A torch was snapped on and shone full in his face. He stood motionless.

"*Ja*. You can go on," he was told as the light was switched off. He went on, to be stopped twice more in the next hundred yards.

At last the darkness fell away and he came out in a rubble-littered clearing in which was assembled a crowd of between three and four hundred people. They were grouped before a crudely made platform that stood in front of a fence at one end of the enclosure. There were two men on the platform, one seated, the other standing. The latter, an elderly coloured man, was addressing the crowd.

Michael approached the platform, stopping to question one of the listeners on the way. The man shook his head. Michael reached a point to one side of the platform from which he could best study the crowd and there he stood motionless, his narrowed eyes searching the sea of faces.

Because of the danger of police observation, light was kept down to the minimum. Two paraffin lamps, one at either end of the platform, although insufficient to reach the gloomy environs of the clearing, served to illuminate the faces of the listeners. These consisted entirely of non-Europeans, although every shade of colour, from the ebony black of the tropical negro to the pale coffee of the coloured, was among them. Women were scattered among the men, their sleeping picaninnies strapped to their backs with shawls. All were listening expectantly, their expressions curious.

The elderly man finished speaking and to a tumult of applause the seated figure rose and stepped into the centre of the platform. He was a negro of outstanding physique and carriage, well over six feet tall with a massive breadth of shoulders. His age was difficult to judge, although he was probably in his late thirties. Unlike the ragged crowd, he was dressed in a well-fitted suit of good quality and taste. He had a strong, resolute face that for all its composure suggested a restive, passionate nature. His bearing was distinctive: his personality immediately holding his audience. He had the deep, full-blooded voice of the negro with a cultured accent that added to its richness.

He spoke in Afrikaans, although Michael knew his English to be equally fluent. He was a born orator: in a minute the motley crowd were in the palm of his hand. His impassioned voice was like music, its every emotion taking expression among his audience. Although there was no hint of violence in his voice, its effect was electric. Long-lost hopes, forgotten pride, sorrow, pity, resentment, suppressed fear: all stirred into life the apathetic faces before him. He was talking of *apartheid*, of his bitterness towards it. Even in Afrikaans faint traces of the picturesque idiom that had once made Zulu oratory famous could be heard.

"It is an unjust thing, my brothers, yet some of you who cannot read do not know its injustice. Some of you have not yet been greatly affected, but do not think it will remain so. In time it will affect each one of you and will brand your children's children as the sons of Ham.

"Think of the worst of these laws. There is the Group Areas Act which will drive us outside the cities. Things are bad enough for you now: under this Act they will be made much worse. Instead of building homes for you here, the Nationalists will drive you into separate locations. An African like myself will be able to live only with other Africans, he will not be allowed to live with Coloureds or Asiatics, who must have their own locations. You will be taken from friends who share your bread. In Johannesburg, the only place in the country where our brothers owned freehold land, they are forced to give it up because of another unjust act — the Natives Resettlement Bill. Land they have owned for over fifty years is taken from them, and they are driven to a location outside the city. Soon this will happen to us all.

"Why is this done? Because the Nationalists refuse to regard us as anything but a migratory labour force. We must do the work of the European but enjoy none of his privileges. We must live like a herd of cattle that can be moved anywhere on the whims of its masters. And will the European provide free transport from these far-flung locations to the place of your work? You know he will not. Already some of you must rise with the moon to trudge your way to work because you cannot afford the bus fares. How much worse will it be then?

"What about the more fortunate ones among you that own little shops and small businesses? What will happen if they are declared to be in a European zone? Will you get a fair price from a European buyer when he knows you have no option but to sell? Will the lion lie down with the lamb? Will the hyena give suck to the stembuck?

"They pass the Bantu Education Act. It is full of words but its meaning is simple. It says there is no place for us in the European community above that of beasts of burden. No longer are the mission schools free to educate us as they wish. Now they either teach us the Nationalist way, or they are made to close down. We have been called oxen, now we are to be taught as oxen, those few of us who are taught at all . . .

"Then there is the law that denied us the right to protest. It is called the Suppression of Communism Act but it is meant to do more than keep down the Communists. They are its excuse. It makes our meetings, which have nothing to do with Communism, illegal. It brands and punishes every man who raises his voice against injustice. Some have said it could make the very words of Christ treasonable. It is a law that has taken away one of the few rights that were left to us before *apartheid* — the right to cry out against our suffering.

"They violate the sanctity of marriage. It is wrong, they say, for a European and non-European to fall in love. And it is wicked for them to marry. So they make it a crime with their Mixed Marriage Act. And so those of you who have sinned by loving the European must now walk with your heads bowed in shame.

"And how do they keep a check on which of you are of one race or another? They come among you like men valuing cattle and to each they give a tag — a registration-card. If you are judged a non-European, this card is your mark of Cain. For ten generations your children's children must walk not in the sunlight but only in the shade . . . My brothers, this *apartheid* is unjust not only to us but to millions of innocent souls crying not to be born . . ."

A quivering sigh ran through the hushed audience. Bowed backs had straightened, dulled eyes flashed into life. The crowd hung on every word as the speaker continued.

"And then we come to the greatest mockery of all, my brothers. The men who have framed these laws tell us they are as much for our benefit as for the Europeans. That eventually the land will be shared out, so that each race may live and develop as it wishes. Ah; if this were so *apartheid* might well be our salvation. But only fools can believe such promises. We outnumber the white man by four to one. Will he, then, give us four-fifths of the land — not the Karoo or desert, but the fertile soil where the grass is green and the cattle fat? Will he give us four-fifths of the industries we have helped build for him? We know he will not; we know these are empty promises to keep us quiet until we are so bound and gagged we can no longer open our mouth to protest.

"And all these laws are in addition to the old ones — the laws that forbid Africans to travel from one town to another without a pass, the laws that keep Indians in Natal, the laws that make us all lepers not fit to share a park bench with our lords and masters.

Laws, hundreds of laws, and so many of us not able to read. We break laws we do not know exist, and then we are thrown into prison where nearly two hundred thousand of our brothers live like dogs."

The speaker towered to his full height over the crowd. His impassioned voice sank dramatically. "What must we do, my brothers? Listen and I will tell you. I have come with a plan that will bring you and your children out of the shadows if each of you will play your part. Listen to me carefully . . . "

Judging his moment to perfection, the negro paused. Another sigh ran through the crowd. Expectancy loaded the air like a static charge. A second more, and the negro spoke again. Now his voice was exhortative, although his words measured and slow. Slowly, carefully, he unfolded his plan and comprehension began dawning on the faces of his listeners.

He had been speaking over half an hour when a group of shadowy figures ran into the clearing. Breaking into pairs they merged with the crowd at scattered points. A minute elapsed, then a sudden harsh voice interrupted the negro's address.

"*Hy's mal!* It would do no good. You are fools to listen. You are wasting your time."

Cries of agreement broke out from isolated points at the rear of the audience, breaking the spell. The crowd looked around, trying to see the dissenters. The negro speaker tried to continue but the heckling grew louder, drowning his voice.

Michael, his eyes riveted on the platform, had not noticed the arrival of the newcomers; but at the first sound of the harsh voice he swung round with narrowed eyes. Hearing it again, he ran round the rear of the crowd, searching for its owner.

The negro speaker, his face set and grim, was standing silent in the middle of the platform. The bewildered crowd was milling about, trying to find the source of the heckling. Suddenly a man ran forward into the vacant space immediately before the platform. He leapt on a box that lay in front of one of the lamps and threw out his arms towards the crowd.

"*Julle is gekke*," he screamed. "This thing will not help you. You are mad to listen. Only one thing will make them take notice — fear. Make them fear and you will make them give. And how do you make them fear? You know — I, Swartz, have shown you before . . ."

Savage yells of approval, like the baying of wolves, came from his supporters hidden in the crowd. The audience stared in fascination at the cat-like figure standing in the lamp-light. He was a Coloured, lean of build, with a thin face, high cheekbones, and cropped, crinkly hair. A knife-scar ran across one cheek, giving his face a twisted, wolfish expression.

The negro on the platform held out an imperious hand. For a moment the cries were stilled.

"Take no notice of this madman," he told them in his deep, resonant voice. "To do as he says would be suicidal as well as wicked. They have money, troops, guns, while you have nothing." He leaned forward, staring coldly down at the vicious face below. "Get back to your kennel, Swartz, and let honest men talk in peace."

Swartz snarled. "Honest men? You talk like a weak woman, Umzoni. You are a — "

A warning whistle sounded from the crowd. Swartz jumped from the box like a startled cat and spun round. He saw Michael, who had broken through the crowd, advancing towards him. His eyes narrowed.

"Who are you?" he snarled. "What do you want?"

"I want you," Michael spat.

Swartz's eyes were wary. "What have I done to you?"

"You attacked a girl in Willisden on Monday night. Why?"

Swartz stared, then laughed harshly. "I remember. A European. Yes; she was lucky. She nearly got something to remember me by."

Michael's eyes, inflamed with hatred, saw nothing else but the sneering figure before him. But Umzoni on the platform above noticed the massive, repulsive negro who had broken his way through the awed crowd and was now approaching

Michael from behind like a great panther. Umzoni went quickly to one end of the platform and gave brief instructions to a party of men standing there. They nodded and slipped away.

"I like Europeans no more than you," Michael threw back. "But that girl is good. She helps our people. She brings them food and clothing. Only a foul swine would attack her."

Swartz's eyes narrowed into slits, flickering for a split-second on the approaching figure of the negro.

"She is a European," he spat. "And if she comes this way again she will get what I would give them all. She will be . . . " The rest of his obscene threat was choked off as Michael leapt at his throat.

The huge negro moved like lightning, seizing Michael's arms and twisting them savagely back, his flat, brutal face grinning with enjoyment. Snarling like an animal, Swartz tore himself away. He smashed his clenched fist twice into Michael's face, then raised his foot to kick. Before he could use it, Umzoni's followers were on him.

Men cursed hoarsely and women screamed as the crowd scattered. Both men fought like tigers. The massive negro felled three men before he was brought down. Swartz, struggling like a wildcat in the arms of his captors, let out a shrill whistle for the rest of his gang. Immediately more of Umzoni's followers threw a cordon round the group. Seeing they were heavily outnumbered, the advancing hooligans faded quickly back among the excited crowd.

Umzoni descended the platform and approached Michael, who was dabbing at his bleeding face.

"What is this about a European girl?" he demanded.

Eyeing the cursing Swartz malevolently, Michael told him. The negro nodded and went over to the gang leader, waving his men aside. They drew back reluctantly, leaving the two hooligans free.

"You are a vicious fool, Swartz," Umzoni said angrily. "We have many friends among the Europeans who sympathize with us and defend our cause. Do you want to turn them all against us?"

"They are all against us," Swartz snarled. "That is the way they deceive us — by pretending they are our friends. What do they do for us? Nothing. A few give us charity — pah," and he spat in the sand. "They let us starve and then give us a bowlful of soup. They treat us as animals and throw crumbs to the floor. Friends!" He spat again.

"It is such as you who turn them away in disgust," Umzoni said contemptuously. "You are blind with hate. You see nothing but evil. Violence will achieve nothing. Only our own people would suffer."

"You will get nothing without violence," Swartz snarled. "People do not give away what they have unless they are made to fear."

"You know our plan. It cannot fail with the support of us all. Why do you keep interrupting my meetings?"

"Because it is the plan of a woman," Swartz sneered.

Umzoni's face darkened. "Because it does not kill, you mean. Because you are a bloodthirsty animal who delights in using your knife . . . " His suppressed anger burst out at last. He moved threateningly forward. "So far I have been patient with you, but now you know what to expect. The next time my men will be waiting for you."

Swartz's face contorted. "You threaten me, you bloody Kaffir swine!" He broke into an outburst of foul oaths and threats.

The negro's followers moved angrily forward. Umzoni waved them back. "Leave the animal, it is diseased," he said curtly. He turned back to Swartz. "Take your filth with you and go. *Opskud!*"

Swartz drew back his lips. He moved away, followed by the scowling negro. Then he turned back, his face twisted in a grin of hate.

"You'll pay for this, Kaffir," he spat. "Remember what I say — you'll pay for it." His eyes burned at Umzoni for a moment, then the two of them had merged into the shadows and were gone.

Umzoni turned to Michael. "Wait for me, please. I will be only a few minutes."

He ran back to the platform and addressed the crowd again, who grew silent at once. "You will not be alone in this thing," he finished. "All over the land your brothers are preparing as you will prepare. But guard your tongues; the Europeans must not know yet. What we shall do will be against the law, but let that disturb none of you. The laws are unjust; the laws are our enemy. Go now and prepare yourselves. Later you shall hear from me again. *Totsiens*, my brothers."

Applause rolled across the clearing in long, fervent waves. Umzoni waved a hand in farewell, then made his way through the milling, enthusiastic crowd to Michael. He drew him aside.

"I am told you know a priest called Father Hendricks. I find his influence very strong among people in these parts. Why is that?"

Michael shrugged. "I suppose it is because he is a good man and the people love him for his goodness." He made as if to turn away. "I must be going now. Thank you for your help tonight."

Umzoni took his arm. "Wait, my friend. I wish to speak to you about this Father Hendricks."

5

"HOW dare you have him round here? How many times do I have to tell you . . . "

The strident voice of Mrs. Dowson stopped Howard short. He grimaced. After an evening stroll, he was making his way back to his room down the cliff steps. Now he paused, to advance cautiously at the sound of quarrelling voices. A few more steps and, to his dismay, he found himself on the site of the quarrel.

It was taking place on the stoep outside his room. The two Dowsons were confronting the maid, Lucy, and a coloured man in his middle twenties. Although the Coloured was now dressed in sports coat and flannels, Howard recognized him as the man to whom Joan Viljoen had been talking in the woods the previous night. Curious, Howard drew nearer. He saw the Coloured's face was badly bruised, with one cheek swollen.

Michael's face was a study of sullen anger as he faced the portly Dowson, whose flow of invective was checked as Howard made his appearance.

"If you haven't gone in five minutes, I'm calling the p'lice," Dowson finished, then turned to Howard.

"We've been having trouble with these two while you've been out," he muttered. "They've been kicking up a hell of a row in her room . . . "

"It's the last time it's going to happen," Mrs. Dowson broke in. She stabbed a dagger-like finger at the sobbing Lucy. "I've warned her before — I won't have her drunken boy friends in the bungalow. They've had a wireless in there and you should have heard the noise they were kicking up. Terrible, it was."

"I heard it before I went out," Howard murmured.

Michael moved suddenly, startling Dowson who jumped nervously back. The Coloured said something in fierce Afrikaans to Lucy, then entered her room, to emerge with a small, portable wireless. With set face, he started down the stoep, scattering the Dowsons as he went.

"Don't you ever dare to come here again," Mrs. Dowson screeched after him. "I'm telling the police all about you and they'll be watching out."

Howard watched the Coloured go by. In spite of his obvious anger he was showing more control than the Dowsons. Howard grew more curious as to his identity.

The Dowsons turned their combined attention on the sobbing maid.

"If you invite that drunken good-for-nothing here once more — out you go," Mrs. Dowson finished. "Now get into your room and stay there."

The girl ran inside and closed her door. The sound of her weeping came through it.

Bert Dowson turned to go. He eyed Howard somewhat shamefacedly as he passed by. "Sorry about the fuss, but I'm not going to have that coloured swine hanging round here at night. It's not safe for the wife. And anyway the noise would have driven you crazy."

He paused for Howard's approval. When it did not come he grunted good night and went up the steps.

Howard went to his room. Mrs. Dowson was standing by his door. He nodded good night to her.

She followed him into the doorway. "It was for your own sake, you know, Mr. Shaw. If we hadn't stopped it, you'd have been kept awake all night."

"I didn't find the wireless over-loud," he said dryly. "It didn't worry me at all."

Her thin lips compressed. "Well; we're not used to the bungalow sounding like a tap-room, and we're not having it."

"Who was the Coloured?" Howard asked. "Her fiancé?"

She made a gesture of disgust. "She's been going out with him for a couple of years, if that's what you mean. The little fool wanted to marry him last year, but I talked her out of it. He's nothing but a drunken wastrel, anyone can see that. I suppose he got those bruises on his face from fighting in some *shebeen*. I asked her what would happen to her mother if she gave up this job. That made her think, I can tell you."

"Does she help her mother with money, then?"

"She gives her something — or so she says. But you can never be sure; they're such liars. Bert keeps telling me to let her go; but it's all right for him — he wouldn't have to do the washing and the rest. You can't get maids easily these days — all of them are going into factories. They pay 'em too much, that's the trouble. All that's left over is the riff-raff . . . "

She moved reluctantly from the doorway. "Anyway; there'll be no more of it. Bert knows where the brute works and is thinking of having a talk with his boss."

Howard paused with his hand on the door. "I very much hope that won't be necessary," he said quietly.

Her lips tightened again. "It's up to them. He's had his last warning. Good night."

"Good night, Mrs. Dowson."

Howard waited until she had gone, then tapped softly on the maid's door. It was opened timidly. The girl stared at him with frightened, tear-stained eyes as he closed the door cautiously behind him.

"I just want to warn you to be very careful," he told her. "Mr. and Mrs. Dowson are very angry and if your friend comes round here again they might get him into serious trouble. So I should arrange to meet him somewhere else. Do you understand?"

The girl fought back her sobs. "Yes, master."

"Mrs. Dowson doesn't seem to think he is good enough for you," Howard went on, watching her. "She says he drinks too much and is always in trouble."

The girl looked up in protest. "He doesn't, master. He is a good man. They do not like him because they cannot bully him. He will not let any European bully him."

"He doesn't like Europeans?" Howard asked.

Fear that she had said too much made the girl lower her eyes.

"You needn't be afraid to tell me," Howard said. "I shan't tell anyone. Why doesn't he like Europeans?"

Her swollen eyes searched his face, then trusted him. "He calls them names, master, and says they are hard and selfish. He frightens me. I am afraid he will get into trouble one day and be put in jail."

"Then Mrs. Dowson is right?"

"No, master. He is kind and generous. He does not look for trouble. It is only that he is proud and does not like being treated as we are treated."

"Who has he been fighting lately? He has been fighting, hasn't he? I saw the marks on his face."

She brushed back her tears. "No one can blame him for that, master. It was a man named Swartz, a *skolly* who has a gang and attacks people . . . "

"Why did he fight him?" Howard asked curiously.

"Because he attacked a European girl in Willisden."

Howard's eyes widened. "A European girl? On Monday night?"

"Yes, master."

After a moment, Howard went on: "Why did he do this — if he does not like Europeans?"

"He does not attack them, master. And he says this girl is one of the good ones — that she goes around helping the poor.

He was very, angry. You see, he is not bad, master. He is a good man."

Howard was thinking of the scene he had witnessed in the woods the previous night. This must have been the reason the Coloured had been talking to Joan, although why he should seek her out to tell her of his intentions was still something of a mystery. But clearly he was a superior type of Coloured. Whatever his general attitude was towards the Europeans, he was obviously capable of passionate gratitude to those who helped his people, for his action in attacking the formidable Swartz was bold to the point of recklessness. It was bitter irony that the bruises he had gathered in the defence of a European should have been used by the Dowsons as his condemnation.

"What were you celebrating tonight?" Howard asked.

The girl stared unhappily down at the bare floor. "I have been away a month, master, and we have missed one another."

"Of course." Howard felt in his pocket and drew out a note.

"Here. Take this and forget all about tonight. I'm sure things will be different tomorrow."

She stared in astonishment, first at the note, then at him. "You're very kind, master. *Dankie*."

Howard nodded good night to her and returned to his room. He was still vaguely puzzled about the meeting he had witnessed between Joan Viljoen and this Coloured. Why had he sought her out and why had she shown such distress?

His thoughts were suddenly scattered by the blare of a wireless from the flat above. He lifted his eyes and shook his head thoughtfully at the ceiling.

6

THE following Wednesday evening Howard made his way on foot to the Mitchells' bungalow. Linda answered the door, radiant in a strapless evening frock of emerald organza. Gold pendant ear-rings set with emerald stones matched her green eyes, the tan of her smooth shoulders, and the pale gold of her hair.

Her voice in itself was a caress. "I'm going to call you Howard from tonight, and you must call me Linda. Formalities become ridiculous if carried on too long. Now come through and meet the others . . . "

Mrs. Erasmus was a brunette in her late thirties. Her face had been pretty once but a tendency to stoutness over the years had blurred its most delicate features, leaving it dull and uninteresting. Her coiffure, while of the expensive variety, only succeeded in giving her hair a starched and lack-lustrous appearance.

The hand she held out to Howard was slightly damp.

Erasmus, possibly five years older than his wife, was above average in height. He was slimly built, with sleek black hair and a dark complexion. He had the gaunt face and deep-set eyes of the fanatic. He bowed slightly to Howard as he shook hands.

"*Aangename kennis, meneer.*"

Howard looked at Linda, who smiled mockingly.

"Sorry, Darney, but you have two ignorant roineks with you tonight. Howard can't speak Afrikaans, either, although he has an excuse. He has been overseas for years and years. Now I have no excuse but laziness . . ." She wandered gracefully over to the cocktail-cabinet. "What will you have, Howard? Whisky again?"

"Thanks," Howard smiled, dropping into a chair. Both Linda and the couple opposite gave him the impression of having had quite a few drinks before his arrival. Erasmus was slightly flushed and his eyes kept resting on Linda with undisguised admiration. It was clear he was infatuated by her and alcohol had driven away the natural caution he would show in the presence of his wife.

At the moment, however, Marie Erasmus seemed unaware of the situation. Alcohol appeared to affect her motor nerves, making her facial control difficult. She wore an inept expression which she was trying unsuccessfully to remove.

Linda brought Howard a glass of whisky, then sank into the armchair opposite him. An air of reckless gaiety surrounded her, setting off her beauty in high relief. Her vivid eyes held Howard's for a moment over the rim of her raised glass.

"You two should have a good deal in common," she murmured, her gaze wandering from Howard to Erasmus. "I did tell you what Howard had come to report on, didn't I, Darney?"

The columnist nodded. "Yes; although you were a little vague about the reasons. May I ask what they are, Mr. Shaw?"

Howard flickered a rueful glance at Linda, then explained. Remembering Erasmus had a column in one of the country's leading pro-*apartheid* papers and would almost certainly hold the same political views, he made his explanation as brief and innocuous as possible. Nevertheless, Erasmus's face had darkened before he finished.

"But your paper is as prejudiced as the rest, *meneer*," he protested.

Howard lifted an eyebrow. "Prejudiced? Why?"

"We have declared *apartheid* a fair policy to all races. The very act of sending an observer on such a mission shows distrust."

Howard smiled wryly. "Let's face it, *meneer*. Few people overseas believe *apartheid* has been designed for the non-European's benefit. In your party's own words, *apartheid* is designed to preserve and uphold white Christian civilization in the Union. I think that makes it fairly clear that it is first and foremost for the European's benefit, whatever other factors may apply."

Erasmus's heavy-lidded eyes had narrowed. "I take it you are against the laws, *meneer*."

"Then you take it wrong," Howard said shortly. "I've been away from this country a long time and I've come back with an open mind. I shall form opinions as I go along."

Erasmus shook his head sullenly. "No, *meneer*. You'll find trouble as all the others have done. You'll find it because your paper wants you to find it. I know those overseas papers too well — they are blindly prejudiced against us. And it is abhorrent they should ask a South African to help them with their prying and trouble-making. I could understand them asking a Kaffir, but not a European. It is like asking a man to be a traitor."

Howard had placed his man now. Here was a blind devotee to the religion of *baaskap*, of white supremacy. The type that believed the possession of white skin was the sole requisite for racial dominance. Not honesty, not intelligence, not culture: nothing but unpigmented skin. A type that because of its neurasthenia was morbidly sensitive to the slightest breath of liberal criticism. A bigoted and intolerant type not uncommon in the Union, or, for that matter, in other territories where white and black shared uneasy domain. It explained the suddenness of the present disagreement.

Only Howard's sense of humour prevented the situation taking an uglier turn. He laughed scornfully.

"A traitor; and you, a journalist, saying it! If critics are traitors, then God help democracy. A patriot isn't a blind fool who mouths platitudes about 'my country, right or wrong'. He is someone who tries to bring it a little nearer perfection by exposing its faults. Criticism is the cathartic of democracy, *Meneer* Erasmus. As a journalist you should know that."

Both men's eyes were locked. Erasmus's face was suffused with blood, his mouth thin and resentful. Linda broke in with a low laugh.

"Howard, darling; you have a turn of words almost like Trevor — although not quite so raw, of course. He has a habit of getting down to fundamentals."

Both men relaxed slowly. Howard turned to her apologetically, only to catch the excited gleam in her eyes. He wondered how much of this encounter she had anticipated when inviting him to the party. Probably all of it, he thought. Her sense of humour was nothing if not capricious.

He smiled wryly. "Actually, I haven't the slightest desire to get down to fundamentals tonight. I hate talking shop on occasions like this."

"Of course you do," she soothed. She turned to Erasmus. "Why, you might find Howard writing in favour of *apartheid* yet, Darney. I was hoping that you might help him with his investigations. There must be loads of facts and figures you could get him from your newspaper . . . "

Howard realized she was not baiting him alone. Beside the sullen columnist Marie Erasmus was having further trouble with her face. During the argument she had ventured to lay a cautionary hand on her husband's arm, only to have it shaken off angrily. Now that the argument appeared over, her efforts to hide her relief were almost comical.

Utterly ignoring the strained atmosphere, Linda jumped to her feet and spun round, her full skirt swirling round her slim legs.

"Come on," she cried. "Finish your drinks and let's get away. We'll use your car, Darney."

When Erasmus did not speak, she gave a tut-tut of impatience and put a hand under his arm. "Snap out of it, for heaven's sake, Darney. It's all over now, isn't it, Marie?"

The woman nodded hesitantly, muttering to her husband in Afrikaans. He nodded abruptly, then walked from the room, followed by his unhappy wife.

Howard met Linda's amused glance. He shook his head. "You don't still intend to go, do you?"

"Of course. He'll get over it when he's had a few more drinks. I don't intend having my evening spoiled as easily as this."

"I can't see it being a howling success. But if you want to go, I suppose there's nothing else to do."

Her green eyes suddenly glowed dangerously. "There is! You can, for example, walk straight out of the front door and keep walking, if that's the way you feel."

Howard held both hands above his

head. "Don't you start now. I've had enough. I'll go quietly."

Linda's anger went as quickly as it came. She laughed and took his arm. "Come on. Let's go and dance it all out of our systems."

⋆ ⋆ ⋆

Berylsford proved to be a select and expensive night club with an excellent orchestra, a sprung maplewood floor, and a good service. The deference of the manager, who personally conducted Linda and Erasmus to their table, suggested they were members held in high esteem.

The evening — at least the first part of it — was not the complete failure Howard had expected. This, he suspected, was due to Linda's influence over Erasmus. Almost on arrival she had whisked the columnist away for a dance, and on his return his attitude towards Howard, although not cordial, was at least civil enough to make normal conversation possible once more. Clearly Linda had been giving him a pep talk.

As Howard had expected Linda proved a superb dancer. She flowed rather than walked and her timing was perfection. Among the many attractive and fashionably-dressed women present her vivid beauty was outstanding.

"Do you know these Erasmus people well?" he asked her during a tango.

She shook her head. "If you're working on the lines that you can judge people by their friends, forget it. I loathe fanatics of any type. But he's a useful acquaintance of Trevor's, so Linda, like a dutiful wife, does her best to entertain him. Actually, I don't see much of him, which is just as well." Her eyes met his quite shamelessly. "He's pretty well gone on me, you know."

"I'd guessed something of the sort," Howard said dryly.

"That might have been one reason he went for you the way he did," she murmured. "The poor thing might be feeling jealous and frustrated. He is at a disadvantage tonight with a wife at his heels, you know."

Howard looked down at her, realizing she was probably very near the truth.

This woman was a witch with men, he thought. Her hair brushed his cheek lightly, the scent of it stirring his nostrils. Her low *décolletage* showed the deep cleft where her tanned neck ran down to the cool whiteness of her breasts. Her lithe body swayed in perfect rhythm to the glide and check of the tango . . .

"Perfect," she murmured, as they left the floor. "You dance very well."

Erasmus, who had not been dancing, rose a trifle unsteadily as they approached. He had been drinking heavily throughout the evening, and his behaviour towards Linda had become less and less inhibited. His inflamed eyes left little doubt of his desire as they wandered over her.

Howard's dislike for him grew, although he had no worries about any possible embarrassment to Linda. Her sophistication could take a great deal more than this. Erasmus's wife proved the problem. With her husband's conduct growing more and more out of hand, she was finding difficulty in aligning her own conduct with Howard. It had been clear she had not approved of him after his disagreement with her husband — whether out of political or connubial loyalty was not so clear — but now the pique engendered by Erasmus's philandering made her want to rejoin in kind. The result was a mixture of cold stares and coquettish giggles, both equally embarrassing to Howard.

"I wish that woman would make up her mind whether to love or hate me," he told Linda during a dance. "The suspense is too much."

"I keep thinking she's going to swoon every time she dances with you, darling."

"Half the evening I'm in heaven and the other half in hell," he said gloomily. "Why must life be like that?"

"I hope," she murmured, pressing closer to him, "that I'm not the hell part."

He met her green, mocking eyes. "You could be, very easily."

* * *

To Howard's surprise the club closed at midnight. Linda, however, had no intention of returning home.

"We're going to Valhalla," she told him.

He shuddered. "It sounds terrible. What do we do there?"

"It's a joint. You meet a motley crowd of arty types and long-haired intellectuals. There's music of a kind, drink at a price, and women given away for a song."

"What about the Erasmuses? Will they play?"

She smiled wickedly. "He'll love it, but Marie won't be so keen."

Valhalla proved to be hidden away down one of the dingy roads leading to the docks. It was a long, low building from which came the high-pitched squawk of a trumpet accompanied by sundry thumps, brays and howls. In front of the door stood a uniformed negro. As Linda and party made their way down the cement path, a European in evening clothes came out, spoke a few words to the attendant, then retired into the hall again, closing the door behind him.

Linda and Erasmus reached the negro attendant first. The boy did not step aside. He shook his head apologetically as Erasmus snapped at him in harsh Afrikaans.

"What's the trouble?" Howard asked the columnist's wife as they came up to the others.

There was relief in her voice. "The boy says the hall is full, that he must let no one else inside." She stepped forward and touched the arm of her husband, who was now arguing angrily with the nervous boy.

Howard turned to Linda. "If the place is full, that's the end of it. It isn't the boy's fault. Let's get back to the car."

"Nonsense," she said impatiently. "I saw people going in as we drove up."

"Maybe you did. They were the last allowed inside."

"You needn't make it so clear you've had enough," she suddenly flared. "You do as you like, but I'm going inside."

She went forward, clearly determined to do as she said. The attendant, already too frightened by the abuse Erasmus was throwing at him to know what he was doing, put his back to the door. He broke into English.

"*Nie*, madame," he begged. "The

master says it is full. No one has to come in . . . "

"Stand out of my way," Linda snapped.

Panic-stricken, the boy threw his arms across the door. Linda, expecting him to draw aside, ran into one of them as she stepped forward. She recoiled with a cry of fury.

"How dare you?" she gasped. She spun round on the two Europeans, her voice almost incoherent. "Did you see that? He struck me . . . "

Erasmus, his face black with rage, ran forward and smashed his fist into the boy's mouth. The boy collapsed with a moan. The columnist kicked at him, trying to find his face. He was kicking like a madman when Howard caught hold of him.

"You damned bully," he gritted. His push, meant to force the inflamed man from the sobbing boy, sent him reeling backwards, to fall heavily over a flower-bed. Cursing wildly Erasmus struggled to his feet. He started forward, then met Howard's eyes. He stopped dead, sober in an instant. His wife ran to him, muttering frantically in Afrikaans.

Linda stepped up to Howard, spots of fire burning in her pale cheeks.

"Why did you stop Darney?" She pointed to the boy who had struggled to his feet and was nursing his bleeding face. "That Kaffir laid hands on me . . . "

Howard's voice shook with anger. "He did nothing but his job. And because of you he got himself a hiding. You're the one that needed it, not he."

She brought up her hand and slapped his face.

His lips drew back. He nodded slowly at her. "I'll let you get away with that because you're half-drunk."

She slapped his face again, viciously. Her arm was suddenly caught; her face drawn up to his. Her breath sucked in sharply at the expression on his face.

"Be careful," he said. "I can hit back. And, by God, if either of you two touch that boy again, I will. Remember that, Erasmus."

Nursing her bruised arm, Linda watched him turn on his heel and stride away down the path.

* * *

Howard walked back to his flat, hoping the cool night air would clear his brain. Mixed with his anger he was aware of an acute disappointment with Linda. The feeling was still with him when he reached Clifton an hour later, vaguely surprising him by its persistence. He descended the steps moodily, to pause in astonishment.

Linda was leaning over the low wall of the stoep, a cigarette dangling from one hand. She straightened slowly as he approached.

"You've been a hell of a time," she muttered sullenly.

"What are you doing here?" he asked.

"What the devil do you think?" she snapped. "Watching for fairies?" Then her mood changed. She faced him squarely. "I came to apologize for that scene outside the Valhalla. It was disgraceful, and I'm completely ashamed of myself. Does that satisfy you?"

"I never wanted satisfying," he said slowly. "I didn't get kicked in the face for doing my job."

"I've apologized to the boy, too," she told him. "And given him five pounds.

Now are you happy?"

He whistled and rubbed his chin. "Five pounds! Yes; I think I am." He paused. "What did Erasmus say to all this?"

"He nearly broke a blood vessel. He wouldn't speak to me all the way home." She hesitated a moment, her eyes falling away for the first time. "I don't know why I behaved like that. I'd had too much to drink, and didn't want the evening to end, I suppose . . . And I never thought the boy would get in my way. Once he touched me — well, you know how we're brought up to detest being touched by them. I went quite crazy . . . And when I saw you attack Erasmus for striking the boy, I wanted to hurt you, too."

"Which you did," Howard grinned.

"Oh, damn you," she said, with a return of her old spirit. "I don't mind hitting you. But, although I'm a bitch, I don't make a point of hitting people who can't hit back. That's the part I don't like."

Howard took a deep breath. "Can I offer you a last drink?"

"No; I'd better be getting back."

"Then I'll come with you."

They went along the beach to her bungalow. The tide was out and the sand soft under their feet. The moon was full, edging the mountains with silver.

As they reached her bungalow Howard remembered and motioned to her arm. "Did I hurt you?" he asked ruefully.

Linda pulled back the sleeve of her coat. "There are two bruises," she told him. Her voice was unusually penitent. "It might be a good thing for me if they stayed there."

The moonlight was full on her. Her hair ran in ice-gold torrents and her eyes were like emerald stars. He moved his head, as if vainly trying to clear his mind of her beauty. For a moment their bodies touched. Then she drew back.

"You've seen enough of the devil in me tonight, Howard. I'm going in now. Good night."

"Good night, Linda."

He watched until she had vanished inside the bungalow before starting slowly back across the beach.

7

THE steaming offal lay red and bloody in the sunlight. The two men picked through it, separating the pieces and arranging them on sheets of soggy newspaper that covered the bare earth. Flies, attracted by the blood, settled in droves.

The site, by its appearance a rubbish dump, was surrounded on three sides by smoking factories. On the fourth side, by the railway, stood a large brick building from which the two men had brought the offal. A crowd of non-European women, who had ceased their chattering at the arrival of the men, had drawn themselves into the semblance of a queue and were now eyeing the offal with expectant faces.

One of the men beckoned the first woman forward. She was a negress clad in a voluminous dress with a black shawl wrapped tightly round her head. Tied to her back with another shawl was a flat-faced piccaninny who was staring around with round, helpless eyes.

The woman pointed inquiringly to a piece of offal. One of the men grunted its price. Shaking her head, the woman picked up another dripping fragment. Again the price was too high. She looked around helplessly. With a muttered exclamation one of the men picked up a piece and thrust it at her. She took it, slowly relinquishing the few coppers from her pocket. She shuffled away, the length of steaming intestine dangling from her hand. The next woman moved forward.

Howard sank back in his seat. Morkel met his eye and smiled wryly. "Seen enough?" he asked.

Howard nodded. Morkel started up his car and drove off.

"Pretty grisly, isn't it?" he said. "It's surprising how few Europeans in Cape Town know of it. We call it the offal market."

"When you mentioned it to me, I was thinking of liver, kidneys and the rest," Howard told him. "After a few years in Europe one forgets what real poverty is like."

"Oh; only the rich can afford luxuries like that," Morkel said ironically. "I don't suppose the crowd we saw there had a sixpence apiece for the day's food for their family. Mind you," he went on, "don't get the impression every non-European in the Cape is as hard up as that. Those in the factories get quite good wages. Most of those you saw are flotsam — the ones out of work and Kaffirs who have drifted from up-country thinking employment easier to find in the city. There's more than thirty thousand of 'em in the Cape Flats."

As Morkel had been talking, the last of the city had fallen away. The road was now lined with pines and wattles, growing from ground that in places seemed pure sand.

"So you want to see the Cape's equivalents of Jo'burg's locations like Maroka, Pimville and Orlando?" the doctor said. "Well; I think we can do as well. We have Windermere, Lower Willisden and a few other prime spots. I thought I'd take you round Willisden, because I know it better than the others. It's a good example, too, because it is almost wholly non-European, and ranges from houses in the better class area to dug-outs and *pondokkies* in the location. The only thing is, you've been through it already, haven't you? Didn't you pick Joan Viljoen up there?"

"Oh; that was an accident. I was only passing through it on my way back from Muizenberg. I saw nothing of it."

"Right. Then we'll make it Willisden."

A few minutes later they crossed the railway and drove down a road lined with old houses and small dirty shops. Barefooted coloured children playing on the road scattered at their approach and mangy dogs slunk into alleys. Morkel pulled up for a moment and turned to Howard.

"This is Upper Willisden. It used to be a fashionable European suburb, but those days are long over. The further one goes down the worse it gets until it's a cess-pool of *pondokkies* and dug-outs. Mind you; it's popular with industry. It's only a few miles from town; the railway is nearby; the land is cheap and labour plentiful. Quite a few factories are moving out. Trevor Mitchell had a tin plate factory built here two years ago. It's down there," and he pointed to a road which Howard recognized as the one in which he had picked up Joan Viljoen.

"I suppose all these houses are as crowded as those in the Jo'burg slums?" Howard asked.

"Just the same. You get as many as six families in some of 'em — sleeping in the kitchen, passages, bathrooms and water-closets. Sometimes two families share one room."

He drove off again. Soon the decayed houses fell away and they were bumping over a rutted, dusty track.

"You can imagine what this road is like in the winter," Morkel shouted.

Howard nodded, staring out at the conglomeration of crazy hovels that stood at either side of the track. Piles of packing-cases, pieces of corrugated iron, even sheets of cardboard: all were thrown together to make primitive shelters. Some were not even above ground but mere dug-outs with a few planks laid on top to form a roof. Among these fantastic shelters half-naked coloured children played while their mothers squatted over fires, doing their cooking. Dogs snarled at one another as they nosed among the garbage that lay in piles everywhere, and scraggy hens squawked and pecked hungrily in the sand.

Morkel pulled up. "Well; here's the location. It goes on for another mile. You're seeing it at its best now. In the winter it's one huge swamp."

The sky was blue and Table Mountain green in the distance but it was not difficult to imagine the location in wet weather. Howard nodded.

"Jo'burg shanty towns all over again. There must be a tremendous amount of disease under these conditions."

Morkel nodded. "T.B. is the worst scourge. We can't even guess how many have it. And we've nothing like enough beds for those who come to us. We have to send 'em back to wait their turn, knowing they'll infect the rest of their family and perhaps a couple more families as well. It's the kids I'm sorry for. Poor little devils, they haven't a chance. They sleep in water during the winter, and those fortunate enough to go to school are lucky if they start the day with a slice of bread in their bellies. If it wasn't for the social welfare people, things would be even worse."

"These places disgrace us all!" Howard said bitterly. He turned to the doctor. "Who owns land such as this?"

Morkel's pleasant face turned grim. "All of Willisden belongs to private owners. Some of those *pondokkies* occupy only a few feet of ground, but the poor devils have to pay as much as a pound or even two pounds a month for a plot. And most of 'em don't get ten shillings more for the whole month's food. You'd be surprised who some of these landowners are, Howard. They're Europeans, of course, but they aren't all Nationalists, believe me. Of course, they keep their names quiet. Their agents do their dirty work for them."

The bitterness in Morkel's voice made Howard warm towards him. Under his veneer, Jannie had not changed.

Morkel threw open the car door. "Shall we take a closer look?"

They crossed the track and entered the location, their feet sinking in the soft sand. They passed near a thin native woman who was nursing a baby to her breast. Her body racked suddenly with a paroxysm of coughing, her eyes rolling unnaturally upwards during the spasm. Recovering, she leaned over the child and spat into the sand.

"There's a T.B. case for you," Morkel said. "She's probably got half a dozen kids and they'll all sleep in that shack behind her. If they aren't all infected now, they will be before she passes out."

Sickened, Howard followed him into a maze of dug-outs and ramshackle huts. From a deep hole nearby came a foetid smell that brought their handkerchiefs to their nostrils.

"By the way," Morkel said, as the smell receded behind them. "Don't come roaming around places like this alone at night. It's just as bad here as in the Jo'burg slums. We've got gangs of *skollies* who would cut their mothers' throats for a tot of brandy. Keep a check on that reckless nature of yours, or your investigations will end up in a ditch somewhere."

"I'll behave myself," Howard grinned.

At that moment an angular coloured woman ran up to the doctor and addressed him in halting Afrikaans. He turned ruefully to Howard.

"Here it starts. Someone has recognized me as the doctor, told her, and now she wants me to look at her little boy. He's in a shack just along here."

They followed the woman into a hovel made of rusty paraffin tins and pieces of board, with a sheet of corrugated iron for a roof. The floor was uncovered sand. On a straw pallet a small boy was moaning feebly. His exposed chest was a mass of red papules.

"Rheumatic fever," Morkel told Howard after examining the boy with gentle hands. "A pretty bad case, too. The poor little chap must be in agony. I'll have to get him into the clinic somehow."

"What shall we do — carry him to your car?" Howard asked.

Morkel thought a moment, then shook his head. "No; I'll go and 'phone for an ambulance." He gave instructions to the woman, then led Howard outside into the sunlight.

"I'll drive off to a 'phone-box. It may

take a little time — there aren't any round here. Do you want to come with me or stay to look around? You don't need to come; there's no work to do."

"Then I'll stay here, Jannie. I can wander around until you get back."

"Right. Don't go far. I shouldn't be more than a quarter of an hour."

⋆ ⋆ ⋆

Left alone Howard wandered deeper into the location. A crowd of children followed him, their small brown hands outstretched for money. He gave them a few coppers, instantly regretting his action when their numbers increased threefold.

He made his way deeper into the maze of *pondokkies*. The narrow track he was taking led him eventually to a piece of waste land, some twenty yards wide, which was enclosed by tightly-packed hovels. As he started across it he noticed half-a-dozen non-Europeans squatting in the sand over a chequered board. From the money lying about, it was clear they were gambling.

One glance was enough to tell him

these were *skollies* of the type Morkel had mentioned. One glance was more than enough. One of the men facing him was the huge negro he had seen in his car headlights the night he had rescued Joan Viljoen . . .

The negro, his massive arms bulging from his shirt, saw him and leaned across to one of the men who was sitting with his back to Howard. The addressed man spun round and Howard saw his face was twisted by a long knife-scar. The Coloured's eyes, as black and beady as those of an uncovered snake, fixed on Howard and recognized him . . .

Swartz moved like lightning. In a second he was on the path ahead of Howard and snarling out instructions to his followers. The negro and another took up positions beside him, the other three blocked the entrance behind Howard. The crowd of children who had been following Howard drew back in sudden fear, some of them running back down the winding track. Round the perimeter of the clearing awed spectators began gathering.

Acutely aware of his danger, Howard

faced the threatening figure of Swartz.

"What do you want?" he snapped. "*Voertsak!* Get out of my way."

Swartz shook his head and grinned, his lips writhing back over stained teeth. He snarled something in harsh Afrikaans.

"I don't know what you're saying. Get out of my way."

With a sneer Swartz turned to the huge, repulsive negro beside him and said something to him. The negro let out a shout of raucous laughter. Swartz addressed Howard in English.

"You bloody witman — I remember you. You hit me in the face last week. Now you pay. You pay for hitting Swartz."

"Get out of my way, you robbing scum, and take your thugs with you," Howard gritted. He took a step forward, to stop short at the sight of the long knife that appeared in the Coloured's hand.

Swartz looked at the grinning negro and laughed exultantly. Howard pulled out his handkerchief and let it fall into the sand at his feet. He picked it up, stood erect again, and took a quick glance round the ring of spectators.

The clearing was ringed with them now but he saw little hope of assistance. Although their expressions were sympathetic towards him, nearly all were women and clearly afraid of the six *skollies*.

Swartz turned back on him and drew the knife expressively across his own throat, then cut it viciously through the air. He advanced a step, going through the motions again. He made a foul gesture that brought a fresh yell of laughter from the negro and the rest of the gang. Then he pretended to throw the knife at Howard. Clearly he was enjoying the cat-and-mouse game.

"Stop clowning, you fool," Howard snapped. "You don't think you're frightening me, do you? Touch me and you'll have every policeman in Cape Town on your heels."

At the mention of the police Swartz's expression changed. He drew a step nearer, then suddenly spat right in Howard's face . . .

Howard stood paralysed for a moment, the warm spittle running down his cheek. Then fury burst like a bomb in his mind, destroying all caution. Leaping forward he threw the sand he was clutching into the Coloured's eyes.

Swartz let out a scream of agony. Dropping the knife he staggered backwards, pawing at his face. Howard snatched up the knife but before he could follow up his attack the huge negro and the other *skolly* with him leapt between him and the screaming Swartz. The negro was clutching a knife, the other thug a bicycle chain.

Howard spun round. The other three *skollies*, who were running forward, stopped at the sight of the long gleaming blade in his hand. He backed slowly away, his retreat being stopped short by the wall of a *pondokkie*. The spectators scattered, to reform and watch again in hypnotized silence.

Led by the hideous negro, the five *skollies* moved in like stalking panthers. Howard felt a sense of unreality. The warm wall at his back, the white sunlight, the blue sky above: all made the brutish expression of the advancing thugs assume the contradictory properties so terrifying of the nightmare.

Swartz stumbled after his men. His

eyes were swollen, tortured slits. Saliva ran in white streaks from his writhing mouth. He wrenched a knife from one *skolly* and turned towards Howard. He stood a moment screaming incoherent curses: a polyglot mixture of foul English and Afrikaans.

Then, under his orders, the line of men lengthened. Cautiously, yet with purpose, they closed in until they were within six paces of the cornered man. In the hushed silence the far-off familiar purr of a car could be clearly heard.

Then the command came. "*Donder hom*," Swartz screamed. The men tensed and Howard braced himself . . .

8

FATHER HENDRICKS opened his refectory door. The bright sunlight made him screw up his faded eyes.

A deep voice greeted him. "Good morning, *Eerwaarde*. You are expecting me?"

"Yes, *meneer*," the old priest said, a trifle breathlessly. "Please come inside."

Umzoni stepped into the room, dwarfing the frail, white-haired old man. He looked around the small room, then nodded towards the second door that led to the priest's bedroom.

"Is it quite safe to talk freely here, *Eerwaarde*?"

"Quite safe," Father Hendricks assured him, going over and opening the door. Umzoni looked into the bedroom, then nodded.

"I am sorry, but one cannot be too careful."

He took the chair that was offered

him. It creaked dismally as he lowered his huge body into it, and the old man watched anxiously.

"Have you any idea why I wish to speak to you in private?" Umzoni asked.

The priest shook his white head. "No, *meneer*. Michael only said you wished to see me."

Umzoni leaned forward, elbows on knees, eyes on the priest's face. "But you do know what I am doing down here in the Cape?"

"Yes, *meneer*. That I know."

The ingenuous answer appeared to satisfy the negro as to the old man's integrity. He nodded. "Then that needs no elaboration. But you do not agree with my work. Is that not so?"

A troubled expression crossed the priest's face. He sighed. "As you ask me, *meneer*, I will answer you. I do not."

"Why?"

The priest lifted his thin shoulders, then dropped them wearily. "Because I fear for our people. I believe they will suffer if they do as you ask."

"Why? There is no blood in my words."

"I know that, *meneer*. But the Europeans will oppose your plan, and then there will be violence."

Umzoni rose abruptly and went over to the window. He stood there silent for a moment, then turned to the priest. "No man knows what will happen. If blood is shed, the fault will not be mine: it will be on the Europeans' hands. Our plan is not unlawful — at least it would not be in a more enlightened land."

The priest did not answer. Umzoni went on, his deep voice challenging. "Do you deny that the laws under which our people groan are unfair? Do you deny they cause misery and suffering? Answer me, Father Hendricks!"

The priest bowed his head. "It would be an untruth to deny it."

"Then what objection can you have to a plan that will give your people and mine the right to live again as free men? There are risks, yes, there are always risks when people oppose tyranny. But we are not going to raise our hands in violence. What, then, is your objection?"

There was a long pause before the old man replied. "I am a Christian, *meneer*, and so do not believe in threats of any kind. And your plan holds threats — not violence I know, but still threats. And men made by force to change their policies remain unconvinced and become enemies. It will be so with the Europeans if your plan succeeds. They will find other ways to keep us down . . . "

"Enemies! They are our enemies now," Umzoni broke in harshly. He made an impassioned gesture, his tall figure towering over the frail priest. "Bah; this talk of Christianity sickens me. I am a Christian myself — yes; I was brought up from childhood in the Faith. And when I came of age my father, who was a Zulu chief, sent me to university in England. I know the European well, *Eerwaarde*. There is much about him I like, but one thing I hate. His hypocrisy over his religion."

"Hypocrisy?" the priest asked.

"Yes. Of all peoples he is the most material, yet he embraces the most selfless faith — Christianity, that makes a curse of money and power. A faith that teaches charity, tolerance, humility, brotherly love . . . This is your European's religion, yet what do we find among him — saints, philanthropists, humanitarians?" The Zulu laughed bitterly. "We find every one of them, big and small, grabbing all he can get, stealing from those poorer than himself, looking after his own skin as he puts it. Each one paying lip-service to Christ while his idolatrous heart is paying homage to Mammon. It is a hypocrisy that sickens me to the soul."

"You are bitter, *meneer*. There are many good Europeans."

The Zulu's voice was fierce, the veins standing out like cords on his forehead. "How can a man help bitterness when he knows such things? Their civilization mocks at their religion, yet we, their servants here, we are taught to be true believers. We must be the things they are not. We must despise money, abominate power, be meek, patient, God-fearing. Can you not see the cunning of it?"

"No, my son. I cannot."

"Can you not see they are using Christianity as a political tool? If we are taught it is an evil thing to rise up against persecution, if we believe we should do nothing but turn the other cheek, then we can never regain our freedom. The very purity of our faith will always keep us in bondage."

"You have no faith at all, my son," the priest said sadly.

"I cannot afford to have faith," Umzoni replied angrily. "Not when it would enchain me. We can only afford to be Christians when they themselves obey the Commandments of their Christ."

The old man shook his head. "And so you argue we should become sinners also. No, *meneer*. I am a simple man — I have not been overseas, nor have I been to university — but I have lived seventy-five years and I have learned that two wrongs do not make a right. It is no use trying to change a man's mind by threats, *meneer*, he must be made to change his heart by love. Only in that way is a man reborn."

"That is nonsense. Throughout history men have fought oppression and conquered it."

"Christianity did not grow on the zeal of its generals, but on the sacrifices of its martyrs," the priest said quietly.

Umzoni brought his fist down hard on

the deal table. "I am not a general. Again I tell you — I preach no violence."

The old man's voice was gentle. "*Meneer* Umzoni; you did not come to defend your campaign — that I know. But you have not yet told me your reason for coming here."

The negro flushed. "Very well; I will tell you now. I have been informed that you have been warning people who attend my meetings that they are breaking the law; that you are trying to stop them co-operating in my plan."

The priest shook his head. "That is not true, *meneer*. I have taken no side whatever. But it is my clear duty to warn these people of the risks they are taking. Some are very simple, many cannot even read. It is only right their dangers should be explained to them as well as their injustices. You do the one, I do the other."

"I had hoped," Umzoni went on, "that you might tell the people it is a Christian thing to risk themselves for the ultimate good of others."

The old man looked up in distress. "You twist and warp things, *meneer*.

Now you make it sound as if I were an obstacle in the way of our people's happiness."

Umzoni moved forward eagerly. "*Eerwaarde*; the revolt against the laws is growing daily — one day it must burst out. The question is which way? By peaceful means, or by bloodshed? Deny the first and you will get the second. Already, in this town and in others, there are wicked men who want nothing less than an insurrection. In the Cape we have Swartz. Every day he grows more dangerous. At every meeting I hold, he and his gang come and try to stir up the crowd's basest emotions. I and the other leaders in our campaign are doing our utmost to keep down this evil force, and believe we can do it as long as we have a better plan to offer the people. But lose us and the people have no one to turn to but the evil-doers. Can you not see that and help us?"

Father Hendricks's face was deeply troubled. He sat a full minute before shaking his head. "A man must be true to his own heart and faith, *meneer*. There are threats in your plan, and as a

Christian I cannot accept threats of any kind."

Umzoni's face set grimly. "So, rather than agree to our plan, you would have the people revolt and die under the Europeans' guns or surrender abjectly to the laws until they become less than animals? How can you, a priest, prefer such alternatives?"

The old man sat upright in his chair, his wrinkled face suddenly alight with faith. "I believe in God, *Meneer* Umzoni, and do not believe He will let such things happen. One day he will make the Europeans relent and open their arms to us."

"They will never relent until they are made to relent," the Zulu said bitterly. "So you will not help me?"

"I cannot," Father Hendricks said unhappily.

"You have great influence in these parts. You know that?"

"It is not I that have influence, *meneer*. It is God."

"Some of my followers will resent your attitude," the Zulu said, staring out of the window. "Some will think the cause too important to be set back by a mission priest. You will make enemies."

"That is one reason I cannot support your cause, *meneer*," the old man said quietly. "All these causes have a way of becoming too important for the people they are meant to serve."

There was a long silence. Umzoni turned from the window at last. The sternness had gone from his face, leaving it almost gentle.

"You have nothing to fear from me, *Eerwaarde*. You are a good man and a brave one, and I admire you. I shall give instructions that nothing must be done to interfere with your work. But the *skollies* who live on blood and hate — they are the ones you must watch." He laughed bitterly. "They hate me for my liberalism. You can gucss how you must appear in their eyes."

"Thank you, *meneer*," the priest said quietly. "I shall be careful."

The Zulu went to the door. He opened it, then stood a moment as if reluctant to go. The old man followed him, moving into the square of sunlight. It shone on his wrinkled face, patriarchal with its white hair and beard. It was the face of a man who had seen and suffered much, but had never lost faith in his God, in mankind, and in himself. Umzoni gazed into it, strangely moved.

He held out his hand. "*Hambe gahle*, Father. If I cannot have your blessing for my work, then give me your understanding. Those of us behind this plan sincerely believe it is for the betterment of the people. I would have you know that."

Father Hendricks put his frail hand into the Zulu's powerful grip. "I do, *meneer*. You may be right and I wrong. Only God knows that. May He take great care of you."

Umzoni's lips parted to speak. Then he shook his head, and turning, walked quickly away.

⋆ ⋆ ⋆

An hour later Father Hendricks made his way towards the location. The vast slum lay ahead of him beyond a clump of trees. He walked into their shade a moment and paused. The roots of the tree under which he was standing rose like knotted veins from the sand, and he placed his feet carefully between them. The shade had a velvet quality, the sunlight outside was a hot shining lake that lapped greedily against the tranquil island.

He leaned against a branch, suddenly conscious of the dull ache in his back and legs. Despite himself, his eyes closed . . . Almost at once the insistent hum of the crickets rose a tone, then died into a murmur. He felt his head nod forward . . . He jerked himself upright, opening his eyes wide. He had not realized he was so tired. Of course, he had not been sleeping well recently . . . It was this worry, this problem that had been crystallized an hour earlier by his meeting with Umzoni. Had he been right? Or did his duty lie in assisting the movement? For weeks the worry had nagged at him. It was hard for an old man to know. If there was only someone to talk to . . .

He made himself step forward again. The white sunlight on the sand dazzled him, bringing tears to his eyes. He plodded on, his feet feeling like leaden weights.

As he drew nearer the *pondokkies* a crowd of ragged children let out excited cries and came scampering towards him. His weariness fell away as they jostled one another in their eagerness to be the ones to hold his hands. He patted each woolly head and spoke to each child in turn before continuing on his way, with the children dancing round him like young dolphins round a parent fish.

It was seldom that Father Hendricks entered Lower Willisden without his escort of children. To them, as to their parents, he was their *eerwaarde*, their father. Men would stand aside at his approach; women bow their heads. To the sick he gave comfort, to the bereaved compassion, to the sinful forgiveness. In his very meekness lay the roots of enduring strength and courage. Humble and devout, unsparing in his efforts to bring happiness into the lives of his fellow-men, the old man drew his resources not from his frail body but from an unflagging belief in his God. Few indeed were there in Willisden who did not know and love Father Hendricks.

He made his way deeper into the location and began his rounds. He was walking along a narrow path not a quarter of an hour later when a frightened coloured boy, running round a bend in the path, saw him and dashed to his side.

"What is it, little one?" the priest asked gently.

Sobbing for breath, the round-eyed boy pointed back along the path and told him. The old man's face set anxiously.

"You must take me, quickly," he told the boy. "No, come; you will be safe with me. Quickly, little one, quickly . . . "

Old man and boy hurried along the path into the maw of the vast slum. By rubbish heap and *pondokkie*, by cess-pool and dugout they went, to emerge in a small clearing. The priest caught a glimpse of shining steel . . . depraved, eager faces . . . a man at bay against a wall . . . then he ran forward.

"Stop," he cried. "In the name of the church, stop . . . "

9

HOWARD stared at the cassocked figure of the old man in amazement, unable to believe his good fortune. Relieved cries of '*Die Eerwaarde*' broke out from the women spectators. They closed in now, forming a breathless circle round the group.

"Go back," the priest ordered sternly, standing between the thugs and Howard. "Go back and leave *meneer* alone."

Swartz screamed a curse at the old man, then turned to his hesitating followers.

"*Donder hom!* What are you afraid of? An old man."

He started forward, only for the priest to step before him. Mad with rage, he lifted his hand clutching the knife. Howard leapt forward, to be thrown aside by the sudden onrush of women. At the sight of their beloved *Eerwaarde* threatened, their fear vanished under a flood of outraged anger. Their rage was a primitive thing, making the blood run cold with its savagery.

A huge, coloured woman grabbed Swartz's arm, screaming at him. "Touch the *Eerwaarde* and we will tear you to pieces, you *skelm*."

Swartz realized his danger in time. Throwing a last vengeful glance at Howard, he turned and pushed his way through the angry, jostling crowd. His five followers, with the huge negro as cowed and sullen as the rest, went after him.

The priest turned anxiously to Howard. "Have they harmed you, *meneer*?"

Howard shook his head, throwing the knife he had been clutching into the sand. "I'm in your debt, Father. You came just in time."

The old man's eyes were moist with tears. "God must have brought me down this morning. Those are wicked men, *meneer*. They disgrace us all."

"How did you know what was happening?" Howard asked.

"Little David told me," the priest said, turning and peering among the gaping crowd. "Ah; there he is."

A small brown face peeped shyly from behind a formidable negress. Howard recognized the child as one to whom he had given coppers earlier that morning. He bent down, thanked the boy, and pressed a note into his hand.

The priest turned to the crowd. “All is well now,” he told them gently. “Thank you for your help.”

Instantly the women began dispersing. Howard rose to his feet. His eyes scanned the old man’s face, admiring the majesty and dignity of age present in it.

“You risked your life for me, Father,” he said.

The priest smiled gently. “I am an old man, *meneer*. My life is not important any longer. But you are young.”

“Is this your parish?”

“Yes, *meneer*. My church is in Riebeck Road, in Upper Willisden. I am known as Father Hendricks.”

A sudden, anxious shout reverberated across the clearing. “Howard! Howard, lad, are you all right?”

Howard turned to see the red-faced, stocky figure of Morkel charging towards him. He grinned. “All in one piece,

Jannie, thanks to Father Hendricks here. How have you heard about it?"

"A woman told me as soon as I arrived," Morkel panted. "I couldn't believe it at first. Attacking a European in broad daylight . . . The bloody, murdering devils . . . "

Howard interrupted his rich flow of language by motioning to the priest. "This is Father Hendricks, Jannie. If it hadn't been for him, I'd be in a bad way now."

The old man smiled shyly. "I know of you, Doctor. You have done much good work among the sick in my parish. I am honoured to meet you."

"Sorry, *Eerwaarde*," Morkel grunted. "This news has upset me. Thank you for helping him."

"I am very happy I was able to do so," the priest said gently. "And now, if you will excuse me, I must finish my rounds."

"Wait, Father," Howard said quickly. "Will you be going back to your church this morning? I would like a talk with you if possible."

"I shall be back in little more than

an hour, *meneer.* I shall be delighted to see you."

Howard turned to Morkel. "Could you drop me off there, Jannie. The church is in Riebeck Road."

Morkel nodded. "I know it. Yes; we can go there. But first we're going to the police, lad. I want that gang of *skollies* under lock and key."

They thanked the priest again, said *au revoir*, and made their way back through the location. The ambulance had taken the sick boy away, leaving no call on Morkel to stay. They drove off to the nearest police station, where they were kept over fifty minutes in furnishing a detailed report.

"They seem to know all about that brute with a scar," Howard remarked as they set off for the mission church.

"*Ja!* But those locations are like rabbit warrens — it takes a military operation to dig a man out of them." Morkel paused, then shook his head. "Man, this has been a shock to me. Thank God you got out of it all right, lad." His words came out with more fervour than he intended, and he began chaffing Howard to hide his embarrassment. "Do you think this is the beginning of the big mutiny you're looking for?"

Howard laughed, yet his reply made Morkel stare. "It might be the first breath of it, Jannie."

"You're not serious, surely. They've always had gangs and *skollies* in these locations. District Six is full of 'em."

"Actually, Jannie, the percentage of criminals from the Coloured populations used to be very little higher than that from the White. I got that from the police the other day. It has only been on the increase since these *apartheid* laws were passed. That could mean something."

"I don't see it," Morkel grunted. "Of course, the Opposition have made the laws sound bad, and the non-Europeans might have lapped it up. But they'll soon realize *apartheid* benefits them as much as anyone else. No, Howard, I can't give you that."

Howard did not argue. "It may mean nothing," he agreed. "But I am keen to have a chat with Father Hendricks. He'll know these people inside out — their hopes, fears, virtues and vices. I've got the feeling he is the man I've been looking for."

They turned down Riebeck Road. Morkel pointed to a large factory on their left. "That's Mitchell's factory — the one I was telling you about."

Alongside the huge building was an enclosed children's playground in which a dozen or more children were scampering about. Next to it was a small wooden church outside which Morkel pulled up his car.

"Here you are. Here is your church of St. Francis," he told Howard.

"I hope the old man's back," Howard said. Followed by the doctor he walked along a sanded path to the porch and peered inside. The church was empty and they stepped into the nave. Plain, wooden benches, possibly enough to hold two hundred worshippers, lay on either side of them as they approached the altar. The church was plainly Catholic in denomination — behind the communion-rail where the altar supported the tabernacle, a small red lamp glowed devoutly. Above it hung the martyred figure of Christ, and on wooden shelves stood cheap alabaster statues, one of the Virgin and the other of the patron saint. Apart from a few flowers in vases there was little else. They turned and went outside again.

"Nice humble little place, isn't it?" Morkel remarked. "Did you notice how spotless everything was?"

Howard nodded. "I'll just walk round to the back. If he isn't there we'll go."

Morkel followed him round the head of the church. Howard knocked on the side door, which fell open at his touch to show an unoccupied room. He turned away in disappointment.

"We can wait, if you like," Morkel offered.

"No. I'll take a run out here another day."

As they approached the car, thcy hcard the excited laughter of children. Morkel turned, then pointed to the playground. "There he is! He must have arrived while we were round at the back."

The priest was leaning over the fence of the playground, chatting to the children who had run up on seeing him. Something he said made them shrill with laughter. Their laughter stopped as they saw the two approaching Europeans. The old man turned, then smiled with pleasure.

"You have managed to come, gentlemen. I am so glad."

"We have been looking round your church," Howard told him. "And we like it very much."

The priest was clearly pleased with the compliment.

Morkel nodded to the playground. "The children seem to be enjoying themselves."

"I was telling them a joke," the old man said mischievously. "It is a bad habit of mine. Sometimes I do it during Bible classes. People have called me irreverent for it, but that I cannot see. To me, God and happiness go together. I never mind laughter in my church as long as it is not profane. Please come with me, gentlemen."

He led them to his room, pulling out his two chairs for them. He looked at Howard timidly.

"After your terrible experience, *meneer*, would you care for a cup of tea?"

"I would," Howard said promptly, then as promptly regretted his words. Sharing table with a non-European was a flagrant violation of the Colour Bar. To Morkel, a Nationalist, it would cut right across his upbringing and tradition. Quickly Howard gave him an opening.

"If you think we haven't time, Jannie . . . "

"No; it's all right," Morkel muttered. "Go ahead."

"Do you go down to the location often?" Howard asked the priest as he turned his attention to his gas-ring and kettle.

The old man looked surprised. "Of course, *meneer*. It is down there they need me most of all."

Howard frowned. "It must be well over a mile. Do you have to walk every day?"

"One soon gets used to it, *meneer*."

Morkel noticed there were only two chairs in the room. He shifted uneasily. "Look; sit here, will you?" he asked the priest who had put the kettle on the gas-ring.

The old man waved him back. "No,

meneer. You are my guests. Please sit down."

Morkel sank back reluctantly. He said little until the kettle had boiled and the priest was making tea. Then he leaned forward.

"My friend, *Meneer* Shaw, says there has been an increase of crime among the non-Europeans lately. Is that true?"

The priest looked troubled. "I do not think there are any more criminals, *meneer*. But the evil ones among us have been bolder lately and some of the younger people are listening more to them . . . "

"Why?" Morkel demanded.

The old man raised his shoulders sadly. "People are growing bitter, *meneer*. They have lost faith in the European; they believe he only wishes to trample them in the ground. They all feel that the laws will eventually take what little they have from them . . . "

"So you blame *apartheid*, too," Morkel interrupted harshly. "Why? It will protect your interests as much as our own."

The old man nodded apologetically. "That may be, *meneer*. I am not a politician. I am only a simple old priest. I am only giving you my impressions, as you asked me to do."

"Your people drink too much," Morkel said harshly. "They drink until their minds are sodden and full of self-pity, until they imagine they are wronged. I'm sorry for the children, yes — but not for the rest. Most of them ask for what they get."

The old man paused in his pouring of the tea, then said quietly: "Of course. One is sorry for the children. They most of all."

Howard noticed with silent appreciation how the priest poured only two cups, which he brought over to them. Morkel's hesitation before accepting his cup was almost imperceptible.

As the old man offered them a cracked cup as a sugar bowl, Howard suddenly realized the extreme poverty under which the priest lived. His clothes, while scrupulously clean, were worn and frayed, and his shoes split and down-at-heel.

"Aren't you having tea?" Morkel frowned.

"With your permission, no," the priest said gently.

"Your playground seems popular with the children," Howard remarked hastily.

A shadow crossed the old man's wrinkled face. "Yes; but I am afraid it will not be there much longer. The people who own the factory are going to put a garage on it."

Morkel frowned. "I'm sorry to hear that." He put down his cup and rose. "Well; I shall have to be moving, I'm afraid. Thanks again for helping my friend, *Eerwaarde*, and good luck to your work."

"Thank you, *meneer*," the old man replied shyly. "I'm very happy to have met you."

Left alone with Howard for a moment, the priest turned to him in distress. "I hope your friend was not offended by my invitation to tea, *meneer*."

Howard's resentment at Morkel's conduct died as soon as it was born. The doctor was to be commended, not criticized. He had gone against his inborn aversions, if not successfully, at least to the best of his ability.

"You saved my life today," Howard reminded the old man. "And Dr. Morkel is as grateful as I am. But let me tell you quickly why I came here." He went on to explain the purpose of his visit to the Union and his need of assistance from influential non-Europeans.

The priest listened with deep interest, his eyes never leaving Howard's face. He nodded, almost eagerly.

"You may come any time, *meneer*. My door will always be open to you."

Howard rose, holding out his hand. "Then good-bye for now, Father. I shall look forward to seeing you again soon."

"So shall I, *meneer*. Go with God."

* * *

Morkel pulled up his car outside his clinic and turned to Howard. "Well; you can't say you've had a dull morning. So you think the old man's going to be the connection you need?"

"I think he is."

"Then it's been worth nearly getting knifed to meet him?"

Howard grinned. "Now it's over — yes."

"When do you expect to get your first article out?"

"Two weeks . . . a month . . . it's hard to say."

Morkel grinned impishly. "From what you've told me, Erasmus is going to give you a nice, friendly review."

"He'll probably never even hear of my stuff."

Morkel's face turned serious. "Don't underestimate him, Howard. He's a fanatic, I know, but he has a tremendous following among the more extreme Nationalists. He could be a dangerous enemy to anyone in your game."

Howard shrugged. "It's too late to worry about that now. In any case, I'm writing for an overseas paper."

"Maybe, but you're *living* here," Morkel reminded him grimly. "Remember what I told you last week — things have hotted up since you were last here. Watch your step, Howard, and watch Erasmus."

At that moment a nurse approached the clinic carrying a large basket from which toy giraffes, rabbits and teddy bears stared with some trepidation into the big, outside world. Seeing the doctor, the nurse waved with satisfaction at her load before vanishing into the clinic.

"What on earth has she got there?" Howard asked.

Morkel had turned brick red. "She's been collecting a few toys from one of the stores. They always give us a few around this time."

"But why? What for?"

Morkel's voice was gruff. "We throw a little party for the coloured kids over Christmas. We have to start begging early; it takes some weeks to get the stuff in. We had a thousand of the little devils queuing up last year."

Howard laughed aloud. "You're a psychological study, Jannie. What with the time you put into this clinic, and one thing and another, you probably do as much for the non-Europeans as any man in the Cape. And yet you support *baaskap*, *apartheid*, and the rest of it. How do you sort it out in that twisted mind of yours?"

Morkel became aggressive. "Easily enough. I look after my dog well, but that doesn't mean I want it to have equality with me."

"You still don't give your dog a Christmas Party," Howard said with twinkling eyes.

Morkel threw open the car door. "Get out and go home, you *roinek*. You've wasted enough of my day."

Howard grinned and went.

10

DURING the next two weeks, helped by Father Hendricks, Howard learned a good deal about the practical effects of the *apartheid* laws on the non-Europeans. Everyone trusted the old priest and through him Howard was given glimpses of non-European life that would have been denied him otherwise. These glimpses enabled him to write his first articles, which were factual ones based on the conditions of the coloured races in the Cape. He had done similar ones of Johannesburg a few weeks earlier.

But, although satisfied enough with this, he was less content about the other and more important purpose of his investigations. Try as he would, he had not yet obtained a shred of proof that the resentment engendered by the laws was turning into a spirit of resistance. The fact that crime had increased among the non-Europeans since the inception of *apartheid*, and he himself had experienced two examples of it, was no proof in itself. A few sporadic crimes by individual malcontents proved nothing unless it could be shown they were part of an active, organized campaign.

True, during his wanderings he had gathered a vague impression that such a campaign might be developing, although on what lines, violent or otherwise, he had no idea. Whispers here, veiled hints there: all had contributed to the nebulous suspicion. But, no matter what he did, he could not find one concrete chip of evidence.

Father Hendricks might have knowledge of such a campaign but Howard felt unable to ask the outright question. He knew the old priest would tell him if he were in a position to tell. There was also the personal problem. It was well known now in Willisden that he, Howard, was a confrère of the priest. If Father Hendricks knew of such a plot and told Howard, who then made it public knowledge through his paper, the old man's safety might be jeopardized.

Howard found these suspicions disturbing.

To understand himself he had to analyse his feelings on the whole racial problem. Why had he taken on this assignment? That was easy to answer — because he believed the Colour Problem the number one problem of the Twentieth Century. But, and infinitely more difficult, what had he come hoping to find? He was not sure of that, although he believed he had come with an unprejudiced mind. But now, after seeing first hand the hardships of the non-Europeans under *apartheid*, he was realizing more and more how empty its claims were that all races would benefit by its laws.

His views, then, were definitely hardening against *apartheid*. How did this affect him, a South African European, in his feelings towards the non-Europeans? If he admitted the laws were harsh and unjust, must he not also admit that some resistance on the part of the oppressed races was justifiable?

The question was an unpalatable one, but he made himself face it. He wanted to believe that liberalism would eventually prevail and the Europeans would voluntarily give more responsibility and freedom to their wards. But he had to agree with his paper that the reverse might well happen — that if *apartheid* went unopposed in the Union, it might well spread to other African territories. Certainly the forces of reaction were more firmly entrenched than for many years. And if to him, a European, the days of Coloured emancipation seemed far hence, how much farther must they seem to the non-European? Could one expect them to wait in patience?

Then what would he concede to them? Certainly not violence. It could bring nothing but misery to both black and white. It would, indeed, be almost a case for *apartheid* — an indictment against the non-Europeans, a proof they lacked the intelligence to find a more civilized way of achieving their emancipation.

What was left; what would he grant them? Vaguely he visualized some sort of constitutional protest — perhaps not constitutional in the South African sense, but a type permissible under normal European governments. But of this, or something similar, he had seen no trace. Either it was so well organized and had such a hold on the non-Europeans that they held it a guarded secret, or it did not exist at all. In the latter case his journey and efforts were in vain.

These doubts made his personal feelings grow more complex. One part of him, the part still influenced by his upbringing, wished to find no defiance among the non-Europeans; and, seeing nothing but occasional outbursts of crime, castigated his liberalism for its delusions. This in turn made the liberal in him search the harder for justification of its belief. The resultant schism in his mind, accentuated by his failure to settle it by finding out the truth, made him increasingly more dissatisfied and irritable.

It was in such a mood that he returned home one evening after a day out on the Flats. Moodily he threw open the door of his room and walked over to his tallboy. On the way home he had decided to look up Jannie Morkel and have a few drinks with him. He opened the tallboy door, chose a suit, then paused. There was the sound of a girl crying — low, racking sobs followed by another girl's reassuring voice. Howard listened, his brow furrowed. The sounds were coming from the maid's room next door. The voice of the speaking girl was familiar. He tried to place it.

A paroxysm of sobs followed. Howard hesitated, then went out on the stoep and knocked on the maid's door. The sobs died into a frightened whimper, then into silence. There was a pause. He knocked again.

The door opened. Howard caught a glimpse of Lucy, the maid, sitting on her bed and staring at him with tear-stained eyes. Then his own eyes widened in surprise. Standing at the door was Joan Viljoen.

"Miss Viljoen," he muttered, taken aback. "I didn't know you were here."

She showed no surprise at seeing him although her face was distressed — whether at his appearance or because of the girl he could not guess.

"Good evening, Mr. Shaw," she said in her low, shy voice.

"I'm sorry if I'm intruding. But I heard the girl crying. Is there anything I can do?"

Behind the girl Lucy buried her face

into her pillow again. Joan made a distressed gesture. "No; I'm afraid not, Mr. Shaw."

Howard drew back uncomfortably from the doorway. "Anyway; I'm next door if you want me," he said.

Joan forced a smile. "I'll come in a moment," she told him.

Howard nodded and went back to his room, wondering how Joan came to be with the girl. A few minutes later there was a timid knock on his door. He let Joan in and waved her into a chair.

"I'm sorry I butted in like that, but I'd no idea you were in there. Can I make you some tea? You're looking tired."

Her oval face was extremely pale, accentuating the dark sadness of her eyes. She was dressed in a simple, navy-blue frock. Her dark head was bare.

"No, thank you," she said, shyly.

Howard went over to his kettle. "Well; I'm having some, so perhaps you'll change your mind later." Curious to know what was her connection with the maid, he gave her a lead. "Has Lucy been having more trouble with the Dowsons?"

Her voice held a note of surprise. "Has she told you about them?"

"I caught them going for her one night," Howard explained, going on to tell her about the quarrel over the wireless. As he mentioned the Coloured, Michael, he watched her closely but her dark head was lowered.

"I guessed they were down on the chap because they didn't want to lose Lucy," he finished. "I suppose they hope to turn her against him."

"They've been doing nothing else for the last two years," she said bitterly.

"You have known them as long as that?"

"Yes," she said quietly. "Michael's father and mother live in Willisden. I had been taking them a food parcel the night you rescued me."

Howard began to think he understood. "I see! You've met all of them through your social welfare work." He motioned towards the adjacent room. "What's wrong with Lucy tonight?"

Joan hesitated. A flush of colour dyed her throat. "She's going to have a baby."

Howard whistled. "A baby! That'll

upset the Dowsons' applecart. Michael is the father, I suppose?"

Joan nodded unhappily. "Mrs. Dowson found out today and is absolutely furious. Lucy is terrified they'll do something to harm Michael."

"But what can they do? He hasn't broken any law, has he? Or is there one I haven't heard about?"

"Mr. Dowson has threatened before to get Michael dismissed from work. I think he knows the owner of the dairy where Michael works."

Howard frowned. "What about Lucy's allowance to her mother? Will Michael keep that up?"

"He will if he keeps his job."

"You have a high opinion of him," Howard said. His mood was still with him and he studied the girl's pale face with some perplexity and a little impatience. "This thing seems to me the best thing that could have happened. They have to get married now, and as a result they both get away from the Dowsons. I can't quite see what there is to worry about."

He judged her silence an expression of

her disappointment in him.

"I suppose I'm not in a very sympathetic mood," he said dryly. "In fact I'm prejudiced against the whole non-European race tonight. I'm beginning to wonder if they deserve all the sympathy people like you give them."

She stared up at him. "What do you mean?"

He shrugged. "I'm beginning to wonder if they are like us at heart. Do they know the sometimes subtle differences between right and wrong? Do they value such things as emancipation and freedom? Or are they content under any system that guarantees them a full belly and plenty of wives?"

"Of course they are like us!"

"Then where is their spirit? When are they going to fight *apartheid*?"

"Do you want them to fight it?"

"I don't know," he muttered, going over to the window, and staring out. "But I do know this: that if they haven't the spirit and intelligence to try, then they're unworthy of sharing in this or any other country's future."

"Yet if they raise a fist against you,

you call them criminals," she protested.

"And quite rightly. If they haven't the brains to think of anything but violence, then they deserve all they get."

"You make it sound as if they can't win whatever they do," Joan said quietly. "You forget how difficult it is for people without education to pit their brains against those with it. But, do you know, Mr. Shaw, I'm growing to hate clever people. I'd rather have one good man like Father Hendricks than ten thousand scheming politicians, generals, and businessmen put together. He'll do more for the world than all of them, and he'll leave something worthwhile behind him. He'll leave love, Mr. Shaw."

Howard smiled wryly. "A few Father Hendricks in each town and we'd have a new civilization. But let's be practical, Miss Viljoen. The average non-European is no more like him than I am. Father Hendricks could shame us into giving him equality, but the others can't do that. I can't help feeling that if they make no practical effort it's because they lack the spirit and intelligence. And in that case we don't want them sharing in the country's management. We don't want to revert back to barbarism."

He made a gesture of disgust as he walked over to the kettle.

"You'll gather from this that the correspondent who set out from England to write a brilliant exposé on *apartheid* and the Colour problem has now got himself one big headache. He can't find anything out and doesn't even know what he wants to find. All he sees is a world split into two halves, one half scheming and predatory, the other spiritless, illiterate and stupid. It isn't a pretty picture."

Her dark eyes were now full of understanding. "You're bitter tonight, Mr. Shaw. You will see it all differently again tomorrow."

He swung round to face her. "Tell me — how would you treat them? Would you give them equality as they are at the moment and let the country sink down into barbarism? Because it would."

"I'm not clever enough to think out policies, Mr. Shaw."

"You're no fool, Miss Viljoen, and in

any case you've no time for the clever people. What would you do?"

"I think," Joan said, and now her eyes were bright and fearless. "I think I would just be very kind to them . . . "

11

THE laugh fell stillborn from Howard's lips. "You'd just be very kind to them," he repeated.

"Yes," she said quietly. "Then they would look up to us, try to be like us, and uplift themselves without our help. Until they were ready for equality, they would be happy with us. And when they had equality, they would share it in friendship. Even *apartheid* would be bearable to them if each one of us was kind."

Howard relaxed slowly. "You're right, of course. Tremendously right. Probably kindness is the only important virtue. Oh; you're right, but — "

He paused at the sound of acrimonious footsteps on the stoep outside. Mrs. Dowson's voice shrilled out.

"Now, you little slut. The master's been to see the dairy people and they're giving your precious boy friend the sack tomorrow. That will teach you to come playing your games in my house."

Howard cursed under his breath. He threw open the door, and confronted Mrs. Dowson.

"I'd like a word with your husband," he said curtly. "Will you ask him to come down?"

Her thin lips tightened at his expression. "If you've anything to say, you'd better come upstairs."

"Upstairs, then," he said grimly. He followed her up the steps and into her lounge. Dowson turned from the window as he entered. It was obvious he had heard Howard's tone and was prepared for trouble. His eyes were sullen and his fleshy mouth loose with nervousness.

"What can we do for you?" he muttered.

"Let's not start by being polite," Howard began savagely. "I hear you've got Lucy's boy friend the sack. Why?"

"What's it got to do with you?" Mrs. Dowson broke in shrilly. "You don't employ her. Mind your own business."

Howard ignored her. "Why did you do it, Dowson?"

Dowson blustered. "The brute kept

coming here after I warned him to keep away. That's why."

"You're a liar. I've only seen him here once. That's not your reason."

"Don't call me a liar."

"I'll call you one again. You got him the sack because you're as mad as hell that you're going to lose a good maid at last. You've kept them from marrying for two years by playing on the kid's good feelings: by telling her Michael won't help her mother, by calling him a drunkard, by doing everything possible to make her doubt him. You've put your damned housework before their lives, which you have nearly wrecked. You're a couple of mongrels."

Mrs. Dowson let out a scream. "Bert; don't let him stand there and say such things."

Dowson licked his lips nervously. "You'd better apologize, Shaw!"

"Apologize!" Howard sneered. "I'm not coloured, Dowson. I can hit back. You're a couple of the cheapest white trash I've met in a long while."

"Get out," Dowson yelled. "And take a month's notice with you."

Howard eyed him savagely. "It's as well we're in here and not outside, Dowson. And it's as well I'm not Michael! Because if I were, I'd pay you a call, Dowson, by God I would. And as there's a Colour Bar, I'd come at night."

He slammed the door and went down to his room. It was empty. He cursed and lit a cigarette. There was a tap on his door and he spun round, to see Joan standing in the entrance.

"I went in to Lucy," she told him. Her eyes were shining. "Thank you for what you said upstairs. I thought it was wonderful!"

Howard gave a grimace. "You couldn't hear it, could you?"

"The ceiling of Lucy's room is very thin," she murmured.

He grinned ruefully. "You heard some choice stuff, I'm afraid. I worked off my bad mood on them. But I'm afraid it doesn't help anyone very much. Do you think Michael will be able to find other work?"

She shook her head. "It's very difficult. There are so many looking for employment."

Howard thought of the vast army of unemployed out on the Cape Flats and nodded. "So they're going to be in trouble shortly?"

"Yes; they are." She paused, then eyed him shyly. "I wonder if you would help them, Mr. Shaw. If you would ask Linda to speak to Mr. Mitchell. He could give Michael work easily."

"But wouldn't it be better if you spoke to him?" Howard asked. Then he remembered the girl's problem.

Her voice became tinged with bitterness. "Mr. Mitchell would only see this as a little more of my sentimental foolishness. I could ask Brian or Linda myself, of course, but neither of them seem to know how to take this work of mine. But they would listen to you."

"All right; I'll ask Linda," he decided. "I'll leave you out of it altogether. These two have had a raw deal from the Europeans and something seems to be owing to them. We'll get Mr. Mitchell to pay a little off the debt. I think he can afford it, don't you?"

A faint dimple appeared beside her mouth. "I think so, Mr. Shaw."

"Right; that's settled. Now what about that tea?"

"The kettle was boiling, so I turned it off," she told him.

"It won't take a minute," Howard said, switching it on again. "Stay for just one cup. Now that I've worked off my temper on the Dowsons you won't find me such a pig. Give me a chance to redeem myself."

"All right," she smiled. "But I must go directly afterwards."

They took tea out on the stoep. Howard started Joan talking about her welfare work, and in her enthusiasm she forgot the time. He had once thought her something of an emotional reformer, but now he saw his mistake. This girl was no high-flying idealist, the type who see the poor as angels in rags, only to turn on them as soon as they find some are as degraded as their garments suggest. She was a realist, who knew the insidious poison of environment, its slow, corrosive effect on the soul. She was the ideal social worker, with deep understanding, kindness, and a stamina of the mind that could sustain its faith even when betrayed by those she had helped.

A wave of warmth that was near affection came over Howard as he sat listening to her. The moon was shining full on her delicate face. There was an ethereal quality about her that was enhanced by the silver light. She was a Madonna of the moonlight, gentle and very lovely.

There was something very pathetic about her refusal to become engaged, Howard thought, for there was no doubt about her affection for Brian. Her behaviour towards the financier's son on the night she had been attacked had convinced Howard of that. And she had only to speak or hear his name for her face to light up. Yet Howard felt she was exaggerating the affair; he found it difficult to believe that Mitchell would take active steps to punish Brian if they announced their engagement. He felt the girl, in her excessive consideration for others, was making an unnecessary sacrifice and denying herself happiness. Like Linda, Howard found himself hoping she would change her mind.

Her sudden gasp as she looked down at

her watch roused him from his thoughts. She jumped up. "We've been talking over an hour."

"I've enjoyed it," he smiled.

"So have I, but now I must be going . . . "

She opened Lucy's door gently, then closed it again. "She's sleeping, thank goodness. I think she'll be all right now."

"I'll speak to Linda about Michael in the morning," Howard promised. "And, if you like, I'll 'phone you at the hospital to tell you what she says."

"Thank you very much. And I do hope this isn't going to make things too unpleasant for you," Joan said, motioning to the flat above.

Howard smiled grimly. "They are the least of our worries. Now I'll run you home."

This he did, in spite of her protests.

* * *

Howard met Linda on the beach the following morning: a swimming appointment he had made some days earlier. She was wearing a white strapless costume that showed to perfection her exquisite shape. Long smooth legs flowed into a body that was all symmetry and grace. Her tanned skin looked as if it had been dusted with gold.

"I have a favour to ask you," he said, dropping to the sand beside her.

Her green eyes teased him. "Be careful. Once you're in my debt anything can happen."

He laughed, then went on to tell her about the events of the previous night, although, as promised, he made no mention of Joan's part in the affair. He had already told her that Lucy's fiancé was the Coloured they had both seen talking to Joan in the woods.

"I thought I'd ask you if your husband would find him work," he went on. "After all, one does feel a certain gratitude to him for picking on the brute who attacked Joan."

"I agree," she said. "Although why he did it I fail to understand."

"I think I can explain that. Apparently Joan has helped his parents a good deal."

"It still doesn't explain why he shouted at her like that in the woods."

"You've never asked her about that?" he inquired.

"No; I've never got round to it. I suppose this must be the reason. He wanted to pick a fight with this *skolly* and she was afraid he would come to some harm. Anyway; he deserves a job, and I'll certainly see Trevor fixes him up. You say he lives in Willisden?"

"That's right."

"Perhaps Trevor will put him in his factory there. I think it can be arranged."

12

TREVOR MITCHELL picked up his brief-case and eased his heavy body from his huge American roadster. Slamming the door behind him he started down the steps to his bungalow. His florid, perspiring face was set and his pale-blue eyes fixed resentfully on the shingled roof below him.

Reaching the bungalow he went round to the stoep. As he had expected, Linda was there, making the most of the last hour of sunshine. She was dressed casually in white linen slacks and a bush jacket. She turned in surprise as he approached.

"You're home early tonight."

Mitchell dropped into a deck-chair and mopped his perspiring face. "I had to cancel our board meeting this afternoon. Old Hathaway's duodenal has started dripping again and he has been ordered to bed." He unlatched his brief-case and pulled out a newspaper, which he handed to her. "It's *Die Volksman*. I want you to look at the back page, at Erasmus's column."

Linda turned the paper over curiously, then frowned. "You know I can't read Afrikaans. What does it say?"

"It says a good deal — about one of your boy friends."

Her green eyes narrowed dangerously at his tone. "Go on. Finish it," she said coldly.

"It appears Howard Shaw has run true to form, after all. The most recent copy of *The World Observer* which contains the first of his South African articles has been withheld from the newsagents by the public censor."

Her eyes widened. "Withheld! But why? What has he been saying?"

"According to Erasmus, the usual rot about the non-Europeans being down-trodden, their heavy infant mortality rate: all the usual maudlin rubbish, in fact." His voice held an angry note. "It's going to make it damned embarrassing for me. People know I'm connected with him."

Her voice was ominously low. "How do they know?"

"How! Through you. You've been seeing plenty of him these last few weeks, haven't you? People notice these things, you know."

A welter of emotions, confused and unrecognizable, suddenly made her want to goad and hurt him.

"I don't see the point. No one in his right senses would believe you had suddenly become a sentimentalist."

His pouched eyes narrowed. "And you should be thankful for it. I've taken life for what it is — a jungle — and I've made myself fit to live in it." He laughed sarcastically. "Not with brawn, my dear — your boy friends have me there — but with the modern equivalent, money. And I think I've done a fairly good job, don't you? You haven't a bad cave to live in."

"Some say a little sentiment makes a fuller man," she said bitterly.

"We all have sentiment, my dear. But some of us keep it under proper control. We don't let it blind us to realities."

"Aren't these bad living conditions realities?" she demanded.

"They are. So much so, that maudlin

sentiment won't alter them. They are the outcome of an inferior race coming into contact with a superior one. Whenever that has happened in history the weak have gone under. The strong must use their strength — it has to be that way or the human race would become so effete it would lose the will to live."

"Is it weak to pity; effete to show compassion? Is that what you're saying?"

"Uncontrolled sympathy can be a weakness," he said coolly. "It would hinder progress by being too careful of the risks to others."

"What is progress for if not for people?"

"Progress is for the strong, my dear. They change civilization; therefore they are the only ones that matter. The weak have to adapt themselves or die. That is the position here in Africa. And the non-European isn't making the grade."

"Has he been given a chance to make it?"

"Why should we give him a chance? Why should we make trouble for ourselves? If we bring 'em up to our level they'll swamp us with their numbers. Let 'em fight for their equality the way we had to fight for ours."

Linda shuddered. "God; you're hard, Trevor. Money, strength, power: those are your criteria of success, aren't they? Or should I just say money?"

"Don't disparage money too much, my dear. Your sex is the last to poke its nose in the air. Yours is the practical sex — and thank God it is. It keeps the world from dreaming itself to death. You measure up a man's worth by his cheque-book because that is where security for you and your children lies. In the old days you chose your mate by his muscles. Now it's his bank balance. But the principle's the same."

She realized she was the last one to deny his assertion and turned sullenly away. His gaze followed her.

"We seem to be growing into a family of social reformers. First Brian's girl friend, and now you. I wonder who'll be next."

"You know damn well I've got no interest in non-Europeans," she said bitterly.

"I'm glad to hear it," her husband

murmured. "For a moment I thought you were becoming one of Shaw's disciples. You have become rather good friends, haven't you?"

"We have. Do you mind?"

"Not until now. I've always trusted you and still do. But this may alter matters. I can't have my name connected with this sort of thing. I can't afford it."

Linda made a great effort to control her rising temper. "I don't believe this of Howard," she told him. "He wouldn't be afraid to say what he thought — I'm not saying that — he might criticize, but he wouldn't be destructive. He would always give alternatives. It's probably Erasmus who is exaggerating the whole thing. I haven't told you this before, but they had a quarrel . . . "

"A quarrel! What about?"

Linda told him. Mitchell listened, his brows drawn together.

"Don't you see?" she finished. "This is Erasmus's chance to get his own back. He can write any lies he likes about the articles if they aren't allowed into the Union for people to read."

"Why didn't you tell me about this affair before?"

"Why should I? It hardly did Erasmus or me any credit."

Mitchell thought a moment. "It still doesn't account for the article being impounded," he said.

"That proves nothing," she said eagerly. "You yourself told me about an English magazine that was banned here because it showed Europeans and non-Europeans dancing together in a London hotel. His article may fall into the same category — something factual which the Government wants to conceal from the people."

His pale, keen eyes were watching her. "Why are you so certain he hasn't done as Erasmus says — criticized the country destructively. That's what these overseas papers want from their reporters. And he has non-European sympathies — we know that. What about the coloured chap he asked me to find work for — the one I put into my Willisden factory?"

Linda's lips twisted. "That proves nothing except that he is decent and has feelings. Everyone knows what trash the Dowsons are, and why they got that Coloured the sack. And as he was the one who picked a fight with the brute who attacked Joan, he deserved some reward."

Mitchell's frown deepened. "This sounds like something else you haven't told me. What fight was this?"

Linda told him what Michael had done after Swartz had attacked Joan. The financier looked puzzled. "But why should he do that?"

She gave a hard laugh. "People can be grateful when they are helped, you know. Apparently they think well of Joan in Willisden."

"Anyway; I'm pretty certain where Shaw's sympathies lie," Mitchell grunted. "And we have more than enough of that nonsense with Joan." He rose, taking the newspaper from her.

"This thing wouldn't be so serious if I weren't so well known out here. But I am, and I can't afford a breath of suspicion around me. Keep out of this, Linda. You know the controversy that has raged over *apartheid*; you know how the Europeans are split in their views.

It's all still there, simmering under the surface. Anyone giving it public criticism will come straight into the limelight. If Shaw keeps it up, Erasmus is going to give him a great deal of publicity — all the more if he doesn't like him. And that means Shaw is going to become pretty notorious out here. I can't afford to become involved, even indirectly."

"I don't tell you that you should throw over some of your friends because their views on life repel me," she said coldly. "I expect the same consideration from you."

Mitchell turned at the lounge door to face her. "Your career isn't jeopardized by my friends — that is the difference. But I'm not going to prolong the argument. If this goes on Shaw is going to become very unpopular, and not only among the Nationalists, and I can't afford to have my name linked with his. I don't dislike him, apart from this nonsense, but business and politics don't mix — not here."

"Business and humanity," she said bitterly.

He nodded coolly. "If you prefer it that way. And now are you coming in to have a drink with me, or are you going to stay out here and sulk."

She turned her back on him. He eyed her a moment, then walked heavily into the lounge.

13

THE initial Erasmus attack on Howard was only the first patter of rain before the storm. As the weeks passed by more of Howard's articles, flavoured now with his impressions were published overseas and censored in the Union, so the venom of the columnist's onslaught grew.

To a foreigner, unused to the emotion engendered in South Africa by any argument on the Colour question, the reaction of the man-in-the-street would have seemed incredible. In no time the name of Howard Shaw was on everybody's lips, to be praised or denounced according to the political views of his critics.

South African though he was, Howard was amazed at the furore. He was also discomforted. Never liking publicity, he soon found it impossible to go anywhere without being pointed and stared at, apart from often being insulted in the bargain. The situation was not improved by his having to move into a Sea Point Hotel after his quarrel with the Dowsons. His daily appearances in the dining-room and lounge became more and more of an ordeal, forcing him to importune his agent for private accommodation.

It was in this hotel lounge one morning that Linda gave her views.

"Between yourselves, you and Erasmus have humanized the political and racial quarrels. People like myself, who find it much too heavy reading, find Erasmus's scandal about you far more to our taste."

"In other words, I'm the chopping block who provides you with meaty reading," Howard scowled. "Frankly, I'm amazed at the fuss people are making over this."

For once Linda's tone was serious. "You've been out of this country a long time — you weren't here to see the bitterness that was stirred up when the *apartheid* laws were passed. It's still there under the surface, and you and Erasmus are bringing it out again. Plenty of people are on your side, Howard, or would be if your articles were published here. There's nothing in them to antagonize anyone unless he is a fanatic — I know that now. But until you do something, Erasmus can get away with his distortions and lies, and make things damned uncomfortable for you. Why don't you answer him?"

"I've no desire to enter into a slanging match with that crank," Howard growled. "I've more to do with my time."

"You owe something to the journalists who have gone to the trouble of reading your articles despite the censor and have defended you," she told him. "You don't have to answer him personally. Surely some paper here will be only too glad to publish the articles. Newspapers thrive on that sort of thing."

"Oh; I've had half the papers in the county approach me," he revealed. "But I gave *The World Observer* the British Empire Rights and can't publish without their permission. I suppose in the circumstances they would give it to me, but I haven't bothered to ask them so far."

"Well, get going and ask," she flashed. "Otherwise people are going to get the idea you're a Communist or God knows what else."

He grinned ruefully. "The path of a liberal is certainly a thorny one these days. I seem to be getting myself into trouble all round."

"You should have known what would happen when you took on the job. Anyone who starts dabbling in racial matters here is asking for what he gets."

Howard's lips twisted. "I suppose so. The formula is to lie in the sun, play tennis, and to hell with tomorrow."

"And it's not a bad formula!"

"Not for those who can afford it," he murmured, offering her a cigarette. "Is this all you came to see me about this morning. To give me blazes for not answering Erasmus?"

He saw he had annoyed her. She made an effort to control her temper, however.

"I came to see if you would take me out to Stellenbosch for the day," she said sullenly. "I've an aunt there I haven't seen for months. The South-Easter is blowing a gale at Clifton, so I can't go on the beach. I'm bored stiff. Will you come?"

He leaned forward. "I can cure your boredom without taking you to Stellenbosch. Come out with me to Willisden."

Her eyebrows arched. "What on earth would I do in Willisden?"

"See how the other half of the world lives. You might find it enlightening."

She stared at him, then her red lips curled. "You think I'm a selfish devil, don't you? And you think I'm made of soft stuff. Get this into your head, Howard Shaw. I may live the easy way and I may enjoy it, but don't get the wrong idea. I'm not as soft as I seem."

"Then you'll come to Willisden?"

"I'll come. But don't think by taking me there you're going to make another Joan Viljoen out of me. I take life as I find it. And it isn't a bad philosophy."

"For those who have, I'm inclined to agree with you," he said, rising to his feet. "Shall we go, then?"

Linda rose disdainfully. "I can't wait. There's nothing I like better than rooting among dustbins."

* * *

Howard turned down Riebeck Road and pulled up his car outside the mission church. Linda stared at it.

"What's this? I came to see slums, not priests."

"You can see the slums later. First I want you to meet Father Hendricks."

Sullenly she followed him into the refectory. The priest smiled shyly at Linda as Howard introduced him.

"It is good of you to come, madame," he said earnestly. "I have wanted so often to thank you for your kindness to Michael."

Linda's eyes had widened on seeing the patriarchal old man and were now examining his face in fascination. For the moment she was too surprised to take notice of his words.

Howard answered for her. "Mrs. Mitchell was only too pleased to help, Father."

Linda looked at him coldly. He realized she had thought his words ironic. She turned to the priest.

"It was nothing," she said tightly. "I don't want any thanks."

The priest held up his hands in

protest. "How can you say it was nothing, madame? It turned the despair of two young people into happiness; perhaps it saved Michael from crime. And it made those who love them happy too. How can you say it was nothing?"

Her voice was bitter now. "Any good it has done is purely accidental. I merely spoke about him to my husband, who employs hundreds of boys. There was nothing personal or generous about it. I did not even know the boy. Please say no more about it."

"As you wish, madame," the old man sighed. "But I would have liked to have given the young couple a chance to thank you. They live just across the way, and Michael will be leaving the factory for lunch at any minute. And I would like you to meet his parents, because they are a sadder case than most, and your kindness has helped them much more than perhaps you realize."

"We could go over now," Howard remarked.

Linda turned on him angrily. "I don't want the fellow fawning over me. You know perfectly well I don't care a hoot about him."

"You won't get this chap fawning over you," Howard grinned. "He doesn't think much of Europeans. But I thought you said you'd come out to see the slums! Is the occasion proving too much for you, after all?"

Her eyes blazed at him. "All right," she said tightly to the old priest. "Let's get it over."

Father Hendricks, clearly worried by her tone, led them across the road and down the narrow alley opposite. Windows stared at them like dead eyes, devoid of hope or salvation. Wooden trellises, dried and warped in the sun, lay at all angles like lifeless arms. Over and around them the wind howled and flung clouds of grit into their faces.

"This is where the upper classes of the non-Europeans live," Howard told Linda dryly. "The rest are down in the location in *pondokkies* and fox-holes."

She gave no sign of hearing him. They stopped outside the last house in the alley. Lucy opened the door, to gasp in surprise at seeing the two Europeans.

Nervously she led them into the front room where she and Michael lived. It was austere to the extreme, having a double bed, two hard chairs, and a bare wooden table. An unpainted wardrobe, obviously hand-made, stood against one wall. On one side of the window hung a piece of sacking that served as a curtain.

Father Hendricks excused himself and went out of the room to see Michael's people, who shared the house. While Linda stared impatiently through the window into the alley, Howard chatted to Lucy.

"Are you still able to help your mother?" he asked her.

She hesitated, then nodded. "Yes, master. And it will be better when I can go out to work again."

Michael entered the house a minute later, wearing an old sports coat patched at the elbows and a ragged pair of flannels. He stopped short at the sight of the two Europeans, then turned and muttered to Lucy. His face cleared at her reply. He looked at Linda.

"*Danke*, madame! I am very grateful to you. And you, too, *meneer*," he went on to Howard. "You have both been very kind."

He turned back to Lucy. "Make madame and *meneer* some tea."

"No," Linda said sharply. "We are going now."

The wrinkled face of the old priest peered into the room, looking at Linda and Howard. "If you would both be so kind as to step this way, you can meet Michael's mother and father."

Michael started at the priest's words. For a moment it seemed he would protest. Then he stood back in silence to let the Europeans pass. As they entered the narrow passage he broke into a torrent of Afrikaans to Lucy.

"Your friend doesn't seem too keen on us meeting his people," Linda said sarcastically to Howard.

Father Hendricks answered her. "Michael is embarrassed, madame. You will understand why in a moment."

They entered a room filled with pieces of old bric-à-brac. The armchairs were drawn round an empty fireplace. A coloured woman with a tired, drawn face, possibly in her late forties, was sitting in one. In the other was a man at least twenty years her senior. He tried to rise as they entered, but the woman put her hand on his arm and gently pressed him back.

"Madame, this is *Meneer* and *Mevrou* Stevens, Michael's parents," the priest told Linda with dignity. To the coloured woman, who had risen, he said, "Ouma, this is the kind lady who found Michael work in the factory." He finished with a few words in Afrikaans.

"*Goeiemore, Mevrou,*" the woman faltered. "*Mevrou was goed vir Michael . . .*"

"She knows little English," the priest told Linda. "I will translate. She thanks you for your kindness to her son, and if ever she or her husband can repay you they will be very happy. She asks God to bless you for your goodness."

Linda, who had lit a cigarette, inhaled deeply. "Tell her I want no thanks. But I'm glad they're happy."

As the priest was translating into Afrikaans, the coloured woman began to cough. One hand clutched at her throat and her face drew up in pain. The priest helped her gently into a chair.

The paroxysm lasted a few seconds, then she smiled up at them apologetically.

"She asks your pardon," the priest said. "Her cough is always worse when the South-Easter blows."

The old man in the chair had stirred and was stretching out a solicitous hand towards his wife. She brushed it aside with gentle impatience and addressed Linda again.

"May she give you something to eat or drink?" the priest asked.

"Thank her, but tell her we must be going now," Linda said.

They moved to leave a minute later. Until now Michael's father had said nothing and Linda had concluded he was in his dotage. But as she said good-bye and reached the door, he turned towards her. Before this he had been sitting with his back to the small window, but now the light fell full on his face. He spoke to her in English — slowly and falteringly as if struggling for words long forgotten.

"Thank you, Mrs. Mitchell. You have been very kind. Perhaps kinder . . . than you know."

It was then Linda realized the old man was a European.

⋆ ⋆ ⋆

Back in the church, the old priest offered Linda a chair. He smiled at her gratefully.

"You will see now, madame, why I am so very thankful to you. Michael has grown up bitter against Europeans because of the way they have treated his parents. Since childhood he has seen his father despised, insulted, and refused work for marrying a coloured woman and remaining faithful to her. And that woman is his mother. Can you think of anything more likely to breed bitterness in a sensitive child? The thing the Dowsons did to him might have been the last straw needed to turn him into a criminal. But your good deed has given him faith again in Europeans."

"I see all that," Linda said. Then she gave an involuntary shudder of revulsion. "But whose fault was it in the first place? It's against nature for a European to marry a non-European. People who do it have only themselves to blame."

The priest sat silent. Howard, who was standing at the window, turned to him. "Tell Mrs. Mitchell that old couple's history, Father. It might interest her."

"If madame cares to hear it, I will . . . "

"Go on," Linda told him. "What else is there?"

Howard turned back to the window. His eyes fell on a European across the road who was going from door to door handing envelopes to householders. The man went down the alley opposite. Howard paid him no more attention, his mind being on the gentle voice of the priest.

"The old man comes from a good English family, madame. He came out to this country many years ago to look for diamonds. While in some desolate place up-country he caught a terrible fever. Seeing he was helpless, his boys stole all his equipment and left him to die. But a coloured girl heard of him and left her home to help him. For many weeks she suffered great hardships as she nursed him, but at last her efforts were rewarded and he recovered.

"It was then, madame, that most men would have given her money and gone away. Particularly a man like this, from a good European family. But he did not. The young girl had fallen in love with him, as we so often do with those we help, and the man realized it. He could have left her and broken her heart, but this he did not do. Instead he gave her the life she had saved. He married her. Perhaps he loved her; perhaps he did not. If he did not, then his deed was the greater. Certainly he loves her now. But, oh, madame, it is hard for us to imagine what that man has suffered over the years. His own race have disowned him — that is bad for any man. But for it to happen because they despise the woman he loves, his wife — that is poison to a man's soul.

"You can see how easy it would have been for him to abandon her. He could have used a hundred excuses. She herself, because she loves him, has often asked him to go. But not once has he faltered, even when his children have been treated as inferiors. These two have faced the whole world together, with only their love to sustain them. But a love that can withstand a lifetime of taunts and reproaches is a very great love indeed. It may be that a wiser man would not have married her — that I cannot say. But I do know that it was the act of a brave and good man, and that one day God will reward them both."

Howard had turned during the priest's story to watch Linda's face. The cynical twist to her mouth had gone. Her eyes were intent on the priest. As he finished speaking, Howard saw the glint of tears under her long lashes. He turned back to the window, pretending he had seen nothing.

He heard her voice, a new voice, low and unsteady. "That is a beautiful story, Father Hendricks. Thank you for telling it to me."

"You can see better now how Michael, a sensitive child, has suffered in seeing the loneliness and unhappiness of his parents," the old man went on gently.

"Yes. He must hate us. I see that now."

"But it does not take much to save a

man's soul, madame. Sometimes a few kind words are enough. You and Mr. Shaw showed him there is kindness and sympathy among Europeans. Now he knows there are two kind ones, he will realize there are many thousands more. And think how his father and mother must feel! Oh, madame. One good deed — what fruits it can bear."

"I hadn't realized all this," Linda muttered. Her voice suddenly grew fierce. She swung round to Howard. "Why didn't you tell me?"

He shrugged. "You never showed any interest."

"How can people show interest if they don't know these things?" she demanded. "Oh; all right. We should come and find out ourselves. But don't forget we aren't all built alike . . . "

Howard motioned towards the alley opposite. "There they are now," he said.

Linda jumped up and ran to the window. The priest followed her. They saw the old couple walking up the alley. The old man's arm was round his wife's shoulders: she was half-supporting him. They walked with painful slowness. As they reached the entrance of the alley a fierce gust of wind sent them reeling against a nearby fence. Carefully the woman guided the old man back down the alley.

"He is old and she has a bad heart," the priest said. "Neither can walk far. But they come up the alley twice a day, at lunch-times and in the evenings."

In silence the three of them watched the old couple vanish from sight. Their weakness was pathetic. In a world of slums, hardship and prejudice, their only protection was one another. And one was old and the other sick. Two frail figures, one white, the other coloured, standing together against a hostile world. Both had committed the unforgivable sin. Both had loved with their hearts: both had loved too well.

Linda turned away, deeply moved. Howard looked after her with twisted face. "They are, of course, enemies of society."

She wheeled around. "What do you mean?"

"*Apartheid* deals sternly with such conduct today. A European can't marry a non-European now, or even live with her. That story you've just heard couldn't happen today unless a man broke the law."

"That is so," Father Hendricks sighed. "The men that rule us are cleverer than I and their reason must be good; and yet I do not know how to explain it to my people here. Because religion teaches love and kindness, and surely if it is wrong to love those of a different colour there will always be hatred in the world. If that old man did wrong by standing by the woman who saved his life, then I am unfit to be a priest because I do not understand what gratitude is or what a Christian should be."

He turned to Linda. "You must not be sad at what you have seen, madame," he said gently. "You must not think of that old couple's suffering; you must think of their triumph. Their love has conquered all. They are not poor — they are rich because each has a great love. And we are richer for knowing them."

Linda made no attempt now to hide her tears. She looked at the priest in wonder, then shook her head, as if trying to adjust her old views with the things she now saw and heard.

"You've put me in a strange state, Father Hendricks. I don't know whether to laugh or cry. I'm sad and happy at the same time. That sounds rather silly, doesn't it?"

The old man shook his head. "No, madame. It is how all good men and women should feel in this world. Sad at the sufferings of others; glad at being able to help them. I think it is right to feel like that."

"You *are* a good man," she whispered. "Howard has told me but I had no idea . . . " She bit her lip and turned away.

Howard stepped forward. "Father Hendricks is a saint," he said briefly. "But even saints have to eat. We'll go now, Father. Perhaps I will bring Mrs. Mitchell again another day."

"But he can have lunch with us," Linda protested. "We can all go together into town . . . " Her voice died away as she remembered.

Howard eyed her mockingly. "With us? Where? He's not good enough. Our politicians say so."

"Please, *meneer*, do not be so bitter," the old man protested. "And do not say again I am a good man. I have as many wicked thoughts as anyone else. Lately they have been troubling me very much . . . "

There was a sudden loud knock on the door. The priest hurried forward and opened it. Michael stood in the doorway, his face agitated and angry. He burst into excited Afrikaans on seeing the old man.

The priest turned to Linda and Howard with distressed face. "Excuse me one moment, Please. There is bad news. I will come back in a minute or two."

He went outside to the excited Michael, leaving Linda and Howard staring curiously after him.

14

FATHER HENDRICKS returned a few minutes later. He appeared dazed at what he had heard.

"What is it?" Linda asked. "What has happened?"

"Oh; very bad news, madame," he said heavily. "So bad I do not know what will happen now."

"What is it, Father?" Howard asked, fetching the old man a chair. "Tell us. We might be able to help you."

The priest turned sorrowfully towards him. "All the people who live opposite the factory have been given notice by their estate agent to leave their homes by the end of April. There are hundreds of them . . . "

"Where will they go?" Linda asked.

The old man lifted his thin shoulders in despair. "That is what I ask, madame. There is nowhere but the location, and that would mean death for some of them. The old people you visited this morning — how can they live in a *pondokkie* or dug-out?"

"Do you know who the owner is?" Howard asked.

"No, *meneer*, but I must try to find out. I must plead with him to change his mind, or at least give them longer. Oh, this could not have come at a worse time . . ."

Howard had been watching the old man's face closely. "What else is worrying you, Father?"

The priest's slight body seemed to shrink within itself. He sat with bowed shoulders, staring blindly at the floor.

"You have something else on your mind, haven't you?" Howard asked. "I've sensed it these last few weeks. What is it? Perhaps we can help you."

The priest looked up longingly at Howard. His wrinkled face was wistful. "Ah; if only you could, *meneer*. People were bitter enough before this news but now . . . I dare not think. But it would not be fair to tell you, *meneer*. You are a European and having to keep it secret might worry you."

Was this secret something connected

with a resistance movement? Howard wondered. He moved nearer the priest.

"We would keep such a promise until you released us from it," he said, looking at Linda, who nodded back. "Tell us and ease your mind. We might be able to advise you."

Father Hendricks sat silent for nearly a minute. Then his shoulders sagged. "I must talk to someone," he whispered. "Not that you can help me — no one can do that. But to talk — that will be such a relief. And I know I can trust you."

He began hesitantly, his voice gathering strength as his pent-up anxieties were vented at last.

"Many weeks ago my parishioners told me of secret meetings that were being held in Willisden and other non-European districts . . . " He went on to tell them about Umzoni and his organization, and the Zulu's plan to get equality for the non-Europeans.

Howard's eyes were glinting with excitement. "What is this plan? Do you know? Is he urging violence?"

"Oh; no, *meneer*. Umzoni does not believe in violence. I only know the broad outline of the plan, but it seems they are trying to organize the non-Europeans into coming out on a general strike . . ."

"What!"

"A general strike, *meneer*. The people are being asked to save their money so they can manage without wages while the strike is on."

"Are people listening? Is there enthusiasm for the idea?"

"Umzoni's meetings are always well-attended," the priest admitted. "And everyone is talking about him."

Howard let his breath out slowly. Linda stared at him.

"Could they get equality with a general strike?"

Howard gave a harsh laugh. "They could get damn nearly anything they wanted with one. Have you ever thought how dependant we are on non-European labour in this country? Without it no ship would be unloaded, no fields tilled, no gold dug, no sewers drained — you can go on for hours. If they all went on a strike together they could probably cripple the country in a fortnight." He swung back on the priest. "Go on, Father. What else?"

"I cannot tell you much more about the campaign, *meneer*, except that Umzoni is calling a day strike shortly to test his organization. The people are being asked to save for this day."

"You've no idea when it is to be?"

"No, *meneer*, that I have not heard."

"But why does this upset you so much?" Linda asked the priest curiously.

The old man lifted his head wearily. "Because for the first time in my life I do not know where my duty lies, madame. For weeks I have warned my parishioners of the dangers of attending these meetings, and because of this Umzoni came to see me — "

"Did he threaten you?" Howard interrupted grimly.

"Oh, no, *meneer*. Umzoni is a good man." The priest went on to describe the Zulu's visit. "But before he left me, he said something that has since worried me very much, for it may be true . . . "

"He said that revolt against the laws was rising like a mighty river, and one day it must burst out. And if it were not given vent in a peaceful way, it would surely take the way of violence and death. I fear he is right. Already there are wicked men who try to inflame the feelings of his followers — men, it is said, who hold evil meetings of their own."

Howard found it hard to contain his feelings at this new revelation. Yet his voice was sympathetic. "I understand. You feel Umzoni's campaign may be necessary as a safety valve, but your faith does not allow you to support it."

The old man looked at him eagerly. "That is so, *meneer*. So far I have withheld my support and some of my congregation do not attend his meetings. But their bitterness towards the Europeans is growing. I try to keep it at bay: I read to them extracts from the newspapers telling of the many kind deeds done by Europeans to our people. I try, and then something like this happens," and he waved a thin hand despairingly in the direction of the houses across the road. "How can I expect people not to listen, at least to Umzoni? I ask myself if he is not right — if it is not better to fight by peaceful means for a better future for the children rather than have slavery or violence."

Howard frowned. "Of course, this ejection notice has nothing to do with *apartheid* or the Government. It is almost certainly a private owner selling his property."

The old man sighed. "I know that, *meneer*, but can one expect the victims to see the difference? To them the same Europeans who pass the laws now turn their women and children into the streets. They will say 'The Europeans hate us — then let us hate the Europeans.' I am afraid now that those who live opposite will not turn to Umzoni but will go to the wicked men. Oh, *meneer*; this bitterness that grows among my people! It is like a great darkness settling over the land. I pray until I can pray no more, and yet every day the light grows dimmer . . . "

The old man almost broke down in his distress. Linda approached him anxiously.

"I wish we could help you with your problem," she said softly.

Father Hendricks lifted his furrowed face, and tried to smile. "You are kind, madame. But no one can help me in this thing — I know that. It is between me and my conscience. Yet, for all I say, it is not likely I shall change my views. As I told Umzoni, I am too old a Christian to believe in threats, whatever their form. But it has been a great relief to talk. You have both been very kind."

Before they left, Howard asked if the priest could arrange a meeting between him and Umzoni.

"This is what I've been looking for, Father," Howard told him. "I shall keep my promise, of course, but if I could get this negro's permission to publish news of his plan, then you would have no objection to my telling my paper, would you?"

"Oh, no, *meneer*. I ask only for his sake."

"I think there's a chance he may agree. Can you take me to a meeting?"

"I think so, *meneer*. There will probably be another in Willisden very soon. But it might be dangerous for you . . . "

"Never mind the danger. So you'll let me know as soon as you hear something?"

"I will, *meneer.*"

The old man saw them to their car. Outside the sun was hot after the cool of the refectory. The heavy pound of machinery from the factory made the air tremble. It towered over the tiny church, an industrial Goliath beside a saintly David. Howard noticed the swings had been taken down in the children's playground and a crowd of labourers were laying the foundations for the garage.

He waved his hand to the priest. "Good-bye, Father. You won't forget about the meeting?"

"I will not, *meneer*. And thank you for coming to see me, madame."

"Thank you, Father," Linda said softly. "I shall come again, if I may."

The old man's face lit up. "Please do, madame. Good-bye, both of you, and go with God."

"He's wonderful," Linda declared, turning back to wave as they drove away. "Quite wonderful."

Howard nodded, his eyes thoughtful. "I thought you'd like him."

"He's a lovely old man." Then she noticed his preoccupation. "What are you thinking about? This underground movement?"

"Yes. It's the thing I've been looking for."

She frowned. "You don't really think anything will come of it, do you?"

"I don't know," Howard said slowly. "I don't think the non-Europeans are ready to be united yet, but then I don't know how strong and determined their leaders are. It's always amazing what a few determined men can do."

Linda shuddered. "They aren't ready for equality, Howard. Some of them are absolutely primitive."

"Some of them are," he agreed. "But if this thing starts everyone who takes a hand in it will expect the same rights." His voice was low, he was talking to himself more than her. "In fact, we're beginning to see what *apartheid* is doing for the country."

⋆ ⋆ ⋆

The following evening Howard had an unexpected visitor. Joan Viljoen called at his hotel to see him. She was dressed in a grey tailored suit and a high-necked blouse — a severe style that suited her, accentuating the melancholy of her dark eyes and pensive face.

She refused his invitation to go into the lounge, choosing to remain in the foyer. She made no preamble but came to the point at once.

"I have only a few minutes, Mr. Shaw. I have been out at Willisden today and heard about the ejection notice. I've come to see if you will help me again."

"If I can, of course. But how?"

"Father Hendricks said you had taken Linda to see him, and she knew about the notice. He thought she seemed sympathetic. Was she?"

"Yes; I think so. You know Linda — she doesn't say much. But she was sorry — yes."

"Will she help us?" the girl asked eagerly.

"Now wait a minute! I'm not saying she is transformed. What do you want her to do?"

Joan drew closer. "Michael told Father Hendricks yesterday evening that he had heard whispers in the factory that the property belongs to Mr. Mitchell. And our society has confirmed it today. They believe he has other land out there, but that is still being investigated."

Howard nodded slowly. "I see. So you want Linda to have a go at him. Frankly, I don't think you have a chance. Finding work for the coloured chap, Michael, was one thing, this is another. This is a business deal probably running into tens of thousands of pounds. He is probably selling the plot for a factory site. He's not going to change his mind when he hears of the misery he's going to cause. He'll know it now; he isn't a fool."

Joan's dark eyes pleaded with him. "Father Hendricks was sure Linda would ask him."

"She may, but don't expect anything, to come of it. What about Brian. Haven't you tackled him?"

A shadow crossed her face. "His father doesn't tell him everything; he knew nothing about it until I mentioned it. And then he said much the same as you, that Mr. Mitchell would look on it as too big a thing for sentiment."

Howard nodded with conviction. "He

will, I'm sure. But I'll ask Linda for you."

"You could point out that he'll probably have trouble in his factory. Most of the men who work there live in the vicinity and some are bound to be affected."

Howard shook his head. "I don't think that will worry him. He could re-staff that factory fifty times over from the unemployed in Willisden. But I'll speak to Linda about it."

She thanked him gratefully, then looked at her watch. "I'll have to go now," she told him. "I promised to meet Brian at eight. He doesn't know I've come here."

"I won't tell anyone," he smiled, walking with her to the hotel entrance. "My story will be that Father Hendricks asked me."

She stopped short. "Oh; I nearly forgot. Father Hendricks said if you go out to him tomorrow night before eight, he will be able to help you. He said you would understand."

She paused on the steps to thank him once more. Howard watched her go, waved, then returned into the hotel. So tomorrow night he would be given his first glimpse of the resistance movement for which he had searched so vainly! His heart beat faster in anticipation.

15

HOWARD 'phoned Linda directly after breakfast the following morning.

"Can I drop round and see you right away?" he asked. "It's rather important."

Her voice sounded unusually hesitant. "Yes; except that you'll find things rather upset. Trevor's in bed with a pain in his stomach, and if it isn't any better this afternoon he wants me to call in the doctor."

Howard understood at once the reason for her hesitation. While she had never admitted her husband's dislike of her association with him, he was aware it existed, if only from the discreet way she kept the two of them apart. He knew her reason. Mitchell was blunt to the point of rudeness: if they were together long he would inevitably bring up his dislike of Howard's articles and his consequent notoriety. It would require only a quarrel between them to make Linda's present position virtually untenable. This she was clearly trying to avoid.

"Then I won't bother you," he said. "But I thought you would want to know what I learned yesterday." He heard her gasp of amazement as he told her who was the owner of the Willisden property. "You might think it is asking too much of you to bring it up, and I wouldn't blame you at all," he finished. "But as you were involved as much as I yesterday, I thought you would like to know."

"I'd have been furious if you hadn't told me," she answered. "I'll do all I can, but I haven't much hope." The familiar bitterness in her voice was clear, even over the 'phone. "He'll probably call me a fool, but I suppose I can take it."

"Thanks. I knew you would try. Now the second thing that might interest you. I'm going out to Willisden tonight — the negro is holding a meeting there."

Her response was immediate. "Tonight! What time will you pick me up?"

"Pick *you* up! You're not going. It might be dangerous for Europeans to be there."

"It'll be no more dangerous for me than you."

"I'm not having a woman on my hands tonight," he told her grimly. "I'll tell you all about it tomorrow."

The receiver fairly crackled. "That's just like you, you heel. You get me interested in something and then leave me high and dry. Two days ago you said it was time I saw how the other half of the world lived — that it would do my selfish soul good. All right; it has. And now I want to see more. I don't like doing things by halves. Take me along, or I'll go on my own."

He knew she was reckless enough to carry out her threat.

"Be sensible," he argued. "They're certain to hold the meeting as far from the nearest police station as possible which probably means it will be in the location. I was nearly knifed there in broad daylight, so think what can happen to you, a white woman, at night. I daren't take you, much as I'd like to. I happen to think something about you." The last sentence slipped out before he could prevent it.

There was silence. He waited, not a little embarrassed. When she spoke all the anger had gone from her voice. She sounded chastened. "I suppose you're right . . . "

"I'll 'phone you at the same time tomorrow and tell you all about it," he promised.

"Yes; please do that. And, Howard . . . " She paused a moment. Her voice was husky. "Howard; take care of yourself. I want to see you in one piece tomorrow."

The receiver clicked and went dead in his hand. He stood staring at it, wishing he could have seen her face.

* * *

Linda left it until the evening before asking her husband about the property. After dinner, which they had early, she went to his room. He was sitting propped up in bed with pillows, reading the evening paper. His red-striped pyjamas accentuated his high colour.

"How are you feeling now?" she asked.

"Not so good," he grumbled. "Keep thinking I must have an ulcer like old

Hathaway. Morkel's late, isn't he?"

She sank into a basket-chair by the bed. "He should be here any time now."

She chatted with him for five minutes before broaching the delicate subject of the ejection notice. Her long fingers were playing with the silken tassels of the coverlet. "I met a friend the other day who said you were selling some land opposite your Willisden factory. Is that right?"

Although her eyes were not on him, she could feel his sudden attention.

"Who was it?" he asked sharply. "Not Howard Shaw?"

"No," she lied. "Not Howard Shaw."

He frowned heavily. "I asked because I can't see how anyone but a prying reporter could have found this out. It's not supposed to be public knowledge."

"Apparently it is," she said, not knowing the truth of her words. She could not resist adding, "It must be if I know of it."

He ignored her sarcasm, watching her closely. "You've never shown interest in my transactions before. Why the interest now?"

She had no alternative but to tell him of her meeting with Father Hendricks, and the old man's distress on hearing the news.

Mitchell nodded sarcastically. "I thought Shaw was mixed up in it somewhere. So it was he who took you out there."

"For months I've been hearing what a wonderful old man Father Hendricks is, and so I asked Howard to take me to meet him," she lied. "And while we were there the people opposite received their ejection notices."

"And having heard I was selling property there, you put two and two together? Quite a coincidence, isn't it?"

"Quite a coincidence," she flashed. "But now, after seeing and hearing a little of the misery of the people there, I feel I must ask you to think twice about selling. Do you realize they haven't a hope of getting alternative accommodation? That most of them will have to go down to the location and live in dug-outs? It'll kill some of the old people."

"A few weeks ago you flew at my throat for suggesting Shaw was getting you interested in the non-Europeans," he said with narrowed eyes. "Now you come asking me to throw over a deal worth fifteen thousand for them."

"I've not changed a damn," she denied hotly. "And I'm not influenced by Howard or anyone else. But I'd be more than a bitch if I didn't mention it now I know the suffering it will cause."

Resentment showed in two spots of red high up on Mitchell's cheeks. "This is the sort of thing I've always tried to keep you clear of. The less women know about these things the better. And I had kept you clear until this damned reporter came along."

Her eyes searched him unbelievingly. "You're not telling me you've been trying to protect me from the facts of life!"

"Some facts don't make any woman happy," he said angrily. "This is one. The property has to be sold — sentiment can't come into it. It's business — a factory is going up there. There's a lot of money involved."

The reluctant admiration faded from her eyes. "There are a lot of people involved, too." She leaned forward suddenly. "I don't ask many favours of you, Trevor. But give these people a break. Don't kick them out into the location. If you can't put the deal off, then postpone it. Give them a few more months in their homes. It's a matter of life or death to some of them."

His blunt refusal died on his lips as he saw her earnestness. He frowned. "Why do you want this so badly?"

Her lips twisted bitterly. "Must I have any other reason? I'm sincere about this, Trevor. I want to help these people and Father Hendricks. Don't spoil it all by thinking anything else, or I'll never forgive you."

"Do you realize what you're asking?"

"Yes; but I want you to do it. It'll help me, deep inside. I want it badly, Trevor."

"And what will it do for me?" he asked. "Or doesn't that matter?"

"I thought it might do us both good," she said slowly. "It might be the beginning of something new in our lives."

There was a long silence. Mitchell's face was furrowed in thought. "Let me think about it," he said gruffly at last.

"It's a big thing. You must see that."

"I do." She turned to go, then paused at the door. "Thank you for listening to me. I hadn't expected you would."

Back in the lounge, Linda went over to the cocktail-cabinet and poured herself a brandy. As she straightened up, she saw her pale face in a mirror. She stared at it with fierce intensity. The mirror seemed to reflect two faces. One she knew, but the other was that of a stranger. As it looked calmly back at her, she felt both exalted and frightened.

Then she turned away. To save the homes of a bunch of unwashed non-Europeans she had virtually promised Trevor to play her part in reshaping their marriage. And she had done it with her feelings towards Howard as they were . . . Why? What was the matter with her? But Trevor wouldn't do it! He couldn't . . . And now she was being a damned hypocrite because she was hoping he wouldn't! With an exclamation she lifted her glass and drained it dry. At that moment the doorbell rang.

It was Morkel. "Good evening, Mrs. Mitchell," he greeted. "Sorry I'm a little late. How's the patient?"

Linda waved a hand towards Mitchell's bedroom. "He's in there, working out how long he has left. Go and put him out of his misery. Then I'll offer you a drink."

Morkel grinned, and went off. He was in the bedroom less than ten minutes. When he returned the grin was still on his face.

"He'll live," he told Linda. "It's his liver that's objecting to all this whisky. I've told him to ease off and given him a prescription."

She motioned to an armchair. "What will you have? A drop of the dog that's biting Trevor?"

He shook his head regretfully. "There's nothing I'd like better. I've had that sort of day. But it isn't over yet, unfortunately."

She was disappointed. She felt like company, and also wished to get Morkel talking about Howard. An old friend, he would know much that would be interesting.

"Just one," she murmured, eyeing him under her dark lashes. "Your patients can't be such tyrants as all that."

"It's not my patients, it's the police," he told her ruefully. "I'm an assistant police surgeon and they want me to stand by tonight. They've got a big raid on."

For a moment the implication of his words escaped her. Then she turned quickly to hide her face, picking up her cigarettes from the armchair. She forced her voice to be casual.

"What sort of raid?"

"The police were tipped off by a Coloured earlier this evening that there is going to be an illegal meeting in the Willisden location tonight, and they're burning up the 'phones to get enough reinforcements in time. They intend having a big round-up."

"What time is this going to take place?"

"The meeting is scheduled to start at eight-thirty, but I doubt if our crowd will be ready so early. But they should catch 'em before it ends." Morkel picked up his medical bag regretfully. "So you see I must keep off the whisky tonight."

Linda said nothing more to detain him and saw him to the door. As soon as he had gone she flew back to the lounge, looking up at the clock. A quarter to eight — there might just be time to warn Howard and the priest if she burned up the road to Willisden.

She went into Mitchell's room. "Dr. Morkel says you'll be all right in a couple of days," she said, managing a smile.

"They always say that," he grunted.

"A friend of mine has just 'phoned to ask if I'll make up a four at bridge," she lied. "You don't mind if I go, do you? The maid is in, should you want anything."

"No; I suppose I'll be all right," he grunted.

She smiled her thanks, then hurried out. Two minutes later she was guiding her car down the twisting coast road. She glanced at her watch and her face set. Tyres screamed as the huge car rolled and skidded round corner after corner.

* * *

With a squeal of brakes, Linda pulled up outside the mission church. Her heart leapt as she recognized Howard's car ahead of her. She ran to the refectory door and tried the latch. The door swung open to reveal an empty room.

They had gone! But why was Howard's car still outside? Wait; Morkel had said the meeting was to be held in the location. *Skollies* could strip an unoccupied car of wheels and engine in minutes. That would be why Howard and the priest had gone on foot. It would also account for their leaving early.

Yet there was still time to warn them if Morkel was right and the police did not arrive until after the meeting had started. But how was she to find the meeting-place? She had only a vague idea where the location itself lay, but knew of its vast size. And, because of its nature, the meeting-place was certain to be well hidden.

She wandered out into the deserted street, wishing now she had told Morkel about Howard. She had not done so because, childhood friend of Howard's though he was, he was a Nationalist and she had felt it unreasonable to expect him to keep their secret.

But now this meeting was police

knowledge, did the secret matter any longer? Was it not likely the police would find out everything now? Certainly Morkel would have done all he could to protect and get Howard out safely, probably with the priest as well.

But it was too late now — she had no idea where to find the doctor. Panic swept over her when she thought of the perils confronting Howard and the old man. Particularly Howard. They were not only physical dangers. Prejudice already existed against him — Erasmus's insinuations had been believed in many quarters. Even if Howard were not charged with seditious conduct for being present at the meeting, the furore Erasmus would raise might well bring out a public outcry for his deportation. His arrest might well ruin him.

Every second was precious and yet to whom could she go for help? Any European would see in her attempt to warn Howard and the priest a move to obstruct the police. For certainly a warning to them would be a warning to the others — Father Hendricks would never leave them to be arrested.

For a moment Linda realized the full implications of what she was trying to do, then she swept her doubts impatiently aside. When the law conflicted with human loyalties, then damn the law. Such was her creed.

A name suddenly came to her. With a sob of relief she jumped into her car, swung it across the road, and drove down the narrow alley opposite. She pulled up outside the last house. Jumping out, she hammered on the door. Michael appeared.

"Michael; do you know where Umzoni's meeting is being held tonight?" she asked abruptly.

Even in the dim light she saw the Coloured's look of shocked surprise. "Don't worry; I know everything, Father Hendricks has told me," she went on. Quickly she explained her problem. "You must show me where to go or both the priest and Mr. Shaw will be arrested," she finished. "Hurry, please."

"Wait, madame," Michael muttered. He ran inside, to return almost immediately with his jacket, into which he struggled.

Linda flung open the door of her car.

"Jump in," she ordered. "You'll have to show me the way."

On Michael's instructions she turned right at the end of Riebeck Road and with headlights full on sent the powerful car thundering into the darkness. In less than two minutes she was forced to slow down as they hit an uneven sandy track. The car leapt like a wild thing. The houses were behind them now, giving way to a dark, wind-swept wilderness of wattle and bush.

"Farther down, madame," Michael replied to her question. "There is a short cut through the location . . ."

Another minute and he motioned for her to pull up. He turned to her. "What do I tell them, madame?"

"I'm coming with you," she said, throwing open her door.

Michael started. "No, madame. There are *skollies* . . . It is too dangerous."

Linda grabbed a duster from a receptacle on the dash-board and tied it over her hair.

"I'll keep my face down and they aren't likely to notice my clothes in the darkness," she told him. Her voice rose as she saw he was still hesitating. "For God's sake, hurry up, man. It's nearly nine o'clock."

They left the car, their feet sinking into the soft sand. A gust of wind buffeted them roughly, then went snarling off among the wattles, leaving an unnatural silence in its wake. Behind them, so far away they seemed in another world, the lights of the city formed a cluster of brilliants under the dark mountain. Above, a crescent moon broke clear, stared down at them agape, then was swept away by a dark onrush of cloud.

The slum drew nearer, dense, shadowy, forbidding.

"You must stay behind me, madame," Michael whispered. "There will be sentries guarding the paths." He stopped, turning to her. "Madame, this is very dangerous. Are you sure you wish to come?"

His nervousness communicated itself to her. She remembered Joan's experience. Fear made her voice harsh.

"Go on and stop arguing!"

In single file they took a narrow path that led into the heart of the location. Cold snails of fear crawled down Linda's spine. She had heard stories of the hideousness of the slum but her imagination had conceived nothing like this. In the crimson glow of the fires the grotesque hovels appeared stained with blood: abodes more befitting demons than men. Every pool of stygian darkness was pregnant with menace; every sound a threat. Figures loomed gigantic in the flaring lights; monstrous shadows lurched out to clutch her. The wind snarled among the hovels, tearing at their crazy walls with savage fingers. Ahead the sky was sullen, stained with crimson smoke. It was like a surrealist's impression of hell.

The path twisted tortuously among the tightly packed *pondokkies* until Linda had lost all sense of direction. A torch was suddenly flashed in her eyes, making her heart leap in terror. Michael answered the sentry's challenge in Afrikaans. After an argument they were allowed to proceed.

"This is a big meeting tonight," Michael muttered, motioning at the deserted *pondokkies* around them. "Many people have gone to it."

"Hurry," she panted. "The police can't be much longer now."

She had already realized it would have been better to have let Michael go on alone. More than once she stumbled in the darkness; once she fell headlong, her hands plunging into something soft and glutinous. She gave a sob of disgust, her stomach revolting. Michael helped her to her feet and they hurried on.

At last a yellow light showed ahead of them. Another minute and they were standing on the edge of the clearing where Michael had had his fight with Swartz. The scene was much the same except that this meeting was considerably larger. Umzoni was speaking from the platform and the two paraffin lamps showed the spellbound faces of the dense crowd.

Linda stared around in amazement. "I hadn't expected anything as big as this," she muttered. "Can you see Mr. Shaw or the priest?"

Michael stared about, then pointed. "There, madame. By the platform. They are standing together."

With a tremendous effort Linda fought back her fear. "Come on. We must get to them."

The attentive crowd, tightly packed at this entrance, resented their intrusion. Gritting her teeth, Linda fought her way forward.

"Let me through," she cried. "Stand out of the way."

The sound of her voice speaking English turned the crowd's attention to her. Men jostled one another to see who was speaking. Somehow she found herself cut off from Michael. The pressure of the crowd became too great, she could move neither forward nor backward. In the struggle the duster fell from her head, revealing her mass of pale, gold hair. Alarmed cries broke out from the crowd.

The pressure around her was so intense now that Linda could not move her arms. The sweet-sour smell of natives came thickly to her nostrils. Dark faces encircled her, hundreds of eyes stared at her from all sides. She felt unreal, part of some grim nightmare.

Suddenly her control broke. "Howard!" she screamed. "Where are you? Howard; for God's sake help me!"

16

FATHER HENDRICKS and Howard reached the clearing twenty minutes before the meeting was due to start. The priest at once introduced Howard to Umzoni, who led the writer to a small *pondokkie* that formed part of the perimeter of the clearing. Its domestic contents had been removed for the occasion, leaving only four wooden boxes for seats and a rough table on which stood a lighted candle.

The huge Zulu treated the humble office with an indifference that was majestic. He waved Howard to a box, then took one himself so they faced one another across the table.

"So you are the Mr. Shaw I have read so much about," Umzoni said in his deep, vibrant voice. "I am very pleased to meet you."

Howard was greatly impressed by the man's appearance. Apart from his massive proportions, his high forehead, wide-set eyes, and commanding voice suggested a man in whom intelligence was coupled with the vigorous qualities of leadership. On all counts — including the vital primitive one of looking the part with his commanding stature — he seemed a natural leader for the non-Europeans.

In spite of this, Howard found the negro's lack of deference towards him, a European, disturbing at first. He had to control his feelings carefully.

"You don't object to my coming to your meeting?" he asked.

The Zulu shrugged his massive shoulders. "Father Hendricks is your passport, Mr. Shaw. I would trust that old man with my life. He assures me you will say nothing of what you see or hear."

"Yes; I've given him my word," Howard admitted. Then he looked at the Zulu keenly. "But, as you've probably guessed, I've come to see if you'll release me from it."

Seeing Umzoni's look of protest, Howard went on quickly. "Let me tell you first what my paper is hoping to do."

He went on to explain the purpose of his investigations, finishing: "You can see that if it can prove that organized resistance is springing up in this country, then it will have a case that will turn other Europeans against *apartheid*, if only on the grounds of self-interest."

Umzoni nodded thoughtfully. "Yes; I see that." Then he frowned. "But surely you realize that we cannot let our existence be known yet. The police would make it very difficult for us to hold our meetings. Already it is difficult enough."

Howard leaned forward. "Yes; but on the other hand you must let the Europeans know sooner or later why you intend to strike. Otherwise the whole thing is pointless. After all, I assume you aren't trying to cripple the country out of spite. You don't want the strike, but you do want emancipation. Right?"

"Of course. The strike is only a means to an end."

"Very well. Therefore you must find some way of letting the Europeans know of your threat beforehand."

The Zulu frowned. "We have considered

all this, Mr. Shaw. We shall let them know as soon as we are ready."

"That's just the point — you're going to find it difficult," Howard said. "What newspapers are going to help you? They aren't going to advertise your campaign for you. And don't forget the Government will have something to say in the matter . . . "

It was clear from Umzoni's expression that Howard had put a finger on one of the organization's greatest difficulties. The Zulu looked at him closely.

"What are you suggesting, Mr. Shaw?"

"I'm going to make a bargain with you. Father Hendricks says you are going to hold a one-day strike to test your organization. Very well. Give me permission to publish details of yourselves and your plans, tell me the date of the strike; and I will promise nothing of it will be released until a few days before the strike. In that way it can't possibly harm you."

"But your articles in *The World Observer* are banned in this country. What use would they be to us?"

Howard smiled grimly, playing his ace.

"You must have heard of the friendship between myself and Erasmus. You can be certain he will see the news is plastered on the front page of every newspaper in the Union. He'll do the publicity for us."

Umzoni's eyes acknowledged their appreciation of the scheme.

"It's a fair bargain, I think," Howard concluded. "But, if you agree, there is one snag. I hope I wouldn't have too long to wait before releasing the news. I couldn't drag my articles out indefinitely."

Umzoni gave a grim smile. "You wouldn't have to wait long, Mr. Shaw. We plan to hold our one-day strike in the Cape very soon — within the next few weeks. It will be followed by similar strikes in the other provinces."

"Can you give me permission yourself?" Howard asked, wondering what the Zulu's status was in the organization.

"Yes; although I should first want to discuss it with my lieutenants." The Zulu pondered a moment. "I must think it over. Will you be staying after the meeting?"

"I could."

"Very well. Let us discuss it again later."

Before they returned to the clearing, Howard asked the question that was worrying him. "Tell me one thing. Is your movement sponsored in any way by the Communists?"

Umzoni smiled wryly as he lifted his massive body from his box. "Not in the slightest, although I have no doubt that is what our enemies will say when they hear about us. No; we are a wholly democratic organization: that I swear." He paused, eyeing Howard curiously. "May I ask a personal question? How do you, a South African European, feel about giving our movement publicity?"

Howard shrugged. "Frankly, very realistically. I'm not making you — you exist. Mind you, I'll tell you honestly that much of me doesn't like the idea of you non-Europeans taking the bit in your teeth. But I'm employed at the moment as a journalist and I'm doing a journalist's job — reporting facts. In any case, I know well enough you'd find some other way of getting publicity if you had to." He smiled. "One could look at it the other way and say I'm doing the Europeans a favour by giving them advance warning."

The Zulu nodded at his words. He followed Howard out into the clearing. The crowd had increased greatly during their absence, being now near the thousand mark.

"I think it would be wiser if you stayed behind the platform in the shadows," Umzoni told Howard. "The people may become uneasy if they see a European among them."

Howard nodded. "I'll stay with Father Hendricks until you have finished." Leaving the Zulu he rejoined the old priest who was standing alone behind the platform.

"Did everything go to your satisfaction, *meneer*?" the old man asked shyly.

"Very well, Father. I said I would see him again afterwards. Will that be too late for you? If it is there is no need for you to stay."

"I will stay, *meneer*. I do not think these meetings last very long."

They lapsed into silence, watching the

proceedings. A coloured man made a short introductory speech, and then Umzoni strode into the centre of the stage. His first few words were enough to tell Howard what a born orator the man was. His deep resonant voice gripped the crowd at once and held them spellbound.

The Zulu's delivery was in Afrikaans. Not being able to understand the language, Howard spent the first few minutes studying the large crowd. Their staring faces showed them to be a mixture of all the Union's non-European races. Although the great majority were Africans and Coloureds, there was a scattering of Malays and Chinese among them. In spite of the blustery wind that kept blowing dust and sand across the clearing, all were motionless, clearly hypnotized by the personality of the speaker.

Howard turned to the old priest. "Can you translate for me, Father? He is speaking slowly."

The old man nodded and began. Howard listened, fascinated. Here was the non-European telling his tale; here was the voice of the oppressed telling of his misery, and his anger.

Emotion was rising in the crowd. Yet the Zulu held it under control so effectively that the hundreds of faces changed as one. From sorrow they turned to pity, from pity to resentment, emotion after emotion sweeping across their faces like gusts of wind across a lake. There was a long pause, and then the Zulu spoke again. A new expression came and remained on the mirror of faces. The unmistakable expression of hope.

"He is telling them now of his plan and what he wants them to do," the priest told Howard. "Do you wish me to go on translating, *meneer*?"

"Only if he gives them the date he wants to have the strike," Howard said, to save the old man's voice.

He watched, fascinated by the Zulu's performance. Until now he had doubted the possibility of anyone achieving an effective unity between the non-European races. They were torn between many factions. The Coloureds tended to look down on the Africans; the Africans themselves were composed of many tribes with ancient feuds. But now, seeing the faces before him, heterogeneous in race but homogeneous in interest and purpose, he began to wonder. If they could produce one or two more leaders with the personality of this Zulu, anything was possible.

Howard noticed Father Hendricks looking round anxiously.

"What's the matter, Father?"

"I am told that nearly all Umzoni's meetings are interrupted by Swartz and his agitators who try to talk the people into violence," the old man told him. "I am wondering if they will come tonight."

Howard's face set grimly. The hard bulge of the automatic in his side pocket felt comforting. Yet any display of firearms in this company could be dangerous. He decided if the *skollies* came his best plan would be to ask Umzoni for an escort for himself and the priest.

During the half-hour they had been listening, the wind had been growing stronger. It was rushing like a mad thing now among the crazy hovels and sweeping in frenzied gusts across the clearing. The crowd were pressing closer to the platform, finding difficulty in hearing even the Zulu's powerful voice.

During one particularly powerful gust Howard thought he heard the cry of a woman. He looked about but could see nothing. Then he felt his arm gripped. Father Hendricks was pointing with shaking finger across the clearing.

"Look, *meneer*. There among the crowd. It is madame . . . "

Howard's heart gave a great thud. At one side of the clearing the crowd were parting, only to turn and press even closer round the object of their curiosity. Umzoni's voice broke off abruptly. Howard saw the pale gold of a woman's hair gleaming among the tightly-packed dark faces.

Then, as he ran forward, he heard her screams.

"Howard! Where are you? Howard; help me . . . "

17

ALL was confusion as Howard fought his way through the crowd towards Linda. Umzoni, who had quickly sized up the situation, raised his voice in a command. At once the pressure of the crowd eased as the curious sightseers fell reluctantly back.

With a sob of relief Linda ran forward, clutching hold of Howard and burying her face in his jacket. He held her tightly, feeling the deep trembling of her slender body.

"What on earth are you doing here?" he muttered. "I told you to stay away. Are you all right?"

"Yes," she whispered, her face still pressed in his coat.

"It was madness to come," he gritted, his relief turning to anger. "You promised me you would stay away."

She took a deep breath and drew herself upright. "Listen," she panted. "I came because I heard from Dr. Morkel that the police intend to raid this meeting tonight. They've found out about it from some Coloured and will be here at any minute . . . "

"The police!"

She seized his arm. "I've got the car on the road. Get Father Hendricks and come quickly. We haven't a second to lose. Michael's here — he knows the way out. Hurry, for God's sake!"

Howard looked around. He saw they were the centre of attraction. Hundreds of dark faces were staring at them. He noticed Umzoni had left the platform.

"Come on, then," he muttered, taking her arm. At that moment Father Hendricks reached them.

"Madame; why have you come?" the old man cried. "This is no place for a white lady . . . "

Howard stepped forward. "Listen, Father. The police are going to raid this meeting. They'll be here at any moment. You must come with us at once."

A look of dismay appeared on the old man's face. "The police, *meneer*! But how do they know . . . ?"

"A coloured man told them this evening," Linda explained. "I heard it from Dr. Morkel and came to warn you both. You must leave at once. I have my car on the road."

"But we must warn the others first," the priest cried. "There are innocent women and children here. I must tell Umzoni. You and madame go, *meneer*. I will follow in a few minutes. You two must not be caught here."

With that the old man turned and hurried towards the platform. Howard hesitated. Linda caught his arm. "We can't leave him, Howard."

"But you?" Howard muttered. "I must get you away."

"Don't worry about me. In any case, I don't know the way back to the road and Michael seems to have vanished. Let's go with the old man. Once he has warned the negro we can go."

They ran towards the platform. Howard pointed ahead. "There's Michael, talking to Umzoni! That's where he went — to warn the others."

As Linda looked she saw the Zulu turn and leap up on the platform. His deep voice called out imperatively, telling the restless crowd of their danger. There was a sudden hush, followed by a gasp of fear. For a moment it seemed the crowd would panic and run. Then the Zulu's calm voice brought them under control. They began to hurry towards the exits and pass through them in some semblance of order.

Howard ran up to the priest. "Come, Father," he said impatiently. "We must get Mrs. Mitchell away and she won't go until you come." He turned to Michael. "Will you show us back to the car?"

Michael nodded. "Yes, *meneer*. Now that the others are warned, I am ready — "

His voice broke off as a police-whistle shrilled out over the turmoil. An authoritative voice rang out, stilling the frightened cries of the crowd. Khaki and blue uniformed figures appeared round the perimeter of the clearing. The remainder of the terrified crowd, still numbering several hundreds, drew back as a police superintendent stepped forward, holding a megaphone to his mouth.

"Stand where you are, and make no move to escape," he ordered in Afrikaans. "I have a cordon of men round the clearing. Remain where you are and you will be quite safe."

Beside Howard, Michael cursed. "Someone has betrayed us who knows us well," he said bitterly. "The sentries have been captured. Otherwise they would have warned us when the police were coming."

The police superintendent had turned to Umzoni, who was standing like an ebony statue in the glare of the lamps. "You on the platform," he ordered. "You will stay quite still and wait for my men."

The Zulu's massive body seemed to swell with incensed pride. His defiance could be felt, charging the air with its passion. He turned his head and saw the group of uniformed men who were closing in on the platform. Letting out a great cry of defiance, he ran along the platform and launched himself among the men with a mighty leap.

His huge body crushed two of them to the ground. Leaping to his feet, he sprang through the gap and ran for the shadows.

The police drew their revolvers and a volley of shots rang out. Umzoni was seen to stagger, then recover and vanish into the darkness. Half-a-dozen policemen raced after him, firing as they went.

The shots terrified the crowd. Until then they had been stunned, resigned to their fate. But many did not see the police were firing at Umzoni because of his efforts to escape, and thought this was to be their punishment. Panic spread like a bush fire among them, driving everything from their minds but the desire to flee. A woman began the stampede. Letting out a scream of terror, she ran madly for one of the guarded exits. Immediately all was mad confusion. Like stampeding cattle, the rest of the crowd followed. There was no thought in their minds of resistance; no thought of attacking the police. Their one desire was to escape, but in their wild terror they trampled underfoot anything that stood in their way.

Police resistance was equally spontaneous. They, thinking in turn they were being attacked, drew their batons and struck at the frantic crowd.

After the initial blows were struck all control vanished on both sides. The police reinforcements, who had been drawn up outside the clearing, poured through the narrow entrances to help their comrades. All the latent passions of racial intolerance spewed to the surface at the feel of baton or stick striking flesh and bone. The air was filled with screams, curses, and the vicious thud of blows.

Linda and Howard, with the old priest and Michael, watched in horror from the wall behind the platform. Fortunately for them there was a thirty-yard gap between them and the mêlée. The crowd, when challenged, had been in front of the platform and at the moment was held there by a line of police. Howard had managed to find a recess in the fence enclosing the clearing and in it the four of them were standing, hidden in the darkness. At their backs the fence was about six feet high. It would have been easy for Howard and Michael to scale it — possibly Linda could have managed it with their assistance — but the old man would have to be lifted over. After seeing the police's reaction to Umzoni's attempt to escape, Howard was afraid anyone silhouetted on the fence might draw a volley of shots. For this reason he bade them stay where they were for the moment.

Yet their danger was great. The frenzied crowd, attacked on all sides by the police, had lost all control. At any time the fighting might break out in their direction.

Beside Howard, Father Hendricks was moaning at the sight of helpless men and women being bludgeoned to the ground. Twice Howard had to seize his arm to prevent his running forward. Linda was watching in horrified fascination. Michael's face could just be seen in the darkness, twisted and bitter.

Howard gave Michael instructions to keep the old priest from going out into the mêlée, then edged out from the recess and slid along the wall, trying to find an unguarded exit. But the fence seemed unbroken at this end of the clearing. Then Howard remembered the *pondokkie* that Umzoni had used as an office. If he could get the four of them into it, they might be able to break through its thin walls and escape. But the hovel was some forty yards away, in the darkness behind the other end of the platform. To reach it they would have to pass through a broad patch of light that was reflected back from the paraffin lamps.

He returned and told the others of his plan. "We'll have to risk it," he muttered. "We can't wait here any longer. Michael, you look after Father Hendricks and I'll see to Mrs. Mitchell. Keep to the fence and run over that patch of light."

Holding Linda's arm, he was about to lead the way when he drew her back into the recess again. The frantic crowd had burst through the cordon of police ahead and were running blindly in their direction. Policemen ran with them, striking out in all directions with their batons. The vanguard of the crowd reached the fence a few yards to the left of their recess and rebounded from it like a wave from a cliff. Screams and groans made the air shudder.

A negro ran right in front of them,

pursued by a policeman. He tripped and stumbled. A baton rose and smashed down on his body. He screamed, rolled over, and tried to grab the policeman's legs. A boot kicked him clear. He staggered to his feet, only for the baton to smash against his jaw, leaving it hanging and broken. He let out a moan and dropped face downwards. The baton rose again and fell with crushing force in the centre of his back. His body arched, then collapsed, twitching like a broken-backed dog.

The policeman, red-eyed, glared around, then ran back into the screaming crowd. Linda clutched Howard's arm, her face deathlike.

"Oh, God," she retched. "Stop it. Dear God; stop it . . . "

Michael was struggling with the priest. The old man's face was agonized, tortured beyond endurance. He was praying brokenly in Afrikaans as he tried to break free.

The desperate crowd were fighting back as savagely. A huge Coloured had snatched a chair from the platform and was swinging it about him murderously.

A struggling, cursing knot of men and women reeled towards the fence. A native man and woman broke free. The woman was carrying a piccaninny in a shawl on her back, the man trying to help her away. A policeman leapt after them, swinging a blow at the man's head. The negro ducked instinctively and the baton swung by him and smashed down on the child. Its helpless, wide-eyed face dissolved in a shapeless mass of blood. The woman let out a ghastly scream, turned, and sprang at the policeman's face. He reeled back, deep claw-marks gouged in his cheeks. In a mad frenzy the negro leapt at him and twisted the baton from his hand. His arm rose and fell with the strength of hate, smashing the policeman's skull like an egg-shell.

Nearby a uniformed figure was slowly and methodically beating to death a negro who had attacked him. His arm rose and fell rhythmically, each thudding blow bringing a bubbling scream from the broken body at his feet.

The old priest suddenly broke free from Michael's grasp. With an incoherent cry he ran forward and clutched at the policeman's arm. The man turned with a snarl, shook off his feeble grip, and was about to strike when Michael, who had run after the priest, leapt savagely at his throat. At that moment a surging horde of struggling bodies swept over them. From the mad confusion Michael emerged with the half-stunned figure of Father Hendricks.

Howard, not daring to leave Linda, was writhing at his helplessness.

"We've got to get out of here," he gritted at her. She did not seem to hear him. Her face was dazed with horror.

Seeing Father Hendricks was able to walk, Howard led Linda along the wall, motioning to Michael to follow them. The fighting had surged back towards the centre of the clearing and there were only a few struggling groups between them and the *pondokkie*.

They crossed the patch of light without being noticed, as did the pair behind them. Whistles were shrilling out orders, trying to get the maddened constables back under control. Howard crept along the fence with Linda close behind. If the *pondokkie* entrance was guarded he would have no option but to make their presence known to the police. This he would have done long ago had he dared. But everywhere race hatred seemed to have taken control: anyone remotely connected with the meeting appeared in danger of a beating. Unfortunately the responsible police officers were all at the other side of the clearing.

To his intense relief the dark entrance of the *pondokkie* was unguarded. Checking Linda, he lowered his head and went inside, half-expecting a baton to descend on him. But the hovel was empty. He drew Linda inside, and then Father Hendricks and Michael.

"If we can break through one of the walls, we might be able to get away," he whispered to Michael. "The cordon of police that were outside ran into the clearing when the trouble started . . . "

A whistle gave a long blast outside. A brilliant light blazed across the clearing. The police had brought up a portable searchlight. It lit up the inside of the *pondokkie*. Michael pointed.

"Look, *meneer*," he said to Howard.

Howard saw that a section of one wall had been smashed away. The thin planking was swinging loose in the blustering wind. He wondered if Umzoni had tried to escape this way.

Howard stooped and crawled through. No police were in sight. He helped Linda and the others out.

"Do you know the way to the road from here?" he asked Michael.

The Coloured stared about, then nodded. "I think so, *meneer*."

"Then come on, quickly . . . "

The screams of pain and terror died behind them as they followed a narrow path among the densely-packed, malodorous hovels. Michael led the way, supporting the still-dazed priest. Linda was holding on to Howard's arm tightly.

She lifted her white face to him. "That was horrible, Howard. Unspeakably horrible. Those people were unarmed. Why did the police attack them?"

His own face was grim, twisted. "The police themselves thought they were being attacked. That's what you get when there is violence between white and black. Raw, bestial savagery."

"I wouldn't have believed it," she said, talking as if in a nightmare. "I wouldn't have believed it . . ."

To their intense relief the car had escaped the notice of the police, who had left their vans farther up the track.

"We had better keep going down this road, or the police are bound to stop and question us," Howard told Linda. He turned to Michael. "Can we go on and still get back to Willisden?"

"Yes, *meneer*. There is a tarred road a mile farther on. If you turn left there, you can get back."

It took Howard twenty minutes to find his way back to the church. In that time Father Hendricks, who seemed crushed by all he had seen, had hardly spoken. Howard and Michael helped him from the car and round to the rectory. Linda ran ahead to light his lamp.

They heard her give a muted scream. Howard released the priest's arm and ran into the room. She was standing by the flickering lamp, staring wide-eyed at the floor. Howard followed her gaze and stiffened.

At the foot of one of the chairs, lying in a pool of blood, was the huddled figure of Umzoni.

18

FOR a moment Howard was too astonished to speak. The entry of Father Hendricks and Michael broke the spell. Michael let out a startled exclamation and ran across to the huddled Zulu. As he knelt beside him, Umzoni groaned.

The shock at seeing the wounded negro roused Father Hendricks from his daze. He joined Michael and with gentle hands probed the Zulu's body for wounds. He looked up at Howard, his face concerned.

"He is badly hurt, *meneer*. Will you help us to carry him to my bed?"

It took the combined efforts of all three men to get the negro in the bedroom. There they pulled him on to the priest's bed. Linda ran out to put water on the gas-ring.

Howard helped the priest to remove the negro's jacket and to cut away his bloodstained shirt. Two wounds became visible: one in the left shoulder, the other across the man's muscular back. The latter looked the uglier wound — a bullet had ploughed a deep furrow between flesh and muscles from which the negro had lost much blood — but the bullet hole in the shoulder was the more serious. The jagged hole was low down and the bullet had remained in the man's body. It did not appear to have punctured his lung — there was no blood-froth on his lips — but clearly it was a wound that needed immediate medical attention.

"We shall have to get a doctor," Howard told the priest. "He's in a bad way now from loss of blood."

Michael answered him. "But a doctor will give him away to the police, *meneer*. And he has taken refuge here to escape them. We cannot betray him . . . "

"Just a minute," Howard broke in. "Do you realize that by hiding him, you are obstructing the law — that both you and Father Hendricks could be arrested?"

Michael turned passionately on the priest. The old man listened, with bowed head and furrowed face.

"You're under no obligation to hide him, you know," Howard pointed out when Michael had finished speaking.

The old man looked up at him. "No, *meneer*, except that, as Michael says, he has taken refuge in my church believing I will help him. And he needs attention."

"The police will see he gets that," Howard reminded him.

Michael's lips drew back. "The police! You saw tonight what they did to our people, to Umzoni who has never preached violence. And you would give him to them."

Linda entered the bedroom with a bowl of steaming water and a cloth. Howard was going to take them from her when she waved him aside.

"I've stood around long enough tonight doing nothing," she told him. Her voice rose as she caught his surprised look. "And this colour business hasn't got such a hold on me that I'd let a man die rather than touch him . . . "

Silently Howard watched her. She spared herself nothing. She pulled the torn skin wide to clean the deep, sullen wound. She took linen from the priest, and with the help of the men put a rough bandage in place. At last it was done. She turned away, her face utterly colourless.

"Thank God the poor devil was unconscious through it," she muttered. Howard caught her as she suddenly swayed.

"I'm all right," she muttered, tearing herself away and going to the window.

All of them turned at the sound of a groan from the bed. The Zulu was stirring restlessly. His eyes opened. For a moment they were dull, devoid of expression. Then memory returned. His face suddenly contorted. He made a tremendous effort to rise. His body lurched almost upright on the bed, then fell back. His bloodshot eyes roved feverishly round the room.

Father Hendricks leaned over him. "Lie still, *meneer*. You are quite safe."

Umzoni recognized him. "The meeting . . . what happened?"

"Do not think about it now," the priest urged. "Close your eyes and rest."

"What happened? I must know . . . "

Michael broke in harshly in Afrikaans. The Zulu's body writhed as he listened:

his hands opening and closing in helpless anger. He looked up accusingly at the priest after Michael had finished speaking.

"And you said it was wrong to call a strike, that it was un-Christian to make such threats! What do you say to this? Defenceless men beaten to pulp, women and children murdered . . . People whose only sin was listening to me." He gave a harsh sob. "Mother of God; have I been wrong and Swartz right? Is violence the only thing that will make them give us justice?"

The old priest's trembling hands pressed him back on his pillow. "You must not talk like this, *meneer*. You are sick in both mind and body. Swartz is a wicked man. You can never be like him."

The Zulu fought for breath, sobbing at his weakness. "Get me well, Father. Get me well so that I may have revenge for my people."

Linda had moved nearer the bed. Umzoni noticed her.

"Who is this?" he muttered.

"A friend of *Meneer* Shaw's," the

priest told him. "The lady who came to warn us tonight."

"I remember," Umzoni whispered. "I must thank you, madame."

"It was Madame who found work for Michael and who dressed your wounds just now." The priest's efforts to subdue the Zulu's bitterness were pathetic.

Umzoni inclined his head weakly. "Thank you again, madame." He shifted his head. "Is Mr. Shaw here?"

Howard stepped up to the bedside. The Zulu stared up at him.

"What happens to me now?" he whispered.

Howard understood what he meant. He shrugged. "You'll have to see a doctor to get that bullet in your shoulder extracted. It's a bad wound, in any case. It must have attention."

Michael broke in harshly. "It will mean your arrest. The doctor will notify the police."

"Then I will not see a doctor," the Zulu gritted. "I will not be arrested. I would sooner die, do you hear? Much sooner die . . . "

He sank back, fighting for breath. His

eyes closed and his head slumped to one side.

Howard lifted back his eyelids to see the pupils turned upwards. He felt his pulse. It was almost imperceptible. He turned to the priest.

"This is ridiculous, Father. I'm going to 'phone for a doctor."

Michael broke into a torrent of fierce Afrikaans. The priest checked him. "*Meneer* wants his arrest no more than you or I, Michael, but *meneer* does not want him to die." He turned a pleading face to Howard. "Is there nothing you can suggest, *meneer*? I shall feel a traitor if he is arrested through taking sanctuary in my church."

"What about Morkel?" Linda suddenly suggested. "He's a friend of yours."

Howard shook his head. "It isn't fair to ask him. Apart from his political convictions, there is his career to think about. By law he must report bullet wounds to the police."

"At least he will see that Father Hendricks isn't involved," she argued.

"True," Howard admitted. He hesitated,

then nodded. “All right. I’ll go and ’phone him.”

“You may have trouble getting through to him,” she warned. “He’ll probably still be with the police.”

Howard nodded. “Anyway; I’ll see what I can do.”

He left them, to return five minutes later. “He wasn’t at home,” he told Linda. “But his assistant is going to get in touch with him through the police and pass on my message.”

“I hope he isn’t long,” Linda muttered.

“Perhaps you’d better be going,” Howard suggested. “You’ve done a fine job tonight, but there’s nothing more any of us can do now. I’ll ring you first thing in the morning.”

Colour flushed her face at his few words of praise. “I’d rather see it through,” she told him.

* * *

It was half an hour before a car pulled up outside the church. Linda ran after Howard into the refectory. Both faced the open door, to relax as a familiar, square-set figure appeared.

"Thank the lord," Howard said. "Come right in, Jannie."

Morkel's bushy eyebrows rose a full inch at the sight of Linda. "Mrs. Mitchell! What are you doing here?"

"I do get around, don't I?" she murmured. "I'll let Howard explain what it's all about while I see how the patient is." She turned and went back into the bedroom.

Morkel eyed Howard grimly. "Just what the hell is going on?"

"Were you in the riot tonight?" Howard asked.

Morkel stared at him. "You've heard about it pretty soon, haven't you? Yes; I was there. I've just come from attending some of the casualties. I've had hell's own job finding an excuse for getting away. But who told you about it?"

"We were there, Jannie."

"You were what?"

Howard explained how both he and Linda had come to be at the meeting.

Morkel whistled. "She did that for you? But why? If she had told me I could have worked a point for you."

"She wasn't free to talk. Just because the police were going to raid the meeting didn't mean they knew everything about it." Howard went on to explain how they had heard of the meeting. He paused, eyeing Morkel. "How much do the police know, anyway?"

"Probably everything by this time," Morkel grunted. "They have made enough arrests and some are sure to talk." He was frowning heavily. "This is pretty near the bone, Howard. You should have told the police everything you heard. It was too big a thing to keep under your hat to appease an old man's conscience."

"If I hadn't promised he wouldn't have told me."

"That's too bad, but it doesn't alter things. And what about Mrs. Mitchell's going to the meeting and warning you? Wasn't that the same as warning the whole meeting? They had been warned, you know, when we arrived."

Howard shrugged sardonically. "Oh; she could have abandoned me for the sake of the Fatherland, I suppose. Only she doesn't seem to have such patriotic ideals, God bless her."

"I don't like it, Howard," Morkel said again. "Imagine what Erasmus would make of it."

"I was only there as a neutral observer," Howard grinned.

Morkel was clearly displeased. "We'll talk about it later. Now who's hurt? The old man?"

Howard shook his head. "No. It's the negro the police fired on tonight — a Zulu called Umzoni. He took refuge here."

Morkel's astonishment was almost ludicrous to see. "That Kaffir who was addressing the meeting! You've got him here! Do the police know?"

"Not yet."

"What's the matter with you, Howard? Have you gone crazy?"

Howard's eyes were suddenly bleak. "Something's the matter, Jannie. I don't seem to know right from wrong any more. But I do know there's a badly-wounded man in that bedroom. Will you fix him up first and argue afterwards?"

Without another word, Morkel picked up his bag and entered the bedroom.

* * *

Morkel stood back from the bed and washed his hands. "There you are," he grunted. "That'll do until the police shoot him again."

"Thanks, Jannie," Howard said.

Morkel shrugged. "Don't thank me. I would probably have got him just the same if you'd reported the case straight away. Now we'll get the police ambulance round and get him to hospital."

Silently Howard followed him into the refectory. Linda was seated in one chair; the priest in the other. Michael was standing restlessly by the window. All three turned sharply.

"How is he?" Linda asked.

"He'll live," Morkel said laconically.

"What are you going to do now?" she asked. "'Phone the police?"

"Naturally. They're combing the town for him."

Michael made a fierce exclamation. Morkel cocked an eye in his direction, then at Howard.

"Your coloured friend doesn't seem to like me."

"He saw the fight in the location," Howard said dryly.

Linda turned suddenly on Morkel. "Were you there tonight?"

He nodded.

"Didn't you think it dreadful?" she demanded, her eyes blazing with indignation. "God knows; no one can ever say I've been a sympathizer of the non-Europeans. But this affair tonight was terrible, a disgrace."

Morkel's eyes fell away. "It was a nasty business, I'll admit."

She gave an ironical laugh. "Nasty? It was butchery. Do you realize that native in there was preaching a pacifist campaign — that he denounced violence of any kind? What are his followers going to think now?"

Morkel shifted uneasily. "It was a pretty shocking affair, I know, but if the Kaffir hadn't resisted arrest, there would have been no trouble. It was the shots that started the panic. The police only got out of hand when they thought they were being attacked, and you can take it from me that every effort was made to get them back under control."

"That's going to console a lot of people, particularly the woman we saw who had her baby's head smashed in with a baton," Linda said bitterly. "As I see it, those people were only attending a peaceful protest meeting that would have been lawful in any democratic country. For that they were beaten up and some of them killed. Don't you think they've had enough punishment?"

"What are you getting at, Mrs. Mitchell?"

"I'll tell you in a moment." Linda turned to the old priest. "Father Hendricks; would you and Michael leave us for a few minutes?"

"Of course, madame," the old man said courteously. He motioned to Michael, who was eyeing Linda curiously, and led him into the bedroom.

Linda turned back to Morkel. "I'll tell you what I'm getting at, Dr. Morkel. I'm suggesting you say nothing to the police about this Zulu."

Howard, who had been listening with growing amazement, started at her words. Morkel's eyebrows shot up ludicrously.

"But he's the one man the police want.

He's the leader. What's your interest in him?"

"I've no personal interest in him," she snapped. "But because he is so important, releasing him is the one conciliatory gesture we can make. If it is known — and Father Hendricks and Michael will see that it is — that certain Europeans saved his life and then let him go free, it will help to lay a good deal of bitterness. And that will be to everyone's advantage, including us Europeans." She eyed him mockingly. "You see, Dr. Morkel, you don't know the whole story."

Morkel was equally sarcastic. "It might help if I were told it, Mrs. Mitchell."

Linda waved a slender hand at Howard. "Take over for a moment. Tell Dr. Morkel in confidence what the priest told us — about the rival organizations and Swartz."

Howard gave Morkel a brief account of the old priest's doubts and fears.

"So you really believe there are firebrands at work?" Morkel asked.

"There isn't the slightest doubt about it," Howard told him. "Umzoni has trouble with them at all his meetings.

The scarred brute who attacked me in the location is their leader. He and Umzoni are bitter enemies."

"Don't you see — they want Umzoni out of the way," Linda broke in impatiently. "Without him they have a clear field. If the non-Europeans are denied constitutional protests, they've nothing to turn to but violence."

"That's one of the greatest weaknesses of *apartheid*," Howard told Morkel. "It doesn't allow a safety valve. And there's far more bitterness than you chaps dream of. Look at that chap Michael. He's a decent-enough fellow, but after what he has seen and experienced it wouldn't take much more to have him handling a knife with Swartz."

"But you can't let these Communists get away with these meetings," Morkel protested.

"They aren't Communists, Jannie. Get that into your head now. They're underdogs fighting for a place in the sun. But they'll become Communists if we go on treating them like this."

Morkel scowled. "I'll listen to the neutrals, if you don't mind. Inventing situations is a writer's job." He turned back to Linda, his rugged face half-whimsical now. "I'm granting you have no axe to grind, Mrs. Mitchell. That's why I'm impressed."

"Let this negro go," she said. "What happens to him later is another matter. While the laws remain as they are, I suppose he may be caught again if he goes on hot-gospelling. But that's another day, another story, and I hope we won't be in it. But as things are now I think we should all go home and forget what we know."

"I see your point," Morkel admitted. "Only don't forget — if the police do trace the negro here your Father Hendricks is going to land himself in a load of trouble."

"He knows that," Howard said.

Linda was all woman now. "There is one last point," she murmured, eyeing Morkel under her lashes. "If the Zulu is arrested, he might talk to the police about us, and that would make things very difficult."

"Very," Morkel agreed dryly. "Were you keeping this up your sleeve?"

Her husky voice was innocence itself. "I wouldn't have dreamed of mentioning it, Doctor, if you hadn't already seen the light."

Morkel grinned ruefully. "You've got what it takes, Mrs. Mitchell. All right. I know I'm raving mad, but I'll do it. Only remember: if I'm struck off the medical register I shall expect the two of you to keep me in comfort for the rest of your lives. And now I'll tell the old man how to look after his patient, and then I'll have to be going. God knows how the casualties are getting on."

As he disappeared into the bedroom, Howard turned to Linda. His eyes held both admiration and surprise. "I never thought you were so deeply affected."

"It isn't a question of being affected," she said curtly. "I just happen to like fair play."

Howard saw Morkel to his car. Neither of them noticed the cat-like figure that watched them from the shadows alongside the factory. As the car drove off down the road and Howard returned to the refectory, the man slid up alongside the church and peered through one of its lighted windows. He started at what he saw, then his scarred face twisted into a grin of triumph. He listened a few minutes, then ran back down the street. His body dissolved into the shadows.

⋆ ⋆ ⋆

Umzoni was conscious when Howard returned. His fever-bright eyes followed Howard as he approached the bedside.

"Father Hendricks has told me about the doctor," the Zulu said weakly. "I am very grateful."

"You owe your thanks entirely to Mrs. Mitchell," Howard told him, motioning to Linda. "She did all the persuading."

"We are all in her debt," Father Hendricks broke in. Michael, who was preparing to return home, added his fervent appreciation.

"I wanted another word with you," Howard said. "Will you let me release the news of your organization now? It can't do any harm after tonight. The police must get the broad outlines of your plan from the people they have arrested, even if they don't get the details."

Umzoni frowned. "We shall see. People may not talk as glibly as you imagine." He paused for breath. Then he nodded. "Very well. If you will give us a fair report you have my permission."

"I shall be fair," Howard agreed, suppressing his excitement. "When is the one-day strike? Won't you have to postpone it now?"

"No; our plans are well advanced. My assistants will handle it if I have not recovered. You shall be told the date as soon as it is decided. It will be sometime in April."

"Right. I shall get through to my paper by land-line tomorrow."

"There'll be a commotion here when the papers find out, won't there?" Linda asked.

"Unless the police find out and release the news first," Howard said. "My guess, however, is that they will keep quiet while they try to stamp it out. I shouldn't imagine the Government would be keen for it to be known what *apartheid* has started."

"Erasmus is going to love you," she murmured.

"Erasmus is going to help me," he grinned. He turned to the priest. "We'll have to get along now, Father. Be very careful — I shouldn't tell a soul who you have in here. If you need me, give me a ring. In any case I'll be round tomorrow to see if you want anything."

"Thank you both for your kindness," the old man said fervently. "None of us will ever forget it."

⋆ ⋆ ⋆

Howard laid a hand on Linda's arm as she was turning to enter her bungalow.

"Before you go in, let me thank you for what you did tonight," he said quietly. "You took a terrible risk for me and because of it you saw some ghastly things. I'm both grateful and sorry."

In spite of her behaviour since the riot, he knew she had been deeply affected. There were lines of strain round her mouth, and the horrors of the night were still reflected in her eyes.

She suppressed a shudder. "I'm not sorry, Howard, although I'm prepared for some unpleasant dreams. I'm under the surface now, instead of skimming along the top. It's harder going, but it's the real thing. It's teaching me things about Linda Mitchell I never knew before. I'm beginning to think I'm the one who should be grateful to you, Howard."

* * *

After a night of hideous dreams Linda awoke with an aching head to her maid's call. A warning bell rang in her mind as she took the telephone from the girl. It was bad news. She felt it as she put the receiver to her ear.

"Hello. Linda Mitchell here."

"Linda. This is Howard. I've just had a call from Jannie. Father Hendricks and Umzoni were arrested just after midnight."

A hand seized her heart. "Was it Jannie? Did he tell them after all?"

"No; it wasn't Jannie. He said it was a coloured informer — someone who must have seen Umzoni enter the church. Swartz or one of his men, I suppose."

Her lips were cold and stiff. "What will happen now? Will they talk?"

"For your sake I'm praying they won't. Father Hendricks is safe enough — that I'll swear. But I don't know about the Zulu . . . "

At his mention of the saintly old priest, Linda's fears for herself fell away. "Father Hendricks in jail," she said slowly. Her voice broke into a sob. "Oh, no, Howard. Not that . . . "

19

FATHER HENDRICKS entered the dock, his faded eyes calm and steady. Alongside his burly police escort he appeared frail, but his face, in its frame of white hair, had a radiance that made the faces of the police and officials look like dull clay.

The clerk handed him a Bible. He took it with the expression of one who recognizes a dearly familiar thing in a wilderness. He gave the oath in English.

Streets, the public prosecutor, eyed him with interest. Streets was in his early forties, although his rounded figure and receding hair made him look older. Good thing there wasn't a jury, he thought. The old man had the look and air of a saint. You could already see the impression he had made on the public . . .

His eyes travelled round the courtroom. It was packed to capacity. Shaw was the attraction, he ruminated. Ever since it had become known he was supplying a defence counsel and would witness himself, public interest had been intense. He picked out Howard, sitting on the third bench. He certainly was sticking his neck out. Over there on the Press bench Erasmus was looking like a waiting hyena . . .

Streets examined the golden-haired woman alongside Howard. Trevor Mitchell's wife — in a non-European court. This was going to cause some scandal. It could only have one interpretation — the rumours had been right. There was something between her and Shaw. And as it was common knowledge at Berylsford how Erasmus chased her around, it wasn't difficult to guess the personal reason for Erasmus's animosity.

Streets was jerked out of his ruminations by the sound of his name. Somewhat pontifically he stepped towards the dock. A hush settled on the crowded court.

"Do you speak English?" he asked the priest.

"Yes, *meneer.*"

"Than I shall question you in English. Have you any objections?"

"No, *meneer.*"

"Very well. Your name is Jonathan Hendricks and you are the priest of the mission church in Upper Willisden. You are indicted on two counts. One of wilfully obstructing the law by giving refuge to an escaped law-breaker, a negro agitator named Umzoni; and another of aiding and abetting this agitator by allowing him to use your church as a meeting-place for him and his followers. Do you understand the charges laid against you?"

"I do, *meneer.*"

* * *

The ponderous machinery of the law moved inexorably forward. The old man bore his ordeal in the hands of the public prosecutor with a dignity and simplicity that affected Press and public alike. Sympathy for him grew with the minute.

The defence counsel, a middle-aged barrister named Griffiths whom Morkel had recommended, turned and whispered to Howard, who was seated directly behind him.

"What does he say?" Linda asked.

"He says it looks as if the police don't know the old man and I were at the meeting," Howard whispered back. "And if they don't, we have an excellent chance."

* * *

The public prosecutor's voice was pained. "You tell me you had no previous dealings with this agitator, and yet the moment he is wounded he makes straight for your rooms! Why should he do this, unless those rooms were well known to him as the den where his plots were hatched?"

The old man was looking distressed at his inability to understand. "But, *meneer*, what is more natural than for a man to take sanctuary in a church? It has happened right down through the ages."

Streets gave a grunt of impatience. "We are not in the Middle Ages now. We are in the Twentieth Century and dealing with an African native, a Zulu. I repeat, why should he come to you unless he knows you?"

"I have never denied that he knows me, *meneer*. I could not support his campaign, but that did not make us enemies. He is a Christian; he knows I am a man of God, and when he was wounded he came to me for succour. How could I refuse it? I would be more unworthy of my God than I am if I did not practice a little of His kindness and mercy. If Umzoni had sinned it was not for me to bring about his punishment. My duty was to help him, and this I did."

Patience was fast leaving the public prosecutor. "You are not telling everything to the court. When the police captured this agitator in your rooms it was found he had been given skilled medical attention. What doctor attended him?"

Howard closed his eyes. Linda hardly dare listen. The courtroom was hushed.

"*Meneer*," the old man said after a long pause. "A doctor did come at my request to attend Umzoni. He obeyed the merciful call of his profession as I had tried to do. He did his work and then he left. That is all I can tell you."

"Was he a European? Do you know his name?"

"I am happy to say he was, *meneer*. Yes; I know his name."

"Then you must tell it to me. If you do not, you can be charged with contempt of court."

The old man shook his white head. "Then I must be charged again, *meneer*," he said gently. "Because no man shall suffer by my hands because he has obeyed his conscience and his God."

There was a deep silence in the courtroom. Tears swelled up through Linda's lashes. The defence counsel seized the moment gratefully.

"Your Honour," he called, rising to his feet. "Those moving words, spoken of another, describe precisely what is happening here today. This priest is being tried by law for obeying the dictates of his conscience and faith. I submit — "

The judge frowned and interrupted him. "Your turn to speak will come later, Mr. Griffiths."

The interruption served to restore Streets' equipose. Sentiment was all right in its place, but not in court.

Besides — and his heart hardened at the recollection — the full story had not yet been told. He turned to the judge.

"Your Honour; I am ready for the defence counsel's witness."

A surprised buzz of conversation broke out as he made his way to his seat. It grew louder as Griffiths rose.

"Your Honour; my witness is at the disposal of the prosecution."

Linda gripped Howard's hand briefly as he rose. Griffiths leaned towards him. "I'm taking a chance, but I think we're all right," he whispered.

Howard went into the witness-box and took the oath. All eyes were on him. From the Press bench Erasmus was watching him balefully. He became aware of the public prosecutor's voice addressing him.

"Your name is Howard Shaw?"

"It is."

"You are at present a reporter for the English newspaper *The World Observer*. You are writing your opinions of the effects of the *apartheid* laws on the non-Europeans. For this purpose you have spent much of your time in Willisden and other non-European districts. Is all this correct?"

"Yes."

"Is it not also true that you came to the Union with the opinion that the *apartheid* laws were unfair to the non-Europeans and have since made this opinion clear in your newspaper articles?"

"It is not," Howard protested. "I came with no preconceived ideas whatsoever."

Griffiths was on his feet. "Objection, your Honour. The question is in no way relevant."

The judge stared over his glasses. "What have you to say to that, Mr. Streets?"

"The question of Mr. Shaw's personal sympathies has a direct bearing on the case, your Honour."

"Objection overruled. Please continue, Mr. Streets."

Streets turned back on Howard. "But it is true, is it not, that your articles have been banned from entry into the Union by the public censor?"

"It is, but I can't imagine why."

"We ask nothing of your imagination, Mr. Shaw," came the dry reply. "Please answer the questions you are asked and do not digress."

Howard's face set. Streets continued. "Do you deny that your recent articles have taken a decided stand against these *apartheid* laws?"

"No. I do not," Howard said grimly.

"So, Mr. Shaw, we establish that your sympathies are now wholly with the non-Europeans."

Griffiths was on his feet again. "Objection, your Honour. These questions are framed to infer Mr. Shaw is a biased witness."

The judge leaned forward. "I think we will leave Mr. Shaw to answer that in his own words, Mr. Griffiths."

Howard chose his words carefully. "Only after studying *apartheid* at close quarters and seeing its effects, did I decide I did not like its laws. But as the Opposition and over half the Union's European population do not approve of them either, I do not feel in bad company. In this limited sense I agree to sympathy with the non-Europeans."

Streets was pleased enough with the reply. "Then it would follow as a natural corollary that you would support the non-Europeans in a move to oppose these laws . . ."

This time Griffiths gave Howard no time to reply. He was on his feet in a flash. "Your Honour; I object most strongly. If such a thesis were supported, half the Union's European population could be accused of sedition."

The judge nodded firmly. "Objection sustained. Such a supposition can in no way be granted."

Streets was not perturbed. He bowed, then walked right up to the witness-box. "In the case of Mr. Shaw, your Honour, my supposition is not advanced without reason. I hope to prove this in a moment."

There was a stir in the courtroom. Erasmus, his eyes glinting, leaned forward. Streets paused dramatically, then dropped his question like a bludgeon on Howard's unguarded head.

"Is it not true, Mr. Shaw, that you were present at this negro agitator's meeting on the night of the raid, as well as being with him later in the church?"

There was a loud hum of excitement.

The clerk's gavel fell. A breathless hush descended.

Howard took a deep breath. "It is true," he admitted.

Again the hum of excitement broke out. Again the gavel fell.

"And was not the priest, Jonathan Hendricks, also with you at this meeting?"

"Yes," Howard admitted heavily.

Streets nodded. "You have forgotten that you have become very well known in Willisden, Mr. Shaw. There was also a woman with you. Unfortunately we have not been able to establish her identity, but that does not matter. You were there, and the priest was with you. Does that sound as if Jonathan Hendricks was innocent of any intrigue with this agitator? Does that sound as if he did not agree with his campaign?" He turned to the judge. "Your Honour; I submit the priest was an active henchman of the negro, and this witness, far from proving otherwise, has established the charge."

The judge looked at Griffiths. "Does the defending counsel wish to cross-examine?"

Griffiths was already on his way. His

expression told Howard how serious he considered the turn of events. On the Press bench reporters were in a ferment of excitement, some already running out with the news. Erasmus's face was exultant.

The gavel dropped. Griffiths faced Howard.

"Mr. Shaw; what were you doing at the meeting?"

"I was there as a reporter for my newspaper."

"And Father Hendricks?"

"He had taken me on my request. He had been worrying that the negro's agitation would bring suffering to his people, and — "

Griffiths broke in quickly. "He did not approve of these meetings?"

"Most definitely he did not. He was so worried about them that one day he broke down and told me about Umzoni. I then asked him to take me to a meeting, which he did."

"And while you were both there as neutral observers, the police made their raid. You managed to get the priest safely home, only to find the wounded negro in the refectory. When Jonathan Hendricks decided that as a Christian priest he was compelled to give the wounded man sanctuary, you returned home. The next morning you heard that the priest had been arrested on a charge of conspiring with the negro, and at once you volunteered as a witness."

Howard nodded. Griffiths turned to the judge. "Your Honour; I submit that this unselfish action of my witness in volunteering to defend the priest does him credit and also affirms his complete faith in the accused's innocence. That is all, your Honour." He bowed and returned to his seat.

The public prosecutor returned to his attack on Howard.

"How does it happen that your friend, the priest, is so well-acquainted with these meeting-places? They are extremely well hidden."

"Father Hendricks is highly respected in Willisden," Howard said tightly. "Everyone trusts him. It is natural enough he should hear about meetings of this size."

Streets switched his attack, boring in

from a new angle. “How long had you known of this agitator, Umzoni, before this meeting in the location, Mr. Shaw?”

“Just on two days.”

Streets nodded. “Two days. But still quite long enough to warn the police.” His voice was bland. “You intrigue me, Mr. Shaw. I am compelled to believe that one who writes as glibly as you on *apartheid* must know something about it. You must have known, for example, that non-European meetings of this sort are illegal. If it is true that neither of you had any sympathy with this agitator, why did you not inform the police the moment you heard of him? Did you not consider it your duty as a Union citizen?”

Howard’s jaw set stubbornly. “The priest told me only on the condition I would keep the knowledge secret. I was told as he was told, in confidence.”

Streets nodded mockingly. “Of course he told you in confidence. And few of us have any doubts why.” He turned to the judge. “Your Honour; I submit that in his zeal to get a scoop for his newspaper this witness withheld information of a dangerous underground movement from the police. He attended a meeting of this movement and later kept secret the whereabouts of its ringleader. I submit this is more than enough to show his unreliability as a witness. I claim his evidence can be discredited on these grounds."

Griffiths was about to rise when Linda leaned forward and gripped his shoulder.

"Things are going badly, aren't they?" she muttered. "Listen; I haven't told you this — Howard wanted to keep me out of it — but I was the woman at the meeting with them. I was with Howard when Father Hendricks first told him about Umzoni, and also when they found him wounded in the refectory. Can my evidence save the old man?"

Griffiths turned a startled face to her. "It should. But do you think you should do it? Think of the publicity and scandal!"

"To hell with the scandal," she snapped. "I'm not having that old man jailed. And Howard's getting into trouble now, too. What do I do? Stand up and tell them?"

"You do nothing until I tell you," he

muttered. He rose to his feet. "Your Honour; a new witness for the defence has just come forward. I beg leave for an adjournment."

The whispered conversation between Linda and the barrister had not passed unnoticed. Griffiths' announcement directly after it made rumours fly like darting swallows round the courtroom.

The judge peered down at the clerk of court, then raised his head. "The adjournment is granted. The court will sit again at ten-thirty tomorrow morning."

* * *

The courtroom was even more crowded than on the previous day. A phalanx of reporters were squeezed into the Press bench. The atmosphere was electric.

Linda's natural composure made her an ideal witness. She was dressed in a black tailored costume and white blouse. A small, black hat, half buried in her mass of pale gold hair, completed her ensemble. She looked cool and very competent.

Griffiths was halfway through his

examination. "And it was at this meeting that the priest first told Howard Shaw about the Zulu's underground movement. You are quite satisfied Mr. Shaw had known nothing of it before?"

"I am certain he had not. We both heard it for the first time that day. He immediately asked the priest if he would take him to one of these meetings."

"And the priest, when telling you of this movement, mentioned his own dislike of it?"

"Yes; that was why he told us. He had been worrying for weeks about it and was desperate for someone to talk to. We both gave our word to say nothing."

"If you had not given your word, he would not have told you?"

"Of course not. As a priest he is bound to respect the confidences of his parishioners."

Griffiths went on smoothly. "When you heard of this meeting you went as well, having a natural curiosity to see this agitator and hear what he had to say?"

"That is correct," she said. This was the weakness of their case. If the police discovered she had gone to warn Howard, they would be in deep water. Apart from awkward questions as to how she had found out the raid was to take place, there was the problem of explaining why she had gone to warn Howard and the priest. This could well be twisted to make it appear both of the men had something to fear from police investigation. In addition, she might be accused of interfering with the machinery of the law. Griffiths had advised them to make it appear they had gone to the meeting together, without actually saying so.

Griffiths went on sympathetically. "And while you were at the meeting the riot broke out."

Her eyes suddenly flashed. "While I was there the police beat up a crowd of unarmed people. It was the worst thing I have seen in my life."

This was a tender spot in the public prosecutor's case. Rumours of the police action had already reached members of the House. Griffiths had wanted her to bring it in, but discreetly. This was too harsh. He saw Streets flinch, and went on hastily.

"And so, with the help of Mr. Shaw,

you managed to escape injury. You took the priest, who had been dazed, back to his church, and there you saw the agitator. Although surprised and upset at finding him there, the priest decided to give him sanctuary. You returned home with Mr. Shaw, to hear the next morning that the priest had been arrested. Is all that correct?"

"Quite correct," she affirmed. Her eyes, flickering past the barrister, fell on Erasmus, who was watching her intently. Throughout the trial she had ignored him. Now, as his face lit up in acknowledgement, she looked coldly away.

Griffiths turned to the judge. "Your Honour; I submit that this second witness agrees word for word with the first. Both agree that the priest had no earlier connection with this agitator whatsoever. In giving sanctuary to him, Jonathan Hendricks acted purely on the dictates of his conscience and his faith. I ask for a judgment of not guilty to be given him."

The judge looked across at the public prosecutor. "Does the prosecution wish to cross-examine?"

Streets had been thinking fast. A further cross-examination of this woman would get him nowhere, he could see that. True, he could accuse her of the same non-European sympathies as he had accused Shaw, but with far less chance of making the charge stick. Shaw carried with him the prejudices created by Erasmus: this woman, the wife of Trevor Mitchell, had no such handicap.

And then there was this business over the police. That was tricky. Heads were rolling right and left at the moment over it. Obviously this woman was itching to vent her indignation. If he went on, she might let it go. Of course, the scandal might come out later: Shaw might give it to the papers himself. But that was another day and outside his province.

Streets decided to leave well alone. He rose to his feet majestically.

"No, your Honour. The case for the prosecution is closed."

⋆ ⋆ ⋆

The judge's voice was dry and precise; his summing-up brief and to the point. The two witnesses came under his fire and he dwelt on them for some time. While there had been an ethical point deterring them from advising the police about the existence of the underground movement, there had been no such deterrent later when they discovered the wounded negro in the church. They could have notified the police at once without breaking faith with the priest. He appreciated that they had sympathized with the priest's wish to give the Zulu sanctuary, but nevertheless he could not align their behaviour with that of responsible citizens.

Of the priest, Jonathan Hendricks, however, he saw no evidence whatsoever of an earlier connection with the agitator. And, while the priest had undoubtedly given succour and sanctuary to an escaped law-breaker, he (the judge) was convinced this had been done from the highest motives of Christianity. Whether these motives in the circumstances were wise was very much in doubt, but there appeared no question of their sincerity. For the same reason he would not press a charge of contempt of court for the priest's refusal to give the name of the medical officer who had attended the wounded negro . . .

Jonathan Hendricks was acquitted without prejudice on both charges.

* * *

There were extraordinary scenes in the courtroom on the announcement of the verdict. Europeans queued up to shake hands with the dazed priest, and with Howard and Linda. Reporters, with the notable exception of Erasmus, clustered around them, taking photographs and trying to get statements.

With difficulty Howard managed to get Linda and the priest outside and into his car. They took the grateful old man back to Willisden, then started back to Clifton. On the way Linda made Howard pull up outside a hotel. She felt a heady intoxication. Happiness seemed to be welling up inside her and bursting like champagne bubbles in her mind.

"I want a drink to celebrate," she

told him. “It was due to me he got off, wasn’t it?”

“Entirely,” Howard smiled. “And God bless you for it.”

“Oh; I’m glad I witnessed for him, Howard. It’s such a wonderful feeling . . . ”

⋆ ⋆ ⋆

“It is worth it,” she said defiantly when they drove on to Clifton. “I know it’s worth it.”

Howard’s face was grim. They had just passed a newsboy’s poster. ‘Financier’s wife and Shaw in court’ had stared at them in crude black ink. Linda had not flinched.

“I had to expect it, hadn’t I?” she murmured.

As they stopped at some traffic lights, a newsboy thrust a paper through the car window. Howard glimpsed the black headlines before the lights changed.

LINDA MITCHELL SAVES
COLOURED PRIEST.
Her night in Willisden
with Howard Shaw.

Linda managed a smile. “It’s a good job Trevor’s up in Jo’burg this week.”

Howard’s face had drawn tighter on seeing the paper. “I’m taking you home to collect your things, and then driving you out to your aunt’s place in Stellenbosch,” he told her. “You must get away for a few days.”

She did not argue as he had half-expected. “Do you think that is best?”

“Yes. And I’d like you to go straight away before the reporters start coming round.”

She nodded. “I suppose you’re right. Brian is staying with some of his relations this week, so I am quite free.” She lit a cigarette and tried to laugh. “It looks as if there is going to be quite a storm.”

20

REPORTERS beseiged Howard in his hotel that evening and the following morning. The telephone rang incessantly, many of the calls coming from editors of newspapers and journals who wanted exclusive articles. One call in the morning was from Jannie Morkel.

"Howard; can you get round to my town rooms between four and five this afternoon?"

"All right, Jannie. I had intended looking you up and telling you about the court case, anyway."

"Right. Now don't forget. This affects you in a big way. See you this afternoon."

* * *

Howard 'phoned Linda before lunch. He was relieved to hear that no reporters had yet discovered her hideout. Then he asked the question uppermost in his mind.

"Has your husband 'phoned you yet?"

"Not yet, although I expect him any time. I left my address with the maid in case he 'phoned through to the bungalow."

"If the 'phone is anything like mine, he won't have a chance of getting through."

"That won't break my heart," she said dryly. Then her tone changed. "You have told your paper about Umzoni and his movement, haven't you?"

"Yes. It should be coming out at any time now."

"So there'll be even more fuss when the papers here get the reports? I've been looking in them and they have given no details of what Umzoni was trying to do. They don't mention anything about the non-Europeans striking."

"I know. Either the police didn't find that out, or they're keeping it quiet." Howard grinned. "Heaven knows what will happen when *The World Observer* blows the lid off. Hold thumbs for me. It might come through today."

Her voice was anxious. "Look after yourself, Howard. And don't be long before you come to see me. I feel lost out here after all the excitement. I want to be with you."

"It's better we keep apart for a few days," he told her. "I'll 'phone you again tomorrow."

* * *

To escape the reporters, Howard went out to Willisden. A steady rain was falling and the drenched houses were huddled together like beggars in threadbare clothes, squalid and deformed.

The old man was in his refectory. It was clear he had been reading the newspapers for he was full of concern for Howard and Linda.

"It is what I feared, *meneer*," he said sadly. "By witnessing to save me you have brought trouble on yourselves."

"How are Michael's parents?" Howard asked, to change the subject. "How is Mrs. Stevens taking this weather?"

It seemed he had asked the wrong question because the priest's face did not lighten.

"They are both very worried, *meneer*. Two men came round to see them yesterday when Michael was at work. They must have been detectives. They asked the old man how long he had been married to a coloured woman, how many children he had, and where they worked. The old man is certain it was in connection with this *apartheid* law."

"But the Mixed Marriage Act wouldn't apply to them," Howard said, shocked at the news. "They were married long before it was passed, and it isn't retrospective. In any case, no one would bother with an old couple like that."

"I went to see them as soon as Michael told me," the priest went on. "And the old man unburdened himself to me. It is the other law he fears — the one whose name I can never remember . . ."

"You mean the miscegenation law? But that forbids unmarried Europeans and non-Europeans to live together. It wouldn't apply to them unless . . ." Understanding came to Howard suddenly. "They aren't married! Is that it?"

"No, *meneer*; they are not," the priest said unhappily. "The old man confessed to me. He said it was because they had never felt the need to marry . . ."

"How do you feel about them now?" Howard asked curiously.

"I think more of them than ever," the priest said without hesitation. "Without marriage ties to hold them, their loyalty has been an even greater thing. It will be a cruel thing if after all these years of love and devotion they are torn apart, *meneer*."

He lifted his lined face up to Howard almost apologetically. "Meneer; I have always obeyed the law because without law there would be much crime and suffering. But this morning I told them I would marry them here in my church."

"What did they say?"

"They refused, *meneer*. They were afraid of getting me into trouble."

"It wouldn't help them. It would be too easy to prove they had been married after the law was passed," Howard said. He shook his head. "It's hard to believe this of the police. It's so unimportant, and so unfair. If they live together they break one law, and if they marry they break another."

"I have promised to make enquiries for them," the priest said heavily. "It is said that if a person lives among one of the other racial groups and is accepted into it, he may be treated as one of them. If so, I can marry them. It would mean the old man would have to renounce his European birth, but this he says he will gladly do. I must find out."

Howard rose and went over to the window. A vision of the old couple helping one another along the alley opposite made his hands tighten at his sides. This thing went down deep, right into the roots. It was a violation of civilization; an attack on the sanctity of old age. He swung round on the priest.

"Let me know if anything further happens," he said. "If these men come again the old man must first make them prove their identity before answering another question. Then let me know."

"What will you do, *meneer*?"

"I don't know," Howard muttered. "But if this thing is true, it must be exposed. It can't be allowed to happen. It may not be the fault of the Government: a few zealous policemen might have over-interpreted the law. In that case a representation to the authorities might put things right."

The priest looked anxious. "I am afraid for you, *meneer*. You have got yourself into enough trouble for us already."

"A little bit more won't make any difference," Howard smiled, making for the door. "I'll have to run along now to see Dr. Morkel. I'll keep in touch with you, Father. *Totsiens*."

"Go with God, *meneer*."

* * *

Howard was shown into Morkel's office immediately on his arrival. The doctor waved him to a chair.

"Well," he started grimly. "I hope you're satisfied with your nonsense the other night. If you'd taken my advice you'd have saved yourself and others a good deal of worry."

Howard flung himself into the chair. "Let's not be wise after the event, Jannie."

Morkel scowled. "I'm not being wise about anything. You don't realize the seriousness of your position. You don't read Afrikaans and you haven't bothered to find out what Erasmus has been saying about you these last few months. Now you've got to take notice." He threw a copy of *Die Volksman* across to Howard. "Take a look at that."

Both the front and back pages were plastered with photographs of Linda, Howard, and the priest.

"You'll have to translate," Howard muttered, eyeing the black type with some uneasiness, his mind on Linda.

"I have," Morkel said dryly, reaching in a drawer. He tossed Howard a batch of typewritten sheets. "Before you go you can thank my secretary for these. She has been working all day on them."

Howard read them through in silence. While expecting distortions and inferences on the familiar Erasmus pattern, he was prepared for nothing like this. Emboldened by Howard's failure to answer him, Erasmus had clearly lost all fear of retaliation. The public prosecutor's case had been elaborately embroidered to suggest by implication that Howard was nothing less than an active member of the non-European underground movement, and that he was a Communist to boot. The tone of the writing was hysterical and exultant.

But the extract that made Howard's face grow pale with rage was where the columnist made mention of Linda. Here he had been more careful — mindful, no doubt, of the powerful Trevor Mitchell — but again a great deal was said by inference. There was no mistaking the accusation. Shaw had secured an influence over Linda Mitchell, a dangerous influence that had dragged her in the filth of locations, underground meetings, and finally to court, to give evidence for a treacherous old priest who had used his church as a secret den for Communist agitators . . .

Howard threw the sheets down on the desk before him. "This man is a bastard," he gritted.

"Maybe, but that doesn't help you," Morkel grunted. "The thing is now — what are you going to do? I'm warning you, Howard, if you don't stand up and fight soon, you're going to be in serious trouble. This court case hasn't done you any good. People who took little notice of Erasmus before are going to start wondering now — after that remark of the judge about 'responsible citizens'. You'll notice the play Erasmus made of that. If you leave things to drift much longer he'll raise such a public outcry the Government will have to take notice."

Howard nodded, tight-lipped. "All right; I'll answer him. By God, I'll answer him."

"Good man. Now you're talking sense."

Howard's eyes were bitter. "Anyone would think these people had consciences like new-born babes. I've just come from Willisden and heard something that makes me feel sick."

He went on to tell Morkel about the two old people. Morkel's face grew perplexed as he listened.

"There must be a mistake, surely," he muttered. "The Act was never passed to affect people like that."

Howard sneered. "Ah, no; it isn't *meant* to affect them. That's the trouble with politicians — they don't think of people as human beings when they frame their damned Acts. They don't realize you can't stop people loving one another by an Act of Parliament! Love is outside man-made laws, thank God. You can't have it turned on and off by a legal plumber."

"Wait a minute, Howard," Morkel protested. "The *apartheid* laws were framed in good faith. The Nationalists genuinely believe it is better for the country if the Europeans and non-Europeans are kept apart."

"I don't give a damn for countries," Howard told him heatedly. "My interest is in people. And the people in this country, like those in any other, depend on one another, and only a blind fool will deny it. I'm tired of all this blather of this thing and that thing being for the good of the Fatherland. Fatherlands to me mean the people who live in them. People make nations: not nations people. Therefore people must always come first."

"No one's going to argue with you," Morkel grunted. "Everyone knows that."

"The hell they do! People are the last thing to be considered these days. Ideologies and Fatherlands come first.

Conservatism, Fascism, Socialism, Communism, Nationalism — the world's full of 'isms'. And the older I get the more I hate 'em all. What are they for, anyway? When will people realize that countries aren't made any better or worse by politics; they are made better or worse by people. The best system ever devised will be a failure if run by crooks, and the worst will make a Utopia if run by honest, decent men — men like Father Hendricks. The salvation of the world doesn't lie in politics: it lies in principles — Christian principles, taught to children at home and at school so they stay with them all their lives . . . We need fewer causes and more Christianity. Father Hendricks has convinced me of that."

He leaned forward impassionedly. "Ideologies breed fanatics, Jannie, and that's what *apartheid* is doing. Making fanatics and devotees who destroy tolerance and reason and truth. We've seen it happen in Spain, Germany, Italy, Russia, and yet we're doing the same thing ourselves. We don't want causes bigger than people — there isn't anything bigger than people. And people don't belong to the State: The State belongs to them. The State belongs just as much to that old couple in Willisden as it does to the Prime Minister and his wife. Every bit as much. I don't know the full story yet about these men who questioned them, so I'll leave that for the moment. But this I do know: that when the love of two people for one another is made a sin in law, then, by God, there's something terribly wrong with that law."

He leaned back, not without self-consciousness. "I'm sorry, Jannie, but this had to come out. I know your political views and I respect them. But you're someone that supports my argument — you, with your Christmas parties for coloured kids. I could stand *apartheid* with people like you running it, Jannie, but we won't get them. We can't. It's a Master Race ideology. Sooner or later it must attract the boys with low foreheads and brass belts."

"There's been a mistake over these old people, Howard," Morkel muttered. "The Act was never meant to be carried out as strictly as this."

Howard shrugged. "Perhaps not. It might be a few zealots trying to win quick promotion, but that doesn't excuse the law. If it had to be framed, it should have been framed better. Remember, this is one case we know about. How many hundreds of others are there? A girl is going to have a baby — the boy intends to marry her. Then the State finds one of them is coloured, so they can't marry. What happens to the girl? What happens to the child? Does the State provide for them? Better — do the politicians? But who cares — it's all for the Fatherland."

Morkel frowned and shook his head. He sat silent.

"There's another thing people seem to forget," Howard went on. "And that's what ordinary people like you and me could do with the laws."

"How do you mean?"

"Think of the smear campaigns we can bring out. We can brand people Communists and have them arrested. Erasmus is trying to do it to me now. Think of the opportunity for blackmail! There must be hundreds, if not thousands, of couples of mixed race like those two in Willisden that one could threaten with exposure. Think of the lives one could ruin! If someone you didn't like was getting married, a dropped hint he was slightly coloured could ruin everything for him. Or one could accuse someone like yourself of having had an affair with a coloured girl. Whether it was proved or not wouldn't matter. He could still be ruined professionally. I can think of hundreds of ways these laws could be used as weapons."

"You've too much imagination," Morkel grunted.

"It can be a nuisance, can't it?" Howard said ironically. Then his mood suddenly changed. He grinned. "You must have had ants in your pants these last two days, wondering if your name would come out."

"I did, damn you," Morkel growled. "I thought I was finished."

"You needn't have worried. Father Hendricks would have died rather than give you away." Howard went to tell him the words the priest had used when threatened with contempt of court.

Morkel was clearly moved. "I must go out and thank him when the hue and cry has died down a little," he said. He eyed Howard curiously. "What's going to happen now between you and the Mitchell family?"

"I don't know," Howard told him heavily. "I don't know . . . "

* * *

But at that moment Linda was having an intimation. Her husband had got through to her at last. He was as angry and blunt as a maddened bull.

"It's taken me all day to find out where you were. The bungalow line has been engaged all day. The one time I got through, that fool maid was out. Why have you gone to Stellenbosch?"

"I thought it better to keep out of the way until the fuss died down," she muttered.

He started in earnest then. "I warned you to keep out of it. I saw the way it was going. And you lied to me; you said you'd no sympathy with the coons. You said that and, by God, you've just stood up in court and witnessed for one. You've admitted going with Shaw round locations, *shebeens*, and heaven knows what else. And you've the nerve to ask me not to kick those bastards in Willisden out of my houses. And I was going to let 'em stay — that's the hell of it . . . "

"They aren't to blame for this," she cried.

"They aren't to blame . . . ! This is the end, you understand? You don't see Shaw again, publicly or privately. If you do, I'll break him."

"What do you think you can do?" she sneered, stung by his threat.

"Don't underestimate me, my girl. I've got money and if necessary I'll use every penny of it. If you think anything about him, keep away, or I'll make him wish he had never been born . . . "

* * *

On the way home Howard saw crowds of people clustered round the newsboys in the city. He caught a glimpse of a poster and grimaced.

SENSATIONAL DISCLOSURES BY SHAW, it read. *National Strike threat by non-Europeans*.

Howard bought a paper and scanned the front page. His face set grimly. The storm looked like turning into a hurricane before the week was out.

21

THE outcry of that day was a whisper beside the tumult that followed on the next. The news that the non-Europeans had a plan to retaliate against *apartheid* by a national strike came like a bombshell to the Europeans: the fact that it was dropped by Howard Shaw made it the more sensational. It was front-page news in every English and Afrikaans morning newspaper, all of whom brought out extra editions as more details came through from England.

By evening the full reports were availablc. By the following day these reports became supplemented by opinions from leading thinkers and economists, and the alarm grew. At first, mixed with the general uneasiness, had been a wide measure of scepticism. But now, as more and more experts gave their studied opinions and showed the essential dependence of the Union's economy on coloured labour, it became clear the scheme was frighteningly sound in principle.

As was to be expected, the Nationalist newspapers took a different tone from the rest. *Die Volksman*, with Erasmus at the helm, gave them the lead. It pointed out that the police, in spite of having arrested an alleged leader of this movement and dozens of his followers, had issued no public statement that such a serious campaign was under way. Surely this could mean one of two things. Either they had found nothing more serious than an isolated agitator venting his grievances, or they had withheld news of the movement in the public interest.

How, then, had Shaw unearthed it? Could the whole thing not be a gigantic scare, a massive falsehood designed to frighten people away from the principles of *apartheid*? Already in his articles Shaw had stopped at nothing to discredit the new laws. Could not this be his crowning falsehood?

That was one interpretation and served as a useful sedative to those nervous Nationalists who saw ruin staring them in the face if such a campaign were successful. But Erasmus had to cover himself. The Zulu's wounds had delayed his trial, but that trial might yet establish Shaw's case. There was also a possibility that the police might yet issue a statement confirming it. A covering proviso had to be made and it was made as damning as possible. If the subversive movement did exist, then it seemed Shaw could only have known of it by being a member himself . . . When all had been clandestine, he had spun his treacherous web with the rest of the malefactors, but as it now seemed all would be uncovered at the trial, he had cunningly turned the situation to his advantage by issuing a threat that sent a chill of fear throughout the nation.

The outcome of all these charges and counter-charges was inevitable. All the bitter conflict over *apartheid* that had raged among the Europeans before the laws had been passed now broke out in redoubled fury. Opponents of the ideology leapt at the opportunity of proving one of their main objections when the laws had been mooted — that they would both antagonize and unite the coloured races. Supporters of the ideology leapt to its defence. Tempers grew more heated; recriminations were hurled on all sides.

From the moment Howard had communicated his sensational news to his London office, he had realized it would probably mean he would be forced to take a stand in the Union. Consequently he had asked permission to use any of the articles already published in *The World Observer*. This had been granted him. Now, spurred on by what he had heard about the old couple in Willisden and by the malicious charges of Erasmus, he planned his retaliation.

There was no difficulty in finding a publisher. Almost every newspaper in the country had already approached him. He chose the two largest of the anti-*apartheid* papers, one English and one Afrikaans, and then made his offer.

As he had expected, it was snapped up. He visited the editors and gave them his plan. He had no intention of joining a slanging match with Erasmus: he intended presenting his case in a series of responsible articles. The earlier of these would consist of those already published in *The World Observer* (although greatly pruned to suit local conditions), which would serve to present the hardships of the non-Europeans under the present laws, hardships that had brought about his own aversion to them. Then would follow his discovery of the two rival factions among the coloured peoples. To conclude, he intended giving some of his own ideas as a substitute for the laws he condemned.

Little work was needed on the earlier articles and they went to Press almost at once in a blaze of publicity. Public interest was intense. In no time Howard was swamped with letters, hundreds arriving at every post. Many were from well-wishers who welcomed his articles and praised their contents. It did him good to read a little of the immense sympathy that flowed among the Europeans for the coloured races in their plight, and added in no small way to his own confidence. He treated the letters of vilification and threats with contempt, although a more timid man might well have been silenced by their ferocity.

With the severe condensations he had made and the huge amount of space put at his disposal, in less than a week he had reached the point in his story where he had first heard of Umzoni. It was now he expected a tremendous sensation. If the revelation of the strike movement had caused such a furore, what would happen when he announced there was a rival movement afoot to start a campaign of bloodshed and terror?

In this sensational article Howard used the argument of Umzoni's — that without a safety valve for their repression, some of the non-Europeans must inevitably turn to the last resort of desperate men, violence. Every harsh enforcement of the law which stifled protest gave whips into the hands of agitators to lash already inflamed feelings.

He was well aware of the risks he was now taking. Enemies would have little difficulty in bringing up a case that he was defending the strike movement of Umzoni. By ignoring his argument that *apartheid* had caused both underground movements to ferment, they would accuse him of wanting one to prosper; whereas his argument was that one movement or the other was inevitable under the present conditions and prudence must allow the lesser of the two evils until the parent evil, *apartheid*, was no more. A subtle difference that was a world of difference, but by its nature open to unscrupulous distortion.

Dangers, indeed, lurked everywhere at this point in Howard's story. His whole case against the laws could rise or fall on it. Its publication was a weapon that could as easily destroy friend as well as foe. The best-hearted people would soon lose their sympathy if they thought the non-Europeans they were trying to help were secretly sharpening a knife to drive into their backs. It might (and certainly would if the threat broke into action) cause a demand for a batch of even harsher laws. On the other hand, if Europeans could be convinced that the laws were driving non-Europeans to such extremes, it might cause a reaction that would uproot those laws from the land. The balance was infinitely delicate.

But it was the truth, and as such it

had to be told. Howard made the point very clear that the agitators of violence and their followers were few indeed and ostracized by the vast majority of the non-Europeans, which was the strict truth. But, astonishingly patient and good-natured as the majority of them were, how long could they be expected to remain passive under the intense pressure now being laid on them? Howard wrote and rewrote the article with painstaking care before taking a deep breath and releasing it to the Press . . .

It landed like a hungry cat among a group of chattering pigeons. The outcry was tremendous. Ironically, it caused the greatest consternation in the strongholds of Nationalism, for these were chiefly located in the country districts where the proportion of Europeans to non-Europeans was much lower than in the cities.

One of the personal effects was a further heavy increase in Howard's mail. From the urgent concern of these letters, it was clear the news had been dynamic. He was encouraged to see that the proportion of letters supporting his campaign had not diminished, so suggesting the article had not had an adverse reaction among those already sympathetic.

As expected, his denunciation came from the supporters of the laws. Once again Erasmus led the onslaught, damning the article as yet another flagrant attempt to discredit *apartheid*. He gave Howard a flat challenge to prove his claims.

It was a difficult challenge for Howard to face. While he knew beyond doubt that agitators of the Swartz calibre were active, he himself had never seen them at work. He needed first-hand proof if his case were not to fall into disrepute, a thing he dared not let happen. From his defiance had come a resurgence of liberalism that was growing by the day. But a few short years ago the liberals had been decisively defeated: their morale was still at a low ebb. They needed the taste of victory if they were to defeat the confident hosts arrayed against them: a taste he alone could provide. His defeat, on the other hand, might well finish them as an effective force.

By force of circumstance and through

factors outside his control, he had become their champion. Opposing him was the formidable figure of Erasmus, behind whom was arrayed the dark legions of *apartheid*. Neither of them was an accredited leader of his cause, yet beside them politicians shrank into insignificance. They had been thrust forward to do battle: they had become the chosen champions. Victory for one might be the death-blow to the cause of the other. Under the breathless eyes of their legions, they grappled, broke, and grappled again . . .

⋆ ⋆ ⋆

Freed for the moment from the mad urgency of preparing his articles, Howard put a call through to Linda at Stellenbosch. Her greeting was warm, velvet with approval.

"You've answered at last . . . I'm so glad, Howard, so glad that I completely forgive you for neglecting me this week. Yes; I know how busy you must have been. I tried to 'phone you on Monday and yesterday, but couldn't get through."

"I've had the 'phone disconnected," he told her. "Otherwise I wouldn't have had a thing done."

"You've put a wonderful case forward," she told him. "But what about these agitators who are trying to incite violence? Aren't you going to take Erasmus up on that?"

Her question confirmed what he had already known. His assertion had seemed presumptive. The public were waiting for his proof.

He explained this to her. "I've asked Michael to help me," he concluded. "He's going to find out all he can, and, if possible, take me to one of their meetings . . . "

Her voice was suddenly anxious. "That's too dangerous, Howard. Swartz knows you . . . "

"We'll disguise ourselves. We'll be all right." He changed the subject hastily. "Is your husband back yet?"

"He's coming back tomorrow. He wants me to stay here for a while. I feel like telling him to go to hell, but . . . Oh; I don't know what to do."

He stood by the 'phone helplessly,

searching for words. Her voice came again, fiercely.

"I'm missing you, Howard. I'm missing you terribly. Try to get up to see me one day when Trevor's in town. Aunt Selina won't give us away. If you don't, I shall come down to you. I'm not staying here like a damned prisoner."

"I'll come up," he promised. "I can't get away just at present, but I'll come the moment this job is finished. By the way; I'm moving again."

"Moving? How do you mean?"

"My hotel manager has complained of my notoriety. He asked me last week to find other accommodation. He must belong to the other camp. Anyway, an agent has managed to fix me up with a little bungalow at Bakoven. It's a cute little place — very ramshackle but right on the beach. I move in next week."

"Bakoven! That's only two miles from Clifton. For a moment I'd the horrible idea you were leaving Cape Town."

"No; I'm still around," he said quietly. "I'll 'phone you again as soon as I get some more news."

"When are you going with Michael?"

"I don't know yet."

"Be careful, Howard," she breathed. "For God's sake be careful."

* * *

Michael 'phoned through later the same day. Howard listened, his heart beating faster.

"Friday night? Right. Then I'll pick you up outside the church at seven-thirty. That'll give us time to fix up our appearances. Good. Thanks, Michael. Seven-thirty . . . "

22

BRIAN MITCHELL shifted uneasily in his swivel chair. A frown marred the clean-cut, pleasant lines of his face.

"You mustn't think of mentioning it to him now," he muttered. "It's hopeless after this court case. He's done nothing else but spit fire and brimstone at the non-Europeans ever since."

Joan, sitting at the opposite side of his desk, shook her head. Her face was grave, troubled.

"He should be proud of what Linda did," she protested. "It was wonderful of her."

Brian's frown deepened. "No; I agree with Dad this time. It has caused a terrific scandal. Everyone is saying Shaw must have some influence over her. And he must have. Before she met him she didn't know the difference between *apartheid* and a game of canasta."

"Isn't she a better person for knowing

the difference? Don't you admire her for going into the witness-box to save an innocent old man?"

Brian shifted impatiently. "How do we know he's innocent? He's coloured like the others. How do we know he wasn't in league with the Kaffir?"

"I know because I know Father Hendricks," she said quietly. "He couldn't tell a lie if he tried. What about Linda? Do you think he could have deceived her if he'd been dishonest? The fact she witnessed for him shows the impression he made on her."

"Maybe; maybe not," he shrugged. "I don't know. But I do agree with Dad that she should have thought more about us. He warned her months ago that his credit could be affected if his name became linked with Shaw's, but she took no notice. Her making a friend of him was bad enough, but witnessing in court with him was the limit."

A deep anxiety, long suppressed, showed now in the girl's troubled eyes. "Do you realize what you're saying? You're suggesting Linda should have kept quiet because your father's money is more important than justice to an old man. You can't mean it, Brian."

Shame reddened his face. His eyes fell away. "You know I didn't mean that. But, damn it all, surely a wife should consider her husband first."

Joan rose and went round the desk to him. She put a timid hand on his arm, a gesture that was almost protective. "People matter more than money, Brian. They must do, always. You'd have done the same as Linda, wouldn't you, if you had known the truth?"

He did not answer. His face was sullen.

Her eyes were frightened now. "You don't answer me . . . Oh, Brian; don't turn hard. Don't change. Please don't change."

Suddenly he looked very young. "I'm not changing. You've got the wrong ideas, that's the trouble. Dad isn't hard; he's just a business man with a tremendous amount of responsibility. You don't understand business. If you did you would understand him better."

She shook her head. "How can I understand him? He is turning hundreds of people from their homes just before the winter. Some of them may die. And he's doing it for money he doesn't even need. I don't want to understand anyone like that, Brian."

"You're not fair to him, Joan. It isn't his fault they haven't anywhere to go. It's just one of those things that are nobody's fault."

"The terrible part of it," she said slowly, "is that you can't see the wrong of it, either."

His distress was genuine now. "I've nothing to do with it. I swear I haven't. I didn't even know about it until you told me."

"But you know now," she insisted. "And if you won't ask him to change his mind, why won't you let me? I'd rather be the one to ask him, in any case, should there be trouble. I must see him, Brian. I'll never forgive myself if I don't. I know some of those people very well, and they're good, honest people. Why won't you let me speak to him?"

He rose abruptly and put his arms around her. He buried his face in her dark hair. She stood motionless with closed eyes, her body trembling slightly.

"Because I want to marry you," he muttered. "I don't want anything to come between us. Why won't you let me announce our engagement? Don't you care for me enough?"

"You don't understand . . . "

"If it's Father you're worried about, all you have to do is give up this welfare work. That's all he has against you; what else can he have? He won't turn on me if you do that. But if you go to him about this ejection notice, anything can happen. Then he might turn on me if I marry you. He might even disinherit me. He's in a wicked mood, I tell you."

Her voice was small, muffled against his jacket. "I know he doesn't like me. I've known it a long time . . . "

"It's only this work you do," Brian argued. "What else could he have against you? If you'd only drop it for a while everything would be all right. Perhaps you could start again later. Once we were married, he might resign himself to your doing it. But you mustn't provoke him now."

Her distant voice came again, as if she

had not heard him. "It has been wrong of me to go on seeing you. I shouldn't have done it. But it's so hard to stop seeing the person you love. It's so very hard . . . "

"Love," he whispered. "You've never said that before. Do you really love me, then?"

"Oh, yes," she breathed. "I love you very much."

His arms tightened around her fiercely. "Then you must give up this work for a while. Give it up and I'll announce our engagement. Forget all about this ejection notice. It isn't as if you had the ghost of a chance of making him change his mind. You'd only be turning him against you for nothing."

It was warm against his jacket. Warm and comforting. It resolved life into a simple thing; it made any action seem impossible that came between the two of them . . . Then reality came back like an icy draught.

She tore herself away. "No," she sobbed. "I can't leave it, Brian. There isn't time. I must see him."

"But you might ruin everything . . . "

She shook her head jerkily. "You mustn't announce our engagement, Brian. I won't let you. It's no use; nothing is any use." Her voice was flat, dull. She lifted her face sadly up to his. "I must try to help those people, Brian."

Brian's face set. He turned away. "All right; if that's all it means to you. He's out at the Willisden factory this afternoon. He'll be there until four o'clock."

She shook his arm in her distress. "Can't you understand? Think what Linda did for one innocent man. Surely we must do something for hundreds!"

His face was white, half-ashamed, half-angry. "I've warned you what might happen. I can't do any more."

She reached up and very shyly kissed his cheek. For a moment his face faltered, then set in sullen lines again. She went to the office door, paused, and looked back wistfully.

"Don't think I'm doing this because I don't care. Because I do. I care very much . . . "

His figure suddenly blurred in her eyes

like a drenched water-colour. She turned and fled down the corridor.

* * *

The tap on the door was not to be denied. It came again, a little louder. Trevor Mitchell looked up again, his scowl deepening.

"Come in," he shouted.

Joan Viljoen appeared in the doorway. Mitchell stared at her slim figure in astonishment. Then his eyes narrowed. He made no effort to rise.

"What do you want?" he asked rudely.

Her face, white and strained already, went paler at his words, but she did not retreat. She advanced over the thick pile carpet to the huge desk behind which Mitchell was sitting. The office was lavishly furnished. Alongside the financier was a huge plate-glass window from which the distant clean blue of the sea was visible over the decayed houses below. An electric fan in one corner hummed, feigning unconcern. Mitchell, red-faced and aggressive, stared at the girl from behind a battery of telephones.

"Did you ask my secretary if you could come in?"

Joan shook her head. "No, Mr. Mitchell. I'm sorry. Should I have asked her?"

"Yes; and see you do another time. I don't allow people to walk in like this. What do you want?"

Her heart sank at his tone. She tried to control her trembling. "I've come about the ejection notice you've given to the people across the road, Mr. Mitchell . . ."

His breath escaped in a sibilant hiss. "How do you know it's my property? Did Linda tell you?"

She flinched at the venom of his words. "No, Mr. Mitchell."

"Then who did? Howard Shaw?"

His hands, red and spatulate, had dropped on the top of his desk, pressing down as if to push him to his feet. She watched them in fascination.

"Who was it?" he shouted. "How have you found out?"

"It's no secret, Mr. Mitchell. Everyone in Willisden knows . . ."

"All your coloured friends know, do

they?" he sneered. "And they've asked you to come begging to me. Is that it?"

Her eyes pleaded with him. "Hundreds of people will be made homeless, Mr. Mitchell. Many will have to go into the location. And winter will soon be here. The older people will never survive it . . . "

"The same sob story Linda gave me," he sneered. His face suffused with blood. "And like a fool I was thinking of giving in until this business in court. Now I wouldn't lift a finger for 'em. Not a finger, do y'hear?"

His tone stung her to retaliation. "Many of your factory hands live over there. Others have relations or friends there. Can't you see it is likely to cause trouble?"

His hands stretched like blunt claws, then closed into fists. "Threats, eh?" He laughed harshly. "It's no good, m' girl. Labour's too cheap around here. Let 'em go into the location. Let 'em rot. What do I care?"

His eyes were inflamed; his face set in bitter lines. His tone surprised as well as frightened her. In the past, while he had often been outspoken with her, he had always observed a fine edge of control. Now his behaviour was brutal, almost abandoned. Was it all because Linda's action had affected his finances? Or did the hurt go deeper . . . ?

Sympathy softened her voice. "Please don't blame Linda for what she did, Mr. Mitchell. If you knew the old priest, you would have done the same. Linda couldn't help herself. And don't blame her for asking you about the ejection notices. It was my fault; it was through me she did it."

He nodded savagely. "I guessed as much. She lied, but I guessed either you or Shaw were at the back of it." His voice shook with rage. "By God; between the two of you, you've set my whole family against me. So far I've sat back and taken it, but not any more. I'm keeping my eyes on Shaw, but that's not enough. There's still you — hanging about my son and turning his guts to water."

Her face was pale, but her eyes steady. "I've never encouraged your son, Mr. Mitchell."

"Don't lie. You've been out with him every other night for months now. What do you call that — discouragement?"

She winced. "I suppose not. But I like him so much . . . "

"Well; you're going to stop liking him now," Mitchell snarled. "You don't think this business of refusing to get engaged has fooled me, do you? You've known I don't like you, and you've thought you'd win me over by acting coy, by pretending my money didn't matter to you. Then, when you'd finally bluffed me and got your hands on it, you'd be able to fling it out to these coloured friends of yours. Clever, but not clever enough. I've found you out, m'girl . . . "

He tore open a drawer and pulled out a folder. "Maybe it's a good thing you came today, after all. I was going to call you in and tell you, anyway. I've warned Brian often enough what a mawkish bitch of a wife you'd make, but the fool has taken no notice. So I've done something about you . . . " He threw the folder at the girl. "Read this! I'm going to give you a week to give up Brian. You can tell him he's too hard for you, too unsympathetic — you can tell him anything you please as long as you keep my name out of it. But you'll give him up and refuse to see him again, or" — and his eyes were cold blue marbles — "well, I'll leave you to guess what I shall do."

Joan had opened the folder and had commenced reading. She gave a sudden gasp of fear. Her body jerked as if it had been pierced by a knife.

"Now you know," Mitchell gibed. "You give him up or I tell everything, and not only about you. Remember that. Now get out!"

Her eyes closed tightly. For a moment it seemed she would faint from shock. When she moved again she was like an automaton from which all thought, emotion, and hope had been drained. She did not look back at his desk, where he watched her with eyes both ashamed and triumphant. She crossed the corridor, descended the stairs, and walked blindly into the street. She felt no pain yet, only intense weariness.

The bright sunlight mocked her, burning her hot eyes. She crossed the road to the opposite pavement that lay in the shadows. The road stretched before her, long, squalid, hopeless. She started down it, walking like an old woman with bent shoulders and bowed head.

23

MICHAEL pointed to a street on the right. “Down this way, meneer,” he muttered.

Howard nodded silently and followed him into a rabbit warren of murky streets. There was no moon, and the occasional street-lamps only served to accentuate the darkness. As they penetrated deeper into the slum the streets became entirely deserted. Their footsteps rang out on the cracked pavements and echoed hollowly behind them. Furtive shadows fled at their approach; cats eyed them balefully from crumbled walls.

It was Friday night. Michael had found out from his fellow-workers in the factory that Swartz was holding a meeting this week in a *shebeen* in the large non-European quarter directly behind Cape Town, and was now leading Howard to it.

Howard had done his best to disguise them both. Michael, wearing a sailor’s roll-collar pullover and with a few lines painted on his face, would pass anything but a close scrutiny; but Howard was not so sure of himself. Darkened hair and dyed skin were the best he could do: he had not the skill to make alterations to his European cast of features. He could only hope neither of them would be seen at close quarters by Swartz or any of his immediate followers.

Howard found himself whispering. "Why is it so quiet? Why is there no one in the streets?"

"It is too dangerous, *meneer*. The police seldom come round here and the *skollies* can do what they like with people."

The road they were taking now was unrelieved by light. From the distance came the faint sound of music and raucous shouting that made the silence seem the more profound. Over the darkened houses showed the glow of the city. Michael pointed to another side street and led Howard down it.

"I think it is down here somewhere," he muttered.

A light flickered ahead of them as a

cigarette was lit. A drunk approached them, lurching heavily across the pavement. The stale, acid smell of cheap wine met their nostrils as he passed by. Ahead a rectangle of light shone on the road and music blared out louder for a moment as a door opened and closed.

"That is the place," Michael said. He put a hand on Howard's arm, checking him. "Let me do all the talking in there, *meneer*. Pretend you are drunk and do not know what you are doing."

Howard shook his head. "I don't want you to come inside. There's no reason why you should take any chances."

"You cannot speak Afrikaans, *meneer*; you would not understand all they were saying. Besides, they might become suspicious and recognize you. I will come inside, too."

Howard eyed Michael curiously. Of all the Coloureds he had met, with the notable exception of Father Hendricks, Michael had interested him the most. A proud and intelligent non-European, he clearly found the humilities of the Colour Bar harder to bear than many of his race. Yet, in spite of this and the persecution of his parents, his dislike for the white race was not a blind thing. He was still able to show gratitude to one of the few Europeans who had helped him and his people.

Michael's next few words confirmed this. Noticing Howard's hesitation in accepting his offer, he turned to him. "Both you and Mrs. Mitchell have done much for our people, *meneer*. We are all in your debt. This is the least I can do."

Howard nodded slowly, knowing too well his need of the Coloured's help. "All right, Michael. I won't forget."

Michael had turned his face away. He spoke into the darkness.

"There is just one thing, *meneer*. Do not blame our people for what you may see tonight. These followers of Swartz are our criminals, our scum. Among them is an animal called Vulisango who carries out Swartz's filthy ideas. Do not judge us on him and the others."

"I won't," Howard promised.

They walked up to a door alongside the darkened building. Michael knocked on it sharply. Howard waited with pounding heart. Was any secret sign required of them? He became aware of a sense of utter loneliness, as if they were a thousand miles from civilization, cut off from it by a vast, stone jungle. Yet theatres, cafés, and comfortable hotels were only a mile away: but a mile that could well be a thousand if their intentions were once discovered. They were alone in a district of long and thirsty knives.

The door opened a few inches. The flat features of a negro peered out at them. Michael muttered in Afrikaans. A long moment and then the door opened wider. It closed hollowly behind them. They were inside the *shebeen*.

Remembering his role, Howard half-closed his eyes, lurched, and allowed Michael to lead him into an adjacent room. The air was dense with evil-smelling tobacco and cheap wine. After the stillness outside the noise was deafening.

Michael led him to an empty corner of the room where Howard pretended to collapse, his ragged cap tilted well over his eyes. Michael sank beside him on the bare, wooden floor. Before Howard could examine the room, a shadow suddenly blocked out the light. Howard squinted upwards, then froze.

A Coloured, slight of build and wearing a lounge suit, was standing above him and staring down. His thin face was utterly expressionless. His watching eyes, as cold-blooded and unblinking as those of a fish, gave him a soulless appearance that was unnerving.

Howard let his head loll to one side. Long seconds passed, then he heard the Coloured rap out a harsh question. Michael answered.

"*Twee bottels Vaaljapie, asseblief.*"

The Coloured gave them one last stare and moved away. Howard felt a cigarette being pushed into his hand. Breathing again, he sat up a little straighter.

"Who the devil was that?" he whispered.

"I think that was the owner, Caspar."

"What did that look mean? Is he suspicious?"

Michael shook his head uneasily. "I don't know. Perhaps he always checks up on new customers. We shall see . . . "

Covertly Howard examined the room and its occupants. It held about thirty non-Europeans, although from the noise entering the open door it was clear that there were other rooms similarly crowded. Half-a-dozen coloured women, obviously prostitutes, sat in chairs, grotesque with their dark faces dusted with white powder and their mouths reddened like raw wounds. Both men and women were drinking straight from bottles. All were in some degree of intoxication, partly from the liquor and partly from the dagga they were smoking.

A negro arrived and thrust a bottle of wine at each of them. Michael pretended to help Howard find his money. The negro took the silver and shuffled away.

In another room a dance-band was playing. A negro opposite Howard suddenly seized one of the women and dragged her about the room, dancing in wild, abandoned steps. The prostitute pulled herself free and smashed her fist into the negro's face. Again and again she struck him, driving his bewildered head from side to side. She flung a stream of abuse at him before rejoining her riotous companions.

Michael nudged Howard's arm. Howard

became aware that the dance-band had stopped playing. A familiar voice had taken its place. It was speaking in Afrikaans but it needed no medium of language to deliver its message. Here, in a voice, was hate. Hate as real as a bloody knife, as savage as the eyes of a tormented leopard.

The occupants of the room made their way in its direction. Howard motioned to Michael and they followed them. They passed into a darkened dance-hall. Around its walls Coloureds and Natives of both sexes were packed tightly. At the opposite end of the room was the band, and before it, standing on a table with a spotlight on him, was the speaker. He was not immediately visible to Howard because of a pillar that stood between them.

The air was fetid with the odours of perspiring bodies, dagga, and cheap wine. Howard pushed through the packed doorway and fought his way along one side of the room. After a moment's hesitation, Michael followed him. The crowd were gaping at the speaker. Dulled with drugs and liquor, they were not yet absorbing all they were being told; but as the harangue continued bloodshot eyes began to smoulder and grunts of assent were heard more frequently.

With the pillar no longer blocking his view, Howard saw the speaker was Swartz. Keeping well hidden among the crowd he listened to the harsh oration and watched its effects on the faces around him. Slowly they began to awaken as the incitation soaked into their sotted minds. In the way of the Coloureds, Swartz interspersed English with Afrikaans as he raved on.

"*Julle is gekke!* Make them fear us! Make them afraid . . ."

Bloodshot eyes began rolling savagely, and the air grew more fetid. Mutters turned to shouts and dark faces became brutal in the dim light.

"Whose land is it? Who has built it? Who runs it today? We do. And yet who takes all the wealth, all the food, all the houses? Who starves our children . . . ?"

Now the crowd were with Swartz as one. The room became alive with hate. It stank like an evil smell.

"Make them give us back which is ours. Make them fear us! How? There are many ways. There is fire. We can burn down their houses, their factories, their farms . . . Oh, yes; fire is a wonderful thing . . . "

As he listened, Howard realized as never before the depths of bitterness in these people. Its expression this night was a terrifying, barbaric thing, and yet even its expression owed much to the Europeans' policy of denial. Granted adequate education, even these people, the very primitive dregs of the non-European peoples, would have had some of their savagery blunted and made less effective. As it was there was no brake on emotion, no curb on hate. They were as wild and uncontrollable as a forest fire.

The address ended in half-incoherent screams of abuse from Swartz, followed by a wild roar of applause. Swartz shouted something in Afrikaans before leaping to the floor. The crowd roared again. A second later a woman staggered into the centre of the room, followed by an enormous negro clad only in a loin-cloth. Howard recognized the flat, repulsive face as belonging to Joan Viljoen's assailant in Willisden.

"This is Vulisango," Michael muttered.

Although a Coloured, the woman was dressed and disguised as a European. She wore a blouse, skirt, and high-heeled shoes, and her skin was painted a chalk-white, giving a grotesque appearance to her negroid features. Simulating fear, she stood staring in mock terror at the huge native who was eyeing her lustfully.

The tableau broke into sudden, savage life. The negro lifted a bare foot and stamped it down on the wooden floor. A throb of drums came in reply from the band, now hidden in the darkness. Tum-tum-tum-tum — they were primitive, barbaric. Drums from the darkness, from ancient Africa. Hypnotic drums, bringing a message of hate, of lust, of destruction. Tum-tum-tum-tum. Tum-tum-tum-tum . . .

The oiled body of the negro began to move to the rhythm. He moved slowly at first, circling the woman who crouched at his feet. Then faster as the drums stepped up their tempo. Faster . . . his face a devil mask of lust. The drums beat louder, mounting to a crescendo. The negro spun dizzily, to land with a savage scream astride the huddled woman. The drums stopped abruptly.

Reaching down, the negro dragged the woman to her feet. He made a swift tearing motion of his hand. The crowd gasped and pressed closer. The negro stared at the woman with gloating eyes before hurling her at his feet again.

Again the drums throbbed. The negro's glistening body was gyrating over the woman in a mad dance almost too fast for the eye to follow. Again the drums rose to a crescendo. Again he screamed and snatched up the woman.

Now the rhythm of the drums was an aphrodisiac. Sweat was running down the negro's heaving chest and saliva was white in the corners of his mouth. The light, shining through the blue dagga smoke, made a devil's grotto out of the hall. The faces of the crowd had now lost all human resemblance. They were bodiless things, floating in a sea of poisonous mist. Transported to hell by drugs, liquor, oratory, and sexual excitement, they were devils glaring through the heated mists of lust and hate.

Now the drums rolled out their triumph and conquest in a mad crescendo. The maddened crowd surged forward. Sickened, Howard turned to his companion.

"Come on," he muttered. "Let's get out of this while we have the chance."

Michael nodded and followed him. All eyes were on the negro and the woman, and they were able to reach and pass through the door unnoticed.

To reach the exit they had to pass an open door on one side of the corridor. Michael went by it without a glance, but something made Howard lift his head as he reached it. His eyes froze on the scarred face of Swartz, who was talking to Caspar, the *shebeen* proprietor, in the centre of the room. The small, vicious eyes of the *skolly* set on him instantly and narrowed. With the skin sliding coldly down his back, Howard dropped his eyes and followed Michael to the door. He could hear no sound from the room, but his fevered imagination conjured up a picture of the agitator searching his memory for recognition.

The next few steps were torture. Grimly he fought back the desire to run. They reached the door. Michael grunted something to the negro doorkeeper, who shrugged without interest and turned the lock. Another second and they were outside, with the night air cool on their heated cheeks and the house a forbidding hulk against the luminous sky.

Howard seized hold of Michael's arm. "Quickly," he muttered. "Swartz may have recognized me. He was in the room we just passed."

They broke into a run. At the same moment the crash of a door sounded behind them and a glare of light appeared like a night monster's eye. Confused shouting could be heard, and above it a harsh voice issuing instructions. Swartz had remembered.

* * *

They ran into a rabbit warren of narrow streets, slipping and sliding on garbage that lay in heaps on the pavements and in the gutters.

"Is this right?" Howard panted. "We

didn't come this way."

"It's darker down here," Michael gasped. "And the main road must lie ahead."

Behind them, like the baying of wolves, the sounds of pursuit grew louder. Swartz's voice could be heard clearly, urging the others on. The two men ran desperately. Reaching a well-lit street, they swung down a turning to the left in the direction of the main road and plunged again into semi-darkness. They ran for fifty yards until Michael, who was ahead, stopped with a curse.

"There's a wall," he panted. "The road ends here."

Pausing for breath, Howard listened. The sounds of pursuit were coming from several quarters now, as if Swartz's party had been reinforced. Shrill whistles confirmed this belief. Michael nodded.

"He has a large gang, *meneer*. They will try to cut us off. We must get over this wall . . . "

Howard jumped and his hands closed on the top of the wall. Something bit deeply into the palm of his hand as he heaved his body upwards. He heard a gasp of pain from Michael.

"Glass!" Howard gritted. "Watch yourself."

On the other side of the wall they found themselves in a narrow alleyway flanked by high walls. They listened, trying to hear in which direction their pursuers had gone. All was suddenly quiet, ominously quiet. They could hear the distant hum of traffic on the main road.

Howard could feel Michael's arm trembling beside his own.

"Where are they, *meneer*?" the Coloured whispered.

"They must know we haven't reached the main road," Howard breathed back. "Probably they have thrown a cordon right round this area and are combing it for us. We can't stay here. Keep that cosh in your hand and use it if anyone comes at us."

He led Michael along the alley. He was tempted to climb over the wall on their right until he realized that beyond it lay the tiny back yards of a long row of houses, and to be caught there would mean disaster. It was better to make their way along the alley and trust to finding a way out at the end. The main road could not be more than a few hundred yards away and obviously Swartz was still in the dark as to their whereabouts. If they could get a little nearer it, Howard decided he would chance using the police-whistle he was carrying. To use it now would only bring Swartz on them, but nearer the main road it might be of assistance. It might even frighten their pursuers away. For Howard had the idea that the present silence was not designed solely to keep them mystified about the gang's whereabouts. Noise might cause some lone policeman or a casual pedestrian to call for a police-car.

They reached the end of the alley and peered into the street. It was fairly well lighted and a hundred yards away a fried fish shop was doing a brisk trade with a gang of coloured youths.

"We've got to risk it," Howard said. "I know they may be watching from one of the alleys, but the longer we stay here the more dangerous it gets. Come on . . ."

They walked down the street to

make themselves less noticeable. At every moment they expected a rush of desperate figures, but nothing happened until they reached and passed the fish-shop. The gang of youths stopped talking as the approached, drawing aside to let them pass. They were another thirty yards down the road when a shrill whistle sounded behind them. Turning sharply, Howard saw one of the youths with his fingers in his mouth, emitting a second whistle. Another of the gang was pointing in their direction. At the same moment a crowd of men poured into the street and made for them.

"Run like hell," Howard gritted. "The road isn't far away."

They raced down the street as whistles sounded behind them. Another gang emerged from a passage ahead and formed a line across the road.

Howard saw a dark alley-mouth on their left and dragged Michael by the arm. They plunged into it, stumbling over dustbins and boxes. Startled dogs began snarling on all sides as they made their way towards the dim opening ahead.

"If we can get out before they close

it up, we have a good chance," Howard panted.

They had no more than twenty yards to go when Howard slipped on a pile of garbage and felt a shock of pain tear through his ankle. He stumbled and fell forward. Michael checked himself and came running back, his face grey with fear.

"What is it, *meneer*?" he muttered.

"My ankle's gone," Howard panted, trying in vain to walk. He thrust the police-whistle into the Coloured's hand. "Run; and blow this as you go."

"But you, *meneer*?"

"Run, for God's sake," Howard shouted, pushing him forward. "I'll try to hold them off until you get help. It's no use both of us staying here. This is our only chance . . ."

Michael hesitated a moment more, then vanished into the street. Howard heard the shrill call of his whistle as the first of his pursuers came running down the alley.

Howard lifted his revolver and waited. The man, a thin, rat-faced *skolly*, stopped dead on seeing it. Behind him two of his companions halted, their narrowed eyes on the revolver. One held a long, bared knife, the other a length of bicycle chain.

Howard watched them intently, thankful for the narrowness of the alley. There was the clatter of running footsteps and another three men appeared out of the gloom. Howard's heart sank as the scarred face of Swartz grinned in hate at him.

"*Vuilgoed!*" the Coloured snarled, drawing a knife from his pocket. His slitted eyes turned on the men ahead of him.

"*Waarvoor wag jy! Donder hom.* Go for him. Kill him."

The men's eyes were on the revolver. Howard stood motionless, his ears cocked for any sounds along the alley behind him. In the distance Michael's whistle could be heard.

The rest followed as fast as lightning. Swartz's arm flickered backwards and down, as fast as a snake's tongue. Howard hurled himself sidewards. The thrown knife glanced viciously off the wall where his body had been. He fired, but his ankle had given way with the abrupt movement and he was falling as he pulled the trigger. Instead of Swartz it was the rat-faced *skolly* who groaned and sank to the ground. Before Howard could fire again the remaining five men were on him.

He swung the revolver with desperate strength. A *skolly* caught it full in the face and collapsed with a scream. Another of them struck upwards with a knife. Howard managed to block the blow with one arm and to smash the revolver across the man's neck. His finger jerked the trigger as he struck and another explosion shattered the darkness.

But the fight was over. Swartz sprang in like a savage panther. Although Howard deflected the knife-thrust to his heart, the blade pierced his upper arm and the revolver fell from his hand. In desperation he caught hold of Swartz's knife arm and managed to tear the blade away. But the other men were on him now, kicking, punching, slashing with chains.

A boot landed full in his stomach as he struggled on the ground and doubled him up in agony. A blow crashed on the back of his head and a white-hot dagger of pain pierced his back. Dimly, through the thundering roar in his head, he seemed to hear whistles shrilling nearby, but the darkness was welling up around him. He heard one final explosion, saw one last flash of brilliant light, then all was darkness and oblivion.

24

CONSCIOUSNESS came back slowly to Howard. At first he knew nothing but pain, a vast sea of pain that swept him through intermittent periods of light and darkness. Then he became aware of faces coming and going in the mist around him, and heard the far-off whisper of voices. Then pain and delirium returned, and the past and present merged into one. He was back in Burma during the war. He was wounded, lying on the steamy carpet of vegetation while the jungle closed in around him. Nearer it came, dense, alive with hate. Green tendrils reached out like tiny snakes, curling round his limbs and creeping up his nostrils. His lungs struggled for air while over him the triumphant vegetation matted a shroud. His head seemed to explode and he lost consciousness again.

His next awakening had a dreamlike quality. He thought he saw Linda leaning over him. He made a tremendous effort to rise. Only his head stirred, but his heart began thudding like a madly-beaten drum with the effort.

"Howard," she breathed. "Can you hear me?"

He tried to speak but was too weak to move his lips. He saw her eyes fill with tears. She pressed her lips against his forehead.

"How dare you let this happen?" she whispered. "I'm very angry with you."

His eyes closed in contentment. Linda kissed him again, then took the arm of Father Hendricks, who was at her side. Tears were rolling down the old man's furrowed cheeks.

"Oh, madame; how I have prayed for this moment! God has been very good to us . . . "

* * *

The following day Howard was able to talk a little, although weakly. Morkel came to see him, shaking his head to hide his anxiety.

"You had it coming, you *domkop*.

What do you mean by going round places like that at night? Have you gone crazy?"

Howard managed a smile. "I had to do something to convince you blockheads," he whispered. "How did I get out of it?"

"A police patrol heard your boy's whistle. The gang ran on seeing them. Another few seconds and they'd have finished you."

"What sort of a mess am I in?"

"You've had severe concussion, a knife-stab that just missed your right lung, another in the upper arm, two fractured ribs, and a few other such trifling cuts and bruises. Otherwise you're in good shape. In fact," Morkel finished gruffly, "you should go on living to be a thorn in our flesh. Take care of yourself, *ou seun*."

⋆ ⋆ ⋆

In the next week Howard's strength returned rapidly. From the nurses he learned how Linda and Father Hendricks had almost lived in the hospital until he had recovered consciousness. One afternoon he asked Linda the question that had been worrying him. To his relief, she shook her head.

"He doesn't know I've been coming; he has been away again. Don't worry," she went on bitterly. "I'm being careful."

She did not tell him why; that she was being careful for his sake, not her own. She had never told him of her husband's threats against him.

There was a silence into which both sank with their thoughts. She knew he desired her; but the deeper things, were they there, too? What would she do if he asked her to leave Trevor? What held her now — his money? Or was it a quixotic sense of duty, an archaic belief in the ancient oath of marriage? Once she would have laughed at thc idea, but of late she had found much in herself to cause her wonder. Yet she doubted her ability to deny herself to Howard if he needed her. Since his injuries she had learned what he had come to mean to her.

He had noticed the bitterness in her voice and had wondered . . . If only he could be certain she were prepared to give up her wealth for him . . . If only he could be certain it was fair to ask her . . . Distrust of himself, lack of confidence born of his illness, caused the moment to pass, to their mutual disappointment.

* * *

Joan Viljoen visited him at the end of the second week. He was alone when she came. He was shocked to see the changes in her. Her cheeks were sunken and wan, and dark shadows lay like bruises under her eyes. Her whole body appeared shrunken.

"I would have come to see you before," she said in her low voice. "But I have not been well. I was terribly sorry to hear what happened . . ."

Howard looked at her with concern. "What has been wrong? I can see you have lost weight."

Her thin fingers picked at his coverlet. "Oh; it's nothing. Nothing to worry about."

Immobilized as he had been for

two weeks, Howard's perceptions had quickened. Something in her voice gave him the impression of utter hopelessness. It came like an icy draught, chilling his mind. He paused, searching for words.

"How is Brian?" he asked.

Her eyes dropped, and he realized he had said the wrong thing.

"He is quite well, I think, Mr. Shaw."

His weakened state would not allow him to contain his question any longer. "What is it, Miss Viljoen? What has happened?"

She attempted a smile. The courage of it made him catch his breath. She tried to speak, but no words came. Unable to face such grief, he closed his eyes.

"Sometimes it helps just to tell other people," he muttered. "If I can be of any use at all, please tell me."

She gave a retching sob that seemed to tear her body. Tears fell down her cheeks, to splash on the coverlet. Then her tightly-closed eyes dammed them back.

"I shall not forget you, Mr. Shaw," she whispered. Then she was gone and

Howard was left staring at the dark stains on his coverlet.

⋆ ⋆ ⋆

On Linda's next visit, Howard's first words were about the girl.

"What is it? She looks terrible. She hasn't contracted tuberculosis, has she?"

Linda shook her head. "No one seems to know what it is. You know she has refused to go out with Brian any more, don't you?"

"Of course I don't know. Why?"

"Nobody knows. Brian is taking it very badly. He won't even speak about it."

"But she always gave me the impression of being very fond of him."

"She was. You couldn't miss seeing it. It's all a mystery to me. Of course, I haven't seen much of Brian recently. He might tell me more when we're back under the same roof again."

"I can't forget the poor kid," Howard muttered.

Neither spoke for a full minute. Then Linda raised her eyes.

"Have they given you any idea how

much longer you'll have to stay in here?"

"At least three more weeks," he grimaced. "Although they say I'll be allowed up during the last week. I intend continuing my articles in a few days. I can't afford to leave them any longer, or the public will be forgetting my case."

"Nonsense. The papers have been plugging you day and night. Everyone is dying to hear what happened to you."

Howard smiled ruefully. "That's the one good thing about this hiding: it should help to substantiate my story. Before it I was worried how I was going to prove what I'd seen. It shouldn't be difficult now."

Her green eyes were reproachful. "It was a crazy thing to do. It was a miracle you weren't killed." She leaned forward curiously. "What exactly did you see? You've never told me, you know."

"It's rather a filthy story," he said, telling her the gist of it. He added: "I don't believe all the incitement takes similar lines to this. This was in a *shebeen*, which lent itself to that kind of filth. There was talk of arson: that was significant. It might be one of the chief weapons of intimidation if violence ever broke out on a large scale. It could do immense damage out here, particularly on the farms."

She shuddered, her mind on the *shebeen.* "Much of that would make people think *apartheid* was too good for them. It would me."

"We have to look at it rationally," he said. "These were the most primitive of the non-Europeans, as well as the dregs. Brutes like Swartz know that the quickest way to increase their numbers is to appeal to this type. To get them they'll use every filthy incitement in the book. It isn't new: the Mau Mau have done it in Kenya. By inciting their followers to break tribal taboos, they bound them together in shame and guilt — that has been the idea behind the filthy oath-taking ceremonies. The victims are left desperate, in their own minds damned beyond redemption; and after that it is easy to get them to murder. This thing I saw was nothing beside their ceremonies, but you can see the similarity of ideas. Racial repression spawns rape — the underdog trying to get his own back on his master. This thing was to show that repression liberated. It used sex, the strongest of human emotions, as a driving force to violence."

She shuddered again. "It's horrible."

"It is horrible, and the vast majority of the non-Europeans are as disgusted as we are. But *apartheid* is driving them nearer this criminal element every day. After all, if we evalue them as not worthy of being civilized, can we blame them if they eventually accept our evaluation?"

As she was going she put a hand on his arm. "Will you spend a few days with me in Donnerhoek for your convalescence? I have some friends there who would love to meet you."

She saw the doubt in his eyes. "It won't gct mc into any trouble," she went on. "Trevor is going up to Rhodesia for three weeks. He leaves next week-end. Brian will stay with his relations, so I'm quite free."

A moment's hesitation and he was lost. "It sounds wonderful," he said.

"Then I'll arrange it." She picked up her gloves, brushing his arm almost imperceptibly with her hand as she moved away.

★ ★ ★

The next week, although still in hospital, Howard wrote an account of his recent experiences — something for which his editors had been waiting with unconcealed impatience. Although he could not describe in detail the foul thing he had seen, he managed to convey something of its bestiality and implications. While making it clear how very few non-Europeans encouraged or indulged in such foulness, he made no effort to conceal its inherent seriousness. By the impact of his civilization, the European had left a moral vacuum in the mind of the native. Western civilization had laughed at the Bantu's tribal laws and derided his gods. It had left him bereft of faith or leadership; left him waiting in pathetic hope for the European to show him a new and better way of life.

That promise, that responsibility, had not been fulfilled. Today it was being denied by law. The moral vacuum was complete, leaving its victims desperate and an easy prey to incitement.

The Coloureds were not immune from such dangers, either, although for a different reason. While some of them were highly intelligent, they were also the most pathetic of all the Union's non-European races. Unlike the Bantu and the Asiatics, they did not even have the splintered staff of an ancient culture to lean on in these troubled times. A new race, created from black and white, too intelligent to take the disintegrating tribal life of the former and denied the civilization of the latter, they had been made outcasts by those who had created them. The result was a steady moral drift into despair and degradation. Who could forecast their ultimate reaction when their cup of unhappiness overflowed at last?

Everything suggested that *apartheid* had enormously intensified the bitterness of the non-European races. It had not given birth to it — the old colour bar had to take the blame for that. But, whereas before *apartheid* the non-European had found in the very makeshift order of the laws hope for their eventual repeal, now, in one devastating blow, all hope had been smashed from him. By nature patient, optimistic, and lazy, he might have carried on indefinitely under the old order, finding excuse for his inaction in his hope. Now he had no hope and so no excuse: he was being forced to protest. And yet peaceful protest was denied him! With millions of such minds all over the country, hopeless and desperate, danger must be apparent even to the blindest of men.

Howard was satisfied with the completed article. It read well, and bearing as it did the seal of personal experience, it was likely to carry a good deal of weight. After all, he reflected, Erasmus lacked the advantage of a hiding to support his assertions. Contemplating the fact with grim satisfaction, he posted the article off to his newspapers.

* * *

Howard had one more visitor before he left the hospital. Michael slipped in during his lunch-hour to give Howard news of Umzoni.

"I haven't long, *meneer*, but there are one or two things I thought you would like to know."

"It's good of you to come, Michael. What are they?"

"It has come out that Umzoni was betrayed by Swartz, both at the meeting and later in the church."

Howard nodded. "I'd guessed that. I think Umzoni must have done, too. But go on."

Michael drew nearer, his voice low. "There is also news from Umzoni."

"Umzoni!"

"Yes; although he is still in prison hospital. He stands trial when he is fully well again. But he is clever; he sends out his instructions as if he were a free man. And he has fixed the day of the strike."

"When is it?" Howard asked eagerly.

"On the twenty-seventh of April, *meneer*. Three days before all of us opposite the factory have to leave our homes . . . "

25

LINDA drove Howard out to her friends at Donnerhoek. They followed the winding road through the university town of Stellenbosch into the valley that lay a few miles beyond. The scenery was magnificent. Cream-painted farmhouses lay among leafy oaks and kaffir plums. Between them stretched the greenery of orchards and vineyards. The fruit season was almost over; the rich earth resting in the late summer sun shine after its labours. Mountains rose round the valley, guarding its peace.

Howard feasted his eyes on the sweep of mountains and sky. After weeks of hospital and antiseptics, the air was intoxicating.

"It looks rather like paradise," he said.

Linda smiled and let the car coast downhill. They ran down narrow lanes lined with flowering gums, their blossoms crimson against the green foliage. Startled doves fluttered aloft at their approach, then settled again, puffing out indignant chests at the disturbance.

They crossed a hump-backed bridge and followed a narrow earthen road flanked by thick trees. Two *rondavels* came into sight, then a long packing-shed, and at last the picturesque outline of a Dutch gable. A huge house, set among spacious lawns, rose before them.

"Here we are," Linda announced, applying her brake. "Welcome to Schoonvallie."

* * *

Linda's friends, a middle-aged Afrikaans couple called Van Reenan, proved both charming and hospitable. Howard was particularly drawn to Van Reenan himself. He was a huge man, with a look of autumn splendour about his gnarled, bent body. He had a pair of twinkling eyes and a ready chuckle.

After dinner that night he invited Howard to have a pipe with him outside, and led him out to the red-tiled stoep that overlooked the valley below. Howard was offered tobacco for his pipe, given a glass of wine by a smiling servant, and then both men sat in silence, looking at the valley and the mountains beyond.

The sun had set behind the house. The valley was in shadow, but the mountain peaks opposite were still tinted pink against the fading sky. A hawk wheeled against them, then fell away into the violet-ash mist of the valley. The silence was tangible; its very nothingness giving it substance. Howard was reminded of the Eastern philosophy: that the only true reality is nothingness. That life is a thought, a dream, and only in the pause between one dream and the next is there true and eternal reality.

The warm fragrance of tobacco drifted towards him. He turned, meeting the farmer's gaze. Van Reenan puffed contentedly again, then nodded to the mountains.

"I see you like our view, *meneer*. I see, too, that you know the value of silence. You are not like most of the townsmen who must blather all the time. Much can be said with silence. This valley, those mountains: they do not talk but how much they tell. It is good to sit out here when one's work is done and listen to their story."

The shadow of the night moved higher. An owl screeched from a clump of trees, accentuating the deep silence. But was it silence? As Howard listened he became aware of a vibrant humming, rising like an organ note. Crickets and beetles in their thousands made the dreamy hum, hypnotic in its insistence. The stars opened their brilliant eyes and looked calmly down. Night had come to Donnerhoek.

The farmer spoke again. "Have you known Linda long, *meneer*?"

Howard shook his head. "No; only a few months."

"We have known her a number of years. We look upon her as a daughter. My son, Piet, first brought her home to meet us. We saw much of her the following year. They became engaged two weeks before he was killed in a blasting accident. It was a sad thing to happen . . . "

From the darkness a wild cat screeched,

stirring a commotion among the fowls that died uneasily into the soothing night. The faint sheen of a rising moon shone silver on the peaks opposite.

"I remember now," Howard said, after a pause. "A friend told me. Only I had not realized he was your son."

Van Reenan's sigh was heavy with memory. "*Ja*; and they were a fine couple." His voice grew harsh. "People said that afterwards she grew hard and worldly, but that is not true. We know her, and she has never changed . . . " His voice trailed off. "But I am growing old. I talk too much."

A servant came out on the stoep with two newspapers. He offered them to Van Reenan, who shook his head.

"Give them to the *meneer*, Daniel."

Howard took the papers, then dropped them beside his chair. "They can wait until later," he said.

"They will be full of arguments about politics," the farmer said, looking down at his pipe. "*Die Volksman* will say one thing and the English paper the other. That is why I get them both. Sometimes I find myself back where I started, which is a relief. But this Erasmus — he does not like you, does he, *meneer*?"

Howard started. This was the first indication Van Reenan had made that he knew his guest's identity. Howard was interested to know what this sagacious old Boer farmer thought of his case but made himself tread warily. The chances were two to one that Van Reenan was a Nationalist.

Van Reenan's pipe glowed red in the gathering darkness.

"*Meneer*; you will have made many enemies by your articles, but you will also have made many friends. I am waiting eagerly to hear the end of your case, *meneer* — your alternative suggestions to *apartheid*. I am interested because I am not happy about these laws. Once I was as bad as anyone. Once I saw only their black skins and laughed at their simple ways. But now I know there are many fine people among them. An old negro who comes round these parts doing odd jobs — do you know what he once said to me when I joked with him and asked him what he was worth? '*Baas*,' he said. 'I am as rich as my kindest thought and as poor as my most unworthy one.' I have never forgotten that, *meneer*."

"And such men as that are never to have a vote," Howard reflected.

Van Reenan turned to him. "That is my thought, *meneer*. I do not say they should all be given the franchise yet — that I do not say. But there must be many among them as wise as this old man. Yet any fool of a European over the age of eighteen can vote in this country today. Eighteen, *meneer*: the most intolerant age of a child's life! The argument used by the politicians is that if a man is fit to fight, he is fit to vote. What nonsense! Then the mad dog should be given the vote, the wild bull, the baboon . . ."

The old farmer leaned forward. "Do you know, *meneer*, the only men to whom I would give the vote?"

Howard shook his head.

"Only those who had children or a garden, *meneer*. It would not matter how small a garden: a window-box would do if there was room for nothing more. But only to such men would I give the right to determine the future."

⋆ ⋆ ⋆

Later that evening Howard asked Van Reenan to translate Erasmus's page in *Die Volksman*. As he had guessed, it contained the columnist's reply to his latest article.

It was in significant contrast to Erasmus's earlier attacks. It seemed he had at last realized the limit of emotional criticism and was now falling back on his own brand of logic. He made no attempt, for example, to deny Howard's experiences inside and outside the *shebeen*. The brutality of the assault had already convinced the public that the writer had seen something clandestine, and Erasmus was too clever a journalist to try to change the public's pre-set conclusions. Instead he uscd both the *shebeen* scene and the assault on Howard as props in his case that the non-Europeans were badly in need of corrective discipline and *apartheid* had arrived just in time.

After this point was made, his tone became almost benign. *Apartheid* was no more directed against the average non-European than the police were directed against the average citizen. Only the law-breakers would suffer under it: the majority would gain. It was the first comprehensive policy designed to give self-respect to all races and to allow them to live without friction inside the same national boundary.

How was this to be brought about? The original *apartheid* laws passed in 1949 gave the clue. The laws preventing sexual intercourse between European and non-European were the first sane precaution. They prevented the problem growing bigger while its solution was being tackled.

Then came the law to give each race its own residential and development area. Surely it was obvious that this would cut down racial friction to the minimum, a thing to the advantage of all races.

Then there was the Suppression of Communism Act. Surely it was the duty of the Europeans to protect the most credible of their wards from the evil cajolery of agitators, particularly those of the type Shaw himself had seen!

And was not the law making the carrying of identity cards compulsory a natural corollary of the other laws? The police had to have some way of knowing to which racial group a person belonged.

Erasmus treated with equal kindness the subsequent and subordinate laws passed since 1949. The worst of these, the Bantu Education Act, he posed as a piece of logical legislation. The mission schools, by giving the Bantu European education, had only succeeded in imbuing him with frustration. The fact was that in the Union the non-European's rôle was that of a labourer. Then was it not better to teach him to be a good labourer, so that he could increase his own earning power, rather than make him a frustrated scholar? Happiness lay in the acceptance of realities; not in a yearning for the unattainable.

Erasmus rounded off his case with a glowing vision: the South Africa of the future when *apartheid* had reached its ultimate goal. Each race was now living in its own development area; each race was living its own way of life (under a benevolent European authority!). From a heterogeneous chaos *apartheid* had created a Utopia.

It was, in fact, a compilation of the things Nationalist politicians had been telling a sceptical world since *apartheid* had been mooted. To the shallow thinker it seemed plausible. But under the hammer blows of reason it broke up badly.

Little imagination was needed to realize how the non-Europeans were suffering by being moved forcibly into their segregated areas. Those with freehold land or property were being compelled to sell — was it likely they were receiving a just price in such a situation? And if total segregation became a fact, if they were herded into reserves or restricted areas outside the cities, how would they reach their work? Already transport expenses formed one of the major items of the worker's budget.

Apartheid's answer was to move industries out to the fringes of the locations or reserves. But were not geographical factors — the nearness of ports, railways, and collaborating industries, to mention a few — of some importance? The idea could be dismissed as ludicrous. Either European industry would eventually have to do without non-European labour, a thing which would cripple most of it, or else vast convoys would have to run day and night, moving hundreds of thousands of workers to and fro from their locations on endless conveyor-belts.

Another point arose here. If *apartheid* were truly conceived for all races, then the development areas into which the non-Europeans were to be eventually sealed had to be proportionate in size to the populations they held. As the non-Europeans outnumbered the Europeans in the Union by four to one, then they had to be given four-fifths of the land — the rich land as well as the poor. Could anyone in his right senses believe this would happen? Could anyone see the slightest indication of its beginning to happen?

No; it was impossible for anyone but the fanatic to imagine that *apartheid* was anything more than a scheme to keep the Europeans a supreme and dominant race; and few South Africans in their hearts believed anything else. Howard knew this and spent little time on the argument. In his answer, which he wrote during the next few tranquil days, he made the point again that the non-Europeans were stirring against the laws, touched briefly on the dangers, then went on to the climax of his case.

For, in the last lines of his article, Erasmus had flung down his final challenge. *Apartheid*, the columnist declared, was a positive thing — the first positive plan ever conceived in the Union to solve the ever-growing colour problem. Any fool could criticize, and many did, but out of the welter of criticism not one alternative plan had yet been mooted. Was Shaw any different from the rest? Very definitely Erasmus did not think so.

This, Howard knew, was the crisis, the last encounter. After this one of them must fall and the legions behind the fallen would suffer a moral defeat. The odds were heavily in Erasmus's favour. Not because there was no answer to *apartheid*, but because the answer lay less in a policy than in a state of mind. A renaissance of liberal thought was needed among the Europeans without which no policy could be a real success.

Mental *apartheid* was complete now: that was the tragedy. Today the white met the black only in the rôle of master. Each to the other was a stranger and daily the estrangement grew. Somehow, if there was to be an equitable solution to the colour problem, these mental barriers had to be broken down. Policies alone were not enough. The spirit of tolerance and goodwill had to be fostered and fostered quickly. The danger was acute that if the white man took too long to sympathize, the coloured man might have learned to hate . . .

Laws, then, were not enough. Not that Howard did not envisage new laws, or that he had no positive plan. He gave these at the end of his article. But policies were meaningless without principles: people had to *want* to make them work. To get his points over without mawkishness, he made them aggressive. The first of them be knew would tread on many sensitive corns.

It was re-education of the Europeans: a

step he regarded as of prime importance. They must be taught to see the Coloured races in a kindlier and more tolerant light. Here the churches had failed miserably in their duty. Indeed, the Union's Dutch Reformed Church was an active supporter of the colour bar. Such an abasement of the Christian Faith he found revolting and said so. The Church must live up to its Christian duty, no matter what the opposition.

Re-education — a vital thing. Adult Europeans could be reached through the Church, the Press, and the Radio. Children could be reached in their formative years at school. Race relations should be a compulsory subject in every school, teaching every European child his heavy responsibility to the coloured peoples at present the wards of his race. The primary rule of good manners — that one is never rude or unkind to those of an inferior social status — should be hammered home. This would greatly ease the friction between black and white in the years of adjustment that lay ahead.

The police came under his fire next. Constant care and surveillance were necessary to ensure that non-Europeans were treated no more harshly than Europeans. Howard stressed — as he believed — that the great majority of the police were decent and fair. But a force of its size must inevitably contain its proportion of negrophobes and these had to be watched. Nothing caused greater bitterness than a harsh and prejudiced police force, and nothing did more harm to law and order.

Howard's next suggestion was a novel one. He recommended the setting up in every town and city of special centres where the Colour Bar was waived. In these oases of neutrality Europeans and non-Europeans could meet on equal terms and learn to know one another. Here would be the natural complement to the re-educational programme: centres where more and more Europeans could experiment with their newly-found liberalism. This idea Howard expounded at length. It would cost next to nothing and could be introduced almost immediately. And the most rabid negrophobe could have no valid objection because attendance would be entirely voluntary.

Next came the legislative part of his programme. Firstly it was imperative that the forces of liberalism took their stand. Erasmus was quite right on this point: it had been painfully clear throughout the Union and colonial Africa that only the apostles of racial supremacy had had the courage to declare their intentions. The liberals had offered weak opposition but had never taken the plunge and declared their own policies. Indeed, they had no policies. This had been the cause of their decline.

The liberals had to decide whether they were prepared to accept the alternative of *apartheid* — economical and political integration. Once they had faced and agreed that the blacks were as necessary as the Europeans to the nation's development, then real progress towards a stable and contented future for all races could be made. This would in no way prejudice the social separation of the races.

With this policy of integration as their basis, Howard unfolded his suggestions. Higher European taxes should be put into force and the increased revenue go into non-European educational and housing schemes. Not the type of education envisaged by the Bantu Education Act, which was clearly designed to keep the non-European in a permanent position of inferiority, but education designed to do the very reverse, for it was that very sense of inferiority that was such a powerful cause of racial friction. Vast housing estates, Government sponsored, should be started immediately, using non-European labour to keep down the costs.

Then wages. Tens of thousands of coloured workers did skilled and semi-skilled work on labourer's pay. This exploitation of labour was a universal thing throughout Africa. But, moral aspects aside, it was short-sighted. If a higher wage structure were built up for the non-Europeans, it would immediately create a greater buying power among them, which, by providing a vast internal market for the nation's goods, would benefit all races alike.

Howard's last argument dealt with the most controversial problem of all: political equality of the non-Europeans.

But it could not be ignored: it was the natural sequel to the policy of integration. Once it was admitted — and it could not be denied — that the non-Europeans were a vital part of the nation, it followed they must be allowed an increased say in its management. But at once one ran into cross-currents of intense emotion.

The European fear was that a general political franchise would mean their virtual elimination from political leadership. This, they claimed, would mean a decline of their nation into semi-barbarism. And their case was strong. Clearly, it was the very nations who had been ungenerous in giving education to their non-Europeans who would suffer the most.

But it was also clear that such a general franchise would benefit no one yet. Illiterate natives could hardly be given a power they did not understand. But that was not an excuse to the Europeans for inaction: it was an indictment. They must start at once the long educational haul that would raise these backward people to the status of responsible citizens.

This would prepare the way for a State in which all races could contribute their own particular genius. But something must be done now for those non-Europeans who had already reached such a standard. It would be proof of the Europeans good faith and it would alleviate the bitterness of these people, who, denied the normal social and cultural outlets of the intelligent brain, were sinking into a miasma of frustrated hate.

Howard's idea was to introduce a Bill that would allow any non-European to win full and equal citizenship rights. To gain these he would have to reach a reasonable standard of educational and social attainment. A panel of examiners would be set up in every town and city consisting of an equal proportion of whites and blacks. A badge of recognition would be given to the successful applicants.

Howard was aware that this idea would please neither race. The Europeans would not like it because it was the thin end of the wedge; the non-Europeans would resent both its implications and its limitations. He reminded his readers of the need for a renaissance of thought . . . Such a scheme would be an incentive to the non-European to uplift himself — it would offer to him that shining thing, hope. And while it would make no appreciative difference to the Europeans' supremacy for years to come, it would accustom them to the novel discovery that some non-Europeans were very much their equal . . .

He ended his article with a warning to all Europeans who held sway over coloured people. This renaissance of thought was as important to their future as to that of the non-Europeans. Racial intolerance led to arrogance: arrogance to moral decay. The European had to think less of himself to save himself. He had to think not in terms of expediency, but in terms of sacred human rights. If he did not, if he thought of nothing but pride and pomp and power, then the seeds of his degeneracy would germinate apace.

And so, at last, Howard's case was closed. With minor modifications he felt it would be applicable to colonial territories as well as the Union. He sent one copy to his overseas newspaper and one to each of the Union papers, with instructions to the latter not to publish until permission was received from *The World Observer.*

He then went out into the sunshine of Donnerhoek.

* * *

The remaining days passed idyllically. Howard was amazed at the change in Linda. Over the last few weeks, indeed since Father Hendricks's court case, she had become a new person. There was no trace of her old cynicism. Her laughter rang true; her gaiety was not forced. They went for long walks together in the mountains and their companionship grew into an even deeper and valued thing.

One evening, two nights before they were due to return home, they went for a stroll up one of the quiet lanes in the head of the valley. The moon was full, floating in silent music over the mountains.

They said little to one another; there was little to say. The night was still, yet full of a hushed, puissant vitality. A jackal yelped in the distance, starting a thousand echoes. The smell of the earth rose thickly to their nostrils, full and rich. They reached a small gate that gave a view across the valley, and both of them stopped as if by mutual consent.

The sheen of the moon lay on the mountains, turning each waterfall into a thread of fine silver. Over to the west, where the sky was darker, a meteor ran a hair-line of light before plunging into oblivion. In the distance the muted purr of a car made itself heard. The twin rays of headlights probed the sky for a second. Then the silence returned, more profound than ever. The air had a quality that banished weariness: an intoxication like rare wine. Linda spoke of it.

"Isn't it wonderful?" she breathed. "Why is it so wonderful tonight?"

"The sages of the East believe there is a mystical element of life in it," Howard told her. "And he who knows the secret can draw youth and strength from it."

"What is that secret, Howard? Tonight I could believe I had stumbled on it. What is it?"

"They say one must think only of good. That in one's heart there must be no hatred. That only love can draw the elixir of life from the air."

"Love!" she breathed. "Yes; of course. When one's heart is full of love, there is no room left for hatred. And hate ages you, but love keeps you young. Isn't that what you mean?"

"Yes," he said, his throat aching with yearning. The moonlight was full on her face, and her beauty was too beautiful to bear.

"I love you like that, Howard," she said, quite steadily. "I have loved you like that since the first night we met. I have always loved you . . . "

Suddenly she was in his arms and he was kissing the moonlight on her face. The earth shuddered under his feet.

"Linda, my darling. Linda, I love you . . . "

Her body pressed against his fiercely; her hair fell in a wild torrent over his hands. They stood together in a delirium of ecstasy. Then, with infinite effort, they drew apart.

"You know he won't divorce me?" she whispered. "You know that . . . "

"Yes. I know."

"Dearest. Oh, my dearest . . . " She caught his face between her hands and drew it to her own. "You have given me back myself; you have made me again the person I thought was dead. I love you, Howard. I'll always love you . . . "

26

THE telephone rang before breakfast the next morning while Howard was on the stoep watching the early morning play of light on the mountains. Linda came out a few minutes later. He started in concern at her expression.

"What is it? What has happened?"

She walked unsteadily towards him, her eyes blind with shock. He caught hold of her. "What is it? Tell me."

"It's Joan. She's dead, Howard."

His eyes dilated. "Joan! Dead!"

"Yes. She has taken some disinfectant, some poison. It happened two days ago. They've only just found out. Brian's aunt 'phoned to tell me. Oh, Howard; isn't it horrible . . . ?"

He was dazed, unable to believe what he had heard.

"Why did she do it?" was the first question he asked.

"I don't know. It all seems so impossible."

His voice was harsh, accusing. "What does Brian say?"

"His aunt says he is in a terrible state. He wouldn't come near the 'phone. I shall have to go at once, Howard."

"Of course. I'll explain to the old people while you pack your things."

Tears suddenly flooded her hot eyes. He held her close, feeling them soaking through his thin shirt.

"Oh, Howard; she was such a nice kid . . . " Then she turned her head and moved away. "I'll go and pack. I won't be long."

* * *

They arrived back in town in the mid-morning. On Linda's instructions Howard drove straight to his bungalow. He threw out his cases and Linda took over the wheel.

"I won't come in," she told him. "I must get to Brian straight away. I shall have to 'phone through to Trevor if they haven't done so already."

"Let me know if there is anything I can do," he said heavily. "I hate leaving you like this."

"I'll 'phone you as soon as I can," she promised.

Their eyes met, then she swung the powerful car away and was gone.

* * *

In an effort to take his mind off the tragedy, Howard pottered about the bungalow for the rest of the morning. Since getting the keys he had only slept in it one night. It was a dilapidated little place but pleasantly situated, sharing a small rock-girt cove with two other bungalows. The mountains seemed even nearer here than at Clifton, appearing to rise sheer from the cliff behind the beach.

Linda 'phoned him after lunch. From her voice he knew she was extremely upset.

"Brian is taking it very badly," she told him. "I've had to call in Dr. Morkel to give him a sedative."

"What does he say? Can't he give any explanation?"

"He can't, Howard. And he's nearly

going mad with grief. He thought even more about her than I had guessed."

"But he must know something. She was sane; she wouldn't commit suicide without a reason. I could see she wasn't well when she came to the hospital. Surely he must have seen the same. He isn't a fool."

"He knew she was unhappy, but she wouldn't tell him the reason, or why she refused to go on seeing him."

"I don't believe him," Howard said savagely. "He's lying. He's done something he's ashamed of, and now he's terrified at the result."

"You're wrong, Howard. Somehow I know you're wrong. He quarrelled with her for not telling him why she would no longer see him, he admits that, but she must have known that was only because he loved her."

"Words can be terrible weapons in the hands of fools," he said bitterly.

"Try to relax, Howard. You've only been out of hospital a short while. Have a rest, and I'll try to get round tomorrow."

"She was such a nice kid," he muttered, unconsciously echoing Linda's own words. “What a rotten world to do this to her.”

* * *

Howard went into town that afternoon. He called on newspaper editors, both of whom were pleased with his final article from which they expected widespread controversy. He was shown a few of the thousands of letters that had poured in since his last article. It was clear that public interest was still at fever heat.

He then went out to Willisden. As he pulled up his car, he noticed the factory garage was completed and in use. Its metal shadow lay heavily over the tiny church.

The refectory door was open and he saw Father Hendricks sitting huddled over his stove. He had an unusual air of sorrow and dejection. Alarmed, Howard knocked and entered.

“What is it, Father?” Howard asked, interrupting the priest’s welcome. “It isn’t like you to look unhappy. What has happened?”

The old man sighed heavily. “It had

to come one day; she was very ill. And I should not fear death. It is peace and happiness and heaven. It is not eternal separation. It must not be that." He sighed again. "This week I have again wondered if I am fit to be a priest because in my sorrow I have doubted."

"Mrs. Stevens?" Howard asked slowly.

"Yes; *meneer*. It was her heart. She was dead in a few minutes."

"And the old man?"

"*Meneer*; there are some things so beautiful that without them life becomes too empty, too great a loneliness. It was so with him."

"You mean he is dead, too?"

"No; but his mind — it is already with her. They have taken him to hospital but he will not be there long. He talks to her as if they were together and young again. They will not be long divided."

Howard gazed out of the window at the narrow alley opposite. The world went on: the factories crashed and pounded, the lorries rumbled, men argued, men lied, men cheated. Something very beautiful had gone from the world and the world was too poor a thing to know of its loss. There was no pause, no intercession.

"How has Michael taken it?" Howard asked.

The priest shook his head sorrowfully. "He has suffered, that poor boy. Only a few of us know how much. I have tried to comfort him but it is as if he had gone mad." The old man's eyes were frightened. "He blasphemes the God who gave him life. He says there is no God, and only ignorant fools believe in Him. I can do nothing with him, *meneer*. I have failed when I am most needed . . . "

"Where is he now?"

"I dare not think, *meneer*. He has been discharged from the factory. I saw Lucy yesterday and she said he only comes home to take money from her. Twice he has beaten her. The poor child is terrified."

"I'll have a word with him," Howard said abruptly, going to the door. The old man looked up anxiously.

"It may not be wise, *meneer*. This hatred of his for the Europeans: it is strong and with him again."

"Don't worry," Howard said. "Good-bye, Father. I'll be round again shortly."

He crossed the road and went down the alley to see Lucy. Her face lightened on seeing him. He noticed a heavy bruise on one of her cheeks.

He refused her invitation to enter the house, coming to the point at once. "What is wrong with Michael?" he asked.

"I don't know, master," the girl whispered. Her swollen body, heavy with child, was trembling violently.

"Why is he behaving like this? Is it because of his mother's death?"

"He has been sullen for a month now," the girl muttered. "But on the day his mother died he seemed to go crazy. Father Hendricks had come round to speak to her. While he was here she had a heart attack and died. Michael went mad — he said terrible things about what he would do to the Europeans. I don't know what happened, master. I did not hear them. Later he cursed the people in the factory and lost his job. I don't know why, master . . . "

Howard gave her two pounds. "Buy yourself food with this — don't give any of it to him. Have you any idea where I can find him now?"

She shook her head. “No, master. He may come home this afternoon, but I am not sure.” Her eyes widened in sudden alarm. “He must not find you here. He is mad; he may do anything.”

“I’ll call round again in a few days,” Howard told her. “If you need anything in the meantime, tell Father Hendricks and he will ’phone me.”

He returned to his car and sat there waiting, hoping to see Michael. Half an hour passed. The factory siren screeched out, signalling the mid-afternoon break. A crowd of coloured workers poured out into the street, to squat on the pavement with mugs of tea in their hands.

Howard was about to give up his vigil when he saw Michael emerge from a side street farther down the road. He jumped from his car and went to meet him. Although only mid-afternoon the Coloured was half-drunk. He would have walked right past Howard had not the latter stepped in his way.

“I want a word with you, Michael.”

At first there was no recognition on the Coloured’s face, only a tightening of his features on seeing a European before him. Then his taut body relaxed and he muttered something thickly in Afrikaans.

"What's all this I've been hearing about you?" Howard asked. "I'm very sorry to hear about your parents, but you mustn't go to pieces. You have Lucy to think about."

Michael's eyes narrowed. He did not speak.

"It's none of my business, I know," Howard went on. "But someone has to tell you. You can't let your wife starve."

"Leave me alone," the Coloured suddenly spat. "I owe you nothing; I paid you back that night I took you to the *shebeen*. Leave me alone."

"I never said you owed me anything. But you have a debt to your wife and Father Hendricks."

"I said leave me alone! I want nothing to do with any bloody European."

"What's come over you?" Howard snapped.

The Coloured moved forward menacingly. "Get out of my way. Mind your own bloody business, white man. *Neut weg! Voertsek!*"

Howard stared at him grimly, fighting

to keep down his rising temper.

"*Voertsek*, you white devil," Michael yelled. "*Voertsek*, or I'll kick you out of the way."

Howard felt himself being pushed roughly aside. There was a shout of laughter from the watching crowd of factory workers. White with rage, Howard fought a grim battle with himself.

He returned to his car, drove round a couple of blocks, and pulled up again. He lighted a cigarette with difficulty; his whole body was still trembling. All the prejudices of his early upbringing had been spewed to the surface during those last few seconds with Michael. He had held the fury in check, but the emotional battle had exhausted him. He sat quite still, shaken and chastened by the experience. He was aware that the part of his mind conditioned by his upbringing was making the most of Michael's conduct, doing all it could to undermine his new faith in the non-Europeans.

A car passed him at that moment, heading in the direction of Mitchell's factory. A few minutes later he heard a man's metallic voice, obviously amplified by some device inside the car, haranguing the factory hands. The address was in English, being meant for the Europeans inside the factory as well as the workers outside.

"You all know of Umzoni, how he was shot and arrested for fighting our battle. You all know his wish, that we should strike in protest of the laws that are making us slaves. The first strike day has been chosen. It is the twenty-seventh of April.

"You will not be alone in this strike. All over the province, in the mines, on the docks, on the farms, in the factories, your fellow-workers will be with you. Many Europeans, who realize the injustices done to us, will be on our side.

"Do nothing violent. Give the authorities no excuse to attack you. Your staying from work will be warning enough."

The voice rose a tone. "And you who employ these men — help them in their cause. Make this strike easy for them. Remember; despotism is on the move, we must all, employers and workers alike, close our ranks against it. Democracy is at stake. Remember what it will mean to you if *apartheid* drives non-European labour into a general strike. Make no mistake — this will happen unless the laws are altered. Help us now before it is too late. Help us to make the strike a success. Remember the twenty-seventh of April!"

On the way home, at the traffic lights at Woodstock, Howard had a leaflet pushed through his open car window.

CITIZENS [it read], DEFEND DEMOCRACY.

STRIKE ON THE 27th OF APRIL.

Don't work,
Don't buy,
Don't sell,

Stay quietly at home on the 27th of April and make the One Day strike a complete success.

* * *

The Mills that grind exceedingly fine were beginning to turn.

27

"OF course I'm not going to help 'em. Do you think I'm crazy? They'll be all the more likely to have a general strike if they get away with this one. Besides, it would look as if we were taking sides, and we can't afford that. There's no time for politics or sentiment in business. No, by George, they're getting nothing out of me — just the reverse, in fact . . .

"Listen, Thompson; this is what I want you to do. Put notices all round the factory that any man who doesn't come in on Friday loses his job. That'll bring 'em in. You know why? Because a lot of 'em will be homeless next week when I've sold their houses. They won't dare lose their jobs as well, or they're finished.

"Right; then that's settled. Get those notices up where they can't miss 'em, Thompson. Once let these fellows get away with a thing like this, and there'd be no stopping 'em. We've got to frighten 'em off this idea of a general strike by showing 'em who is the boss . . . "

* * *

Everywhere dark-faced, grim-featured men were mingling with groups of non-European workers. Everywhere the message was the same.

"This will be the day you have been saving for. Strike on Friday the twenty-seventh. Strike, but show no violence. Strike for Umzoni. Let the Europeans see we are united. Do it for your children's sakes; do it for the future . . . "

And sometimes voices were raised to the employers sitting inside in their offices. "Let your workers off for the day. It is as much your fight as theirs. You know you cannot do without us, any more than we can do without you. Help us and we shall not forget . . . "

Some employers listened, grave-faced. Others 'phoned for the police.

"*Ag*; they'll never do it. They can't stick together like that. In any case, they can't afford to miss a day's pay."

"Don't be too sure. They're starting to fight back in the most dangerous way they can. This is more serious than most people realize. They're all working together: the Coloureds, the Natives and the Asiatics. Nothing like this has ever happened before . . . "

"Aw; these scares always fizzle out. What's on at the Plaza tonight?"

"This chap, Shaw, couldn't have picked a worse time for his article. Have you read it? My God; he hits out at everything and everybody . . . "

"Have you read Shaw? You know, I like that idea of a neutral meeting-place where there is no Colour Bar. A place where one could chat on equal terms with a non-European. What a wonderful safety valve it would be . . . "

"Really, this fellow Shaw has gone too far this time. Dash it all, he could have been a little more selective about whom he attacks. I mean, one doesn't mind his hammering the Nationalists, but now he has lumped us all together. Re-educate the Europeans! The damned cheek . . . ”

“My dear; he actually suggests giving Kaffirs equal rights. I know he said only the educated ones, but what difference does that make? They’re still black, aren’t they? Fancy sitting next to one in the bioscope! Or being next to one in church! I’m going to write to the newspapers . . . ”

“We’ve never considered that angle, have we? Educate the Europeans! There’s a lot in it, Bob. Look at our crop of youngsters today: they’re a hundred times kinder to their animals than to the non-Europeans. There’s an animal clinic in Cape Town now that cost £15,000 to build. And that’s while Coloured kids root in dustbins for food in Willisden and Windermere . . . ”

“They should kick the bastard out of the country, or else throw him in jail. A couple of years in Roeland Street would straighten him up . . . ”

"He's right. We need them just as they need us. And he's not suggesting social integration. As a matter of fact, from the psychological angle, there is far less likelihood of miscegenation once the non-European has lost his sense of inferiority . . ."

"Liberal economists have told us that for years. If we raised the living standards of our non-Europeans we would boom. Think of it! Their average income is round about £45 a year. Think of the increased buying power if that was stepped up to three or four hundred. After all, there are over eight million of them . . ."

"I've often thought of that. Think of the appalling waste of brains and labour. Potential fitters and turners only allowed to sweep out workshops: potential accountants running errands for office boys. In our firm the tea boy is a qualified schoolmaster. The waste of it . . ."

"The *skelm*. If a man hasn't any pride in his race, what good is he? The

Germans didn't degenerate because they believed themselves the Master Race. They nearly conquered the world. If it had not been for the jealousy of England and America . . . "

Words. Millions of words. And as they were spoken the last weeks of April slipped away. On the slopes of the mountain the bush was dry from the heat of the long summer. The lizards lay somnolent among the warm rocks. It was quiet up there, as silent as an empty cathedral.

But in the city at its feet, in the tiny houses and factories, the ants that were men scurried about ceaselessly. To and fro they went, living their little lives. Children were born, youths became men, men loved, and children were born again. Men did good and men did evil. And when their little act was over, men died — the one act common to them all.

One of these was an old man who had known contempt, derision, and despair. A man who had travelled a long, harsh road down which he had been whipped and stoned. A man whose pilgrimage had led him into the stony desert of loneliness, but where he had never faltered. A man who had found himself and so found his God by being true to his heart and his conscience.

And because of this, life, which had tormented him over the long years, relented at last. He was allowed to die, soon after the one for whom he had suffered had died. And after his death — because his son, who was drinking in a *shebeen*, heard of it and made his wish known — he was not buried where Europeans are buried, but instead laid in the humbler cemetery of the coloured folk, where lay his wife. He was put by her side. As it had been in life, so it was now in death. No colour bar could hurt and grieve them now. They had passed on to a land where the laws were different — where men are judged not on the colour of their skins but on the purity of their souls. The old couple were very safe now.

28

APRIL the twenty-seventh was another mellow autumn day. Among the lower pine plantation of Devil's Peak that overlooked the industrial suburbs of Woodstock, Salt River and Observatory, it was more restful than ever. The distant sounds were not there: the far-off rumble of lorries and machines, the shrill hoots of sirens. As the sun rose higher the city remained inert in a restless, fevered sleep.

Housewives looked in vain for their morning milk. Factory executives saw their machines silent and idle. Ships lay in harbour, rising and falling on the sullen swell, their cargoes untouched in their holds. In a hundred ways, in a thousand ways, the city and the countryside around it lay paralysed.

Only a few factories operated that day. One of these was in Willisden. In the hearts of at least half its workers a lonely battle was fought that morning. In three days one's own family or one's relations would be thrown out into the street, to be homeless with the winter fast approaching. Could a man risk losing his job as well as his home? Was it right to bring despair to the eyes of one's wife and hunger to one's children? Was any cause, even this one, as important as that? What should one do . . . ?

But wait. That is Solomons over there, and he is going. See, he has his lunch-tin in his hand. And running to catch him up is Gentry . . . Then they have won. They have won because we are too poor. To strike, to fight back, one has to have money, one must have food for one's belly. "Yes; I am going, mama. Yes; I will be careful. Yes; that I will be. *Totsiens*, mama . . ."

⋆ ⋆ ⋆

Into the factory the long stream of workers entered. One by one, step by step: the time clocks checking their arrival. In the offices the tensed faces of the European executives began to relax.

"You've got to hand it to Mitchell.

He's a shrewd devil, that's how he has got where he is. There's hardly another factory operating in town, and yet look at us. We've got at least two-thirds of them in."

In the factory the main switch was thrown and metal wheels began clanking out their mockery to the workers around them.

"Strike, strike, strike! Strike, strike, strike . . . !" Men clenched their hands and sank teeth into lips at the sound of it.

* * *

"Well, that's fine. Just as I thought." Trevor Mitchell put down the receiver, slapped his thigh contentedly and swung round on his son. "That was Thompson from the factory. Everything's quiet there and Slabbert, the foreman, seems to be having no trouble with the men. Over four hundred of 'em have come in. He can get by with them."

"Do you still want to go round?"

"Yes; I want to be there over the lunch-hour. That's the danger time. Once that's over there'll be nothing to worry about. You can take me out there in that new sports car of yours. How's it going?"

Interest stirred on Brian's pale face. "Very well. It was awfully decent of you . . ."

Mitchell's plump hand waved deprecatingly. "Nonsense, my boy. It was time you had a new one. Well; I think we'd better get moving. I've a couple of other calls to make first, so we won't be there much before twelve as it is."

* * *

They arrived in Willisden at a quarter-to-twelve. After a brief chat with Barker, the secretary, Mitchell took Brian into the works manager's office. Thompson, a thin, dark-haired man, rose deferentially as they entered.

"Well; how is it now?" Mitchell asked. "Still quiet?"

"Still quiet, sir. They're a bit sullen, of course, but I think it's going to be all right. I've told Slabbert to take it easy with them today."

“Have you had any agitators round yet?”

Thompson shook his head. “No, sir.”

“Lunch-time’s the time to watch,” Mitchell grunted. “They’ll have their needle in this place once they hear we’re operating. If they do come, I want ’em moving at once, understand? I think I’d better stay a while with you. What time do you go to lunch these days?”

“Twelve-thirty — the same time as the clerical staff. The men break at twelve.”

“You’d better stay here today. Can you send out for some lunch?”

“I’ve brought it,” Thompson told him. “Most of the clerks and typists have done the same. They didn’t want to go out in case there was any trouble.”

The financier nodded. The minute hand of the electric-clock on the wall moved nearer twelve o’clock.

* * *

Outside the factory, in the alley at its side, groups of men were collecting. Men whose eyes moved shiftily and who dropped words from the corners of their mouths. Men who had an air of vicious purpose about them, a look of malignity on their gaunt faces. Michael was there, his face half-covered by a ragged cap. He stood apart from the others. His eyes, as savage as those of a hungry wolf, were fixed on the factory.

Just before noon a car drew up at the entrance to the alley, pulling away immediately its two passengers had jumped out. They were Swartz and Vulisango. The waiting men stiffened expectantly. Swartz stopped by Michael and muttered to him in Afrikaans. Michael answered with a curt nod. Swartz passed on to the other *skollies*. Vulisango followed him, his repellant face evil with anticipation.

★ ★ ★

The banshee wail of the factory siren rose and fell. The clank of machinery stopped abruptly as the main motor switch was thrown off. Men began streaming out from the gates on to the pavements. There was no life or laughter in them. They broke up into sullen groups and sat on the pavements to eat their sandwiches. Among them, unobserved at first, slipped the men from the alley with whispers and threats.

Mitchell was staring out through the office window. Suddenly he gripped Thompson's arm and pointed.

"You see that chap in the cap over there? Isn't that Stevens, the coon you pointed out to me — the one Shaw recommended? I thought you said you'd given him the sack."

"I have, sir."

"Then what's he doing out there?" Mitchell grunted. "Call Slabbert, will you?"

Thompson hurried out, to return with Slabbert, the foreman. Slabbert was a stocky, square-headed fellow with close-cropped, ginger hair. Mitchell pointed Michael out to him.

"That's him all right," Slabbert grunted. "But I don't know what he's doin' round here."

There was a sudden hush outside, then a man's harsh voice. Through the window they saw the sinewy figure of Swartz standing in the middle of the road with the curious factory hands crowding around him.

"Now do you see what I mean?" he shouted. "Now do you see why striking is no use — why Umzoni was a fool and a weak woman? Why are you here today? Because of injustice. Because in three days you are to be kicked from your homes. Because you will lose your jobs if you strike. You will never beat the European this way. You will only learn what a swine he is. There is only one way to get your rights — to fight for them!"

There were mutters from the listening men. A few cries of assent were heard. Mitchell turned sharply on Thompson.

"You hear him? Get outside and move him, you and Slabbert. Hurry, or he'll have the lot of them."

Thompson hesitated. His face had turned pale.

"Go on!" Mitchell shouted, staring at him. "What's the matter with you?"

Slabbert was already on his way. Thompson followed him slowly. Mitchell looked after him in disgust as he picked up the telephone.

"The fellow's as yellow as a quince," he grunted. "See his face?"

"Do you think they'll be safe?" Brian asked. "That Coloured looks a pretty tough customer."

"Tough be damned! They're all talk. A couple of policemen will shift the lot of them. Slabbert himself will probably handle 'em. What the devil's wrong with this 'phone? Operator, where are you? Operator."

There was a sudden uproar outside. Brian ran to the window. Slabbert's loud coarse voice sounded over the din.

"That's enough. Get inside, the lot of you."

"*Voertsek*," Swartz yelled back. "Get inside yourself, you bloody white man."

Another shout came from the *skollies*, a mixture of merriment and menace.

"You bastard!" Slabbert screamed. A door slammed and the crowd jeered again.

"They really mean business," Brian said breathlessly. His father cursed, slammed down the receiver, and pushed him to the door.

"Go and find out what has happened

to the 'phone. We must get hold of the police."

Slabbert and Thompson brushed by Brian in the corridor. They entered the office. Thompson's face was ashen with fear. Slabbert was cursing.

"Have you 'phoned the police?" Thompson asked Mitchell.

"The 'phone isn't working," Mitchell told him tersely. "My son has gone to see what the trouble is."

Brian returned a few seconds later. "They're all the same," he told his father. "The switchboard girl says they went dead a few minutes after twelve."

Thompson looked at the others in terror. "They've cut the line. My God; they've got us now."

Mitchell was staring through the window. "Where's that coon, Stevens, gone?" he growled. "I can't see him among the crowd. I wonder what he's up to."

He turned from the window, his pouched eyes narrowed. "He knows the place well. I wonder if he cut the line. He might still be inside the building."

Slabbert nodded and ran out into the

factory. Brian turned to his father in surprise.

"But why should he? You did him a good turn. He can't blame you for his getting the sack."

"He's a bad devil," Mitchell muttered. "I've heard all about him from Slabbert."

Slabbert burst into the office, his eyes wide with astonishment. "The factory's on fire! Two of the boys saw that bastard Stevens throwing petrol on the benches and walls."

They ran to the factory door, then drew back. A sheet of flame, roaring with unnatural ferocity, was sweeping across the floor towards them. Slabbert slammed the door closed.

"The place will be burned out in no time," he grunted. "We'll have to get out through the main entrance."

They ran back into the administration section, to be surrounded immediately by panic-stricken typists and clerks. The flustered secretary ran up to Slabbert.

"You'll have to send one of your boys to call the police," he told the foreman. "Some of the girls are getting hysterical. The noise outside is frightening them."

Slabbert grinned. "They'll be a damn sight more hysterical when you tell 'em the factory's on fire. I've no one to send. All my boys are outside now, listening to the sermon."

Not lacking in animal courage, Slabbert was enjoying the temporary leadership the situation had given him. The works manager was speechless with fear and Mitchell had now lost a great deal of his bluster.

Brian took his father's arm. "We can't stay here," he said. "Hadn't we better all go to our cars and drive off to the police? There are enough cars to take everybody. We'll be safe — they daren't attack us."

As if to deny his words, there was a deafening roar from the crowd outside. Mitchell paled.

"Better wait," he muttered. "The police must hear of the fire soon. That crowd's dangerous."

There was a sudden hysterical yell behind them. "Fire! The factory's on fire . . ."

In a moment the corridor was filled with a mad, scrambling crowd of clerks and typists struggling to escape. Brian and his father were swept with them through the entrance into the street.

The street was now packed with people. It seemed half Willisden had heard of the trouble and come hurrying to see it. In spite of the incitement, no attacks were made on the Europeans as they left the building. Swartz's *skollies* tried to get at them, but the rest of the crowd, workers included, held them back. Insults were thrown, but that was all. The frightened Europeans made their hurried way to their cars. Brian's car was parked some way down the road and he pushed his father through the dense crowd towards it. As they passed the factory building they saw flames glowing through the windows and dense smoke pouring out through its roof. The roar of the fire could be heard clearly over the shouts of the crowd . . .

Swartz, hemmed in by the crowd, saw them go. He pointed them out to Vulisango, who was at his side. The huge negro nodded, his blubbery lips agape with anticipation. The two of them fought their way through the packed crowd.

Brian and his father reached their car without incident, both breathing more freely when they were inside. Brian was reaching for his ignition key when a Coloured shouldered his way through the surrounding crowd and leaned over the open car. It was Michael.

His face was twisted in a snarl of hate as he stared down at Trevor Mitchell. "Bloody white man," he spat.

Suddenly, without warning, he sprang on the car bonnet and yelled out to the crowd around.

"*Hier is hy!* Here is the man you want. Here is *Meneer* Mitchell. This is the one who starves your children and makes your women weep. And you let him go. You forgive him . . . You forgive him when he drives you from your homes, when he charges you for a rotten piece of sand only fit to dig a grave in. *Meneer* Mitchell — who grows fat on the flesh and blood of children . . . "

The faces round the car were threatening now. Brian watched them in fascinated terror. His father moaned in fear. "Hurry up, for God's sake. They'll tear us to pieces."

Brian revved up his engine but the crowd were packed tightly ahead of the car. He looked helplessly at his father. "I can't run over them," he muttered.

"*Meneer* Mitchell," Michael yelled. "Who rents those *pondokkies* to you. Who never spends a penny on them because only the Coons and Kaffirs live in them. *Meneer* Mitchell: who kicks you into the gutter if your rent is one day late. Oh; you never see him. Someone else does his filthy work for him. But I know him. I have good reason to know him. *Meneer* Mitchell . . ."

"Come over here," the financier muttered, pulling Brian from the driver's seat and taking his place.

Michael looked down and showed his teeth in a grin of hate.

"Don't try to drive away yet," he snarled. "We'll say when you can go."

Desperately the financier threw in the gears. Michael leapt to the ground as the car lurched forward. Men and women scattered in all directions. Brian felt a bump and heard a woman's frenzied scream. The crowd let out an enraged yell.

Suddenly two men leapt into the car. Brian saw one was a huge negro. The other he did not see, his terrified eyes being on his father, whom he tried to protect. He was torn savagely from his seat and hurled to the ground. Dazed, he tried to rise as a terrified scream came from the car. He heard the thud of blows and the helpless screams of his father. Through it came the piercing, hopeless wail of a woman.

Brian made one last effort to rise, reached one knee, then saw the gleam of a knife. He clutched at the door of the car . . . there was a last scream from his father that bubbled horribly away . . . then he was tossed half-senseless to the pavement as the crowd ran before the attack of the police.

* * *

He lay a few moments before lifting himself painfully to his feet. The road was almost deserted: the police pursuing the crowd down side streets and alleys. In the distance came the sound of shots and the screams of the injured and the dying. A siren wailed up the road as a fire-engine pulled to a halt outside the blazing factory. The heat from it could now be felt on the road. Great tongues of flame were sweeping through the garage and licking at the little church huddled alongside.

Brian saw and heard none of these things. His eyes were fixed in horror on the whimpering figure of a Coloured woman who was kneeling almost under the front wheels of the car. In her arms was a silent child, its body broken and still. On the road, mixing with the dust, a red gout of blood was running into the gutter. The woman moaned, rocking backwards and forwards in a paroxysm of grief.

Brian rose to his feet to go to her. A shout sounded behind him, and as he turned his eyes fell on the slumped figure of his father who was hanging over the driving wheel of the car. From a gash in the back of his jacket a dark stain was spreading ominously.

A policeman ran alongside him and grabbed his arm.

"Come along — you can't stay here!"

Brian pointed to his father and the moaning woman on the road. "My father, and her . . . I can't leave them . . . "

"I'll get them into an ambulance," the policeman told him. Blowing a whistle he beckoned to an ambulance farther down the road. It moved towards them.

"You'd better go along," the policeman told Brian when the others had been carried inside. Blindly Brian entered, and the ambulance pulled away, its siren screaming like a lost soul . . .

* * *

And behind them they left terror, agony, and hate. For, in the way of these things, the innocent were the greatest sufferers. Violence begot violence, fear begot fear, and like a pestilence both spread to the guiltless. They in their suffering cried out at the injustice and in their hearts the seed of more bloodshed was sown. Only in the few — and it seems there can be only a few whose hearts are incapable of bitterness — was there nothing but sorrow. One of these stood outside his little church and in silence watched the flames devour it. The fire-engines were busy on the garage and factory; there was no time to spare on a tiny, wooden church.

With eyes that held all the sufferings of mankind, Father Hendricks watched the fire devour the simple thing he had loved so well. The end came suddenly. The roof collapsed and the flames leapt high in the air, like devils triumphant at the destruction of their ancient enemy. And then, because there are some things no human heart can endure to watch, the old man turned and with bowed back shuffled away down the lonely road.

29

"HOWARD, is that you? Linda here. Thank God you're home. Something terrible has happened. Brian has just 'phoned from hospital. There has been a riot outside the Willisden factory and Trevor has been stabbed. Yes; it's serious. Will you take me: I haven't a car here. Yes; I'm ready now. Please hurry . . ."

⋆ ⋆ ⋆

In the hospital it was quiet: they could hear the distant sound of traffic. Linda's white face stared at Howard across the waiting-room.

"Why is Brian so long? I must see Trevor. He mustn't die without my seeing him."

"They'll let you see him," Howard muttered.

Her shocked voice ran on. "I can't believe it. To be knifed in the back like this. God; it's horrible. He wasn't a politician; the laws weren't his fault. Why don't they hurry up . . . ?"

A nurse appeared in the doorway. "Please come now, Mrs. Mitchell."

Howard gripped Linda's hand tightly, then she followed the nurse and was gone. A few seconds later Brian entered the room. His face was dazed with shock. Howard put an arm round him and tried to lead him to a seat.

"Come and sit down," he urged. "Would you like a cigarette?"

Brian shook his head. His eyes were staring wildly round the room. Howard watched him in alarm. Coming so soon after Joan's death, this shock was enough to turn the boy's mind.

"He's dying," Brian said suddenly. "He lost consciousness while I was in there." There was a strange harshness about his voice, a stunned bitterness that Howard did not fully understand. He stood silent, undecided on the right words to use.

"I'm going," Brian said, almost defiantly. "Please tell Linda."

"Shouldn't you stay — in case

anything happens?"

"I'm going," the boy said again. He turned and ran from the room. The seconds stumbled by.

Linda appeared with a face devoid of all expression. "Please take me home," was all she said. The air of finality in her words told Howard the rest. They were half-way to Clifton before she spoke again.

"He was unconscious when I went in," she said bitterly. "And he died while I waited."

She did not speak again until they reached her bungalow. She sat staring white-faced through the windscreen. He waited silently. She turned to him at last.

"They murdered him. You realize that, don't you?"

He bowed his head without answering.

"Oh; he was no angel," she cried. "He had his faults. But he was too good to die with a knife in his back."

He was acutely aware of her hostility. He could not speak.

"Why don't you defend them?" she cried. "You and Father Hendricks are good at that — at painting them in glowing colours and convincing gullible fools like me. Trevor tried to tell me you were wrong, but I believed you because I wanted to believe you. You, with your deluded, credulous love of the underdog! You, with your altruism! God help me," and she choked over the words. "I even found a job for the man who killed him."

He started at that. She laughed hysterically.

"You didn't know it was your Michael who roused the mob to put a knife in his back, did you? Brian said it might even have been he who used it. That's the gratitude these people have. I hate them now. They killed him, but you aren't guiltless with your articles. You know that, don't you?"

He winced. She went on slowly now, as if to herself.

"I never loved him, but women can live with a man if they respect him. And I respected him well enough until you came along. I never questioned his ideas — they had all worked well enough. It wasn't until you came along that I began thinking differently again — the way I had thought as a girl. You, with your talk about justice and the inherent decency of all mankind. Or was it Father Hendricks or Joan who said that? I can't remember . . . "

Her voice rose in anguish as she turned to face him. "You can't help thinking something of a man you've lived with for years — not when you know he loved you and gave you all he could give. I think he would have withdrawn that ejection notice for me if I hadn't gone to court. It wouldn't have been so bad if we'd parted friends, but last night" — and she sucked in her breath at the memory — "we had a terrible quarrel over you. That was why I wanted so much to speak to him once more. And now he's dead. Dead — and I'll never be able to tell him I'm sorry . . . " Her sobs were dry, harsh things that racked her body.

She composed herself and turned her face to Howard again. "I'm sorry. Some of us see things one way and some another. Perhaps I shouldn't blame you. But you do understand why we must say good-bye now, don't you?"

He tried to speak, but his throat was dry and closed. She held out her hand. It touched his briefly, then moved quickly away.

"Thanks for everything, Howard. I'm sorry it has to end like this, but there isn't any other way, is there?"

Her eyes wandered over him, almost wistfully, then she was gone and he alone in the car. Good-bye! It has to be good-bye because the people you influenced me into helping have killed my husband, and if we lived together a thousand years, every day of it we would see his body like a drawn, bloody sword between us . . .

With a curse he came to life and drove like a madman out to Willisden. There was no plan in his mind, nothing but an insane desire to find out at any cost why this had happened. Was she right; was there no gratitude in these people? Must the laws be harsh to keep them peaceable? Was his newly found faith to be shattered into a thousand splinters?

He pulled up outside the church and

stared in horror at its gutted ruins. Dear God; not this. This had been more than a building: it had been a shrine, hallowed by a thousand acts of love and faith. A thing like this could not perish if there was a God and He was just to man. As he stared at the ruins, something broke inside him and bitterness seared his soul like vitriol. This church had been a challenge to all who sneered that goodness could not live among these slums and people. Were these ruins, then, a symbol?

Like a crazed man he jumped from the car and ran down the alley opposite. The door was open and he burst into the front room. Lucy was lying sobbing on the bed.

"Where is Michael?" he demanded harshly. "Tell me, quickly."

The look of welcome faded from the girl's face. She stared up at him fearfully. "I don't know, master."

"Don't lie. Where is he?"

"I don't know, master," she sobbed. "Someone said he ran away with Swartz. If I knew I would go after him myself . . . "

"Where would Swartz go? Into the location?"

"I don't know, master. Some say he has a hide-out up the other side of the mountain. But I don't know . . . "

Howard scribbled his address and telephone number on a sheet of paper and handed it to her.

"If Michael comes back to you, go out to a 'phone-box and ring me. Immediately, do you understand? Here's the money."

"Yes, master," she muttered.

Without another word Howard left the house and returned to his car. His mind was dulled now, worn out with disappointment. He drove back to his bungalow. He had not been there five minutes before the telephone rang. It was Morkcl.

"Howard? Man; I've been trying to get you for the last hour. This is a shocking business about Mitchell. I was out on a case when he was brought in. How are his family taking it?"

Howard told him. Morkel was sympathetic. "I'm sorry for the boy. He's gone through enough recently. But I felt all along these chaps could never organize a peaceful strike . . . "

Morkel did not pursue the point when Howard made no reply. "But that isn't all I 'phoned about, lad. This hasn't been released to the Press yet. Umzoni has escaped. The police-van that was taking him from hospital to jail this afternoon ran into an ambush. There's been a bit of smart intelligence work somewhere. The police didn't have time to draw their guns before the coons were on them. They were bound and gagged and left inside the van. I thought you'd like the news red-hot."

"Thanks, Jannie. It's good of you to 'phone."

"What's the matter, lad? You sound half-dead."

"I'm all right," Howard muttered. "I'll drop round to see you tomorrow."

He put the receiver down and tried to think what Umzoni's escape would mean. But there was no room in his mind for anything but Linda and her parting words. That and his bitterness, which scourged him like a thousand whips.

* * *

The wind began rising towards sunset. It moaned over the cliff behind the bungalow and sent the manatocka trees reeling in torment. Fishing boats in the bay took warning and turned for home, fighting in the spindrift that was torn in white sheets from the sea. The bungalow creaked and groaned as if in agony.

Unable to relax, Howard went out on the beach among the rocks. Ignoring the buffeting wind, he stood looking back at the mountain that rose in massive folds behind his bungalow. Somewhere up there were Swartz and Michael — Michael, who, after acknowledging his debt and the debt of his people to Linda, had so brutally betrayed her. Beside it, Howard's own betrayal faded into insignificance. He knew the fight it had been for Linda, but he knew also the glory of her victory. He had seen it in her eyes, heard it in her voice, after she had witnessed for Father Hendricks. She had found herself again, and her happiness had been a living thing.

And now reaction would turn her soul

to brittle glass. His hands clenched as he stared up at the mountain, wishing some guiding finger would point out Swartz's hiding-place so that he could find Michael and wring from him the reason for his treachery.

What reason? The triumphant sceptic in his mind sneered at him. How much proof did he need to convince him of his delusions regarding the non-Europeans? In his despair he called on the memory of Joan Viljoen to help him; tried to find faith in her faith, but his shoulders sagged. She was dead. The world she had believed in so ardently had killed her, as it killed anyone whose faith was greater than his reason.

With heavy steps he trudged across the sand to his bungalow. He entered the lounge, to halt in amazement.

Two men stood in the centre of the room, facing him. One was Umzoni, dressed in an old pair of trousers and a tattered shirt. He looked older: his face was drawn, with the skin tight over his high cheekbones. There was a grimness about his eyes and mouth that Howard had not seen before.

Howard found his voice. “What are you doing here? What do you want?”

The Zulu made no apology for his uninvited entry. His reply was simple and direct. “I need your help, Mr. Shaw.”

“My help! What do you mean?”

“I want you to come up the mountain with us. To watch. And then to come back and report in the Press what you have seen.”

“I don’t understand you,” Howard said curtly.

The Zulu motioned towards the window. “The curtains — will you close them, please?”

Howard hesitated, then drew the curtains across. He switched on the light.

Umzoni stepped closer. “It is this way, Mr. Shaw. It was Swartz who warned the police about my meeting, hoping to get rid of me and at the same time cause bitterness among my followers.” The Zulu’s voice was harsh. “He could hardly have been more successful. But that was not all. It was he who told the police of my hiding-place, so getting Father Hendricks and me arrested. And it was he who turned the strike into a riot today, so undoing all I have worked for . . . ”

“I know most of this and I’ve guessed the rest,” Howard broke in abruptly. “I wanted to get my hands on Michael, but he’s gone off with Swartz. They’ve taken to some hide-out up the mountain. It would take a battalion to find them.”

“We can find them,” Umzoni said grimly. “After the riot some of my men captured one of Swartz’s *skollies*. They made him talk.” The Zulu pointed to his companion, a small, wizened Coloured of indeterminate age who seemed in awe of the giant negro. “Pretorius here knows the mountain well and thinks he can find the hide-out. It seems another man has gone with them — an African called Vulisango whom I know of. They are hoping to hide up there until the hue and cry dies down. We are going after them. But we must hurry. It is believed the police captured one or two of Swartz’s followers. If so, they might also learn of his hiding-place. I must reach him before they do . . . ”

“Why?” Howard asked.

"Why?" The Zulu's voice suddenly turned hoarse with passion. "You ask why, when all I have worked for may have been undone! I could have lived overseas as a respected citizen. Instead, I made it my life's work to try to emancipate my people. I came back and have lived ever since as a hunted rat. Time and again I have hated, time and again I have felt the desire to strike back against the Europeans. But each time I held back the devils within me. Never once have I preached violence: never once has a drop of blood been shed by my followers, except in self-defence. The strike today was peaceful everywhere, except in one place — in Willisden where Swartz brought his hyenas . . . "

The veins were standing out on the Zulu's forehead. "My movement will take the blame for that riot. The Europeans will use it as propaganda to prove our motives were not peaceful. That is why I thank God I was rescued today and was able to get your address through Michael's wife. It gives me a chance to kill that propaganda, if you will help me."

"How?" asked Howard, curious now.

"I want you to witness that we non-Europeans here do not let murderers and thieves lead us in our struggle. I want you to witness how we deal our own justice to those that live by the knife."

"Do you include Michael?"

"I do not know why he turned traitor. I hope to find out. But the others — "

"You intend to kill," Howard finished, staring at the unarmed negro.

Umzoni's face was an ebony mask of relentless purpose, his eyes implacable. "If God gives me the strength, yes."

⋆ ⋆ ⋆

High above Bakoven the wind was a wild thing, sweeping in fierce gusts from the towering peaks ahead. The sun had set and below the darkness was spreading like mist and welling slowly upwards.

Umzoni was setting a killing pace through the thick bush. Howard, not yet fully recovered from his injuries, felt his legs aching and his heart pounding. The small coloured man was in real distress. Twice he stumbled and fell, and at last could go on no longer without rest. He sagged down on a rock, struggling for breath.

Umzoni eyed him impatiently, snapping a question in Afrikaans. The man lifted his head and pointed to a rocky buttress that rose sheer from the foothills ahead of them. The Zulu turned to Howard with gleaming eyes.

"He says the hide-out is somewhere along the base of that buttress. If he is right, we are getting close to them. Come . . . "

Howard motioned at the gasping Pretorius. Umzoni shook his head impatiently. "We can leave him here. I shall not need him any more." He spoke to the seated man, who nodded.

"He will make his own way back," Umzoni told Howard. "I cannot waste any more time. Listen! What was that?"

The mad wind had dropped for a moment. In the hush Howard heard the distant sound of a police-whistle. It was followed by another, from a different direction. Then the wind came booming back through the ravines, drowning all other sounds.

"Down," Umzoni muttered, crouching

low among the bushes. Howard followed his example. The Zulu cursed.

"I thought this might happen. His followers have given him away. Can you see the police?"

Howard was peering through a clump of rocks. Far below them, just visible in the rising gloom, he saw a line of tiny, uniformed figures making their way up the steep, bush-covered slopes. He pointed them out to the Zulu, who nodded, saying:

"There is still time to reach Swartz first, but I must hurry." He turned to Howard. "I had hoped this would not happen. Now it is better you go back. You must not be seen with me."

"You can't tackle two men by yourself — three, if Michael helps them," Howard muttered. "Go on. I'll follow you."

"This is not your fight, Mr. Shaw. You have done enough for us already."

"I'm not doing this for you or anybody else," Howard gritted. "I'm here because I want Michael."

Umzoni studied his bitter face, then nodded. With a last word to Pretorius, he began running up the mountainside, crouching and taking advantage of all available cover. Howard followed him. They had gone about a hundred yards when they noticed a sullen red glow staining the mountain above them.

Umzoni halted a moment. "Swartz," he growled. "He has seen the police and started a bush fire to hold them off until he gets away."

Howard's face tightened. He knew the savagery of bush fires. In this wind the vanguard of the flames would reach the speed of a racing horse.

Umzoni pointed to the right. "We shall have to go round it. Come!"

There was no arguing with the vengeful Zulu, although there was great danger that the fire would beat back and trap them. Changing direction slightly, they plunged on. The glow ahead of them grew brighter. From the length of the fire it was clear it had been started at a number of points. As they struggled on, a pin point of light appeared a few hundred yards to the right of the main fire. It flickered, then waxed ominously.

Umzoni's voice sounded triumphantly over the howling wind. "There's one of them now. Look!"

A tiny figure was silhouetted against the new fire before vanishing into the dark background.

The Zulu redoubled his efforts. Sweat poured down Howard's face in his efforts to keep pace with him. Bushes tore at his legs, boulders rolled under his sliding feet. Umzoni paused a moment, pointing at the dark gap between the two fires.

"We must go faster. We must get through before the two fires meet."

Howard saw with alarm that the recently started fire was being blown sidewards at frightening speed. The gap between the flaming infernos was closing by the second. If it closed before they passed through, their lives would be in great peril. With the original fire already below them on their left flank and encircling their rear, they stood every chance of being cut off. The noise of the fires could now be heard over the roar of the wind as a deep and ominous thunder. Clumps of pine trees yards ahead of the conflagration, with their natural oils turned to gas by the intense heat, were exploding like giant, kerosene-soaked torches.

With hearts pounding and lungs struggling for air, the two men ran for their lives. Smoke drove over them in dense clouds, biting their eyes like acid. Sparks were now showering over them, the wind flinging them forward like incandescent hail.

Out of sheer exhaustion, they had to pause for breath in a shallow *donga*. The air was purer down there, the smoke and sparks were cascading over their heads. But they dared pause only long enough to clear their choking throats. The *donga* bank ahead prevented their seeing how much of the gap between the fires was left, but behind them the original fire had eaten back, cutting off their retreat. If the gap above were closed, it was doubtful they would survive.

"The police will never get through: they'll have to outflank it," Howard muttered as they climbed up the bank of the *donga*.

Back in the mad turmoil of wind, smoke and flame, it was a few moments before they could see the gap. Then, to their intense relief, the smoke lifted for a second and they saw a narrow corridor of darkness still remained. It was no more than a hundred yards ahead. But the heat from the advancing fires was intense now, searing their faces. With bursting hearts they ran forward.

The noise was deafening now, the crash of exploding pines like the detonation of high explosive. They could no longer see: the smoke was almost solid. With closed, burning eyes they stumbled on, covering their faces to protect them from the intense heat.

Suddenly the ground fell away from them. They rolled down a steep bank into a clump of bushes. As Howard picked himself up he realized what had happened. The narrow gap they had seen between the two lines of fire was actually a deep *donga* that ran across the mountain, then turned at right angles and bisected the two walls of fire, for the moment holding up their fusion.

Umzoni had fallen heavier than Howard and was dazed for a moment. When he had recovered Howard explained the position.

"I don't think the fire has bridged it

yet. If it hasn't we have a chance of getting through."

They stumbled along the stony bottom of the ravine, holding their breaths as they rounded the bend. Both gasped in relief when they saw the fire had not yet blocked the *donga*. Yet the sight was a fearsome one. Both banks were crowned by flaming trees that swung in the wind like gleeful devils. The whole *donga* was bathed in blood-red light. Clearly its vegetation could not resist the fierce heat much longer. As the two men neared the line where the two fires above faced one another, a clump of small trees directly ahead of them suddenly exploded into flames.

"Quickly," Howard shouted. Scrambling from rock to rock they made their way round the trees. Now the fire was on all sides of them. The heat beat down mercilessly. Howard felt the skin of his face tightening like parchment. His eyes felt as if they were being shrivelled to cinders. White-hot ash, blown by the wind, fell over the men, scorching their hair and clothes. Every breath was an agony.

A belt of pine trees lay across their way. A white jet of flame licked through them. Covering their faces with their arms, the two men ran desperately forward. There was a moment of intense heat, then a merciful gust of cooler air. They were through the fire at last.

They ran another thirty yards, then dropped, completely exhausted. Behind them flames were lunging through the trees like liquid jets, making a white-hot barrier across the *donga*.

* * *

It was a full minute before either man could speak. Then Umzoni struggled to his feet.

"They may get away," he gasped. "I must go on . . ."

Howard followed him up one side of the *donga*. Hundreds of acres were burning below them, a seething carpet of flame and white-hot ash in which incandescent trees and bushes writhed like tortured souls. The mountain buttress, now rising only a hundred feet above them, was stained red in the glare, but in the shadow of its fissures and crevices a thousand men could have hidden unseen. There was no sign of Swartz and his companions.

"I think they would run this way," Umzoni said, pointing ahead.

Howard saw his argument. Knowing the police could only reach him by outflanking the fire, Swartz would probably run with the wind, relying on it to drive the fire ahead of him and so protect his flank. That was the logical assumption. Whether Swartz had acted on it was another matter.

Umzoni climbed from the *donga*. "I am going to take the chance," he told Howard. "We can't stay here much longer or the police might outflank the fire and come on us. They can't be very far behind."

Howard nodded and followed him. They climbed the remaining hundred feet of steep talus and reached the foot of the buttress that towered vertically into the crimson sky. A narrow contour path ran along its base — a path used by mountain fire-watchers — and along this Umzoni set a brisk pace.

They had not gone a hundred yards before a fragment of rock face splintered ahead of Howard and something ricochetted shrilly into the darkness. Umzoni turned a startled face back to Howard. At the same moment another bullet smashed into the rocks.

"No; it can't be Swartz," Howard shouted in reply to the Zulu's question. "It's from some of the police below the fire. They've probably mistaken us for him."

The range was extreme: over a thousand yards uphill with the drifting smoke making conditions even more difficult. Yet the firing was remarkably accurate and grew heavier by the minute. Howard realized that the crimson rock face behind them was in favour of the marksmen. Bullets ricochetted shrilly at all angles and pieces of splintered rock flew like shrapnel.

Just as Howard was going to call to Umzoni to jump down to the sloping talus, whose bushes offered some cover, the path rounded a shoulder of the buttress and gave them protection. They paused, but only for a second. Umzoni let out a triumphant yell and pointed ahead. A hundred yards along the path a man had suddenly leapt to his feet on seeing them. The firelight caught him clearly — there was no mistaking the cat-like figure of Swartz. He ran swiftly away and vanished round another bend in the winding path.

Ignoring the bullets that began raking the rocks again, the vengeful Zulu started after him. Howard hesitated, then followed. Bullets smashed before and behind the running men. Howard felt the wind of one by his face, another sent an explosion of rock splinters waist high at him, almost knocking the breath from his body. The path was uneven, in places rockfalls had broken it away. They stumbled on, the thunder of wind and fire punctured by the banshee wail of ricochetting bullets.

They reached the rock shoulder round which the fleeing Swartz had vanished. A twenty-foot stretch of the path had broken away at this point: they could only go forward by climbing over huge boulders. Below the talus fell steeply to the fire that had eaten back to within fifty feet of the buttress. Above towered the crimson rocks, forbidding with their black shadows.

To Howard's relief the firing ceased again as they clambered round the bend. Once more the rocks sheltered them. In single file they climbed over the boulders, sweat from their efforts and the heat of the fire stinging their eyes.

Umzoni was the first to regain the path, being a few yards ahead of Howard. He had not gone five paces before a massive shape dropped on him from the rocks above, swinging a huge knobkerrie. Howard let out a yell of warning, throwing himself backwards at the same time. His instinctive action saved his life. He missed the knife thrust that was aimed at his heart but not the impact of a plunging body that drove him to his knees. Retching for breath, he clutched at his assailant, seizing the arm that wielded the long knife. A foot kicked him savagely. Blinded with pain, he hung on. A blurred face, satanic in the crimson light, was inches from his own. As his eyes cleared he recognized the twisted, vicious features of Schwartz . . .

30

IT was the huge negro, Vulisango, who had attacked Umzoni. He had dropped from the rocks, aiming a blow from behind that would have crushed the Zulu's skull if it had not been for Howard's warning. Umzoni jumped aside and the blow landed on his upper arm. The pain stung him to madness. For a second the two men glared at one another, then Umzoni went in like a maddened bull.

Vulisango swung the knobkerrie again, but the Zulu brushed it aside as if it had been straw. His great hands dropped on Vulisango, gripping like a vice. Locked together, the two men staggered along the path.

It was a battle of Titans. Both men, with their shirts ripped from their backs in seconds, were of much the same build, massive of chest and shoulders. On the crimson wall behind them their shadows, huge and grotesque, joined in the death struggle with them.

Unable to break the hold Umzoni had on him, Vulisango lowered his head and buried his teeth in the Zulu's shoulder, tearing bloody flesh away in his teeth like a savage dog. Growling with pain Umzoni let his arms slacken for a second. Instantly fingers stabbed at his eyes. As he ducked his head, a foot swung upwards. He twisted, catching the boot on his hip.

Pain flamed in his brain. He let out a roar like a wounded lion and hurled himself again on Vulisango. One of his powerful arms wrapped itself round the negro's neck, levering up under his chin. His legs locked themselves round the other's body.

They fell heavily but nothing would have broken that grip of the Zulu's. The muscles of his back and shoulders stood out in shining black ridges as he increased the pressure. The sinews of Vulisango's neck looked as if they would burst through the skin as the negro tried to resist the fearful strain. Slowly his head was drawn back . . . back. Terror came into his bloodshot eyes. In a mad frenzy of desperation he threshed his body about like a landed shark, but the grip held, the relentless pressure increased. His bulging eyes flooded with blood; his teeth splintered in a sudden paroxysm of agony.

Umzoni, his face contorted with the enormous effort, was kneeling now on the negro's back. Inch by inch Vulisango's head came back, his back bent like a bow. The Zulu drew back his lips and made one last, tremendous effort. There was a sudden, sharp crack, like the snapping of a dry stick. Vulisango's body suddenly went slack, like that of a broken doll. His legs kicked, his back arched once, then he lay quite still . . .

The sweat was pouring in rivulets down Umzoni's face and chest. Behind him the fire was igniting the small bushes that grew barely twenty yards from the path. The Zulu remained kneeling a moment with bowed head. Then, at the sound of running footsteps, he turned, started, and leapt to his feet with a growl.

* * *

As Howard stared into the wolfish face of Swartz, anger ran like fire through him, bringing back his strength. Here was his arch-enemy: the leader of the forces that had defeated his faith. Here was the one who had seduced those Linda had helped, so destroying her newly found happiness and turning her from him.

Swartz had torn away from his first desperate hold and was now crouched before him, knife in hand. Neither of the men was on the path: they were amid boulders and thick bushes. Behind Swartz, on the path above, the two negroes were locked in battle, their figures gigantic in the blood-red glow of the fire.

Howard dropped his hand into his pocket for his revolver. Seeing the movement Swartz snarled and leapt forward, stabbing upwards with his knife. Howard managed to get his revolver out, but his hand had seized it by the barrel and there was no time to reverse it and fire. Using it as a club he struck at the Coloured's knife arm. Swartz gave a yell of pain and the knife spun away. Before Howard could press home his advantage a vicious kick landed on his shin. Groaning with pain he dropped on one knee, only for another kick under the heart to send him sprawling, the revolver falling from his hand into a thick bush.

He saw the gleam of the knife not two yards from him as Swartz leapt for it. With a desperate effort Howard rolled over and seized the Coloured's arm as it rose with the razor-sharp blade. Over and over they rolled, kicking, gouging, biting, with the knife held rigidly between them.

Before his face Howard saw the glinting blade and behind it the glaring, white-rimmed eyes of Swartz. Their bodies were motionless now, every ounce of energy being concentrated on the possession of the knife. All other things became as nothing: the knife was the focal point of existence. Seconds, hours, ages passed while muscles screamed with unbearable pain and lungs pumped vainly for air.

Howard was conscious of a strangely detached feeling. While one half of him fought with an animal fury, the other half watched the knife with an interest that was almost academic. The feeling grew as the seconds passed and the knife wavered this way and that. Yet all the while the muscles and sinews of his body were screaming in agony.

Then, at last, the knife began to move. Slowly at first, then more quickly. Swartz's eyes, veined with blood, dilated with terror. Summoning the last of his strength, Howard threw his weight down. Suddenly all resistance went from his arm. The knife plunged down — to bury itself into the earth.

Swartz had released his hold on the knife and rolled aside. Before Howard could recover, he had jumped back and away. He leapt up on the path, only to see the mighty figure of Umzoni rise to bar his way. The expression on the Zulu's face was like that of a great cat who has cornered his prey at last. As Swartz leapt off the path to the steep talus, Umzoni let out a roar and went after him, bounding from rock to rock like a hungry lion.

The diagonal onrush of the Zulu drove Swartz down the talus to the very fringe of the fire. In his terror his flight was blind; he did not notice how the ground fell sharply away behind a clump of bushes. Bursting through them he felt his feet suddenly slide away. Unable to check his fall, he rolled down through the burning bush into the very heart of the fire.

His screams came through the thunder of the wind like sharp needles, stabbing into the brain. He rose from the white-hot ash, and in his agony ran farther into the fire. He became a living torch, writhing and pirouetting in a hideous dance of death. Then, mercifully, it was over. He fell, jerked upright once, then collapsed. His charred body merged with the ash around it.

* * *

Umzoni stood a full minute, an ebony statue in the crimson glare. Then he turned slowly and made his way to Howard, who was fighting with his revolting stomach.

"It was an end I would have wished no man," the Zulu said in his deep voice.

They made their way back to the path. As they reached it, Michael came stumbling round a shoulder of the rocks. He was holding a hand to his head. Blood was trickling through his fingers. He looked amazed at seeing them. Then he noticed the dead body of Vulisango lying beside the path, and his eyes lifted to the grim face of Umzoni.

"The other one is in there," the Zulu growled, pointing to the fire.

"I tried to stop them," Michael muttered. "The other thing was different, but this was murder. I tried, but Vulisango hit me . . ."

Howard moved nearer the Coloured. All his bitterness had flooded back on seeing him.

"Why did you kill Mr. Mitchell?"

The financier's name seemed to bring Michael out from his daze and sting him into madness. His face suddenly contorted.

"I didn't kill him," he spat. "Some bloody swine, maybe Swartz, maybe Vulisango, took that pleasure from me. I am sorry because I would have liked to have buried my knife in his belly and twisted it."

"Why?"

"Because he was a swine! A dirty, filthy swine."

"It was he who found you your job. And what about Mrs. Mitchell? You once admitted how much you and your people owed her for saving Father Hendricks. So, in your gratitude, you cause the death of her husband and the destruction of his factory. You help to cause a riot that killed heaven knows how many innocent people. You destroyed Father Hendricks's church and probably broke his heart in the bargain. And, although you probably don't give a damn about it, you've destroyed all Mrs. Mitchell's and my faith in your people. Why did you do all this?"

"Answer Mr. Shaw," Umzoni growled. "He and Mrs. Mitchell have suffered for us. Why did you do this thing?"

Michael looked at the Zulu sullenly. "I cannot tell him."

Howard's body was trembling with his efforts to control his temper.

"You must have a reason — a tremendous reason! Why did you want to kill Mr. Mitchell?"

Michael drew back his lips. "I can give

you hundreds of reasons. Go and look at the land he rented to people in the location. Most of it was his. He was a profiteer, living on the blood of children. Then there was Willisden — didn't you hear about the people he was kicking out into the streets?"

"But you don't kill a man for these things. You aren't savages."

"No; we aren't savages, *Meneer* Shaw. We are people with feeling like yourselves. And that is why you can't go on kicking us around. Sooner or later we are going to hit back . . ."

"You still haven't given me one reason for killing a man," Howard shouted. "You haven't told me why you left Lucy to mix with scum like Swartz and Vulisango."

"I could give you a thousand reasons for wanting to kill him," Michael snarled. "But you are white; I have nothing to say to you. I have risked my life for you and settled my debt."

"And what of me?" The deep voice of Umzoni was ominous. "Once you said my work was good, that you would help me. Is this how to keep your promise?

Today you may have done untold harm to our people. We will be called savage and treacherous, and the laws may be made even harsher."

Michael lowered his head. "For you I am sorry," he muttered. "But the Europeans are different. You do not understand . . . "

Howard's control broke. He seized Michael by the collar, dragging him forward.

"There must be something else, damn you! People don't murder for the things you have told me. If they do, they deserve all they get. What else is there?"

Umzoni eased him away from the struggling Coloured. "He is not worth your anger or mine, Mr. Shaw. And there has been enough violence tonight. Let him go." The Zulu waved a contemptuous hand at Michael. "Go and leave us, animal — if you can find a way through your fire."

For a moment it seemed Michael would speak. Then he turned and stumbled away down the path the way Howard and Umzoni had come. Umzoni shouted after him. The Coloured shook his head and went on, to vanish round a bend in the path. Umzoni shrugged.

"I warned him about the police. I can do no more." He looked along the path in the opposite direction. The fire had moved higher; in a few minutes it would make escape impossible. He turned to Howard.

"I must go now. What will you do — return home?"

"After making my peace with the police. What can I tell them about you?"

"You can tell them everything; they will not catch me. And you promise to publish all you have seen this night? You will let the Europeans know that I, Umzoni, have punished those who would have brought fire and blood to the land?"

"I'll let them know," Howard promised.

The Zulu's voice was vibrant with feeling. "Thank you for all you have done for us, and for your help tonight. You have more than justified my faith in your race."

Howard's lips twisted. "I wish I was

left with the same faith in your people, Umzoni."

"You are blaming us for the deeds of a few," the Zulu said quietly. "Yet we are asked not to blame you for the deeds of many."

Howard laughed bitterly. "True."

The Zulu held out a huge hand. "Will you shake hands with me?"

"Gladly."

"Are you going to carry on with your work?" Howard asked as their hands clasped.

"Of course. Apart from Willisden, the strike was a success. Yes; we shall go on."

Umzoni's hand tightened again, then he stepped back. "We may meet again, we may not — only the stars know that. But it has been good to meet a man. *Hambe Gahle*, my brother."

Howard watched the huge Zulu stride along the path. In spite of his tattered clothes, he walked with the majesty of a prince. He paused at a shoulder of the cliff and looked back. The fire shone on his massive body, bloodstained, half-naked, magnificent. He lifted an arm in one last salutation, then vanished from sight.

Strangely moved, Howard turned back along the path and made his way towards the police.

31

THE sea was like silver lamé and the air fresh with the tang of salt. Out near the horizon a yacht caught the morning sun, its sail as white as a gull's turning wing. The beach lay without footprints or blemish, sleeping after its union with the sea.

Howard turned slowly from the stoep. He felt the hard rustle of an envelope in his pocket and winced at the reminder. Its message held no ambiguity. Jane had always called a spade a spade. His mother was dying and wanted to see him. Perhaps it was already too late, perhaps his journey might be in vain, but that was the way of some journeys.

He took a last look round the little bungalow in which he had spent so little time, then locked the door and climbed into his car. The way to England was clear: his air passage booked. His story to the police had been proved by their finding the dead body of Vulisango, and it appeared that Michael, who had surrendered to the police, had confirmed all he had said.

There was little more to be done, he thought bitterly. He had visited Lucy again and given her a few pounds. He had not seen Michael again; there had been no time to arrange a visit to the jail where he was awaiting trial. But he no longer cared what the Coloured's reasons for his treachery had been. His bitterness had dried like salt on the soil of his mind, leaving it barren of interest or emotion.

He had seen Father Hendricks. It had taken him two days to find the old priest and then only with the aid of the Mission Authorities. The old man was staying in a hostel, waiting for a vacancy in another mission. Howard had not stayed long. To see the frail old priest, with all he had known and loved destroyed, waiting patiently to take up another burden had been too moving an experience. And there had been no bitterness in him. Only a sorrow that grew deeper as he sensed Howard's own disillusionment. Not wishing to give him more pain, Howard had left before too much of it was revealed to the old man.

"Write me, Father. And take great care of yourself."

"May the Good Lord bless you. And may He give you peace of mind and great happiness. Go with God, for I love you as if you were my own son . . ."

The old man had wept then, and Howard had walked quickly away. Now, thinking about him, he felt a rush of emotion that for the moment eased his bitterness. While one man like Father Hendricks existed on earth, surely the world was still full of hope and promise. Then a vision of the priest's gutted church came to him, and his lips tightened again. The world did not deserve them: there lay the tragedy.

Jannie Morkel had been downcast to hear he was leaving.

"Come back soon, lad. We need more of your type. You've done us a lot of good."

Howard had laughed bitterly. "Good! Don't be kind to me, Jannie. I can do without that."

"I'm not being kind, lad. You've made

people think. They aren't so sure of themselves any more; they aren't so arrogant. I know. I'm a Nationalist. You're taking this thing the wrong way, lad. The trouble out at Willisden wasn't your fault. Some of it was ours. I mean that, Howard — honest to God. Give my love to Jane, and good luck to your mother, God bless her. *Totsiens*, Howard."

Howard was aware of the irony as he left Morkel's clinic. Jannie was slowly beginning to believe in the very things in which he himself had lost faith. He could draw no comfort from the knowledge. The shock of events had been too great; Linda's accusation had burned too deeply.

He spent the rest of the morning and early afternoon clearing up the last of his affairs. He kept his promise to Umzoni, who had escaped the police, and gave a full report of the Zulu's recent words and deeds to his newspapers. He said his farewells, he walked in and out of offices signing his name, he laughed, he smiled, and yet his mind was a thing apart, walking alongside him like a weary, heavy-footed prisoner without hope or comfort.

Five o'clock came and the streets were full of people. The day's work was over; people were going home. Men to their wives; lovers to their sweethearts. They hurried by, shoving, bustling, running, going home. Thousands of them and he felt unbelievably alone.

Reaching his car, which he had arranged to leave at the dealer's the following morning, he climbed into it and drove away — anywhere to be out of the city. Lost in his thoughts he found himself automatically taking the familiar road to Clifton. Was he, fool that he was, still hoping to see her he wondered.

He did not stop at Clifton, however. He turned up the road that led to Kloof Nek. The sun was low over the sea now and the naked oaks were silhouetted black against it. A squirrel ran across the road ahead of him and fled up a tall pine. The shadows were deep and cool here, but rising sheer above the trees the craggy summit of the mountain was tinted a delicate rose in the setting sun. A descending cable car was caught in its crimson rays, the wire from which it was suspended looking no thicker than a gossamer thread. Reluctantly and almost sullenly, he turned the car at the top of Kloof Nek and took the road over Signal Hill.

This had been one of their favourite drives in the evenings. Often after coffee they had come up here to look over the coloured, twinkling lights of the city. Bitter-sweet memories came back as he stopped the car on the crest of the hill. There was the city, the city that was so lovely. The city that was bounded by the blue sea on one side and the green mountain on the other. One could not see its inhabitants from here: its Europeans, Natives, Indians, Malays, Coloureds . . . nor could one hear their anger. One could not see the politicians or hear their didactic wrangling. One could not see the slums. One could only see the city that was so fair, with its golden bay sweeping so gracefully to the mainland where the Drakensteins rose like blue smoke into the sky.

It was a city full of love and lust, wealth and wretchedness, sobriety and sin. Yet from above one could only see the things that were so beautiful and seemed to hold such promise. The Fair Gateway to a continent, the Tavern of the Seas, the meeting-place of many races in which could be born a new conception of man's duty to man. The Fairest Cape in all the world . . .

* * *

He sat while the sky darkened, until, in one sudden flash, millions of lights appeared on the roads below, sweeping in dazzling arcs towards the distant mountains. He did not hear the car that had crept so uncertainly along the road behind him. His eyes were on the city and his thoughts beyond expression. Only when her hesitant approach ended, when she stood at his elbow, did he see her.

"I had to find you, Howard. It's very important. I had to tell you before you left . . ."

Silently he opened his car door and she sat beside him.

"I've been looking everywhere for you," she whispered.

His sudden rush of gladness had died away, leaving helplessness in its wake. She had been right; the thing that had happened could not be undone. Though she might forgive him and live with him, his own guilt would always lie between them. One might escape the condemnation of others but there was no escape from oneself.

Her eyes were pleading into his own. "Help me," she whispered. "You must help me to explain. Don't look like that. I didn't know then. How could I know?"

"Nothing has changed," he said slowly. "You were right; I realize that now. Don't forgive me. Don't try to forgive me."

"You don't understand," she said. "Everything has changed. Everything is different now."

"The dead don't come back," he said harshly. "Death is the one great finality. Nothing can alter it. And your husband's death was the beginning and the end of everything. You said so yourself."

"No; it isn't, Howard. The reason for his death — that is the thing that can change everything. Can't you see that?"

"The reason for it?" His eyes were hard with self-aversion. "We both know the reason." His laugh made her wince. "My altruism; my credulous, deluded love of the underdog. My shameless incitement! Those were the reasons."

She shuddered. "Don't, please. How was I to know what had happened? How could I have guessed anything so horrible?"

He turned slowly towards her. "What did happen? What else is there to know?"

She lifted her pale face to him. "About Trevor. About what he did. Oh; it's horrible, Howard. And it's worse now he is dead. It's like digging up his body for all the world to see. That's why Brian has been so long in telling me. Trevor was his father . . . "

"What did Brian tell you?"

"The truth about Joan. Why she committed suicide . . . "

Linda paused, gathering strength. The sun had gone down behind a mist on the edge of the sky. The air was hushed and trembled slightly.

"Trevor confessed to Brian before he lost consciousness," she began. "That was the reason Brian was so upset that day. You remember, he didn't wait for me."

"Yes, yes. Go on."

"It was Trevor who killed her, Howard."

Howard stiffened. "Your husband! Killed her?"

"Caused her to commit suicide. You see, he had found out her secret." Her arm alongside his own was trembling violently. "He had found out she was coloured . . . "

"Coloured!" The word was like an explosion. It sent a blinding flash through Howard's brain, dazing him.

"Yes. And Trevor had found out. You know what coloured parents are like. If one of their children is white, they give him his chance and let him go among the Europeans, even if they never see him again. They all do that. That's what had happened to Joan."

A vision of the girl's gentle, sad face passed before Howard's eyes. His voice was like a threatening knife. "What did he do to her?"

"He found out all about her by using private detectives. Then he told her what he would do if she didn't stop seeing Brian. He said he would tell the police about her parents. One of them was a European and they weren't married, so he threatened them under the *apartheid* laws."

"Good God."

"And, of course, he threatened to expose her, to Brian and all her friends."

"Did he ever tell Brian about her colour?"

"Not until he was dying. There wasn't any need. She had already stopped seeing him."

"Where do her people live? Who are they?" The air was tight in Howard's lungs; his brain was too dazed to accept the obvious.

"They were the old people in Willisden you took me to see."

"Then Michael . . . "

"Is her brother. That's it, don't you see? That's why he hated Trevor so much. Joan must have told him everything before she killed herself. And after she took the poison and after their mother died of shock, he went crazy. Don't look at me like that, Howard. I didn't know anything about it. Oh, God; don't look like that."

"So he didn't only kill Joan. He killed both of the old people as well."

It was all clear to Howard now. It explained the scene in the Kloof Nek woods that Linda and he had witnessed. It had been Michael's own sister who had been attacked by the *skollies*. Michael's anger had been with her as well as Swartz because he would have wanted her to sever her connections completely with her own race, something she had steadfastly refused to do. Apart from the danger of attack by *skollies*, while she had gone on helping non-Europeans there was always the chance that the secret of her birth might be discovered — something which had happened.

It explained Joan's refusal to become engaged to Brian. She had loved him deeply, and had not been able to resist seeing him. But that had been all the happiness she had allowed herself. Her love, for Brian's sake, had not allowed her to marry him, even though he had pleaded with her so ardently. And Howard knew now that nothing would have changed her mind.

But Mitchell had seen her as a dangerous influence on his son, as well as an embarrassment to himself. No doubt, in putting detectives on her, he had hoped for rather than expected some startling disclosure, although he may have had a nascent suspicion of the truth. However, the result must have surpassed his wildest hopes. It had been these private detectives of his who had frightened the old couple in Willisden.

The rest could be guessed. Sensitive and intense as the girl had been, she must have suffered deeply from her inability to marry Brian, and her suffering would have been increased by his repeated accusations of indifference on her part. On nerves as tightly drawn as hers, the sudden hammer of Mitchell's threats had proved too much. Faced with the danger of her parents being brutally separated, faced with the fear of Brian being told her secret, tormented by the vision of his turning away from her in revulsion, she had taken her life.

It explained Father Hendricks's visit to the old couple when Mrs. Stevens had had her fatal heart attack. The old priest, who would know the girl's secret, had heard of her death and gone round to break the news. The shock had killed Mrs. Stevens and broken the old man's heart. And Michael, with his whole family destroyed, had known the identity of the man responsible. Tormented beyond human endurance, he had turned to Swartz for revenge. And it had been his loyalty to his sister and her secret, even after her death, that had made him refuse to tell Howard the reason for his apparent treachery.

The tragedy went even deeper than it appeared. Harsh though the laws were, they would almost certainly not have been invoked against the old couple, even if Mitchell had told the police. But the financier had used the laws as Howard had once warned Morkel they could be used — as an instrument of blackmail and intimidation against the guileless.

"What about Michael?" Howard asked bitterly. "Does he have to die to complete the story?"

"Brian is getting him released," Linda

whispered. "He has told the police he made a mistake with his identity. They don't believe him, but they can't prove anything. Michael is going back to Lucy. And we've had the ejection notice withdrawn; the people can keep their homes. Oh; don't look like that, Howard. I didn't know anything about this." Sobs racked her body. "How can you live with a person and know so little about them? How is it possible?"

Slowly the implications of all he had heard were coming to Howard. Linda's lovely, tear-stained face lifted up to him.

"There is something else you must know. It's rather wonderful. Lucy told me. The non-Europeans in Willisden have been making a collection for Father Hendricks. They are going to buy material with thc money and build a new church for him themselves."

Howard sat very still, listening.

"You were quite right about them," she whispered. "They're just as kind and decent as other people, if they are given a chance. There's no real difference in them. They let me help them with a donation. I was afraid they wouldn't accept it, but Lucy helped me . . ."

Howard thought of the old man's joy, and the surge of emotion washed away the last of his bitterness. The cause he had supported had not proved unworthy after all. Father Hendricks' devotion had been repaid, and Linda's new faith restored. Her happiness would return, and because of its nature be with her always.

They sat together, watching the last saffron of the sunset fade into the deepening night. Suddenly, as if the sky were a screen, Howard saw his mother's house again. It was spring there now: the hedge round the garden was white with blossoms. In the evenings, if one were patient, one might hear the last sweet song of a blackbird, trembling on the still air like a magic flute.

"Your agent told me you had received bad news from home," Linda whispered. "Is she very ill?"

"Jane thinks she is dying," he said simply. "That's why I'm leaving tomorrow."

She gripped his arm tightly. "I'm so sorry . . . "

A pause, then she cried out: "I'm coming with you. You can't leave me. I'll come on the next 'plane."

He nodded. The silence came again, like warm velvet.

"Will you come back?" she asked, when the night had drawn around them, holding them together.

He took a deep breath, and lifting his head looked down on the shining city below.

"Yes," he told her. "I want to see more. Not that we are likely to see the end of it. But the next phase and the next — yes, I want to see them."

Her arms tightened around him. Outside, the evensong of the crickets rose like an organ note. The lights below were like a myriad gems, bracelet after bracelet sweeping out into the darkness. To the west a solitary star hung in the afterglow. Out at sea the lighthouse on Robben Island shone its defiance to the approaching night.

She felt a shudder run through him. He turned to her and his eyes were wistful.

"It's a lovely land," he said slowly.

"Sometimes it's so lovely it tears the heart in you. God; in a land so light, how is it so many men cannot see."

She held him tightly, and they floated together in the darkness between the city and the stars.

THE END

Other titles in the Ulverscroft Large Print Series:

TO FIGHT THE WILD
Rod Ansell and Rachel Percy

Lost in uncharted Australian bush, Rod Ansell survived by hunting and trapping wild animals, improvising shelter and using all the bushman's skills he knew.

COROMANDEL
Pat Barr

India in the 1830s is a hot, uncomfortable place, where the East India Company still rules. Amelia and her new husband find themselves caught up in the animosities which seethe between the old order and the new.

THE SMALL PARTY
Lillian Beckwith

A frightening journey to safety begins for Ruth and her small party as their island is caught up in the dangers of armed insurrection.

THE WILDERNESS WALK
Sheila Bishop

Stifling unpleasant memories of a misbegotten romance in Cleave with Lord Francis Aubrey, Lavinia goes on holiday there with her sister. The two women are thrust into a romantic intrigue involving none other than Lord Francis.

THE RELUCTANT GUEST
Rosalind Brett

Ann Calvert went to spend a month on a South African farm with Theo Borland and his sister. They both proved to be different from her first idea of them, and there was Storr Peterson — the most disturbing man she had ever met.

ONE ENCHANTED SUMMER
Anne Tedlock Brooks

A tale of mystery and romance and a girl who found both during one enchanted summer.

CLOUD OVER MALVERTON
Nancy Buckingham

Dulcie soon realises that something is seriously wrong at Malverton, and when violence strikes she is horrified to find herself under suspicion of murder.

AFTER THOUGHTS
Max Bygraves

The Cockney entertainer tells stories of his East End childhood, of his RAF days, and his post-war showbusiness successes and friendships with fellow comedians.

MOONLIGHT AND MARCH ROSES
D. Y. Cameron

Lynn's search to trace a missing girl takes her to Spain, where she meets Clive Hendon. While untangling the situation, she untangles her emotions and decides on her own future.

NURSE ALICE IN LOVE
Theresa Charles

Accepting the post of nurse to little Fernie Sherrod, Alice Everton could not guess at the romance, suspense and danger which lay ahead at the Sherrod's isolated estate.

POIROT INVESTIGATES
Agatha Christie

Two things bind these eleven stories together — the brilliance and uncanny skill of the diminutive Belgian detective, and the stupidity of his Watson-like partner, Captain Hastings.

LET LOOSE THE TIGERS
Josephine Cox

Queenie promised to find the long-lost son of the frail, elderly murderess, Hannah Jason. But her enquiries threatened to unlock the cage where crucial secrets had long been held captive.

THE TWILIGHT MAN
Frank Gruber

Jim Rand lives alone in the California desert awaiting death. Into his hermit existence comes a teenage girl who blows both his past and his brief future wide open.

DOG IN THE DARK
Gerald Hammond

Jim Cunningham breeds and trains gun dogs, and his antagonism towards the devotees of show spaniels earns him many enemies. So when one of them is found murdered, the police are on his doorstep within hours.

THE RED KNIGHT
Geoffrey Moxon

When he finds himself a pawn on the chessboard of international espionage with his family in constant danger, Guy Trent becomes embroiled in moves and countermoves which may mean life or death for Western scientists.

TIGER TIGER
Frank Ryan

A young man involved in drugs is found murdered. This is the first event which will draw Detective Inspector Sandy Woodings into a whirlpool of murder and deceit.

CAROLINE MINUSCULE
Andrew Taylor

Caroline Minuscule, a medieval script, is the first clue to the whereabouts of a cache of diamonds. The search becomes a deadly kind of fairy story in which several murders have an other-worldly quality.

LONG CHAIN OF DEATH
Sarah Wolf

During the Second World War four American teenagers from the same town join the Army together. Forty-two years later, the son of one of the soldiers realises that someone is systematically wiping out the families of the four men.

THE LISTERDALE MYSTERY
Agatha Christie

Twelve short stories ranging from the light-hearted to the macabre, diverse mysteries ingeniously and plausibly contrived and convincingly unravelled.

TO BE LOVED
Lynne Collins

Andrew married the woman he had always loved despite the knowledge that Sarah married him for reasons of her own. So much heartache could have been avoided if only he had known how vital it was to be loved.

ACCUSED NURSE
Jane Converse

Paula found herself accused of a crime which could cost her her job, her nurse's reputation, and even the man she loved, unless the truth came to light.

BUTTERFLY MONTANE
Dorothy Cork

Parma had come to New Guinea to marry Alec Rivers, but she found him completely disinterested and that overbearing Pierce Adams getting entirely the wrong idea about her.

HONOURABLE FRIENDS
Janet Daley

Priscilla Burford is happily married when she meets Junior Environment Minister Alistair Thurston. Inevitably, sexual obsession and political necessity collide.

WANDERING MINSTRELS
Mary Delorme

Stella Wade's career as a concert pianist might have been ruined by the rudeness of a famous conductor, so it seemed to her agent and benefactor. Even Sir Nicholas fails to see the possibilities when John Tallis falls deeply in love with Stella.